...she crooked up her mouth, and gave him a sassy grin. "Fine."

Fine. That one word and Lonesome Wolf realized he had been outmaneuvered. He chuckled at this singular woman with a stubborn streak wide enough to rival the Texas sky... with the gentle sound of the privileged South peaking through her voice despite the rugged reminder of life in the West surrounding her... and with a dangerous spark of mischievousness in her green, green eyes.

He'd have to watch himself or he could easily fall for her. He certainly hoped the Good Lord didn't intend for him to stay long enough for that to happen, because if there was one thing he knew, it was the type of trouble he could bring to her door if he allowed himself to get too close to her.

– Lonesome Wolf, **Chapter 1**

Reviews for Lonesome Wolf:

"...not your ordinary romance... Lanna Webb creates the raw tensions of a romantic novel embellished by masterful descriptions of a credible frontier setting."

-- Grant P. Ferguson,
Young Adult author & illustrator

"If you like western/frontier romance, this book should be on your reading list."

-- Whit McClendon,
Fantasy author

I cannot say enough good things about it. It will be one of my all time favorite fiction books.

-- Amazon reviewer

OTHER BOOKS BY THE AUTHOR

KLEIN CREEK:
>Lonesome Wolf, BOOK 1
>>*~ also available in eBook & LARGE PRINT*

>***Coming Soon:***
>Reynolds, Book 2

&

TEXAS RANGERS:
>Kilgore, Book 1

LONESOME
WOLF

A Klein Creek Novel:
Book I

Lanna Webb

Dabar Publishing
Angleton, TX 77515
www.dabarpublishing.com

ISBN: 978-0-578-41448-5 (paperback)
ISBN: 978-1-953551-00-9 (large print)
ISBN: 978-1-5323-9615-1 (eBook)

Dedicated to

Richard Wilcher,
English Professor and Mentor Extraordinaire:

Without your encouragement and belief in me,
I'm not sure what my life would look like.
I can say I'm sure this project, among so many
other good things, would have never happened.

Thank you for all the
happiness, success, and fulfillment
your impact on my life produced.

I'm looking forward to telling you all about it
when we meet again on God's Golden Shore.

- Lanna

DEAR READER,

I am unbelievably happy to share this work with you.
May you be blessed as you read it,
and may my words bring glory to God!

LANNA WEBB

CHAPTER ONE

Texas Hill Country, 1868

The shriek of an Apache war cry shattered the peace of the afternoon.

The chilling echo of its unearthly sound worked its way down Jacob's spine, carrying a shiver along the way. Swiftly, he turned, hardening his mind to what may come, and kicked his horse into a full gallop toward the unmistakable promise of bloodshed.

As he got closer to the squall of the Indians, he unsheathed his rifle and reined in between two mesquite trees on a small rise. He took in the scene. Looked like three … no make that four Apache braves attacking a small cabin. He heard a rifle shot and was relieved to know that whoever was in the cabin was able to defend himself. The Indians appeared armed with only knives and bows and arrows. *Only.* That was the wrong word. He had seen an awful lot of death and mutilation caused by those weapons. But at least the man in the cabin had a gun.

Jacob, acutely aware of the scene unfolding around him, reacted with every sense both heightened and detached. The Apaches' voices rang in his head intermingling with the swish of blood rushing through his veins. The air stilled and the sight of the Indians, declaring battle against the inhabitants of the home, stood out against the backdrop of a graying summer sky. The scene tried to change, desperately attempted to morph itself into a memory long ago hidden away. He knew that any distraction could prove fatal, so he blinked hard, ruthlessly clearing his mind of the heart-rending images of his past and focusing on the present.

He nudged his horse forward, scraping through the mesquite to get into position. As he brought his rifle up against his shoulder, Jacob saw one Apache go down and one get alarmingly close to the cabin. Just as he took aim, another rifle shot cut through the air and the warrior fell. That left two attackers, who were making their way to the side of the house and up onto a porch. Jacob sighted one in. The Indian dropped even before the report of the rifle stopped sounding. The only remaining brave was moving swiftly toward the back of the cabin. Jacob put a bullet in him as the Indian was rounding the corner, just before he made it out of sight.

A sudden grief overwhelmed him, as it always did, at the loss of life. He hated the thought of shooting a man, loathed the knowledge that he had sent a soul to its judgment, but he knew all too well what the Apaches' intentions were, and he couldn't stand by and let them murder in cold blood the inhabitants of the cabin. The images that had battered at his mind before the short fight crowded in once again, attempting to overtake his thinking, his emotions. Now, however, was not the time to let them in, and so he pushed back against them and forced himself free. He let out a long, ragged sigh while his world shifted and realigned, bringing all the pieces back together to form a unified whole based on the here and the now. And here and now required his full attention to assure the area was secure.

Jacob, all senses alert and trained on his surroundings, approached the small home – from the front, out in the open, and with his hands raised out to the side, sweat pouring down his back from the unrelenting Texas heat and the excess adrenaline that had nowhere else to go. Before he even saw the figure at the window clearly, Jacob called out, "Hello, the cabin! Do not shoot!" He paused, waiting for some kind of answer.

Finally, a voice called back, "Who are you?"

Jacob faltered for just a moment at the sound of the voice, a woman's voice, so feminine yet so clear and strong, and then he tilted his head toward the dead Apache. "Obviously, I'm a friend."

To his surprise, he heard laughter, shaky and nervous sounding but beautifully melodic in such sharp contrast to the harsh crack of rifle fire that had so closely preceded it. In a moment, a woman's head appeared in the open window. He was too far away to see anything but her long, auburn hair, so Jacob walked his horse forward until he could speak without yelling. When he came close enough to make out her features, he felt a catch in his chest. She was one beautiful woman. He cringed at what the Apache would have done to her had they taken her.

He could see by the look on her face that she was more than curious about the way he looked, but she didn't ask. That was okay, he was a little curious about her, too.

She motioned behind the house and said, "You can wash up at the pump. Supper's all but ready."

He hesitated, not wanting to offend her by seeming ungrateful and yet not wanting her to do something that made her uncomfortable, notably inviting a man like him to stay for a meal out of a sense of debt. He regarded her with a look that conveyed his feelings on the matter. "I'm much obliged, ma'am, but it isn't necessary –"

Her face had disappeared from the window, but her voice rang out from the cabin's interior. "I hope you like stew."

He couldn't stop the small smile that felt so foreign playing at the corners of his mouth. The frontier sure bred all kinds of folk. Then he looked over the yard at the fallen Apache, and any hint of mirth died an instant death. Pointless. All the death creeping around the hills and valleys of this rugged country was so pointless. He couldn't reconcile how a land filled with people who fed strangers and stepped in whenever help was needed could also be home to so much sorrow.

He raised his voice to be heard. "I need to check the area and give them a proper burial. Keep your gun handy."

She came back to the window for a brief moment, her face masking whatever thoughts she had about the drama that had just played itself out on her homestead. "I'll have supper on the table by the time you get back." She hadn't even blinked as she'd met his gaze, and at the end of her declaration she turned on her heel and disappeared into the shadows of the cabin's interior.

⌘

After he ground-tied his horse, Jacob grabbed his rifle and ammunition and, with one hand on the knife in his belt, made a methodical check through the woods that flanked the homestead. The place was beautiful and, despite the upsetting events of only moments before, peaceful. The cabin was situated near the edge of a gentle, grassy slope that led unguarded to a creek. He walked halfway into that shallow valley to check each way as far as he could see down the creek's length. Everything looked quiet. Heck, everything *was* quiet aside from the soothing sounds of nature – the soft, low rumble of the water mixed with the rustlings of wildlife just beginning to stir again after the disturbance of gunfire. The scene was downright comforting. A man could feel at home in a place like this … that is, if he had a mind to feel at home anywhere.

Jacob took his time, searching the area. Finally, he saw the subtle signs that the four braves had left behind, not enough to alert most trackers but enough that he could tell hints of where they had been, from which direction they had come. He saw no sign of others, and, unfortunately, it was coming up dusk and he couldn't search as far out as he would've liked. He would stick close to the area tonight to make sure that the woman was, for the time being, safe. That is, unless her husband came home in the meantime. But Jacob hadn't seen any tracks that belonged to a white man, not a one. And as he'd taken in the place, the presence of it, he'd noticed the tell tale signs of neglect and disrepair that indicated lack of a man, or lack of a man who worked. It just didn't *feel* like there was a man to come back home; it felt like she was out here surviving on her own. The thought of it knotted his stomach at the same time it stuck in his craw. Not that this land always left men alive to provide and protect. He turned back and walked up to the yard, determined to put these thoughts behind him. Then he saw a cross beneath a lone oak tree, out of sight from the cabin but nearby, all the same. Near enough to visit but far enough not to be a constant reminder of grief. He had just found the answer to his question. He shook his head at the wanderings of his mind. It was no matter to him one way or the other.

He took the walk back to the house slowly,

stretching out his weariness. He'd been in the saddle for far too long, and the Texas sun was a merciless thing. He cranked up a bucket of water from the pump. A rinse and hand washing would feel good. A dip in the creek would feel better, but that luxury would have to wait; he had a call with grave digging to answer. Jacob, wet from the sweat that had been drawn from his body, sweat beckoned by both the searing heat of the day and the nerves churned up by the shoot-out, peeled off his torn shirt. He picked up the bucket and leaned over, pouring the cool well water over his long, ebony hair and smooth, chiseled features. He let out an easy sigh as the water rinsed away trail dirt from his face and neck. Shaking his head like a dog sloughing off water, he headed to the cabin. As he was pulling his shirt back on, he knocked on a side door. The woman creaked open the door just enough to peak out at him. He carefully looked over her face and when he caught a glimpse of the metal of the gun she had in her hand, he relaxed a fraction, grateful that she seemed both calm and cautious.

"Everything okay?"

She nodded. "Everything's dandy. I was just about to serve up tea and cake."

Her dry assessment brought forth a rusty chuckle from him. "All right. That was a stupid question. How's this? Where's your shovel?"

They both sobered at the grim reminder of what had occurred, what they had both had to do. She pointed to a lean-to against one side of the barn. They stared at each other for a moment with a strange mix of ease and discomfort. And then she shut the door.

As he went to get the shovel, he stepped over the dead Apache that lay sprawled on the porch steps. The brave was just a kid, probably not even fourteen and yet a warrior still. Jacob knew the harm the boy had meant to do, and yet he couldn't help but mourn the waste of a young life. He closed his eyes for a moment. This was surely not the way he had anticipated spending his day.

⌘

It was late evening before he finished burying the bodies. He set aside their weapons. Apache arrows were known to shoot straight and true. They and the knives could prove useful to him, or to the woman for that matter, and were too valuable to bury simply because they came from the enemy. *The enemy.* Too bad one man could think of another that way. But today, these men had been the enemy. An enemy that were small in number and possibly had the rest of their party out somewhere in the hills.

Jacob camouflaged the grave, hauling and spreading out the excess soil over a large area. He made sure the top was covered with twigs and pebbles and placed several large rocks over it to make sure no animal came along and dug them up. He was pretty sure he had gone deep enough to prevent that, but the possibility was always a concern.

He walked back to where his horse grazed lazily. As he got his saddlebags for soap and fresh clothes, he saw the woman was standing in the doorway with her gun, watching him with solemn eyes. He noticed that her attention strayed to the blood on him. She didn't say a word about it, but her eyes met his and held them for a moment in understanding. Only when she broke contact did Jacob walk away. This time, he did go down to the creek. He couldn't wash quickly enough after the grisly chore. The water was unbelievably cold and fed his soul after a day he hoped to soon forget. A short time later found him clean, dressed in fresh clothes, body aching, and back at the kitchen door.

The woman invited him in.

Jacob stood stock still for several long moments, moments during which the woman watched patiently without fear or any visible sign of distress. In fact, if he wasn't mistaken, he detected a hint of amusement in her eyes. He looked down at his only clean shirt, regretting that it was made of buckskin. He caught sight of his dark, work-worn hands and passed one of them over the back of his neck, where his damp, black hair hung well past his collar. Finally, he was able to force his mouth to speak. "You…" The first word came out rough and hard, so he cleared his throat and began again. "You don't have to ask me in, ma'am. I sure appreciate your offer of food, but I'd just as soon take it out here on the porch."

"It's okay. You can come in."

Frontier hospitality was one thing. This situation was altogether another. He knew it was customary for a stranger to be offered a place at the table, but he was having a difficult time allowing her to make that offer to him, all things considered. He shook his head, and this time took the direct approach. "I don't think that's a good idea, ma'am."

She ignored him, pushed the door open wider, and asked if he would like coffee. He hesitated for a good, long while but finally the pull of food and a place to sit, and an inner prompting he couldn't deny, pushed him inside the room. He wouldn't know for some time what those few steps would mean.

⌘

She gestured to the table with a dishtowel and he sat, laying his belongings on the floor beside him. She put the coffee in front of him and he pulled the mug toward himself, willing the bold aroma to cleanse the sickening scent of blood from his senses.

He waited patiently for the woman to sit down, taking the time to will away the awful images from his mind, to pray that he would be able to eat after what he had just experienced. To his surprise, his stomach growled loudly to announce its anticipation of the meal, an actual meal, set before him. "Smells mighty good, ma'am." And it did, savory and warm.

"Thank you." The woman sat across the table from him and shot him a measuring look. "Would you say grace for us, please?"

Jacob wondered if this were her way of seeing just how civilized he was. She certainly held his eyes with a challenge in her own. He returned her direct look, suppressing a grin at the subtle inquisition. "Yes, ma'am, I'd be honored."

After the prayer, the woman passed him a bowl of venison stew and biscuits and saw that he was set to eat before she began to fill her own dish. The fact that she would honor a man like him in such a way touched something deep within him that had long been buried. The feeling was not altogether unpleasant. He tried to rebury it anyway.

Once they had settled in and were eating, Jacob spoke. He posed his question carefully and hoped his tone was friendly and comfortable. "I don't mean to pry, ma'am, but I saw a wooden cross out under that oak yonder." He saw her stiffen, and she turned her head and looked in the direction of the grave as if she could see it through the cabin wall. He asked the question though he felt sure he already knew the answer. "Your husband?"

She nodded and went back to eating. "My

husband."

Jacob held back the barrage of questions that logically followed this news, like how had it happened, how long had it been, and why she was still here, out in this untamed land, alone. Instead, he changed the subject altogether. "This stew is delicious. Best food I've had in a long while. Where did you get the meat?"

She looked at him with scrunched eyebrows. Then, relaxing them, she sent one side of her mouth up in a quirky smile and said, "It's venison. Comes from a deer."

Jacob chuckled. This time it came out sounding less unused than the time before. "Right. Another stupid question. I meant to ask who shot it." Although he saw her demeanor was still easy and friendly, he knew immediately by the look in her eye that he had tread on touchy ground.

"I know what you meant," the woman spoke evenly, allowed a slight pause, and then continued. "You might not have noticed, but I'm quite handy with a gun, sir." The teasing smile was gone and the challenge was back.

Jacob searched her face. He was again hit with her beauty. And he felt the sudden need to apologize, to let her know he believed in her. "I noticed. Sorry." And then, in case he had truly, well and good offended her, he added, "I don't know why I even asked."

She looked at him for quite some time. So long in fact, that he was becoming uncomfortable under her stare. Many men had stared him down without so much as a blink in response from him, but this woman gave him the overwhelming urge to fidget. Then again, those men hadn't had eyes so brilliantly green and piercing as this woman's. Just before he thought he was going to have to look away, she spoke. "No harm done. I suppose you know what it's like to have people misunderstand who you are or what you are capable of doing."

Hmm. An arrow straight to the heart. He could respect that. It brought a rare, genuine smile to his lips. "Yes, ma'am. I reckon I do."

⌘

They spoke little more during the meal, but an easy companionship had been forged and wove itself through Jacob's spirit. Interesting.

When supper was over, the woman calmly rose from the table and decreed, "The dishes will wait. I need to see to my chores before it gets dark."

Jacob reached over and put a hand on her arm. It was meant only to get her attention. Had he thought about it, it was a gesture he would have declined to offer. But it was done. And he couldn't take his hand away. It felt like it was lashed to her arm with rawhide strips. To his surprise, she didn't so much as flinch, although something in her eyes came alive at the touch. What was that he saw? Probably something best left there. Jacob forcefully directed his thoughts back to the matter at hand, to his reason for touching her rather than the sensation of the touch itself. "Let me see to the chores. Please."

She thought on it for a moment, nodded, and said, "There's milking, minding the chickens and horses, and bringing in water for tomorrow. You can take care of your horse in the barn. There is an empty stall and some oats."

And still he touched her. He had to will his hand from her ... and himself from the cabin.

⌘

Clara washed the dishes with a vengeance. The poor things were taking the abuse for the edginess she was having trouble shaking. The shock from the attack on her

11

home still coursed through her. And the feeling left over from the touch of the man's hand on her arm was so far from the peace in which she usually walked, firmly and with confidence, that she was at a total loss as to how to escape it. The overwhelming need to offer this obviously lonesome man a place to stay had grasped a hold of her and would not let go. It would not be an easy time, this she knew. And yet she would face it with God's strength and grace. She waited as she prayed and sighed deeply when she began to feel peace wash over her. Then she set the last dish in the cupboard.

⌘

Jacob walked over and picked up Fella's reins, wrapping them in a wide loop around the saddle horn. Then he turned and headed for the barn, with that buckskin horse of his following right behind him. Once he adjusted to the dim light of the setting sun that made its way inside the open door, he looked around the barn. It was nice, very nice. And so were the horses stalled there. In addition to the sturdy-looking pair of workhorses, were a gorgeous bay mare and a striking gray stallion that seemed out of place on this humble homestead. There was probably a tale associated with that discrepancy – there always was. And it never really mattered to him what the tale said because he wasn't around long enough for it to make any difference. He told himself he wasn't interested this time either.

Jacob led Fella into one of the remaining stalls, leaving an empty one between him and the other horses. He set his rifle down, hung the saddle and his saddlebags over the stall wall, dropped his bedroll onto the floor of the barn, and brushed down his buckskin gelding. Tonight he felt an extra measure of relaxation in the action that sloughed off some of the stress the day had left behind. He patted Fella affectionately on the nose as he secured him in the stall before leaving him a little water, a few oats, and an open stall and barn door. The horse would come out by the cabin when he was finished.

As he went about the business of milking the cow and gathering eggs, his mind raced with thoughts of this woman. Something about her was hard and strong, and yet a serenity exuded from her that was almost overwhelming. And those eyes. He needed to stop thinking about her eyes. He wondered again what her story was.

That's when it occurred to him that he didn't even know her name.

⌘

His knock on the door was answered before it was finished. He searched the woman's gaze for any sign that she really didn't want him there but saw none. He couldn't explain why he felt pride in this fact, but neither could he deny it.

Stepping inside was like walking into a bank of fog, the feel of being surrounded by something of which one has no control. He didn't remember the cabin having this feel about it when he'd taken his supper here and wondered vaguely if it was truly a change in the cabin or a change in him. Whatever it was, it was a comforting feeling, like walking into … peace. He could feel his muscles one by one letting go of the layers of tension that had built up over the past hours, days, maybe even years. Yes, if he stayed here long enough, he felt sure that it, whatever it was, would reach far enough to touch the years – *not* that he would be staying that long.

Oblivious to whatever was happening inside him, the woman slid a bowl of berry cobbler and a glass of milk in front of him. When she sat down, he looked up and met her eyes. Those eyes could defeat a man. They did appear more relaxed than they had earlier, although they were just as piercing. Blaming it on weariness, he gave in and allowed himself the luxury of a few moments of just looking into two rings of clear green. He had no idea what she was thinking and he really didn't care, not right then. He just wanted to lose himself in her eyes, just for a short time, a little reprieve from his life. Finally, he broke the spell by speaking. "Mind if I ask your name?"

"Clara Jane Henson." She rolled her eyes as if embarrassed by her formality. "Clara," she amended. "Please, just call me Clara. And yours?"

"Jacob."

Her right eyebrow rose. He waited. He wondered if she would ask – and unlike he had with countless people before her, he hoped she would. He couldn't explain why, but he wanted her to know. Funny how he'd spent much of his life keeping himself from others and a few moments with this woman and those blasted eyes and he was ready to lay bare his soul. He resisted the lure.

When he offered up nothing further, she did ask. "Is that your *real* name, *Jacob*?" He could see the testing in her ... and the gentle teasing. It was a compelling combination.

He couldn't help but grin. "No, ma'am. I was given that name when I was nine years old."

Again he waited.

And again she asked. "And before then?"

"Before then I was called Lonesome Wolf." Saying it aloud after so much time was like soaring back through time to a childhood home. He wasn't sure whether or not he liked the journey.

Luckily, her voice cut in. "Lonesome Wolf. Hmm.

Seems a weighty name for a child." She paused, perhaps waiting for an explanation, one he wasn't about to give. "How do you say it in your native language?"

For a moment he just stared at her, set a little off-balance by the question, by the fact that she even thought to ask it. His voice came out softer and huskier than he intended. "Waya Natsiya.*"

"Waya Natsiya." She spoke it as if she were trying it out. He was thoroughly unprepared for the effect of hearing her say his name in the language of his people; it flooded his chest with a searing heat and stirred something ... something. And the way she surveyed him – his clothes, his hair, his face – unashamed of his awareness of her scrutiny, intensified the feeling. When her eyes made their way back to his, she pronounced her assessment, "I sense the name fits you. Pity, that." She slid an unfocused gaze off to her right as if in consideration of her own statement. When she finally looked back at him, she raised her cup to her lips and asked, "What's your tribe?"

Glad for the change of topic, he readily answered, "Cherokee. But, as you've probably guessed, I've lived many days among white men."

Clara flashed him a smile. "Yes, that became apparent as soon as you opened your mouth to speak. I would say you've spent many *years* among white men, Lonesome Wolf." Still she smiled, and her smile reached out with painless tendrils and wrapped itself around his soul. He felt himself smile back.

He cleared his throat more to remind himself of who he was than out of necessity. And who he was was not a man who should be smiling back at this woman. Still, it was reluctantly that he admitted the hour. He needed to be leaving, not that he would be going far, not before he knew the Indian situation, but she didn't need to know that. He took a quick glance around the room and away from the woman. "Speaking of being a lonesome wolf, I should be heading out. Daylight's already gone."

Before he could even stand, Clara casually waved him off in a gesture dismissive and yet inviting. Only a woman could pull off something like that. "Nonsense. Unless you have somewhere pressing you have to be, you'll stay here for the night.' She shrugged. "I have an extra room. It's the least I can do…" her smile was small and sad, "for your saving my life and all."

Jacob felt his eyes widen and heard himself stumble over his words. "I … I can't stay here alone with you. You know that. Folks wouldn't think it proper in the least."

Clara studied him curiously for a moment and then laughed a clear, easy laugh. The sound sent cascades of warmth and beauty tumbling about the cabin. She spoke with a shake of head, "Proper. Funny. It isn't proper for a woman to work the livestock, yet my cattle would've died had I neglected them. It isn't proper for a woman to shoot a gun, but I would've been dead had I not done so today and many other times before to put meat on the table. Proper should be what the Bible teaches, not some set of rules set by people quite full of themselves." She was picking up momentum, mentally taking up arms against the injustices of society. It was captivating. She was captivating. "Believe me, there is no respect in this land for *proper* via the standards of society. Out here, society-proper can get you killed." She threw both of her hands up in the air. "Besides, you'll have your own room and you'll be protecting a helpless woman from the evils lurking about in this untamed land." She stopped to offer up a sassy smile. "If that isn't proper, what is?"

Jacob laughed aloud, liking the way the rich, deep sound that vibrated the walls of the cabin was a perfect foil to the woman's light, airy laugh. "You will never make me believe that you are a helpless female." He was about to decline her offer when one word shattered all other thoughts. *STAY.* The voice boomed inside his head. The idea came uninvited, and he tried his best to dismiss it. Taking care of a woman was not in his plans, or what he had that passed for plans. If only he didn't know so well the source of that voice. But his spirit did know it and had learned to listen. Disobeying God never turned out well. Still, his brain had its doubts. He was just working up a good argument for himself when he thought about how nice it would be to sleep in a real bed. He immediately shook off that notion. There was no way, *no way*, that he would stay here in the cabin with her. It was too dangerous, for both of them, an Indian staying in the house with a white woman. But, he had absolutely nowhere to be, and he'd been planning on hanging around close by anyhow. And, it wouldn't hurt her to have a man's presence close up to the house, even if it were for one night and even if that man were him. But mostly, he knew to obey the Voice. He gave a sigh of defeat and conceded. "Okay, I'll stay here tonight. I appreciate your hospitality.

And that's when he heard the baby's cry.

⌘

He knew his jaw was slack, but he couldn't hide his shock. His gaze followed Clara as she strode with purpose to one of the two doors off the main room of the cabin. He noticed the crib through the open door. When Clara returned, she held a small bundle as if it were the most precious of packages. She moved to Jacob's side of the table, a look of pure joy upon her face, and showed him a beautiful green-eyed baby with coal black hair and pudgy arms and legs that pumped with glee.

"This is my son, Nathanael. Nathanael, this is Lonesome Wolf." Clara smiled at Jacob, who tried his best to smile in return.

He was unable to prevent the shudder that coursed through him at the thought of what would've happened if the Apache braves had entered this home. "I ... I didn't know you had a child here."

Clara gave a little shrug. "I wasn't quite up to performing the introductions earlier." Her eyes softened. "But I am now." The smile she sent down to her son spoke of more than just happiness, it held all of those maternal emotions like pride and love and a fierce loyalty that left Lonesome Wolf feeling like an interloper.

He forced himself to acknowledge the child, to smile, even though his worry over the situation had multiplied. If he could've walked away, he would have, but he didn't want to insult this woman who had been through so much and yet opened her home to a man like him with unrestrained hospitality. And he couldn't shake the sense that he would be abandoning them if he did so.

Clara easily settled into a rocking chair in the living area of the room and, with a blanket thrown over her shoulder, began nursing the baby. "Now, come, Lonesome Wolf. Have a seat and tell me what brings you to these parts." It was a gentle command, with just a hint of pleading threaded amongst the words. He of all people knew how lonely a person could get, so Jacob, or Lonesome Wolf as he was once again beginning to think of himself, moved to sit in a chair near the woman.

Before he spoke, he took in the cabin in detail. He recognized the action for the stalling tactic it was, but he also felt genuinely drawn to this place. It was rustic yet had a feeling of home. Simple, yet the details testified to the care someone had put into the place. The wood plank floor, even and swept clean. The stone fireplace, positioned along one wall with the bedrooms on either side behind it so they could draw warmth in the cold months. The rag rugs adding splashes of color and comfort. The rocking chair of exceptional workmanship. Even the sturdy shutters tightly secured over glassless windows, no doubt in response to the earlier attack as the evening could have used the breeze, warm though it would be, that the open windows would've let in. Each detail joined together to create a home filled with warmth and invitation.

"Have I overstepped?" Clara's question quietly interrupted his inventory. "I only meant to make conversation, perhaps get to know each other a little. But if you don't want to talk about yourself, I'll honor that."

He looked over at the woman. Even in the dim light of the kerosene lamp, he could tell how intense was her beauty. And the picture of her caring for her baby brought feelings he didn't know existed, feelings of longing for a home and family, useless feelings. He looked away.

He had to clear his throat before he could speak. When he did, he intended to say as little as possible without coming across as rude. "You asked what brings me to these parts." He shrugged and shook his head. "Nothing in particular. What I mean to say is I don't have any specific business near here... or anywhere in truth." He leaned his head back and stared for a long moment at the rough ceiling of the cabin as if it held scenes of the places he'd been and the things he'd witnessed. Wanting to shut them away, he spoke again. "I've traveled a long way, but sometimes I feel like I've gone nowhere." His gaze rambled uncomfortably around the room, and the words that came out next surprised him. "I have no home."

So much for intending to keep quiet.

Lonesome Wolf closely watched Clara after his impulsive declaration. All he saw in her expression was compassion, and he heard it in her voice when she whispered, "I'm sorry, Lonesome Wolf. May God grant you a home, and soon."

He made himself give her a smile, false though it was. "He's offered me a home for the night. For that I'm truly thankful – to Him and to you." To put a swift end to the topic, the solemn mood, and any chance the situation had of getting any more out of control, he silently apologized to God and said, "But I just can't stay." Surely God would understand that Lonesome Wolf had to put this sentimentality behind him.

She regarded him soberly, and he knew he was hiding nothing from her. "God told me to offer you the room." She tilted her head and turned the power of her beguiling eyes on him. He braced himself when those eyes shifted to a stubborn set. "And you will use it."

"I will not." her boldness surprised the words out of him a little more defensively, and a bit less demandingly, than he wished.

"You will." Head tilted up, jaw firm, Clara looked like she was settled in for a showdown.

Lonesome Wolf crossed his arms over his broad chest. Clara could not out-stubborn him. "I am not staying inside this cabin with you, Clara." This time, his words firm, commanding even.

Her eyes assessed his for a flicker of time. "Fine! You can stay on the porch!"

"Fine, I'll stay on the porch."

Clara huffed out a dramatic sigh and breathed in a dramatic breath. Then she crooked up her mouth, and gave him a sassy grin. "Fine."

Fine. That one word and Lonesome Wolf realized he had been outmaneuvered. He chuckled at this singular woman with a stubborn streak wide enough to rival the Texas sky... with the gentle sound of the privileged South peaking through her voice despite the rugged reminder of life in the West surrounding her... and with a dangerous spark of mischievousness in her green, green eyes.

He'd have to watch himself or he could easily fall for her. He certainly hoped the Good Lord didn't intend for him to stay long enough for that to happen, because if there was one thing he knew, it was the type of trouble he could bring to her door if he allowed himself to get too close to her.

Clara put Nathanael to her shoulder and burped him. Then she sat him on her lap, talking to him as he cooed back to her. And despite the warning thoughts running through his mind, Lonesome Wolf couldn't turn away from the scene, couldn't stop the warming of his heart that the beautiful child ignited, couldn't keep himself from watching them with a tender admiration. After a short while, he realized Clara was looking at him.

"Have you any children, Lonesome Wolf?"

He was shaken, but her eyes steadied him. The "no" he breathed out barely registered to him.

"Hmm." She studied him closely, taking in one feature at a time until her eyes reached his again. "You watch him with the eyes of a father."

He didn't know how to respond, and he couldn't hold up under the woman's piercing eyes, so he looked away. It was less than a moment before he was compelled to look back at her.

She must have sensed his uneasiness because she switched tacks. In an act that showcased what he would soon fondly refer to as Clara's boundless curiosity, she turned her face but slid her eyes his way and asked a question as if she didn't look directly at him it would be less ... well, nosy. "So, do you miss your family?"

As far as he was concerned unrequited curiosity built character.

"Haven't had a family in eleven years. I rode out one day, and I haven't stopped riding since." And that was all he planned to say on the matter, but his gaze migrated to the empty fireplace, his mind's eye watching long dead flames dance and pop in flares of yellow and orange. Lost in the image, he gave up a quiet confession. "It felt like I left pursuing as much as fleeing, but I have no idea what I was hunting or if I'll ever find it."

The weight of Clara's scrutiny yanked his eyes back to hers. The corners of her mouth barely curved upward in a poignant smile. "Lonesome. Wolf."

He looked away from her. Yes. He was aptly named.

CHAPTER TWO

Lonesome Wolf spread his bedroll onto the hard packed ground by the side porch. He sighed with a weariness he hadn't noticed until he lay atop the thick blanket Clara had insisted he borrow. Tired though his body was, his thoughts wouldn't quiet so that he could sleep. He couldn't let go of the attack that afternoon or of the feeling that those braves had not been a small band of four. Tomorrow he would follow the signs farther, far enough to find a bit of peace about the matter. Or far enough to read the true tale.

It wasn't, however, thoughts only of the Apaches that troubled him. The entire evening seemed like it had happened in another time, another place. He replayed his conversation with the woman, with Clara, in his mind. He'd never been so affected by another person before. It was like she possessed something within her that he needed.

The word he'd heard so clearly resounded in his mind. *STAY.* Was that truly what God wanted him to do? He wasn't at all sure that it was what *he* wanted to do. He was kind of partial to the idea of riding out at sunrise and leaving this appealing woman and her baby far behind...

and saving them all from the trouble surely to come if anyone caught him alone with her. White folks in this part of Texas didn't take too kindly to the red man.

He had seen it happen with Indians who dared get close to a white woman. Physical attacks. Harsh looks that so often preceded pushing, spitting, tripping, laughter. Hangings. Suspicious glances, worse somehow than ones that clearly sprung from hatred, worse because they spoke silently of unease, of ignorance not soon to be rectified, of fear. A flit of pain striked across his ribs on the left side, a remembrance of what happens when the wrong person gets the wrong idea about a man simply because his skin is dark. The memory-pain disappeared quicker than it had hit, but the hurt that followed it was much, much worse.
If only she hadn't stopped and smiled at Franklin, if the old Creek hadn't stopped, too. If he hadn't spoken to her, if they hadn't walked down that boardwalk in the wrong direction, if he hadn't made her laugh, if she hadn't put her hand on his arm and looked at him with eyes sparkling, if he hadn't reached over in his old-man way and patted her hand, if she hadn't been born into a family with a brother who hated seeing her with an Indian so fiercely that he would rather see her lying on the side of the street, knocked down from the boardwalk, would rather hear her cries of begging as he slid the whip from its place by his saddle and lifted it up over his head only to bring it oh-so-much-more-quickly down, would rather hear her pleads and apologies and promises as he felt the leather slice –

Lonesome Wolf rolled over, trying to find enough comfort despite his troubling thoughts. It was quite some time before sleep could overcome his mind.

⌘

Clara placed Nathanael in his crib and kissed him

lightly on the forehead before slipping between the covers of her bed. She blew out the lamp on the bedside table and settled in for the night.

Except her mind wouldn't settle. It was consumed with the events of the day. The attack had shaken her. She'd never known such fear, and it threatened to overwhelm her.

She couldn't stop her mind from travelling the never-ends-in-a-good-place road of what-ifs. What if she hadn't kept her rifle loaded like Tremont had told her to but Rob hadn't wanted her to? What if the attack had come before she'd had the chance to spend long hours of many days loading and unloading and of aiming and of shooting and of becoming familiar enough with the gun that wondering what to do with it was not part of her reaction to hearing that eerie sound pierce the peace of her cabin? What if Nathanael had woken up during that tense moment when she had seen her first attacker and he had seen her? What if the man had not shown up just when she needed saving in a way she never had before and hoped never to again? What if he had been like them instead of the good, kind man she already knew him to be? What if, instead of helping her, he had pulled a bow from behind himself and aimed it at her as she met him at the window and –

"No!" The word tore out from her soul in an attempt to stop the bombardment of all the horrid things that could've happened but hadn't. That hadn't because God had chosen to save her, to send her a protector.

As the rush subsided, she was left with two words. A name. Lonesome Wolf. Waya Natsiya.

She began to pray. To pray that the man would accept her hospitality and that God would change the name of this Lonesome Wolf.

⌘

She awoke just before dawn fully broke. Nathanael saw to that. Although she wasn't about to complain to waking up to the beautiful sound of "Mama, Mama, Mama," she might have asked to sleep in just a little while longer. The corners of her mouth lifted easily as she heard Nathanael's morning-time chant and saw the smile of love peeking out from above the rail of the crib. She dressed quickly, talking quietly to Nathanael while she did so to keep him happy. Then she took the baby from his crib and got him ready for the day.

As she made her way into the living area, she looked at the closed door of the cabin. She walked to it and peered outside. The bedroll was picked up, the blanket was folded and laid on the small wash table on the porch, and the man was gone; it was almost as if no one had been there at all. She took in the empty spot where he'd slept and felt a pang of hurt.

Silly woman, she chided herself. *What exactly is it you thought was going to happen? That he would stay? When he so obviously wanted to run from you?* She considered the ridiculously self-involved thought and swiftly dismissed it. It wasn't her the man was running from – that fact was clear. But he *was* running. And whatever he was fleeing had left a dark mark on his peace. *And you, you had... what? Some foolish idea that you could simply give him some of yours? Just like that? Just open your arms and let it float out for him to grab?* And what made her think he would just take it? Just look at her and be so overcome with a desire to suddenly heal himself? *Silly woman.* And here she was missing a man she didn't even know when she should be mixing up her biscuits. *Silly, silly woman.* She swiped the back of her hand across her cheek to wipe off what some might think was a tear but surely was only a drop of water that had appeared there from somewhere and left a smear of flour behind itself.

It was as she moved to the stove to begin breakfast when she heard the distinct ring of ax on wood. Even though she was the only one who could see her, she tried desperately not to let herself show how relieved she was. Despite her best effort, she lost the battle with a smile. She had no idea it was so beautiful it caused even the streak of flour to look appealing.

⌘

The troubled sleep he'd gotten the night before had done nothing to settle Lonesome Wolf's mood. Never before had he felt so much like his insides were heading off in two different directions. A part of him felt more at peace than… well, than he'd ever felt in his entire life. And yet the better part of him was so unsettled his skin was fairly crawling. While watching the sun rise that morning, he had finally admitted to himself the source of his anxiety. He was afraid.

As he chopped wood, he faced that idea. He shamefully realized that the fear was not only in regards to the very real threat of what his heritage could bring down upon all of them, but also to the emotions swirling in his gut. All these long years he had worked so hard, been so careful. He hadn't allowed himself to get close to anyone. He had forgiven God for things best forgotten, but decided long ago that he wouldn't come to care for another person when the pain of losing them was just too great. Always before he'd been able to stay somewhere for a time, work as a ranch hand or some such, and leave before he got emotionally involved with the people there. Even during the time he'd spent with Franklin, he'd been careful to learn from the old man but not to get too personal, not to get too attached. He'd been so vigilant. And now this woman and her baby threatened to work their way in past his defenses... and it had taken them only one evening. And now he was supposed to *stay*? He wasn't sure why God would ask such a thing of him.

He looked at the small stack of firewood. It would do for now, more than do, but he wanted her to have a store of firewood in case he left soon. The less she had to chop later, the better. He'd already milked the cow and seen to Clara's horses, putting them out in the pasture for some exercise. He'd also saddled Fella, leaving him ground-tied by the side door.

Now for breakfast. As he made his way toward the cabin door he smelled the distinct smell of biscuits baking. His stomach rumbled in answer to their call.

When he reached the door on the porch, he hesitated. Should he knock or just go in? As he stood there pondering, the door opened and Clara smiled up at him. His breath caught in his chest and he coughed to cover the slip.

"You can just come on in, no need to knock. If that's what you were wondering," she called to him as she went back to the stove.

He moved through the narrow doorway, shoulders almost touching either side, and stepped into the kitchen. Clara worked while carrying the baby, bouncing him as she went. She looked over her shoulder at Lonesome Wolf as she tried to wipe her hands off on an apron. "I need to milk the cow, and then I'll get the rest of breakfast on."

"Cow's milked," he said as he reached outside for the pail of rich white liquid and set it on the counter.

Clara smiled at him and shook her head. "Cow's milked. Wood's chopped. You gonna do my laundry later?"

Lonesome Wolf laughed. "I will, ma'am, but I can't guarantee the outcome." He paused and then added hesitantly, "But I'll hold the baby while you finish breakfast, if you'd like."

⌘

Clara couldn't hide the amusement from her eyes. She wondered just how comfortable this man would be holding a baby. She laughed a little inside at the idea of his playing nursemaid to an eight-month-old. Even so, she passed Nathanael over to Lonesome Wolf without hesitation and nodded toward the rocker. "If you want to rock him, he should go back to sleep for a couple hours."

She watched as the big Indian took the baby with a tenderness that some mothers didn't possess. He pulled Nathanael in close to his body and carried him slowly but with confidence over to the rocker, talking quietly to him the whole way. The chair had obviously been made for Clara, not a grown man, but Lonesome Wolf fit himself into it and set it gently into motion. Before she'd finished frying the eggs and bacon, Nathanael was asleep.

Whispering loudly to her, Lonesome Wolf asked, "Where should I put him? Or do you want me to hold him 'til you're done?"

Clara pointed with the spatula to the open door of her room. "You can lay him in the crib there. And you don't have to whisper; you won't wake him." She smiled and Lonesome Wolf carried the baby with slow, concentrated steps into the bedroom.

Fascinated, she observed him as he took the baby and placed him in the crib. And then she watched as this man she'd known for not even a day leaned over the side of the crib and kissed her baby. Unbidden, a tear rose to the surface and traced a path down her cheek. She turned quickly back to the stove and wiped her face.

As she placed breakfast on the table, Clara didn't look at Lonesome Wolf lest her feelings show. Exactly what those feelings were she really didn't know, but they overwhelmed her and she thought better of sharing them. When she sat down to eat, he reached over and took her hand. Her eyes shot up then, but his head was bowed, and he was saying grace. She quickly bowed her head and joined him. He released her hand at the sound of his "Amen," but Clara could still feel the burn of his touch for some time after.

⌘

The breakfast dishes were cleared and in the washtub. Clara wiped down the table, and Lonesome Wolf quietly began to wash the dishes. Clara was going to have none of that.

"What are you doing?" She sounded offended, and a tad skeptical of his abilities.

"It's called washing dishes," he said with a mischievous grin. "This way they're ready to use again next time you need them."

Clara rolled her eyes at him and swatted him with a dishtowel. "Very cute. Move over and let me."

He shook his head. "I'll wash. You can dry and put away."

His tone brooked no argument, and she must have realized he wasn't going to budge because she moved to his side and they worked together in silence for a few minutes before she quietly asked, "The Indians yesterday, what were they?"

"Apache... Mescalero," he answered simply. Wondering how candid he should be, he scrubbed a plate until it squeaked. He decided she needed to know the truth, probably already suspected it. "Clara, they may have been part of a bigger party. There could be others close by or headed this a way."

"I know," was her solemn reply.

"I'm going to have to leave you as soon as we're done to scout out the area. I don't want to go and leave you alone with the threat so real, but it's got to be done."

"I know," she repeated, this time with a touch of tenderness.

He looked into her eyes for far too long a time and then, staring at the sudsy dish in his hand, issued her the warning, "Don't go outside today. Keep the doors locked and the windows latched, but keep an eye out, too. Check through the peephole and the cracks in the shutters every little bit, and stop what you're doing and listen pretty regular. A man, or woman, should be aware of what's around him." He waited for her to agree before continuing, "I'll be gone most of the day. I'll make sure you know it's me when I get back."

Clara didn't respond. She didn't even look at him. Rather, she stared at the back wall of the cabin as if there were a window there. When he spoke her name softly, she took a breath and gave him a small smile. "I'll be listening for you."

"I won't leave you alone tonight, I promise."

When she simply looked at him with green eyes tightened with apprehension, he gathered up his guns and headed for the door. Just before he walked through it, Clara stopped him with a loud, "Wait!"

She began moving about the kitchen, wrapping biscuits and bacon, "Here. You'll get hungry." She handed him a bundle of still warm food wrapped in a kitchen towel. "And Lonesome Wolf," she met his eyes and the worry in them almost felled him, "you be careful."

⌘

He walked slowly from the cabin, searching as far into the distance as his sight could reach, as far into the trees as he could see. He moved his eyes slowly from side to side searching for any movement. If there were still Mescalero out there, he wanted to see them before they saw him. He moved cautiously, setting each moccasined foot down easy before it bore his weight, making no sound as he moved farther and farther from Clara's home. Every several feet he paused, putting ear to wind to hear any sound that wasn't native to the land. He was especially watchful when he stepped from the woods and into a spot of open, rolling hills where it would be easier to see but easier to be seen, too. At least there he didn't have the murmur of the trees to mask his hearing.

He passed through the open space without incident and entered once again into the West Texas woods. The ground in the area was littered with rocks and twigs, and a body had to be careful not to make too much noise. It was a slow going process, but a calming one despite the danger he was searching for. If he did, in fact, have any kind of home, it was this – the outside, the woods, the land.

He saw the flickers of movement just before he heard the snuffling. Four horses were standing in a small unit. Four horses belonging to four dead Apache. Four horses that could, with twitching ears or a warning whinny, signal the rest of a raiding party. Four horses that might be there to lure him to them. One thing Franklin had taught him was that patience could save a man's life, so he stood stock still for long minutes, listening and watching for movement. Then slowly, he made wider and wider circles around the horses grazing in the small clearing, until finally, he determined that there was no trap. He left the horses where they stood until he could come back for them when he finished his search.

He stopped for a long while when he entered another section of woods. He took in the shrubs, the low hanging branches, the trunks, and the scurry of small critters moving about the ground and rustling the trees above. The wind had picked up and blew a gentle symphony of oak, cottonwood, and mesquite leaves. A beautiful sound but not one good for scouting.

He spent the entire day making a wide circle around Clara's cabin. He checked the woods, the arroyos, the creek sides, the shallow caves carved into the cliff edges. He checked everywhere he would've hidden had he not wanted to be found.

His search was long, cautious, and thankfully, turned up no sign of any other Indians nearby.

CHAPTER THREE

The day was half gone and Clara had been praying for most of it. She thanked God for His peace and for sending her help at just the time she needed it. For it *had* been God's work. The likelihood that someone was close enough to her cabin just when she needed him was too remote to be anything but a miracle. She shuddered at the thought of what would have happened if Lonesome Wolf hadn't shown up when he did. The thought was like a shotgun blast that scattered images through her mind. Images of the man who had helped save her out there all by himself with the possibility of Indians lying in wait. Images of herself and Nathanael here alone. Images of... She needed to take her mind off her worry.

She set down her mending, moved Nathanael back over to his blocks, and decided to can some of the tomatoes she'd picked yesterday. She had been planning on canning them with the ones she picked today, but since she wasn't leaving the relative safety of the house until Lonesome Wolf told her she could, she decided to go ahead with the chore. It wasn't much of an activity to help take her mind off the situation, and it would be hot as blue blazes, but it would have to do.

She was taking supper off the stove and putting a cloth over it to try and keep it as warm as possible for Lonesome Wolf's return when she heard him holler, "Ma'am! Hello!" She was relieved at the lack of stress in his voice. "I'm back! Come see what I brought."

Clara grabbed the baby and rushed to the back door, throwing it open so hard it banged off the kitchen wall. Her worry disappeared in a rush of excitement. Lonesome Wolf had returned to the homestead leading one black, two bays, and an appaloosa. Presumably the Indians' horses. All good stock. All probably stolen, but there was nothing to be done about that.

"You didn't find anything?" she asked, just to be sure.

"Nothing but these." He waved his hand through the air, presenting the horses to her.

"They're wonderful," she breathed out as she followed him out to the back pasture. Nathanael pointed at the horses and babbled the whole way. "I've always loved horses. Used to ride like the wind when Mother wasn't around."

Lonesome Wolf grinned. "I noticed you have some more-than-decent horseflesh. That mare of yours is something else."

Clara nodded. "She was a gift from Robert for our wedding. Best present I ever got besides this here." She hefted Nathanael high in the air, enjoying his baby giggles.

"I was going to talk to you about breeding her with that Stallion you have. He's a beauty, and well-tempered. You'd get a good foal. For that matter, you've got three more mares here, you could breed them all. I'd wait and see how this guy here," he gestured to the bay he'd hobbled when he first rode in, "acts around us before I bred him. He gave me a touch of trouble on the way in." His grin said it was more than just a touch of trouble. "Anyway, you could sell the foals come next spring and make some money. You probably know someone who could help you find a buyer when the time comes. Somebody who knows everyone around these parts and how they treat their horses. "

Clara laughed. "Oh, yeah. If something goes on around here, Jim Kearney knows about it." She watched as Lonesome Wolf one-by-one introduced the horses into the pasture, making sure all parties accepted each other. When he returned to where she stood, she told him, "If you think it's a good idea, then I'm in agreement."

"Alright. We'll discuss it later. I can at least tell you what to talk to this Kearney fellow about."

After he had watched a while, making sure everything was set with the new horses, Lonesome Wolf turned to Clara. "Any chance you have something to eat in there? I'm famished."

"I just finished up supper. You're right on time." She grinned at him and winked. "Must be a habit."

⌘

Clara's hand stilled on the plate she was drying and looked up at Lonesome Wolf. She watched him for a long while, seeming to weigh her words before she spoke them. "I think you should stay." He said nothing. "With me." He smiled. "What I mean is …"

"I know what you mean," he said, glancing down at her. "I was wondering how I was going to invite myself to stay at a woman's home."

"Good." She nodded decisively. "It's settled then."

"But I'm not staying in the house." He put as much finality in his voice as possible, and still she made a face and started to speak. But, when he raised an eyebrow and shot her a warning look, all she ended up saying was, "We'll see." Then she shook her head. "Good thing we don't live in town. Folks would talk."

And that was one of several things that worried him.

⌘

He was heading out to the barn for his bedroll, thinking that maybe he'd sleep in an empty stall and take advantage of a fresh pile of hay instead of lying another night on the baked dirt of the side yard, when Clara came racing after him, Nathanael giggling on her hip at his mother's fast, bumpy pace. Lonesome Wolf stopped and let her catch up to him. As she neared, he could see the excitement in her eyes, and he felt his curiosity begin to mount when Clara thrust Nathanael at him and took off for the barn.

Bemused, he looked down at the baby as if perhaps the little boy had an answer for his mother's behavior, but Nathanael only smiled and slapped his hand against Lonesome Wolf's cheek. "You don't know what has gotten into your mother either, huh? Well, lot of help you are." He grinned at the baby's giggles and was about to speak to him again when Clara's voice rang through the waning light of the evening.

"Are you coming or not?"

He looked at Nathanael and taking the baby's toothless grin as encouragement enough, strode into the barn after Clara.

"There it is!"

He followed her voice into the tack room and saw what she'd found. A rolled up tick sat on a high shelf amongst the nails and tack oil.

"Get it down, would you? But hand me the baby in case there are critters in it."

Chuckling, he passed off the baby and didn't even try to hide his amusement when Clara moved to just outside the doorway. Apparently the fearless woman had an aversion to critters. Reaching up, he gingerly brought down the thin mattress, holding it by one corner in case a family of mice had made it a home. He wasn't much on critters himself. He twirled it around and, though he could plainly see where the material *had* been chewed away, no rodents were currently in residence that he could tell. He was surprised to see feathers escaping the tear in the fabric.

"It's for you!" Clara bounced on the balls of her feet as she watched for his reaction. "I didn't even think about it last night, but Cletus's old bunk is still in the little room on the other side of the barn." At his silence, she went on to explain. "We hired a hand named Cletus to help out. After Robert died, Cletus went to the neighbor's with most of my cattle. But his little room and bunk are still here." She held out a triumphant hand indicating the tick he still grasped by a corner. "And you, sir, have a bed. A real, honest to goodness, bed."

"Your hand had a feather bed?" he asked, incredulous.

She blushed, and Lonesome Wolf felt a stirring of some dark emotion swirling like a muddy, green vortex in his belly – an emotion that he did not in the least bit like and refused to name. He did allow himself the admission that he hoped he never had to meet this man called Cletus.

Clara's voice broke through his thoughts before the irrational feeling could gain a firm hold. "It was his Christmas present that first year. Robert said I spoiled the help, but Cletus was more family than help. And he worked so hard. And, well, I grew up with feather beds, and we had one and it didn't seem right that Cletus had to go without, so…" She shrugged and turned on her heel to cross the barn only to pivot full circle, grab the lantern by the door, and hold it out expectantly.

When Lonesome Wolf didn't immediately comply with her implied wishes, Clara huffed out an impatient, "Take it and light it, would you? It's getting dark."

Chuckling, he lit the lantern and followed her to a door to what he had assumed was another storage room but was clearly a bunkroom – the tiniest bunkroom he'd ever seen, but a bunkroom nonetheless.

He set the mattress on the bunk that sat along one wall and the lantern on a small table along the other. There was perhaps one stride between the two pieces of furniture, if one had stubby legs.

She turned to him and beamed, "Welcome to your new room! I have some bedclothes in the house that fit the bunk mattress. I'll launder them tomorrow so they're nice and fresh, but tonight you'll have to make due with a blanket." At his continued silence, her smile dimmed. "Is it okay? I mean, you said you wouldn't use the spare room, which I think is just plain silly, and I know it isn't very spacious, which the extra room *is* by the way. I mean, it isn't like –"

Lonesome Wolf held up a hand to stop that train from leaving the station again. "It's great, Clara. It's… well, it's more than I've had in a long while. Thank you."

She nodded, smile back in place, and then left to retrieve the blanket he'd used the night before, a now-sleeping Nathanael in her arms. She came back without the baby but with arms full of the blanket, a pillow, a tin pitcher of water with matching cup, and a small piece of linen. She set the items on the table, wrinkling her nose at the dust and grime on the tabletop. "I'll have to do something about that," she murmured more to herself than to him. A second trip to the house produced a wet kitchen rag and a broom. Lonesome Wolf was pretty sure that she'd forgotten his presence entirely. She wiped down the table like she was expecting an inspection of her work and beat the tick as if she were trying to bash to death any living thing unlucky enough to have crawled inside it. Then, with a continued brisk efficiency that he was coming to expect from her, she snapped open the blanket and commenced to cover the bludgeoned mattress.

As he watched Clara fix up his bed, he acknowledged the warring thoughts battering against each other in his head. He wondered how long it had been since he'd slept on a feather mattress and laid his head on a pillow. A very long time. Too long. It spoke of a comfort with which he'd become wildly unfamiliar.

Unsettled, he had to fight the urge to flee this taste of home life all while longingly eyeing the comfort of the bed and the care of the woman readying it for him. It seemed he'd experienced more emotion in the hours since meeting Clara than in the many years past. It was unacceptable. He gave himself a stern command to stop *feeling*.

At long last, with Clara safely back in her cabin, he quietly closed the door to his room. Climbing into the bed felt foreign… and wonderful. He let his muscles relax, could feel the tension leave them. He smiled as he thought of stubborn Clara with both arms filled to overflowing with things for his room and shaking her head at his offer to help. He'd just stood around while she set things to right, and then she'd bid him goodnight and left as swiftly as she'd trailed him outside earlier.

The woman was something else; that was for sure. She had to be to make it out here at all, much less to stay on after her husband died. He couldn't believe she'd taken care of things on her own for so long. Whatever she had been before she came here, she was a true woman of the West now. Even so, he was thankful God had sent him here to help her. The thought of helping her brought to mind Cletus. He frowned, wondered why *Cletus* hadn't stuck around to see to her after her husband died. He liked the cowboy less and less the more he thought about him – and it wasn't all to do with the feeling a bit like jealousy that coursed through him at the mention of the man's name. *Cletus*. Cattle or no cattle, the man should've stayed here and helped her. Maybe he felt like it wasn't proper since she was a widow and they'd be out here by themselves. It wouldn't have been an unheard of situation, not by a long shot. Survival overrode delicate sensibilities in this land that tested one's mettle in ways that could prove life or death.

He tried to push from his mind the fact that he *was* out here alone with her. Clara's voice flitted across his mind. "*Good thing we don't live in town. Folks would talk.*" He looked at the situation from both sides. True, it wasn't exactly the best choice of things, but it was better than leaving a woman to fend for herself. Especially considering the attack of the day before. What kind of man would he be if he walked away from her now?

But what kind of man was he to stay? Would it prove, in the end, to cause her more harm than good to have a Cherokee staying in her tiny, little bunkroom?

After chewing on the idea forward and backward, he settled on trusting God, whatever happened, and drifted off to sleep.

⌘

As they ate breakfast the next morning, Clara stole quick glances at him from under her eyelashes, her interest in this stranger now peeked. She'd tried not to notice yesterday just how handsome he was, but she couldn't deny it now. His features were strong. Black eyelashes surrounded his dark eyes. She snuck another look. Straight nose. Square jaw. Another peek. Sleek black hair that hung loose just past his shoulders. A longer, more assessing gaze. Tan skin that did nothing but accentuate his features.

Just as she bit into a biscuit slathered with honey, Lonesome Wolf spoke. "Something on your mind?"

She looked him full in the face and noted a slight look of amusement. Apparently she'd been caught looking. The biscuit seemed to expand in her mouth. She held up a finger as she chewed … and chewed. His amusement only grew. He took a big bite of egg and smiled around his fork. Finally, she was able to swallow the biscuit. She lifted her chin and held his eyes. "You're very handsome."

He choked. Now it was her turn to be amused. He had, after all, asked her what she was thinking. If he thought to embarrass her, he'd failed miserably. She, on the other hand, had definitely embarrassed him. She wouldn't have thought that one could see the blush on an Indian. He had stopped choking, but he still didn't look at her.

They went back to eating in silence.

After the chore of morning dishes was done, Clara had noticed that Lonesome Wolf's blue chambray shirt was wet all along his left shoulder and arm. She shook her head at him. "How did you manage to get your shirtsleeve so wet?"

Hesitating before he answered and then deciding that now was not the time to start being dishonest, he replied with as light and dismissive a tone as possible, "Oh. I had a run-in with a mesquite tree the other day. Prickly things."

Clara scowled at him. "The other day as in the day you came to my rescue?"

He shrugged, not wanting her to feel responsible. "It's nothing to worry about. Just a few scratches."

"Not unless they get infected." She threw down her dishtowel and gave him a stern look worthy of sheriff to outlaw – or mother to small child. "Take your shirt off."

"Excuse me?" He almost choked on his spit.

"I said take your shirt off so I can clean and treat those *scratches*, if in fact that is all they are."

"I washed them last night, Clara," he said, trying to hide a smile and thinking that no way was he taking off his shirt and letting her touch him. "I'm fine."

"Well, I'm not. Now take your shirt off and sit down." She turned to the cabinet and as she took out a bottle of whiskey, a tub of salve, and some clean cloths, she ordered, "That shirt had better be off before I turn around."

He didn't think he'd ever been more tempted to laugh. Somehow, he did not think Clara would find the humor. He also had serious doubts as to how wise it was to cross this woman. So, contrary to what he had just thought, he obediently sat down and took off his shirt. And began the agony of the torture that was Clara touching him. He wasn't sure which burned more, the gouges – because they certainly were more than scratches – from the mesquite thorns or Clara's fingers brushing against his arm.

He decided it would be much better to focus on the negative than on anything that felt nice. After all, he'd made it through this many years surviving by looking at the negatives. And this situation was ripe with them. First off, he found himself attracted to her in a way that was as sharp and painful as the mesquite thorns, because nothing could ever, ever come of it. In fact, he reminded himself again, if the wrong person saw him here it could mean trouble for her, or him, or both of them. Second of all, she seemed to genuinely care, and people who cared made others want to care. Caring was not an option for him, and he didn't want it to become one. And thirdly, she was impertinent. And bossy. And beautiful. Which brought him back around to point number one.

By the time she had cleaned, doctored, and dressed his arm, Lonesome Wolf had worked himself into a flat-out foul mood. As soon as she tied off the bandage, he leapt from his chair and stalked outside, pulling his shirt on as he went and leaving a surprised Clara standing in the kitchen.

~~~

Whether to ease his own frustrations or by way of apology to Clara, Lonesome Wolf spent the better part of the day working around the home place. It was plain to see the woman had done the best she could under the circumstances, remarkably well, actually, but she hadn't been able both to care for a baby and do the work of a man. It was fine with him, the more to keep him busy and out of the house. The place had much potential, and Lonesome Wolf found himself assessing future additions as well as needed repairs.

As he worked, he felt the sun's wrath as it created rivulets of sweat that ran down his back and face. He'd braided and bound his hair with a length of leather string to keep it out of his way and away from his sticky skin, but the act was little defense against the Texas weather. Still, he felt an almost kinship with the heat, as it was forever intertwined with the land, a land he'd travelled much and long viewed as his home, the whole expanse of it.

While Lonesome Wolf sat atop the roof mending holes and losing himself in the menial task, he thought again to that morning. He gave a shake of his head at his behavior toward the confounded woman. He'd have to be nicer if he was going to stay here, and someone needed to stay here to help protect her. He wasn't sure what God had in mind with assigning him that particular task, but he'd learned long ago to be obedient. It'd saved him on more than one occasion.

Two days before, it had saved Clara and the baby, as well.

⌘

At supper that evening, Clara was ever welcoming as she set the table and filled plates. He waited patiently for her to throw a serving spoon at him and tell him to dish up his own food, but she acted as if she had no recollection of his rude behavior that morning. She asked him to pray again, served him first, and then fed Nathanael bits and pieces of her supper, talking amiably the entire time. Lonesome Wolf felt a keen sense of relief at first, but as the meal wore on his clothes began to bother him, as if they suddenly didn't fit right. And the food that was so delicious to begin with began to taste like the dust of an arid Mexican plain. At last he admitted the unwelcome truth that he couldn't let it go on, ignoring the situation, nor could his conscience allow her to let him get away with it. He was going to have to say he was sorry, no matter how much neither of them seemed to wish it so. Living right was often quite a bit uncomfortable. If he had to do it, he would rather apologize soon and get it out of the way.

To that end, he set his fork down and cleared his throat. "Clara, I owe you an apology for my behavior this morning. You were mighty kind to help with my cuts and I didn't even say thank you. So..." he hesitated, thinking this wasn't coming out quite like he thought it should. His request for forgiveness sounded as begrudging as it felt. "Uhm..." he cleared his throat again and made himself look her in the eye as he forced out, "thanks."

She tipped her head to the side, a wary smile barely edging up the corners of her mouth. After an endless length of time, she asked him the one question he knew he couldn't answer. "Why did you leave like that?"

He shook his head and ignored the rasp in his voice when he told her, "It doesn't matter." And it didn't. Couldn't. Father God in heaven help him, it *wouldn't*. "I'm sorry. That's the important thing. If I'm going to be working here for a time, I don't want strain between us. It was disrespectful, and I'm sorry."

For a long moment he thought she would argue, could see the want of it warring on her face, but finally she nodded and waved it away with her fork in the air. "Apology accepted. Think nothing more of it." But he would, and he was afraid she would, too. He felt even worse when she said, "Tomorrow, give me the shirt you ripped and I'll mend it."

CHAPTER FOUR

Lonesome Wolf led the pretty bay mare out into the pasture and released her. Her deep red coat shone with the afterglow of a good currying, and she loped around, happy to be free of the saddle and the burden of a man on her back. She sidled up to Fella and snuffled loudly. Lonesome Wolf laughed as his gelding sidestepped her. He checked to make sure the new stallion, which Clara had taken to calling Marvin, was behaving himself. He was an ornery horse if he'd ever seen one, and maybe more trouble than he was worth. Lonesome Wolf would have to try extra hard to make that one tame enough to stick around.

He'd been at Clara's for almost a week and had been able to spend a considerable amount of time checking out the property. She owned quite a spread. The creek ran fairly close to the house, coming from farther away toward the northeast. The few heads of cattle remaining could easily be handled within the boundaries of a barbed wired pasture not far from the barn. But the entirety of land could hold a much, much larger herd. She'd been keeping her horses stalled in the barn, but Lonesome Wolf left them out in the pasture for the most part and had taken to riding each of them in turns so they could get good exercise. He was out there with the new horses a lot, anyway. Of the whole lot – minus Fella, of course – Clara's mare was his favorite. She was a first rate cow pony. He felt sure she'd throw a nice foal. It'd be a fairly simple way for Clara to earn some money. Although if she wanted to get the most out of it, someone should train the horse before she sold it. He could do it, but he doubted he'd still be here come spring.

He shook his head, thinking he probably wouldn't even be here come fall. He was again beginning to doubt the wisdom of staying at all. Had he not been sure that God had told him to stay, he would have fled. And fast. He wasn't her husband, and he couldn't live on here indefinitely. And he didn't want to risk becoming too involved, too attached.

He sighed deeply. It was an argument that twisted and turned in his head, going first one way and then the other. He just wouldn't think about it right then. He whistled sharply, and Fella's ears perked up and the buckskin obediently trotted over to him. He would saddle up and go for a good long ride.

⌘

The smell of coffee permeated the air and all but overpowered the smell of the blackberry pie that Clara was dishing up for dessert. As she served him, she talked. He could tell by the softness of her voice that she was going to say or ask something personal before the words she spoke were finished. But, at some point during his ride, he'd determined to be nicer, more open, so he let her ask. And he answered.

"How did you end up wandering around on your own, Lonesome Wolf?" she asked in that way she had that inspired confidence.

"When…" He cleared his throat and started over. "When I first rode off, I took nothing but what I had with me when I set off to hunting that morning. I had a rifle, a bow, and thankfully my horse – I rode a sorrel back then named Sampson." He felt a small smile begin to grow at the memory, but he ran a hand over his lips to wipe it away before it could fully form. "I had no thought as to where I was headed and, after two days on the trail, no recollection as to how I'd gotten to the creek I made camp by. I didn't know where I was. Heck, I didn't even know in which direction I'd gone."

Lonesome Wolf shook his head in an effort to dislodge the thoughts creeping up on him. He sighed heavily, breathing out the melancholy and breathing in the peace in the air of Clara's cabin. Somewhat fortified, he went on. "As I rode out on the third morning, I felt a disquiet in my spirit. I reined in Sampson to listen. I don't, to this day, know how I heard it, other than that the good Lord brought it to my ear, but I heard a cry. Whimpering, really. I came up on a boy crouched against a White Oak along the banks of the creek. Poor kid. He had his knees drawn up and his face pressed against them, and he'd covered his head with both hat and arms so much so that it muted his cries. It also shot his ability to hear anyone approach." He paused, just long enough to make sure Clara was listening, before he firmly stated, "A man should always be aware of his surroundings." He looked hard at Clara, trying to communicate the seriousness of the lesson. "Always." He waited until she nodded dutifully before he went on.

"It was when I finally spoke to him and he let out an ear-stabbing scream and jerked his head up that I realized it wasn't a boy at all, but a young girl. Turns out she was only eight years old." Lonesome Wolf chuckled. "Man, she was a feisty one. There's not anything much more ornery than a kid with something to prove. Even worse if it's a girl."

Suddenly, he remembered his audience. "No, offense, ma'am." Lonesome Wolf grinned. "But… you know the type I mean."

Clara nodded her assent primly. "I think I might." She took a sip of her coffee, eyebrows raised expectantly in an effort to encourage him to continue on.

"Well, it was a good ten, twenty minutes before I could convince her that she in fact did *not* know where she was going and needed my help." He shook his head, thinking back to the young lady. "Man, but she was a stubborn one. Turns out that she'd set off the morning before in an effort to prove to her father that girls were just as useful – her word, not mine – as boys. Seems her father paid more attention to her brothers than to her and she was feeling a little left out. Apparently her ma had died birthing the youngest son and there was only one crotchety old great-aunt to teach her how to be a lady. Only thing was, the girl agreed with her father that hunting and riding herd was more important than being able to crochet."

Lonesome Wolf took another bite of pie and washed it down with some coffee. He picked the story back up just before Clara could prod him to continue. "At any rate, Maddie, that was her name, was lost as a goose. She'd spent the whole day and night with nothing to eat and no idea how to survive out by herself. It took me two and a half hours to track her backwards and find their ranch. I wasn't so good at tracking back then."

At this point in the story, Lonesome Wolf turned into himself, staring out across the cabin's main room but seeing only what was in the distant past. Clara must have recognized something in his face because she waited patiently for him to return to the present. After several minutes he took to eating the pie again. When his piece was gone, he set down his fork, waved off the offer of a second piece, and began speaking again as if he had never stopped. "Her dad saved my life. The aunt wanted to see me hanged for 'committing unknown crimes' against her niece. I thank God that He gave the father enough sense to actually listen to Maddie to see what went on. When I returned her home, he'd immediately sent me out to the bunkhouse under the watchful gaze of three very large and heavily armed men. But in the end, when my version of what happened matched Maddie's, he couldn't thank me enough for rescuing his impetuous daughter."

Another sigh signaled a shift in tone. "He offered me a job as a ranch hand. Yates, that was his name. He taught me how to ranch in exchange for my teaching his kids, including Maddie," Lonesome Wolf grinned at the memory, "how to make it on their own in the woods, on the trail, wherever." He grew serious suddenly. "We all learned a lot in the six months I was there. We learned a lot about how to do things, but not about each other. I stayed for *six months* and no one knew me any better when I left than when I rode in." But he knew them.

"Why did you leave?"

Lonesome Wolf startled. Clara's voice must have broken the spell he seemed to have fallen under. "The aunt started causing problems, spreading stories, lies, around to the neighbors. It was causing problems for the family, so I decided it was time for me to leave." His careless shrug belied the sentiment that clearly shone in his eyes.

Clara cleared away the dessert dishes, allowing Lonesome Wolf a private moment before she pressed on.

"So, you became a ranch hand after that?"

An odd look crept into his eyes and he stared at her overlong before he answered, "Mostly, yeah." As if he knew he had planted curiosity where he didn't want it, he quickly went on. "I found work fairly easily after that, even though I was an Indian. Mr. Yates had taught me well, and my skill outweighed my skin if I could get far enough as to be able to show my work. After that it was mainly a long series of brief stays at one ranch or another. I'd hang around until something happened, and then I'd move on."

Clara found herself intrigued by this Godly, honorable man who had apparently gone through life under suspicion simply because of his heritage. "What kind of things happened that would make you move on?"

There was another uncomfortable silence. Finally, his answer was, "You ask a lot of questions, woman."

She grinned impishly. "That's one of the reasons I wasn't a very good debutante."

⌘

It had been over a week since the attack, and Lonesome Wolf figured enough time had passed that it was okay to approach Clara about learning to shoot the bow and arrow. She might never have to use them, but if even one time in her life the knowledge came in handy, then it was well worth the time it took to teach her.

He paused after shoveling in several bites of the beans Clara had reheated for lunch. "I thought we could practice this afternoon with the bow. What do you think? While Nathanael is down for his nap? We could set up close to the cabin so you can hear him if he wakes up before we're through."

Her answer was strong and sure, even a little excited. "Excellent. I'll rock the baby while you do the dishes."

Clara reached for his bowl and he barely caught it before she whisked it away. He mock scowled at her. "Hold your horses, woman. I'm not finished eating yet." He looked into her bowl and saw half of her beans still in it. With what was probably an overdone frown, he scolded, "And neither are you. Sit down and finish eating. It'll be there when we're done." The grin he'd been trying to hold back broke through. "I knew you'd be excited."

"Good, Clara. Hold it just like that, with the arrow pointing down. Now, bring it up and pull back the bow at the same time. Don't shoot it yet. Just practice pulling back on it."

Clara got it on the first try. She was going to be as good a shot with a bow and arrow as she was with a gun.

"Perfect. Now, put it back down again and let up on the tension. We'll do it one more time. This time, when your bow is up and ready, aim at that piece of wood. Don't look down the arrow shaft. This isn't a gun. Just look at where you want to hit and then release in a smooth motion."

She hit dead center the first release.

When he turned and looked at her, she had a rascally smile on her face and she was wiggling like a little kid. Something dawned on him. "You've done this before." It wasn't even a question.

She nodded and her smile went to full bloom.

"Clara Jane. Shooting a gun, riding a horse, shooting a bow."

"I have many talents."

"And you're ornery. No wonder you weren't a good debutante."

⌘

Just before noon several days later, Lonesome Wolf entered the cabin, carrying in a chicken with a freshly wrung neck and plucked feathers. He dropped it into an empty pot on the counter, washed his hands and arms in the washbasin by the back door, and went to Clara who was sitting in the rocker with the baby. Nathanael was crying and she was in tears. He knew she'd been up much of the night with the fussy baby and recognized an exhausted mother when he saw one. He walked over to the rocker and took Nathanael from her arms. Then he took her hand and pulled her to standing. She immediately fell against his shoulder. For a moment he forgot to breath. He put his arm around her, relishing the feel of her against him, of her leaning on him for strength. It made him think about … He blinked. He would have to refrain completely from such thoughts.

He unwrapped his arm from her and spoke softly. "Clara, why don't you go lie down and I'll take Nathanael outside with me for a while."

Clara shook her head. "I can't ask you to do that for me."

"And why not?"

"It's my job. I'm his mother."

"Yes, but you're tired. And you're not here alone anymore. Let me help you." When she didn't reply, he led her to her bedroom door, gently laid his hand on the small of her back, and nudged her inside the room. "If I can't handle it, I'll come get you. But you need to rest."

Reluctantly she nodded, crossed to the bed, and flung herself down on it.

Lonesome Wolf turned to the baby and whispered, "How about you and I go for a walk." He continued to speak softly to him, and as they left the cabin he gently bounced the baby up and down and patted his back. Once outside, Lonesome Wolf grabbed a tin pail from the porch, walked to the well, and brought up a load of water. He took a clean handkerchief from his pocket and dipped it in the bucket. He twisted it tightly, and when he put the corner into Nathanael's mouth, the baby clenched his jaw. Lonesome Wolf kissed the child's cheek and cooed to him gently, "Just as I suspected. Trying to get a tooth are you? Well, let's see if we can make you and your mama a little better, shall we?"

Pail in one hand and a more relaxed Nathanael in the other, he made his way to Clara's garden. He knelt down at the end of a row and pulled out a carrot. Then he walked away from the cabin and down to the water. Once there, he tucked Nathanael in the crook of his arm and washed the carrot. They both got a little wet, but the heat of the July sun made the frigid water feel refreshing. Lonesome Wolf filled the pail and then sat on the creekbank. When he reached to take away the wet handkerchief, Nathanael protested. "Patience, little one. I promise this will be even better." He snapped the ends off the carrot and tossed them aside. Then after dipping the handkerchief in the cold water, he placed the carrot inside, tightly twisted the cold, wet handkerchief around the carrot, and then handed it back to Nathanael. The baby instantly shoved it into his mouth and bit down.

Within seconds Nathanael grew quiet. Lonesome Wolf smiled and carried him to sit in the shade under a group of cottonwoods. As they settled against a tree, Nathanael watched Lonesome Wolf as the Indian talked quietly to him. After a short time, the baby was smiling around the carrot. He reached up with his chubby little hand and patted the big man on his cheek. Lonesome Wolf's chest felt tight and hurt with a sharp, intense pain. He loved this child. Only a few short weeks with him, and he loved him. He trusted God but didn't understand why He'd brought him here to grow attached to these people only to make him leave again one day.

When he again looked down at the baby in his arm, he saw that his eyes were drooping heavily with a need for sleep. Poor little guy was probably as tired as his ma. He carried baby and the pail of cold creek water back up to the cabin. By the time they reached the small home, Nathanael was sleeping soundly. Lonesome Wolf slipped inside and laid the child in his crib without sound so as not to wake Clara. Then he went back into the living area and fitted his large frame into the rocker. When Clara awoke after a three-hour nap, that's where she found him, sitting in the rocker and staring into the empty fireplace.

"What's on your mind, Lonesome Wolf?" He startled. He'd neither heard nor seen her come into the room. She cocked one eyebrow up into her forehead. "And a man should be aware of what's around him, should he?"

He chuckled. "He should. A couple of weeks off the road and I've already lost my edge."

Cautiously, she asked, "Is that what's on your mind? Being on the road?"

"In a way I guess. It's more *not* being on the road that I'm thinking about."

She nodded and sat beside him. He didn't want to discuss the topic further and was glad when she changed the subject. "Thank you for the nap. I was about at my wits end. How did you finally get him settled down? And how do you know so much about babies?"

"I'll show you later. And haven't I told you that you

ask too many questions? Now, are you hungry?"

"Oh, my! I forgot all about fixing your lunch. You must be starved!"

He smiled at her. "I can feed myself, Clara. Not that I prefer to do it, but I can." He didn't tell her that he hadn't eaten. "Besides, I asked you if you were hungry."

"I'll be fine until supper, which I should probably set to making. I was going to make venison stew today, but we're out of venison. How does an early meal of fried chicken sound, instead?"

"Delicious. I'll go tomorrow and try to bring in a couple more deer. I'll smoke them and then show you how to tan the hides if you like."

She laughed. "Only if you show me what to do with them after they've been tanned."

"Deal." He almost said something more, but just shook his head, instead. "I'm going to exercise the new horses before supper."

Clara eyed him as he headed out the kitchen door. She wondered what was on his mind. And if there was anything she could do to help.

CHAPTER FIVE

A rifle shot cracked the stillness of the warm summer morning. Lonesome Wolf rose from his hunter's crouch and headed toward the deer. It was a nice clean shot, right through the head. He had hooked a travois up to Fella, so he drug the animal there, taking sticks and small rocks along with him. As he set out to change spots and hopefully get one more deer, Lonesome Wolf mulled over his current situation. It was strange to feel as if he were settling down after so many years of wandering around. True, he'd taken jobs at ranches here and there for months at a time, but he'd never felt like he was settling into home. He really didn't know what to think of feeling that way now. It *wasn't* his home. And yet he felt like he had a place here.

The whole thing did nothing but create discord in his mind. And truth be told, thinking about it was bordering on an obsession. Part of himself argued that he needed to saddle up Fella and get the heck out of there, while another part felt deprived of air at the thought of riding away.

It was that woman who did it.

They'd experienced an instant kinship of some sort. It was like she'd always existed in his life. She and her son. Lonesome Wolf smiled to himself when he thought about

Nathanael. He was as calmed by Lonesome Wolf's presence as he was by his mother's. And when the baby smacked him in the face and smiled at him… Nathaniel had totally and completely taken up residence in Lonesome Wolf's heart; he might as well admit the truth of it. Then again, was that a good thing? No matter that it felt so now, it wouldn't feel so good when he was riding away from Nathanael and listening to the baby cry for him. He felt torn, not knowing what he should do. And then he heard it again. The single word command in a tranquil yet resounding voice – *STAY*. And he knew, no matter how much these people's lives, or their hearts, threatened to entangle themselves in his, for now he must stay. An instant peace drifted down upon him like a soft snowfall on this dry, hot day. He smiled and willed his mind to rest in the peace he'd been given and enjoy his hunt.

He took in a deep draught of air, appreciating the rich scent of earth. He let his ears take pleasure in the scuttle and scurry of the squirrels in the trees and looked up and thanked God for such a beautiful, expansive sky. An eagle flying high above a craggy hilltop caught his eye, and he wondered if the eagle's aerie was hidden up there somewhere amongst the jagged rocks.

His thoughts were cut short when he heard a low rumble off to his right. He didn't even have to look to know that it was the distinctive warning sound of a mountain lion. With a calmness born of experience, he turned and lifted his rifle in time to catch the cat in a ready crouch. Just as the muscles in the cougar's legs flexed to pounce, Lonesome Wolf fired his gun. It had all happened in the span of only a few seconds. If he had hesitated – or missed – he would've been in a heap of trouble. Breathing out a breath to slow his now-racing heart, he put the animal on the travois and decided it was time to call it a day.

He headed back in the direction of Clara's cabin. Perhaps he would come across another deer on his way back. He'd thought of the perfect gifts for Clara, and he needed to make sure he had enough hide for the project.

⌘

Clara, Nathanael on her hip, set the last plate on the table just as Lonesome Wolf walked through the door for lunch. "You have amazing timing, you know that?"

He grinned. "I try."

They sat down and asked the blessing over their ham sandwiches. Clara, while chewing, was trying to get Nathanael to eat a bite of mashed up fried potatoes left over from breakfast. He kept turning his head away and saying, "Oof, oof."

Clara swallowed and set down the spoon. "Honey, I don't know what 'oof' means." She looked over at Lonesome Wolf. "He's been saying that all morning. I haven't been able to figure out what he means."

Nathanael reached his hands out to Lonesome Wolf and repeated, "Oof, oof."

Lonesome Wolf got up and came around the table to take the child. As he settled back in his chair, Nathanael laid his head against Lonesome Wolf's shoulder and patted his chest with his little baby hand. He continued saying, "Oof, Oof," until the realization of what the baby was saying hit. He smiled and whispered in the baby's ear, "I love you, too, little one."

Clara gasped and jumped up from her seat, "Lonesome Wolf! He's saying your name!"

He quietly answered, "I know," and laid his head against Nathanael's. Getting too close was far past a lost cause. The peace he'd felt during his hunt threatened to come apart, but Lonesome Wolf worked to push aside the doubts and focus on the joy of the moment.

Clara walked around the table and leaned in to kiss Nathanael's cheek. She was so close to Lonesome Wolf that he stopped breathing. She slowly pulled away, smiling into his eyes, then returned to her seat and ate, but Lonesome Wolf just sat there with the baby lying on his shoulder. After several minutes, he could tell that Nathanael had fallen asleep. He rose and went to put him in his crib. When he returned to the kitchen, he walked past the table, leaving his lunch uneaten, and went out the door.

Clara stopped him with her voice. "Are you okay?"

Without turning to his head, he said, "I'm going out for a ride. I'll be back later," and he left, knowing that Clara would notice that he hadn't answered her question.

⌘

Two hours later Lonesome Wolf came to the cabin dripping wet with sweat. He grabbed a towel and dunked it in the pail of fresh water Clara kept by the back door. He wiped his face and neck with it as he entered the cabin. Clara watched him from where she sat on the couch reading, but decided to let him be until he wanted to talk. After a few minutes of standing in the kitchen, he asked Clara, "Did you save my sandwich?"

She nodded even though he wasn't looking at her. "It's on the counter under that dishtowel."

"Thank you." He brought the sandwich and a glass of water over to the low table in the living area and sat on the floor next to Clara to eat it. After a couple of bites he looked up at her. "What're you reading?"

"The Count of Monte Cristo."

"Will you read to me?"

"Of course." And so Clara began to read. A few

pages in, they heard Nathanael awaken. Lonesome Wolf shoved in the last bite of his sandwich and went to get the baby. He brought him back with a blanket and a couple of toys. Reclaiming his seat by Clara, Lonesome Wolf pushed aside the table, spread the blanket in front of him, and set down baby and playthings. He took a long drink of water, and then leaned his head against Clara's leg and closed his eyes. It took all within her to keep her voice steady. She wondered what had possessed him to do something so intimate, but he was in such a strange, quiet mood that she simply accepted it without question. She wasn't sure if he could hear her over the tripping of her heart, but she kept reading.

Lonesome Wolf relaxed listening to the rise and fall of her voice as she spoke the words aloud. She could feel the tension leave his body as she read. She carried on, wanting to continue to soothe his hurt, whatever it was. Without thinking, she switched her book to her right hand, reached with her left, and stroked his hair. She took a strand that had fallen forward and, hooking it beneath her finger, brought it back across his shoulder to join the others. He often kept his long hair braided, but today it was loose and she ran her fingers down it in long soft caresses. Every once in a while she would lift her hand to turn the page, and then she would continue her comforting gesture. After several chapters, her throat was getting dry and her voice was suffering. She closed the book and placed it in her lap, but she continued to run her hand through Lonesome Wolf's hair. After some time, he reached up and stilled her hand, clasping her fingers in his. He lifted her hand to his mouth. Her breath stilled as he gently kissed it then held it against his cheek.

After a long while, Clara asked softly, "Do you

want to talk about it?"

"Not right now. Can we just sit here for a while longer?"

"Of course." There was no other answer she could give, or would want to, or would fit the feeling permeating the air of the cabin.

Lonesome Wolf placed Clara's hand on his shoulder and released it, then reached out and, kissing Nathanael, pulled him into his lap. They sat there together until long after supper should've been eaten.

⌘

The next morning after a quiet breakfast, Lonesome Wolf lingered over an extra cup of coffee. Every few seconds, he glanced up at Clara. Finally, she reached a hand and covered his. It seemed like a bold gesture, but she was pretty sure they had crossed that line yesterday. He turned his hand over and held hers, gently rubbing his thumb over the back of her hand. Then he released it and, taking hold of his coffee, took another drink.

When he looked up at her again she asked, "Do you want to talk about yesterday?"

He gave her a half grin. "Which part?"

It took her a moment to realize he was flirting with her. She couldn't help herself but smile and flirt right back. "Whichever part you care to discuss."

Laughing, he shook his head. "You are something else, Clara Jane." He looked over to where Nathanael sat on the floor with his blocks, then turned back to Clara and met her eyes. "Those eyes," he said so softly she almost didn't hear. "I'm surprised that you even have to ask me about yesterday, Clara. It seems you can look at me with those eyes and know everything about me."

Clara wasn't sure how to respond. Well, that wasn't

altogether true. Something about the way he said it sent a little shiver skipping along her spine. But she wasn't sure how to respond *to him* about it.

Before she settled on anything, he was talking again. "I've thought before how hard it would be to leave here. But yesterday, when Nathanael said my name, or what he could get out as my name ..." Lonesome Wolf smiled at the memory, a brief smile that soon faded. "It just hit me that he knows who I am. I mean, you said he'd been saying it all morning. He was calling for me even when he couldn't see me. Like he *knows* me. It'll be difficult to walk away from him."

Clara sat very still for a moment. She studied Lonesome Wolf with a critical eye for a long while before she asked him, "Are you planning on leaving, Lonesome Wolf?"

"I ... uh, no. I just mean that ..."

"If you aren't planning on leaving, and I," she made sure she met his eyes, "I'm not planning on asking you to leave, then where exactly does the problem lie?"

Lonesome Wolf sighed and let his head fall back to rest on the chair. "Clara." He paused for a long while. When he looked at her again, the anguish she had seen yesterday was back. "Clara, in the past eleven years, I haven't become attached to anyone. No one. Not a single soul that I minded whether I ever saw again. Until I came here, all the people that I have ever cared for were dead." He closed his eyes and hung his head. He set his elbows on the table and ran one hand back and forth through his hair. He didn't raise his head when he spoke, and Clara could barely make out his words. "I'm not sure I can handle this." With that, he got up from the table, grabbed his hat on the way out the door, and was gone. Again.

⌘

Lonesome Wolf lay awake for hours that night, for the second night in a row. He and God had been having long talks in the wee hours. No matter how many reasons Lonesome Wolf gave God, no matter how many arguments he put forth, God kept coming back with the word *STAY*. About four hours into that second night, Lonesome Wolf conceded defeat. If God wanted him there, for however long or short a time that would be, then he'd stay there. He'd just have to guard his heart against becoming any more involved, try to separate himself from the feelings he'd so foolishly let creep up on him. For, whatever else might exist between them, Lonesome Wolf was still an Indian and Clara still was not. So, he'd accept her friendship, but that was it. He'd stay but remain apart. And he'd do his best to relax and take in the joy God had provided for him here in this place. He closed his eyes and rolled over on his side, falling asleep with visions of the sources of that joy flickering behind his eyelids.

⌘

The raging inferno that was the sun seemed bent on scorching everything it could get its rays on. About an hour before lunch, Lonesome Wolf came through the cabin door declaring how intensely hot it was outside. Clara looked up from her sewing and smiled. Nathanael was playing contentedly on the floor with a tin plate and cup. It was noisy business, but he was certainly occupied with it. Every time he slammed the two dishes together, his eyes blinked and his body jumped … and he slammed them against each other again and again and again. Lonesome Wolf walked over and picked up the child, clattering dishes and all. Nathanael beat Lonesome Wolf's head with the cup and repeated his new mantra of "Oof, Oof, Oof." Lonesome

Wolf gently took the cup from Nathanael's hand and kissed the little boy until he giggled.

Then he turned to Clara. "Is it terribly important that you sew that now?"

She raised an eyebrow to him and answered, "Well, that depends."

"I thought we could go for a picnic, down by the creek. I'll help you gather up a blanket and some food and we can take it and settle in the shade down by that little waterfall at the headwaters. The water is shallow enough there that we can wade around, get Nathanael out in the water to play. What do you say?"

She replied, "I say let's have ourselves a picnic," and he could tell by the brightness of her eyes that she was excited.

The walk down to the waterfall was uncomfortably hot. Clara squinted against the bright sun and wiped sweat off her brow. "My, but you weren't kidding about the heat. Even a warm breeze would bring a welcome relief."

"The cold creek water will help. Can you wait to eat until after the creek?"

"Oh, yes. Creek first, as fast as we can get there."

Clara spread the blanket out under the shade of a cottonwood, put the picnic basket in the middle of the blanket, hoping to keep the food free of pests, and then sat to take off her boots and stockings. Lonesome Wolf caught sight of Clara's boots.

"Clara Jane!"

"What?" She looked around her for the danger but found none. She repeated, more inquisitively this time, "What?"

"Are those *men's boots*?" He put as much shock and outrage into his voice as he could.

Clara had the grace to blush. "They are," she confirmed, sticking her nose in the air "So what?"

"So I am scandalized!" He shook his head in mock shame. "What will the other debutantes say when they see this?"

Clara threw a boot at him, laughing. "I told you I wasn't a very good debutante!" She took off for the creek, bare feet peaking from beneath her skirts.

Lonesome Wolf, enjoying her sense of humor, sat down to pull off his boots and roll up his jeans. He had to grab an escaping Nathanael who was speed crawling across the grass. Baby in hand he stood and watched as Clara knotted up her long dress to keep it from getting wet. By the time she was done, her dress was up around her knees, showing off her strong, shapely calves. That woman had no idea how beautiful she was. Lonesome Wolf willed himself to look away from her legs. Clara caught his eye when he looked up and, blessedly ignoring where he'd been looking, called to him to come in. "The water feels magnificent! What are you waiting for?"

When he and Nathanael joined her in the creek, she pronounced, "This was the best idea you've ever had, I must say." She grabbed his arm to stabilize herself as she sloshed across the rocky creek bottom, and her hand grasping the muscles of his forearm burned hotter than the Texas sun. For a moment, the only thing that existed was her hand on his arm. Everything else had faded into a blurry existence. It was at that moment, standing there in the middle of the cold and rushing waters of Clara's creek, that he realized he was in love with her. He wasn't sure exactly when it had happened – somewhere between the day he'd ridden in, when he'd first seen her beauty and heard her tinkling laughter fill the cabin, to this moment here, watching her enjoy the simple pleasure of the water and feeling her touch against his skin. He knew then that any idea he'd had about guarding his heart or separating his feelings were thoughts come too late.

When he looked at her, he saw that she was speaking. "… until I can see his face before you show him the water. I want to see his reaction."

It was worth the time and energy of the entire excursion, and the weighty discovery he'd made, to see Nathanael's face when Lonesome Wolf stuck his hand into the cold water splashing over the little waterfall. The baby seemed not to be able to decide on which thought to show, his shock at the temperature of the water, his intrigue at the falls, or his happiness in splashing water all over the adults and himself. By the time they left the falls, all three were sopping wet, but none of them cared.

Hunger did eventually drive them out of the creek and onto the picnic blanket. As they spread out their lunch, Clara was laughing and smiling almost as much as Nathanael.

Lonesome Wolf grinned at her, "You look like a kid at Christmas morning. I'm happy we came."

"Me, too. Thanks for suggesting it. I don't know why we get so bogged down by life, the daily chores and worries, and forget to enjoy ourselves with these kinds of treats more often. You should promise me that you'll try and remind me."

Lonesome Wolf thought for a moment about what she'd said. "Clara, are you unhappy with your life?"

She looked up at him with green eyes that were shining with joy and said, "Not anymore."

CHAPTER SIX

After supper, they sat together at the table, resting from the days work. Clara set down her coffee cup and watched as him as he bounced Nathanael on his knee. "Why did you leave home? You said you left with only what you'd taken hunting with you? Why?"

Lonesome Wolf almost shot down her question, more out of habit than anything else. The words, however, were bubbling up on their own, ready to get out. "My Indian village was struck with cholera when I was nine years old." Images pushed against his mind trying to get out, to be seen, to be *remembered*. Just as he thought he was going to lose the tug of war, he heard the baby drowsily chanting, "Oof...Oof..." It was the sound of *now*. He closed his eyes and listened as the chatter ran down and Nathanael leaned back and lay his head on Lonesome Wolf's chest. He took a moment to savor the little life he held. When he opened his eyes, he saw that Nathanael had already fallen into the gentle sleep of a child who knows he is loved. Rising quietly, he took the baby to his bed.

He began speaking before he reached the table, before Clara has a chance to ask anything more. It would be much easier to simply state what happened than to answer more of Clara's curious questions. "A lot of my people died, including my parents, my brothers, and my baby sister." He could see words of condolence coming from Clara, so he stopped her with, "Every family was hit hard. A white couple, friends of my family, took me in, nursed me back to health, taught me about our Savior. I lived with them for over seven years. Then," he allowed a sigh to escape but pushed quickly through, "they were killed by a band of Comanche while I was out hunting." He pushed aside the question as to why he was about to reveal so much of himself – a self he'd spent years protecting from others – and before he could stop, he was spilling the past he'd kept so closely guarded for so long. "I came home to a burned down cabin and smoldering barn and … death, everywhere. I buried them. My mother and father, who had taken in a young Cherokee boy and raised him as if they had birthed him, my two younger sisters who loved me like I was truly their brother and looked up to me like I was a hero–" He heard the crack of his voice, but forced out "and" before clearing his throat. "And they all were dead. When I rode in, the smoke was still hovering around. The heat from the burning house was so intense I could barely get close to the... to their… to them. I buried them," he repeated softly.

The quiet in the little cabin rang loudly in Lonesome Wolf's ears. He couldn't take it. If it didn't stop, he would sink inside himself and he didn't trust himself to ever come up to the surface again. "Say something," he demanded. When she only looked at him with those blasted eyes of hers, he raised his voice louder. "Say something, Clara. Ask me one of your questions." At her continued look of confusion, he pleaded with her, "Ask me one of your questions."

Clara's voice broke through the quiet as she softly

asked, "That's when you found the little girl?" His shoulders sagged and his breath began to return to normal. She lay her hand on his and slowly, slowly intertwined them. "When you went to that ranch you told me about?" When he attempted a smile and nodded, nosey woman that she was, she continued by asking, "What did you do after you left that ranch?"

He paused a long while but, having somehow committed to this sharing, and wanting badly to be sharing something else, he told his tale. "The next place I worked was a smaller ranch, smaller but less hospitable. I was there two months before a new hand, newer than me, accused me of stealing three dollars. The bunkhouse was split in their support, and the boss wasn't strong enough to stand up for an Indian even though he knew I didn't do it. So I paid the hand the money and rode out."

Clara's eyes flared with the injustice of it, but before she could say anything Lonesome Wolf started speaking again. Maybe if he shared enough, she wouldn't make him look at things he could not change.

"The place I worked that gave me the most was a huge spread up near Oklahoma." His expression turned grim. "I was good enough to work at their ranch, but not good enough to mingle with the other cowhands. So, I slept outside because I wasn't allowed in the bunkhouse."

"Why'd you stay?" There was no judgment in the question, only Clara's undeniable – and unendable – curiosity.

He shrugged. "The pay was good." He gave a short humorless laugh. "I got paid less than the greenest of greenhorns, but the pay was still good." He almost wished he didn't have to tell her this next part. "I'd been there for four months when the owner's son got killed by an Apache.

I was immediately, and quite vocally, dismissed."

"But, you aren't Apache!"

Her indignation made him smile despite the subject. "Apache, Cherokee, Navaho, Sioux. An Indian is an Indian in most people's eyes." He had meant the words to sooth her, but he was not successful.

Clara was incensed. "But that's outrageous! How could they –" he stopped her with a gentle hand laid over hers or just a moment, and the he smiled wryly. "It's okay, Clara. You don't have to fight those battles. They're over and done, having been fought… and are, won or lost, in the past. I appreciate your support though." Now his grin was genuine and something deep inside of Clara's eyes responded to it.

Distracted, she seemed to almost not hear his quiet murmur, "Working at the ranch was one of the best decisions I made."

After a moment, what he had said must've sunk in because her brow crinkled. "How can that be the case?"

He leaned back and rested his intertwined fingers over his stomach. "You know how God can bring good out of bad?"

"Absolutely."

"Well, I wasn't the only one let go that day. There was an old Creek Indian – well, old to me because I was still just a kid – anyways, he was fired that day, too. We set off together. I rode with him for years. Heck of a guy."

Clara could surely see his fondness for the old man in the warmth of his eyes. And she just couldn't stand not knowing about him. "What was his name?"

"Franklin." Lonesome Wolf grinned, knowing what Clara's next question would be.

"And what was his *real* name?"

He laughed outright. "Clara, sweetheart, you are something else."

Blushing at the pet name that had slipped out, Clara couldn't help but chuckle at herself, and still he knew he wasn't appeasing her curiosity any. He waited her out. He didn't have to wait long. "Well?"

"Well," he picked up his fork, ready to dive into the cobbler dish set in the middle of the table, and put an end to his contributions to the conversation. "I'm up for only so much talking about my past in one day."

"Okay." She nodded – seeming to be, temporarily at least – satisfied.

And she was... temporarily. She waited almost until he had finished the cobbler when she asked her next question. "How much Cherokee do you remember?"

Wondering where in the world this conversation was going but willing to go there for her, he answered, "Quite a bit. I didn't truly learn English until I was nine, and even then I'd meet with friends from my village and talk to them. And, of course, my new parents knew much of the language." He paused and then knowing he was committing himself to whatever it was she was getting them into, asked, "Why?"

A moment of silence followed and then, as if the matter had already been decided without his input, Clara stated, "I want you to teach me some, just a few words and phrases."

His fork froze in midair and he stared at her. "What? Why?"

She shrugged. "So you won't lose it." It sounded like a question, and a pathetic one at that.

He tried to keep the corners of his mouth from moving upward. "Ah, so purely for my sake?" When she nodded with too innocent eyes, he chuckled and shook his head. "I doubt your motives, but I'll teach you a bit." His answer clearly tickled her, and although he had no idea when she would ever need to speak Cherokee, he was happy to make her smile.

After the supper dishes were put away, they began their first lesson. Lonesome Wolf asked her where she'd like to start.

"That's easy. First I want to learn to tell my son that I love him. Then we can move to things like pleasantries and numbers and colors and animals and such."

"Whoa, now!" He held up a hand, whether in warning or surrender he wasn't sure. "Just how much time do you expect us to spend on this?

She scowled at him and said, with total seriousness, "As much as it takes."

"Gvgeyuhi."

"Huh?"

Lonesome Wolf grinned and repeated the word more slowly. "Gvgeyuhi. I love you." As soon as he said it he felt a burning fist try to strangle him. He cleared his throat, trying to dislodge the feeling, and willed himself not to show his discomfort. When Clara repeated him, both in Cherokee and in English, their eyes held each other's for some time before Clara broke away. He silently prayed that she hadn't seen within him, but he doubted she'd missed it. He doubted her eyes missed anything. He felt the overwhelming need to break the silence that had permeated the cabin. Clearing his throat a second time, he said, "It means much more than a simple English 'I love you.' But if you mean love like the Bible defines it – giving of yourself, putting others ahead of yourself – then the translation would be true."

sooff

Clara picked up the baby lying in her lap. She looked at Nathanael and said the word softly, reverently. Lonesome Wolf made himself repeat it so she could hear it correctly. She listened, speaking over and over until hers sounded much like Lonesome Wolf's.

At last, her green eyes shone in triumph. Victorious, she said, "Now, how do I greet someone?"

⌘

The days were passing in a nice routine. During the day, he worked with the animals and repaired things while Clara spent her time doing household chores and caring for Nathanael. On rainy days, particularly sweltering afternoons, and some evenings, they would often find refuge for a short while on the porch or under the live oak closest to the cabin. There they would read aloud together from one of the few books Clara owned. After supper the last few nights, they'd played with the baby until he fell asleep and then had their slowly progressing Cherokee lessons – it wasn't an easy language to learn, but Clara was determined to do it. At the end of the day, she would retire and Lonesome Wolf would head out to what he had taken to calling his bunkhouse.

It would have been a comfortable life for a family, had they been one.

The afternoon wasn't quite as hot as days past, and a breeze, albeit a warm one, was blowing. Lonesome Wolf had just stepped out of the barn when, in the distance, he heard the rumble of a wagon and the accompanying sounds of a rider on horseback. Quickly stepping back into the shelter of the barn, he peaked out the door and down the cabin drive. The approaching wagon was filled with a family, probably friends of Clara's coming for a visit. There was a man and woman, a couple kids, and another man, younger, who rode beside the wagon on a good-looking horse.

Feeling like a yellow-dog-of-a-coward for hunkering in the shadows, he set down the pail in his hand and emerged from the dimness into the daylight, resolved to walk out the trust he had so recently given to God. He barely crossed the threshold when Clara came running out of the house letting out a squeal like he had never heard, a giggling Nathanael bobbing in her arms. "Lonesome Wolf!" She yelled to him over her shoulder. "Come meet my friends!" She covered the baby's ears with her hand and yelled "Lonesome Wolf!" again.

"I'm right behind you, Clara." He spoke to her, but he was keeping a keen eye on the two men as Clara's company neared the cabin.

Clara, impatience evident in her bouncing feet, waited long enough for the wagon to roll to a stop and the driver to set the brake before she, not even looking behind her, handed a squirming Nathanael to Lonesome Wolf and rushed to greet her friends. The man reached up to take a baby about the same size as Nathanael from his wife so she could climb down from the wagon, but Clara ignored his outstretched arms and nabbed the baby before he could. The fellow riding the horse dismounted smoothly then sauntered over to help a little girl out of the back of the wagon. An older boy had already jumped over the side and was standing in front of Lonesome Wolf with a look of awe on his face.

"Are you an Indian?" The words were full of childlike wonder and spoken in that way kids had of saying things their parents wished they hadn't.

Lonesome Wolf wiped his mouth to hide his smile. "Yes. Yes, I am." Not knowing what else to say, he asked,

"What are you?"

The boy scrunched up his nose and said, "I'm a white man. Can't you tell?" and then he scampered off to climb a tree. When Lonesome Wolf raised his eyes from the little critter, he was met with looks of close scrutiny from the other visitors. Only Clara was completely oblivious to the underlying discomfort. She was busy making blowing noises to the baby instead of paying attention to what was going on. He cleared his throat and spoke her name to get her attention.

She looked at him questioningly before she remembered she was the hostess and, therefore, in charge of introductions. She carried them out seemingly without a clue that her guests might not be too keen on meeting her new friend. "Oh! Lonesome Wolf, this is the man I was telling you about, Jim Kearney. This is his wife and my dearest friend, Lydia."

The woman, Lydia, stood very still, assessing him and holding tightly to her daughter's hand. The little girl was hiding behind her mother's skirts, eye's wide and still as stone. Lonesome Wolf caught himself before he made what could be a huge mistake – an Indian had no right to look at a white woman or her child – and quickly turned his attention back to the men. When he did, his gaze met the glaring eyes of the young cowboy who'd ridden in on horseback. Knowing he couldn't show a sign of weakness nor of threat, a sign of nothing that made him look anything but confident and steady, he didn't look away until Jim stepped up to him.

Lonesome Wolf casually held out his hand and, thankfully, Jim shook it. In fact, it was the... *heartiest* handshake he'd ever experienced. He smiled in what he hoped was a friendly manner and said, "Pleased to meet you."

"Yeah, you, too." The greeting sounded distracted, but not insincere. Then Jim cut his eyes over to his wife and they shared a long look. "How do you know our Clara?" The question was obviously aimed at Lonesome Wolf, but the man didn't let go of his wife's eyes until it was halfway out. Even then, he spared only a glance at Lonesome Wolf before regarding Clara keenly, as if he expected her to be the one to answer. When he saw she was too busy kissing the baby's hand in little nibbles and not paying a lick of attention to him, Jim looked back at Lonesome Wolf.

Lonesome Wolf tried to shoot Clara a look, too, but she was ignoring him just as much as she was Kearney. He'd have something to say about that later. He forced himself to relax his shoulders and make good conversation. "I've been helping Clara out a little, doing some work around the place."

"I see," was all Kearney said to that. Then he called out to the young man without taking his eyes off Lonesome Wolf. "Lowell, come meet … uh, Lonesome Wolf." It would have been humorous how awkward the Indian name sounded on Jim's lips if anything else about the situation were funny. Jim gestured back toward Lowell with his thumb. "This here's Lowell. He's one of my cowhands."

Lonesome Wolf extended his hand to Lowell who only sneered at it and then at Lonesome Wolf. The cowboy turned away without saying hello and went over to Clara, who was talking nonsense to the baby and trying to appear not to be watching what was going on.

The young man tipped his hat with two fingers and, sounding innocent as a Sunday preacher but looking oily as a rattlesnake, drawled, "Afternoon, Miss Clara. How d'ya do?"

"I'm doing fine, Lowell, and you? How do you do?" Clara sounded polite, but she was paying more attention to the baby than she was the cowboy.

"I come to see what I could do to help ya out."

"Oh, well, isn't that nice, Lowell. To be honest, I'm not even much sure what needs done these days. Lonesome Wolf here's been making all kinds of repairs and doing all kinds of chores. You could ask him if there's anything he could use some help with." Her voice was just a tad too bright and she refused to look the young man in the face. If anybody had been looking on, they would've thought Clara was talking to the baby.

Lowell stood before her like he was waiting on her to come to her senses. When she didn't, he turned a black look on Lonesome Wolf, who worked hard not to grin at Clara's pointed nonchalance. The cowboy swiveled on his heals. "Boss, it okay if I head back to the ranch?" He paused long enough to make sure his message was clear. "Since there ain't nothin' for me to do here?" He started out for his horse before Jim had the chance to give him his leave.

"Oh, Lowell, are you leaving?" Clara sounded like she was genuinely disappointed to see him go, but Lonesome Wolf knew better. "You should at least stay and have some pie."   That made the cowhand hesitate as he was circling his horse around to leave, but in the end, he stuck to his guns. "I thank you, Miss Clara, ma'am, but I best be getting on." He clicked to his horse only to pull up on the reins and stop him. Turning in the saddle and taking the time to give Lonesome Wolf a thorough looking-over, he added, "But when you see he ain't doing a good job for you, you send word and I'll come right over and fix things. You know he ain't gonna do you right. Them Indians are just—"

"Lowell," Kearney said his name like he was tired of saying it. "Shut your mouth and head back to the ranch."

Lowell scowled, first at Kearney and then at Lonesome Wolf, then he tipped his hat to Clara as if he considered himself polite company and lightly kicked his horse into a lope.

They had all stood around awkwardly for a moment, and then in unison they all jumped back into greetings as if they'd silently agreed to pretend the surly cowhand had never been there.

Once all the hugging and squealing was done, Clara invited everyone in for pie. Now, they were sitting around the table letting the awkwardness seep back in.

"So, where exactly is your place? Does it border Clara's?" It was the only thing he could think to say, other than, *What do you think of the fact that Clara has an Indian living on her land?* Although, he could pretty much guess that they weren't morally opposed to the idea. After all, the ranch hand who'd been with them had all but challenged Lonesome Wolf to a duel at noon, and Jim Kearney had sent him to bed without any bread. So, Lonesome Wolf felt fairly safe in thinking that he was, to a degree, among friends.

Strange, how he felt guilty. Guilty of what, he wasn't sure, but when Clara set a huge piece of pie in front of him, he wasn't sure he was going to be able to stomach it.

"Oh, don't I wish!" Until she answered, he'd forgotten he'd asked Lydia Kearney the question. "Wouldn't that be wonderful, Clara?" Lydia clasped her hands together at the idea, suddenly at ease. "Think of how much time we could spend together then." She turned her kind, sparkling eyes on him. "No, Lonesome Wolf, I am afraid we live on the other side of town. We don't get out here as often as we'd like, although Jim gets out more than I do. He can ride over on his horse in a fraction of the time it takes all of the rest of us to creak along in the wagon."

"And, Jim," Clara said, as she sat at the table, "don't think that I don't know what a sacrifice it is for you to come over and help me out or to send Cletus over to help. I know you have plenty enough work for him to do for you. I appreciate it more than you could know."

Jim had just taken an enormous bite of pie. He turned an amusing shade of pink and waved off Clara's thanks like it was a pesky horsefly.

Lonesome Wolf almost had time to grin at the man's embarrassment before Clara began to regale the other couple with his bravery from the day they'd met. Personally, he thought that Clara was the brave one, but she didn't seem to want the praise any more than he did. He told them how calm she'd been that first day, and he was going to say more, but he backed off his praise before the conversation turned into a battle for one to out-praise the other. Unfortunately, he wasn't quick enough to stop Lydia and Jim from exchanging a look that Lonesome Wolf recognized as *knowing* – he wasn't sure exactly what it was they thought they knew, but he was positive he didn't want them to know it.

When the pie was finished off, the ladies moved to the living area and the men headed outside. Lonesome Wolf readied himself for what might pass between the men without the womenfolk around.

The two men ambled over to the oak tree by the house. Standing in its shade, they watched the two elder Kearney children running around the yard, the little girl squealing in delight at something her brother had done. The smile hadn't fully made its way onto Lonesome Wolf's face when Jim Kearney turned to face him and cleared his throat. Lonesome Wolf met Jim's eyes evenly and with a composure born of a peace that had suddenly settled over him.

Jim pushed his hat back and dropped a glance down to Lonesome Wolf's gun strapped to his thigh. "I have something I feel like I need to say to you."

"And what is that, Jim?" Lonesome Wolf kept his voice strong and even

"I have worried over Clara since Rob passed." Following the admission, he said, "Now, I believe worryin' to be a sin, and I've given the situation over to the Lord more times than I can count, but I've worried." The little girl ran into her father, grasping his pant-leg tightly in her little fist, and then she ran off just as quickly as she'd come. "And now here you are, proof He heard me." Jim was smiling, but Lonesome Wolf didn't know if it was because of the Lord's faithfulness or the child's antics. After a moment the smile faded, and Lonesome Wolf braced himself. "But I wouldn't be doing my duty as someone who loves Clara if I didn't tell you that I think it's a very bad idea for you to stay here." Jim adjusted his hat and the sigh that escaped him seemed to be pulled from deep within his soul. "Still…" he held Lonesome Wolf's eyes with a steadiness that bespoke strength of character, "I'd thank you to stay awhile.

It wasn't the reaction Lonesome Wolf had readied himself for. In fact, it took a moment for his brain to catch up and make his mouth talk. "Thank you, Jim." He tried not to stumble over his words. "You don't know what that means to me. Not just for my sake, but for Clara and her…" He hesitated to voice it.

Jim did so for him, casting it at him with a raised brow. "Reputation?"

There was nothing to say except, "Yes."

Jim shook his head. "We're in untamed land, Lonesome Wolf. And it ain't safe for a woman and child alone. Heck, it's not always safe for a man." He adjusted his hat, settling it back straight on his head. "I don't doubt for one second Clara's integrity. And I feel … I see in you a man of God. There may come a time when the situation has to change, but for now you're where you belong." He spat on the ground and squinted off into the distance. "Just don't make me sorry," he said, and not once looking at Lonesome Wolf, he walked away.

"Never," Lonesome wolf whispered to his retreating form, "never." And he meant it.

⌘

"Do you like Jim?"

The Kearney family had barely started off in the wagon before the words seemed to bounce out of Clara.

"I do. He's right friendly… and honest." Clara grinned. Lonesome Wolf looked at her out of the corner of his eye. "You knew he'd take me aside, didn't you?"

Clara nodded, scrunching up her nose. "I figured. I'm sorry." She reached across the table to refill his coffee cup and continued, "If I'd known they were coming today, I would have forewarned you. But they've never been anything but very good friends to me."

"Well, you're blessed to have good friends, especially out here in the middle of nowhere." Lonesome

Wolf rose from the table and stretched. "I believe I'm going to turn in for the night." He placed a hand on her shoulder and let it slide off as he walked away. "Thank you, Clara, for introducing me to your friends."

"You're welcome." She paused for a moment to savor the intimate gesture. "Next, I'll introduce you to Tremont."

"Tremont?" He looked startled and a little bit disgusted.

"Yes. I'm a bit surprised he hasn't shown up here in the last couple of weeks."

He grunted in return. Yes, he definitely looked disgusted.

"What's that ugly look for?"

His pout was so big he looked like a petulant little boy. She chose not to tell him so. And she chose not to laugh at him when he *sounded* like a petulant little boy as he grumbled out, "Just how many men are you friends with?"

She could feel how far her eyebrows rose. The devil just grinned, so she smacked him with a dishtowel. "I'll take you to see him later, IF you can learn to behave." She purposely planted a coy smile on her face. "I think you'll very much enjoy meeting him." The curiosity in his eyes was dancing around, but she wasn't in the mood to relieve him of it. Let the man suffer.

CHAPTER SEVEN

It was a brilliant morning. Lonesome Wolf stood in awe once again at the splendor of God's creation. He loved to watch the sunrise, especially standing here on this particular hill. On this particular homestead. As the sun cleared the horizon, he turned and walked back to the cabin, thinking that he might teach Clara more Cherokee after breakfast.

Before he could share his plan, however, Clara announced amid the smell of bacon and fresh biscuits that she'd be making a trip to town. "I need to stock up on food supplies. I also need to get material for winter clothes and a new thicker blanket for Nathanael. If there's anything you need, you can add it to my list and I'll pick it up if it's to be found."

Lonesome Wolf studied her for a short time. He had some questions about this trip. "How far away is… Klein Creek, right?"

Nodding, she broke off a piece of biscuit and handed it to Nathanael. "About six miles, why?"

"And you plan on making this trip with Nathanael, on your own?" He was pretty sure his eyes told her what he thought of the matter.

She took a deep breath, let it out slowly, then spoke

very patiently, as if she were speaking to a small child. "Lonesome Wolf, I've been making trips to town by myself for over a year. And I've taken Nathanael with me for almost nine months." She touched the hand that held his fork and stopped him from taking another bite. "I'll be okay."

"I'm going with you." He went back to eating as if that settled the matter.

"I'm not so sure that's a good idea."

Her words irritated him, so he caught her eye and held her look long enough that she'd see he was not going to argue with her about it. "It's a better idea than you going alone."

He had just begun thinking he'd won when she said his name again, only this time it sounded worried. "Lonesome Wolf." He set his fork down in defeat and listened to her. "They could refuse to serve you, or charge you double, or worse. I don't think it's a good idea."

It was his turn to adopt the parenting tone. "Clara, I've been through many towns. I'm not afraid of what people might or might not say or do to me."

She sighed heavily and her lovely eyes filled with concern. He tried to look at things from her side. Where he came from, the Cherokee were mostly treated as the whites. Mostly. Many of his people lived there, and most of them were educated. They intermingled and intermarried. Here there were still at least small bands of Indians who spread havoc. Here it didn't matter if he was Cherokee and not Apache. And here it was Clara who would be hurt by association. He couldn't risk his actions hurting Clara. But that didn't mean he could in good conscience let her go alone – no matter that she'd done so in the past. He folded his arms and stared her down before making his offer.

"Let's compromise. I'll ride with you *to* town but not go *into* town with you. That way I feel better about your safety and there won't be trouble with the townspeople. Deal?"

She slowly tilted her head from side to side as she considered his plan. Finally she nodded resignedly. "Deal."

"Okay." He pushed his chair back and stood. "I'll go hitch up the wagon and saddle Fella while you finish the dishes." At an odd look from Clara, Lonesome Wolf paused. "What?"

"Your horse's name is actually Fella?" She stared at him and then burst out laughing. "All this time I thought you were just calling him a fellow. I had no idea that was his name! It's kind of like naming a boy Son, isn't it? 'Come here, Son. How are you today, Son? Whoa there, Fella.'" Covering her mouth and throwing her head back, she laughed.

"I'm so glad I could amuse you. Now get ready." He went out the door, smiling. He *was* glad he could amuse her. He loved the sound of her laughter. And the beauty of her smile.

⌘

After waiting for her to nestle Nathanael in a crate filled with blankets for cushion and toys for company and nailed securely to the back of the wagon seat, Lonesome Wolf approached her with several gold coins. Clara shook her head. "I don't need your money."

"I didn't ask if you needed it. I want you to take it and use it."

"I have plenty of money in the bank and a healthy credit at the Mercantile. I sold off an entire herd of cattle when Rob died, and I haven't hardly spent any of it."

"I don't care if you're the wealthiest lady in all of Texas. I cost money to house and feed. Take it."

"You don't cost that much."

For a while they had a standoff of wills. Lonesome Wolf won out with his declaration of, "If you don't take it, I'll walk into the Mercantile and add it to your account myself." She took it. She saw him attempting, and failing, to hide his victory smile and knew he could probably hear her mutter under her breath, but he just mounted Fella and said nothing. Smart man.

They hadn't gone very far when Lonesome Wolf surprised her by asking, "You've been taking this trip for over a year? Is that how long your husband's been gone?"

It shouldn't have surprised her that he asked. He'd been a lot more patient about learning things about her than she'd been with him. She shaded her eyes with her hand so she could see him through the sun and nodded. "Yes, my husband, Rob, died over a year ago. Snakebite." And, although he asked no more about it, she told him. "It was awful. He was clearing rock out of the backyard and was bitten on his upper arm. I found him when I came home from visiting Lydia. His arm was swollen like you wouldn't believe, and he was already dead. He hadn't even made it to the back porch." An unwanted feeling washed over her. She shook her head to dispel it. "I didn't know I was pregnant then. When it set in that I was really and truly alone, I cried. I felt … afraid … to be on my own."

For a long while, Clara sat gazing off at the land around her. For a moment, Lonesome Wolf saw a woman who was vulnerable. She breathed in deeply and slowly let her breath out. When she looked back at him, the peace and strength that seemed a part of her being had returned to her eyes.

"I had Nathanael there in the cabin by myself. I've

never been so scared in all my life." She gave a small, soft smile. "But God saw us through."

"I don't know what to say," was his inadequate response.

She cut her eyes over to him. "Don't say anything. Just enjoy the ride."

Enjoy the ride and think about it; that's what she meant. Think about how God sees his people through even the toughest of situations. It wasn't encouraging to consider the fact that heading into town made her think he needed to be reminded of God's provision, His protection. But he thought about it anyway.

The less than six miles to town felt more like fifteen with all of the hills they traveled up and down. Plus they'd had to stop so Clara could tend to Nathanael. At least the weather was mild. It didn't get really hot until over two hours later, and by then they had neared the outskirts of town. They had passed no one on the way in. When Lonesome Wolf saw the town, he realized why. It was barely more than a few buildings gathered together. The term small and sleepy seemed too big and too fancy for the little town. That was fine by him. Even so, he distanced himself from Clara when the buildings came in easy sight.

⌘

Clara tried not to hurry too much through her business in town. Funny, she generally dawdled as long as possible to make the most of her visits, especially since she was left alone for days, or even weeks, at a time in the cabin with only a baby for company. But today, she was anxious to get back to Lonesome Wolf. She even wished that it wasn't the first Saturday of the month when she met Lydia and their friend, Deborah. Typically, they spent the better part of the day visiting and picnicking by the creek.

She'd just have to let them know she couldn't stay today.

She had walked into the general store about ten minutes earlier with her list in hand and was now tapping her foot while Mr. Keller finished with another customer before he was able to fill her order. She didn't see Mrs. Keller anywhere. The poor woman must've taken sick again – she seemed to do that an awful lot. Used to be the Keller's daughter, Ellie, would help out, but now Ellie was working at Klein Creek's first official café, Miss Rose's. Just as Clara handed over her list to Mr. Keller, she heard a throat clearing behind her. She hesitated to turn around until a familiar voice politely entreated, "May I have a word with you, Mrs. Henson?"

Stifling a groan and an eye roll, she bowed to the inevitability of speaking to Carl Schmidt, the town's blacksmith. She knew from months of experience that ignoring the fellow would only serve to make him try all the harder to gain her attention. And so, with every bit of the politeness she'd been taught as a Southern lady, she turned with a smile on her face. "Why, Carl, how've you been since I last spoke to you?" *Which was last time I came to town and every time before that during the last six months,* she thought petulantly. Heavens, but the man must have a guard posted to alert him when she arrived within a mile of the place.

"How about we sit on the bench outside while you wait for your order, Mrs. Henson. It's still in the shade this time of day."

Clara nodded, knowing it would do no good to argue, and followed Carl outside. She really should tell him, again, to call her Clara, but she hardly cared anymore. Oh, he was nice enough, she supposed, but he was far too interested in finding a mama for his rambunctious boys. It really was a shame that Ilsa Schmidt had died in childbirth late last winter, taking what would've been the couple's first daughter with her. But even though she felt sorry for the blacksmith, she didn't feel sorry enough to take on Ilsa's role as wife and mother to the Schmidt clan. If only she could politely get Carl to understand that simple fact. Unwittingly, she let a sigh escape her.

"Is everything well with you, Mrs. Henson?"

Okay, three times in one meeting was enough. "Please, Carl, call me Clara. Everyone else in town does. No need to stand on such formal ceremony in such a small town."

Uh oh. Clara conceded that she might have committed a tactical error in pressing the familiarity, for Carl suddenly had a gleam in his eye that made her more than a bit nervous. When he hesitated to speak again and that tell-tale blush began to sneak its way up his neck, she knew for sure what was coming and wished she'd let Lonesome Wolf accompany her into town, consequences or not. But she hadn't, and so she faced Carl, steeling herself to be firm – kind, but firm – in her response to the bulky blacksmith's advances, respectful though they were, and let him have his say.

"Thank you … Clara. I, uhm, well, I was just wondering… I know you come to town at the first of every month to visit with your lady friends and all, and I thought that maybe next time you came we could, well, that is to say that you could maybe set aside a little time to maybe have some dinner." Having gotten that far, Carl appeared to pick up steam and rushed ahead. "I realize, ma'am, that might put you gettin' home later than usual, and I'd be happy to see you back to your cabin safe-like." At this point in his seemingly well-rehearsed petition, Carl

Schmidt's face turned from pink to red. "I would, of course, bring my boys along for that ride as escorts so that nobody could say ... well, so that nobody would say anything against ... well, just because." Here, Carl paused and took a deep breath. Clara thought he was finished and opened her mouth to speak only to be graced with the final, and apparently most embarrassing, piece of his little speech. "I would have someone minding them during the dinner so that you and me could, uhh, get acquainted ... I mean *talk*." Carl blew out a breath like he'd just trekked uphill carrying a fifty-pound pack.

Clara felt a little sorry for him and almost ... *almost* accepted his sweet invitation. However, she knew that any indicator she was in the least bit interested would be like intentionally starting a stampede, and self-preservation kicked in. "Carl, while I'm very honored by your request and flattered that a man like you would think of asking me out for dinner, I must decline your offer. I truly appreciate all you've done for me and for my family, before and after my husband died. And I view you as a friend, a very good friend, but only a friend."

She realized she had made another mistake when she saw relief flood his face. "Well, goodness, Clara, I just look on you as a friend, too. You ought to know that. Thing is, well, my boys, they need a woman's influence. Young kids sometimes need the gentleness that a man like me just can't give them."

"I thought Mary Ellen Brantley was helping you watch out for your sons, even beginning to teach them their letters and sums. Are you unhappy with her help?"

"Unhappy? No, ma'am. Mary Ellen ...I mean Miss Brantley," he turned pink again, and Clara thought things were getting mighty interesting. "She works wonders with my boys, gets 'em to behave like nobody's business. But she only sits 'em, she ain't a mama. My boys need a mama. Clara, look, I wouldn't bother you but there ain't another widow woman around here under fifty besides you. Well, Mrs. Gentry, but she and her poor Sam, God rest his soul, they never had any kids."

Talk about having one's ego set right. Clara almost laughed aloud at the thought that all this time she thought Carl carried a torch for her, and really all she'd been was the only one in fifty square miles to meet his limited criteria. She placed her hand on Carl's forearm, and letting only the tiniest of smiles escape, she said, "Again, Carl, I'm flattered, but I just don't think, as much as it may seem otherwise to you, that I'm the answer to your troubles. But thank you for thinking of me." At that she rose, glad to be free from trying not to hurt Carl's feelings. "I'll see you around?"

Carl thought for a moment, twisting his lips this way and then that, before nodding, obviously having come to what she thought was the right sort of conclusion. "I understand, Clara." Her illusion of freedom from Carl was broken when he looked at her hopefully and threatened... ahem, said, "I'll see you around."

Clara wasn't so sure she'd heard the last of Carl Schmidt on this matter, but she was off the hook for today, anyway.

⌘

Finally, Clara returned to where Lonesome Wolf had been waiting. Her wagon was loaded with supplies, and the baby was asleep in the back. It had seemed so normal, waiting on Clara so they could head home... that is, to Clara's home. Only, it *had* started to feel...

He shook off his useless wanderings and tried to

pay attention to Clara and her account of the visit to town, in which obviously she got great delight. She gave Lonesome Wolf a detailed rundown of every item bought, its purpose, the cost, and every woman she spoke with during her short stay. As she was nearing the end of her list she looked over at him. "Are you even listening to me?"

His guilty grin was answer enough.

She raised her brows and pertly reprimanded him, "I will have you know that for a woman on her own out here in these hills there aren't many things that happen to break the monotony of one day from another. You should cut a girl some slack and let her prattle on about her shopping."

His grin widened and he looked down at her from his mount. "I thought I was letting you prattle on."

She laughed. "I guess you were, but you could at least pretend to listen."

His grin turned into a smile. "I *was* pretending."

She reached out as if to swat him. "You're ornery, you know that?"

Lonesome Wolf chuckled and they rode on in easy conversation. Fifteen minutes later, they reached a small river and stopped for lunch. They ate on the wagon seat and chatted about things of no consequence. After lunch and a short rest in the shade, they continued on their way.

They'd ridden for about ten more minutes when Clara burst out with, "Look! *Awohali!*"

He followed her finger pointing into the air and spotted the eagle soaring above. He looked back at her with wide eyes. "Very good! I'm impressed." Clara had quickly progressed past simple greetings and was now naming things, mostly animals and items around the house. It felt good to use his language again, and he was enjoying the lessons at least as much as Clara was.

The rest of the trip passed quickly as Lonesome Wolf pointed out things and Clara tried pronouncing them. They laughed at some of her mistakes, a few of which completely changed the meaning of the words. Some of the meanings Lonesome Wolf kept to himself.

Once they reached home, they had the task of unloading the wagon. Clara was surprised at how much more quickly it went and how much easier it was handling the bigger items with Lonesome Wolf helping her. He'd been here only a few weeks and yet she'd already come to depend on him for help with many things. She shook her head. Someday he'd ride away and she'd have to go back to doing for herself. The thought of his leaving troubled her in far more ways than the thought of having to do the full load of work again.

Her countenance must have revealed some of her feelings because Lonesome Wolf stopped her with a touch to her arm. "Are you okay?" He looked genuinely concerned. "Clara?"

She looked up at him and willed herself to smile. "Just letting my mind wander. I'm fine." But she wasn't sure she would be fine when he left.

⌘

One particularly squelching afternoon a couple of days later, Clara declared a halt to all work. Lonesome Wolf was on his way out, but she stayed his hand as he reached for the latch to open the cabin door. He turned a questioning face to her, and she smiled. She was so beautiful he almost forgot to listen to her words. "It's entirely too hot for you to go back outside and work. You'll smother in this heat and humidity. This afternoon we'll rest. You can work later."

Lonesome Wolf didn't even have to weigh his options. He had to admit that spending the afternoon relaxing with Clara was the far better alternative to going back out and working in the hot sun trying to tame the cantankerous stallion Clara had dubbed Marvin. He turned around and leaned back against the door, his shoulders falling just shy of touching each side. "And what, do tell, do you have in mind?"

"Well, I say we grab a blanket, spread it out under the live oak by the house, and read aloud!" She didn't even wait for him to agree. "I'll get the blanket and toys for Nathanael and you, sir, may decide on a book from our fine selection." With this, she swept her hand in front of the lone shelf in the main room; a shelf that was made of smooth, fine wood and the contents of which were almost revered by Clara.

As he went to select a story, it hit him for the first time how truly out of place the shelf and the books were in this rustic cabin. The collection of books with their gilded leather covers would be more in place in a grand library or a wealthy man's study. It made him wonder how the items found themselves in a small cabin in the Texas hills. "Clara?"

She called out from her bedroom, "Yes?"

"Where did you get these books?"

She swept back into the room, a blanket folded over one arm and a flush of pride on her face. "I brought these books from my family home when Rob and I moved out here." She paused and her eyes lost focus as she looked at some place in the past. "Growing up, I loved to read. And we had a massive library to rival all libraries. I'd sneak inside and choose a book and find a nook in the house or a limb outside in a tree and read and read until I got caught and had to do chores or eat or whatever other necessity I was overlooking to walk through whatever imaginary world I had joined. Jane Eyre was my favorite." Something changed in Clara's expression, and Lonesome Wolf almost thought he detected a flash of anger in those green eyes, but it came and went so quickly he couldn't be sure. "I was allowed to bring only five books with me when we moved here. I spent hours deciding which ones I'd choose." She looked at Lonesome Wolf with that twinkle once again dancing gaily amongst the greens of her eyes. "And today, you will choose. Which world will you select for us to explore this afternoon?"

The way he saw it, Jane Eyre was the only right choice to make.

CHAPTER EIGHT

It was a mild summer day when Clara, Nathanael, and Lonesome Wolf set out to visit Tremont. Lonesome Wolf had to admit that his curiosity was more than a little peaked, especially considering the almost conspiratorial way Clara was acting. Her mischievous grin wouldn't go away and that spoke of some sneaky victory.

As they neared the large cabin set back amongst trees, all became clear. The wagon came to a stop and Clara jumped down and called out, "Osiyo!"

Lonesome Wolf had little time to wonder at her use of the Cherokee for hello. Soon a huge man made of solid muscle appeared from the door of the cabin and rushed out, took Clara up in his arms, and swung her around as if she were a child. Her laughter carried through on the warm breeze and made Lonesome Wolf smile. The large Indian set her down and said, "Tsilugi. Dohitsu?"

She beamed up at the man and replied, "Dohiquu, Nehenaha?"

"Dohiquu." With the greetings completed, the man beamed at Clara with pride and approval. "Now, where did you learn that?"

Clara looked over her shoulder and pointed toward the wagon. It was only then that the man seemed to notice

Lonesome Wolf, who was climbing down, Nathanael in his arms, and making his way over to introduce himself.

The two men shook hands. "Tremont, but you can call me Red Eagle." The big man rolled his eyes. "Clara insists."

Lonesome wolf could see how the man had been given the name. He had a bearing about him of a fierce warrior, a chief with striking cheekbones and authority surrounding him like a touchable thing. And yet he was obviously what many would call a half-breed with enough white in him that his hair was a deep, deep red. A deeper red, even, than Clara's. Yes, this man's name seemed to suit him just as much as Lonesome Wolf's did. "An honor to meet you, Red Eagle. Lonesome Wolf."

"Pleased to meet you, Lonesome Wolf. I see you're a good teacher."

Lonesome Wolf smiled. "More like Clara's a good student. I didn't understand her determination before, but now I see why she was so eager to learn. It's been a privilege to teach her the language of my people."

"Come, let's get inside out of this sun. I have a gift for Nathanael." And with that, Red Eagle turned and re-entered the cabin.

Lonesome Wolf was surprised when he stepped inside. The main room of the cabin was tidy and organized. A large wooden screen with hides stretched out across it partially separated the living area from a kitchen very similar to Clara's with the exception of a sturdy and ornately carved set of table and chairs. The furniture in the living area was equally impressive. Two rockers, almost identical to Clara's, and a beautiful carved sofa with plush cushions were situated around a rock fireplace topped by a carved wooden mantel.

Before Lonesome Wolf could comment, Red Eagle was bringing something out from one of the rooms in the back of the house. Clara's eyes lit up with excitement, and she clapped when she saw the gift. "Red Eagle! I cannot believe you did this!" She grinned at the older man. "Not that I'm about to not accept it!"

"I know he's still a bit small for it, but he'll grow into it sooner than we can blink." Tremont beamed as he set the tiny rocking chair on the ground. "It's made just like his mama's."

Lonesome Wolf watched Clara and Red Eagle relate to each other. The man could easily have been Clara's father, the way he treated her and with the affection that so obviously shown through his eyes. To know that Clara was treasured so warmed his heart, and yet made him feel somewhat like an outsider intruding on a family moment. A worrisome feeling of jealousy began to worm its way inside. Ruthlessly, he squashed it.

As if Clara knew his thoughts, she turned to include him, "Oh, Lonesome Wolf, isn't it marvelous! We can help him until he gets steadier. Here, help him sit in it and see what he thinks."

He knelt down before the little chair and sat Nathanael in it, being careful to keep his hands on either side of the baby. The little boy placed his chubby hands on the armrests, smiled up at Lonesome Wolf, and squealed. Lonesome Wolf chuckled, "I'd say he likes it."

The door to the cabin flew open, and a young girl sailed in. Lonesome Wolf felt his jaw drop open and immediately clamped it closed. The girl looked to be about twelve years old, with light skin and strong dark features. She was the most beautiful child Lonesome Wolf had ever seen. She dashed across the room and fairly leapt into Red

Eagle's arms. He received her much as he had Clara. In the little girl's wake followed a graceful woman with a basketful of vegetables. She smiled at Red Eagle and an intimate look passed between them. The woman walked over to set her basket on the kitchen cabinet and then came to join the group. Red Eagle introduced them. "Lonesome Wolf, this is my wife, Deborah, and my daughter, Rebecca." They all exchanged greetings. Red Eagle turned back to Lonesome Wolf. "Maybe next time you can meet my sons. We have twin boys, Jeremiah and Ezekiel. They're out on a hunt right now. Probably won't be back until tomorrow. Too bad. They're good boys, I'd love for you to meet them."

Mrs. Tremont clasped her hands together and interrupted, "Would everyone like some cookies and fresh lemonade? Come on over to the table and Rebecca and I will serve you up." She guided everyone over to the kitchen area and the visiting began in earnest.

Lonesome Wolf did his best to stay with the conversation, but his mind was intent on focusing on the implications of this family. They seemed so happy and so… so right. He watched Clara as she chatted with her friends. She must've felt his eyes on her because she looked over at him and smiled a warm, reassuring smile. He smiled back, aware that something had just changed between them.

⌘

"Y'all need to go into town?" Tremont led his guests out to their wagon with a friendly air but a keen eye.

Clara shook her head. "We just went. Why?"

"Thought next time I go you could come with me. I could introduce Lonesome Wolf around." He smiled, his eyes crinkling at the edges. "Not too many Indians like us living in these hills. And there's no need for you to spend the years that I've spent establishing a decent reputation. I'm not trying to talk myself up, but if they know you're my friend, they'll trust you. Better, anyways.

"I'm humbled by your offer, Red Eagle. Thank you."

Red Eagle nodded and patted him on the back. "I'll come by and get you next time I ride in. Y'all be careful and holler if you need anything! Dodadagohvi!"

Clara looked at him with clear displeasure. "I don't know that one yet."

The big Indian chuckled. "Bye, Clara."

As they pulled away and headed home, Lonesome Wolf, turned to Clara with an amused look on his face. "Now I see why you hold such an interest in Cherokee."

"At first, yes, I confess. I wanted to learn as much as I could before… you left so I could speak it with Tremont. I had no idea how much I'd enjoy learning it from you."

His mind wanted to close off his heart to the look in her eyes, but his heart saw it first and held on tightly. He looked away from her and back to the road. "I've enjoyed teaching you. You've learned very quickly." Without thinking, he looked back at her and smiled with pride and an affection he wasn't altogether sure he should share with her. He quickly looked forward again, away from those all-too-perceptive green eyes.

He was forcing his mind on something other than the idea that he'd enjoyed the pupil more than the teaching when Clara's clear voice jolted his very being. "I've enjoyed the teacher as much as the teaching." She was smiling at him, but he couldn't muster one in return. Her comment unsettled him, and given his feeling that her eyes

shot right through him and saw into the depths of his mind
and soul, he resolutely kept his eyes forward.

⌘

When they returned home, Lonesome Wolf sent
Clara and Nathanael in while he took care of the horses. He
worked distractedly the entire time, having to retrace steps
and check to see if he'd done things he usually could do
without thinking. His mind was going so fast right now it
was bypassing the moment and speeding onward, leaving
him in a sort of weird haze. He shook his head, trying to
slow the tide, and decided to take a ride to clear his mind.
The third time he had to backtrack in putting on the saddle
– something he could've done in his sleep, and pretty near
had a time or two – he stopped and stilled himself before
the Lord. Resting his arm across his saddle and his head on
his arm, he breathed out slowly. And then he waited. The
normal sounds of the barn reassured his ears that all was
well. He breathed in the scents of hay and horse and
leather, and rested in the comfort of their familiarity.
Before long, the barn air seemed thick and warm and filled
with the presence of God. He could feel his body slowing
down, relaxing, responding to the feel of the nearness of
the LORD. The animals all settled down as if they, too, felt
the presence. Heaving a sigh of relief, he closed his eyes
and willed his mind to remain still and just let God do His
God thing.

He wasn't sure how much time had passed before
he could begin to put forth his thoughts before God. Once
he began, they seemed to all flow out of him. He had
wanted to stay in this place, to enjoy being with people, to
get to know them, even like them… without getting so
attached to them. But he'd failed. He wasn't just attached
to them – he *loved* them. He confessed that loving them felt

much better than being alone, and he could see possibilities where before he thought only impossibilities existed. Still, he didn't know God's will for his future. He prayed that whatever it was, the Lord would protect his heart, for it had been fragile long before he'd come here. If it were to break one more time, he didn't know that it could mend.

As he said, "Amen," he thought back over his prayer and couldn't remember exactly what he'd said. Only two things stuck in his mind. First, he was scared. And second, he loved Clara.

⌘

After supper the next evening, Lonesome Wolf suggested a walk outside. Clara happily gathered up Nathanael and the trio set out. Before they'd even made it down the porch steps, Lonesome Wolf had taken the baby in his arms. Nathanael began to babble and pump his arms and legs excitedly when they neared the barn, and was chattering wildly by the time they were actually in the barn with the horses.

Lonesome Wolf took the baby's plump hand and helped him pet Fella as they passed by him on the way to the back of the barn. Clara watched, heart warm and overflowing.

She shook her head and followed the boys down the row of horses. "That boy loves horses. Before we know it, he'll be riding the property from corner to corner all by himself."

Lonesome Wolf opened the top section of the back doors. They leaned against the bottom gate looking out onto the pasture. "I've been thinking. What would you say to me building a corral here off the barn? It'd provide space for the horses to get some exercise without having to put them all the way out in the pasture. It'll also be a good place for training if you'd like to start raising some horses of your own in the future. I'm finally making some headway with that crazy stallion –" he looked sideways at Clara, who was giving him a mock glare, "I mean, Marvin. And having a paddock to work him in would sure help." He eyed her carefully, like he thought she might possibly say no to his generous offer. "What do you think?"

She thought about it for only a moment before she replied, "I hate for you to go to the trouble, Lonesome Wolf. It sounds like an awful lot of work." She knew the sparkle in her eyes gave lie to the protest of her spoken words.

"It wouldn't be that difficult, and you have plenty of trees for lumber. It isn't like I have too much to do around here. You wouldn't want me to waste away from boredom would you?"

She laughed. "I would certainly not want to be responsible for that, no. And I'd really appreciate a corral, if you don't mind."

"Done." He paused while Nathanael spoke a long stream of gibberish and nodded to the baby like he understood every word. When the boy smiled proudly, Lonesome Wolf chuckled and went on, "There's one more thing. How would you like to extend your porch around to the front of the cabin? I could cut the timber when I start the corral. It'd be an easy addition and you'd have a place to work or read outside even in the rain."

He could tell the idea thrilled her, but she started to protest anyway. "Lonesome Wolf, I can't ask you ..." He raised both of his eyebrows to her and she changed her answer midstride. "Why, yes, that would be lovely, thank you."

"Good, I'm so glad that you see fit to agree." He

grinned at her, mischievousness and something else altogether lighting his eyes.

Clara desperately wished that he wouldn't smile at her like that. She could feel her cheeks growing warm under his gaze. She should probably tell him that she changed her mind and that it wouldn't be proper to allow him to do so much for her, but she hoped the extra work would keep him around for a good, long while, so she said no such thing. Instead, she muttered loudly enough for him to hear, "Like I had much choice."

He muttered right back, "Smart woman." And then he shot her another of the playful grins she had grown to love so much.

⌘

"Okay, grab the boy and a blanket and come with me."

Clara looked up from her mending with a jolt of surprise. She'd been so lost in her thinking that she hadn't even heard him come in. "Where are we headed?"

"Outside to read. I've worked enough in this heat for one afternoon, and you got me so into that story we've been reading that I confess I'm in dire need of knowing what happens next." He paused. "Unless you're too busy. I'm sorry; I didn't even ask if you were busy."

Clara quickly returned her sewing to the mending basket and stood. "Never too busy to read. I'll grab the blanket and you get the book."

He read aloud while she corralled Nathanael. She loved to listen to the rich flow of his voice. Even though the story was at a tense part, his voice relaxed her. She wondered if he sang as beautifully as he read. Too bad they didn't have a church in town to attend so she could find out. Not that that was the most important reason to have a church. Besides, she supposed if she wanted to hear him sing she could simply ask him to do so. Would he?

"Okay, Clara."

For one moment she thought she had inadvertently voiced her request. She looked up at him, but he was studying the book. That's when she realized she hadn't been paying attention to what he'd been reading. She'd just been listening to the sound of his voice and letting her mind drift.

"Who is this woman?"

A bit chagrined, she asked, "Which woman?"

"This woman in the attic. You said this was a favorite book, so I know you know who she is. And what about Grace Poole? Who is she?"

Clara shook her finger at him and laughed. "No, sir. Handing out information about the book before the author wanted you to know it is strictly forbidden."

Lonesome Wolf made a face. "Forbidden by whom? If I don't mind, and Nathanael doesn't mind," he chucked the baby beneath his chin and smiled at him, "then why should you mind?"

"Because, Mr. Impatience, as you so aptly pointed out, this is one of my favorite books, and I want you to experience it as it was meant to be experienced – suspense and surprises and all."

He looked off to the side and heaved an exaggerated sigh but gave in. "Fine. But just wait until I have a secret and you want to know it." He slanted his eyes to the side to look at her. "When that time comes, my lips will be sealed."

Laughter bubbled up inside Clara and she gave it free rein, enjoying the too-infrequent sensation. "Deal. Now keep reading."

"Actually," Lonesome Wolf cleared his throat, "my voice is a bit tired. You read for a while."

Clara's brows immediately scrunched into a frown. "I hope you aren't coming down with something. Here, take a few sips." She handed him the canteen of cool water they'd brought with them.

Lonesome Wolf drank and then turned the canteen to help Nathanael take a drink.

Clara felt the press of tears as they fought their way to the surface, but she blinked them back. If he saw her crying, he'd ask her what was wrong. And then she'd have to explain…. explain what the sight of this man, of this *good* man, loving her son did to her heart. And she knew beyond a doubt that the man involved was in no way ready to hear those thoughts. She wasn't even sure she was ready to think too heavily on them herself.

⌘

"Wanna go for a walk?"

"You know I do. Let me put these last few dishes up and grab the baby." Clara set the plates in the cupboard and turned around to see that Lonesome Wolf already had Nathanael. "Tell me, am I ever going to get to carry my son on a walk again?"

"Not while I'm around." And he sounded like he meant it.

They stepped out into the evening. Nathanael clapped his hands and smiled one of his baby smiles that grabbed onto the heart and didn't let go. Lonesome Wolf squeezed him close and kissed his cheek. When the baby replied with a little giggle, Lonesome Wolf starting kissing him as fast as he could, tickling his belly. The baby's giggles were contagious. Suddenly, Nathanael grabbed Lonesome Wolf's face with both hands and gave him one open mouthed, slobbery baby kiss after another. He wouldn't let go. He kept kissing him and kissing him. Lonesome Wolf was trying gently but desperately to free himself but to no avail. Clara burst out laughing, and soon, all three were dissolved into bellyaching laughter. The more Nathanael chortled, the more the two adults laughed. Soon Clara had tears streaming down her face.

She swiped a hand across her cheeks. "Oh, my. That was the funniest thing I've ever seen. I do believe that baby loves you."

"The feeling is altogether mutual."

The warmth in his voice touched Clara. "I can tell." She sighed contentedly and turned her face into the slight breeze. It was warm but the still air was warmer, so the breeze was appreciated. She gathered her hair in her hands and lifted it off her neck, enjoying the relief of the wind on her bare skin. She could feel Lonesome Wolf staring, so she looked at him out of the corner of her eye. "What?"

"I'm sorry?"

"You look like you want to ask me something. What is it?"

He chuckled. "I was wondering about your hair. I rarely see you wear it up, but when you get warm you always lift it off your neck to catch the breeze. I was just wondering why you don't just put it up."

She looked at him for a long while as they walked down toward the water. She was thinking thoughts she shouldn't be thinking. One of them slipped out without her permission – "You don't like my hair down?" She immediately regretted her brazenness. "You don't have to answer that. I used to wear it up. Every day. It was the proper way for a lady to wear her hair." She felt sure her eye roll said what she thought about that. "First my mother insisted, then when she was gone my brother insisted, then I got married and Rob insisted. Now I'm on my own, so I get to choose. And," she grinned at him, "in case you haven't noticed, I am not all that into social proprieties. It's why I wasn't a very good debutante." She grinned at their private joke then shrugged. "I like it down and so I wear it down. I don't know why wearing hair down is thought inappropriate anyway."

Lonesome Wolf was quiet for a moment, but his eyes never left her hair. Finally, he said, "I think I know why it's considered improper." His voice held a husky note but he didn't care.

Her cheeks turned pink and she wouldn't look at him, but she rolled her eyes in true Clara fashion and grumbled, "Great, now I suppose *you* are going to insist I wear it up."

"Me? I would *never* insist you do anything you don't want to do." He grinned teasingly, feeling quite close to her at the moment. "I'm smarter than that.".

Clara laughed. "Thank you."

He should've known the topic wasn't closed. Clara hadn't asked enough questions to drop it.

"Please, enlighten me. Why is it the proper way for a lady to wear her hair is up in an uncomfortable, difficult to manage bun or some such?"

He considered how to respond and then *if* to respond. He decided to take the coward's way out – answering without answering. "I'd rather not say."

"What kind of an answer is that?" she huffed. "Just tell me."

He sighed, and, knowing he had no choice but to tell her now that he had, for some unthinkable reason, brought up the subject, said, "I think long, thick hair with waves" *like yours* "when worn down causes a man" *like me* "to imagine things like how his fingers would feel in it and how it would look when it's spread out on –" He shut himself up.

Clara stopped and faced him. He didn't want to look at her, but he did. Her bottom lip was caught firmly in her teeth trying without success to trap a smile, and her right eyebrow quirked up. She looked incredibly, painfully beautiful. Lonesome Wolf eyed her, a slight smile on his lips. "And, just for the record, I like your hair down." His smile disappeared and a dark look of passion crossed over his eyes. "In fact, I prefer it down."

Clara held his eyes for a moment, even as the blush she'd felt hiding just under the surface came to life on her face. When Lonesome Wolf's lips turned up in a mischievous grin, she shook her head, put her hands on her hips, and looked out across the water. "This is what I get for being too forward. I'm going to have to stop asking so many questions."

He leaned his head back and laughed. "That'll be the day!"

She turned back to him with a mulish look. "I could do it if I wanted to."

"But you don't want to. And we don't want you to, either. Do we, Nathanael? It's part of your appeal." He moved toward the cabin. "Now come on, let's go gather the eggs and see how many Nathanael can drop before we reach the house."

She followed him up the small hill. "I want to check that hen that's setting, anyway."

Again, he wrongly thought he had put an end to the

conversation. It wasn't but a few steps later when Clara shamelessly asked, "So, you think I'm appealing?"

"I think you're too ornery for your own good, that's what I think."

CHAPTER NINE

Saturday dawned brutally hot without one solitary cloud to give any hope of a few minutes reprieve from the glaring summer sun. And Clara had planned a trip to town.

"I'm not so sure, Clara. It's already scorching. I broke a sweat watching the sun rise. If it's this hot now, it'll be dangerously so come early afternoon. You and the baby shouldn't be out in that heat. It isn't worth the risk."

Clara paused while buttering her biscuit to think. "I know you're right, about the risk, but I really wanted to get some new material for a few things I want to sew, and it's the first Saturday of the month. I've been looking forward to my visit with Lydia and Deborah. There has to be a way to go safely."

Right about then, Red Eagle and his wife showed up at the cabin door. After a brief discussion of the trip to town it was decided, mostly be decree of Red Eagle, that not only should Clara go but, if Lonesome Wolf was going to stay around for any length of time, he needed to get to know the townspeople and would, therefore, also be taking the trip. They would beat the weather by creating a makeshift shade for the baby with a rigged up blanket, by taking time during the worst of the heat to picnic at the river where it passed behind the general store, and by heading home later in the day when the sun was at least fractionally less brutal.

And so it was that Lonesome Wolf met the townspeople of Klein Creek.

He didn't go in blindly, as Clara spent a good portion of the ride telling him about pretty much every person within a hundred miles of the small town. Clara made sure to describe how each person looked, what family they had, how each family member looked, everyone's basic personalities, the latest news, and any other information she could bring to mind. He wasn't sure if she was talking to benefit him in his first journey into local civilization or if talking just plain calmed her nerves. Reason aside, the talking passed the time so quickly that they reached the little group of buildings affectionately known as *town* far sooner than he expected.

The men hopped down from their respective wagons and secured them to the hitching post in front of the general store, as this would be their meeting place. Lonesome Wolf walked back to help Clara from the wagon. When he set her on firm ground, his hands froze at her waist. Holding her so closely was entirely improper in general and possibly deadly in town, and yet as long as she was looking into his eyes, tethering him there with brilliant green, he couldn't let go. Behind him a throat cleared, Clara broke eye contact, and Lonesome Wolf dropped his hands away from her waist as if he'd found himself holding a rattlesnake.

She quickly left to join Deborah in the general store, abandoning him there alone with Red Eagle. Ornery woman.

⌘

As Red Eagle stood at the back of his wagon and

unhitched a bay horse he had brought to have shoed while in town, he turned with solemn eyes to Lonesome Wolf. "I'm not going to say anything about what just happened because I don't think it has to be said." He raised a brow at Lonesome Wolf that would've been stern had the blasted man not been trying rather unsuccessfully to hold back a grin.

He started walking off toward the livery but suddenly stopped and turned back to Lonesome Wolf. "It'd be a good idea if you called me Tremont while we're in town. It seems to put folks a little more at ease. And I don't know if you have a white name, but if you do, now'd be the time to use it. And if you don't, now'd be the time to get one."

"Jacob." Oddly, the name seemed foreign to him after so many weeks as Lonesome Wolf. "My white name is Jacob." Red Eagle looked relieved as well as chagrined. Lonesome Wolf had to laugh. "I understand. It's not my first time in a small town."

Red Eagle nodded, his expression a sort of grim that indicated shared experiences. "I'm sure you do understand. And, uh, I'm glad to see you're armed. Shouldn't need to use it, but it ain't a bad deterrent."

"I take my pistol everywhere, and I have my rifle with the horse and a knife in my boot, but I don't start trouble. It'll all work out one way or another." He stopped Red Eagle with a hand to his arm. "I appreciate what you're doing for me, *Tremont*."

"Thanks, *Jacob*. It's a pleasure." But from the look on his face, he thought this would be anything but pleasurable. "Let's get this over with."

As they neared the livery, Red Eagle told Lonesome

Wolf about the man who ran it. "He's a nice guy. Was a corporal in the war. Getting on up in years, but he can still handle a horse like a dream. Never seen a livery master treat other people's horses so good." He leaned over and spit in the street. "This small town don't have a whole lot of use for a livery by itself, so he also does handyman work. Right nice feller."

They entered the livery and Lonesome Wolf took in the familiar smell of hay and horses, he breathed a sigh of relief from being out of the sun.

An older man, slightly bent but still walking proud, greeted them. "Mr. Tremont! What brings you into town?"

Tremont cocked his head toward the bay. "Got me a horse here that threw a shoe up in the north canyon somewhere. I'm thinking he might like a matched set again."

The old man nodded as he said, "Can do. Can do."

"Eldon," Tremont made sure he had the old man's attention, "this here's Jacob. Jacob meet Richard Eldon – we all just call him Eldon – Klein Creek's master of horses, all-around fix-it man, and husband of the best cook in all of Texas."

"That last part's the truth, least-ways," Eldon said as he patted his skinny belly, "not that you can tell it from my scrawny carcass." He held out his hand and shook Lonesome Wolf's without ceremony – it was always a test of a man's makings as to whether or not he'd shake hands with an Indian. Eldon turned further into the livery, leading the way to a ring where he tied Red Eagle's horse's reins. "Let's take a look here, darlin', and see what he done to ya. Yes, sir. Gonna need a new hoof. Be done right away. If'n ya got any other business t'town you just go on 'n do it. She'll be fine as frog hair by time you get back." He patted the horse affectionately on her withers and rubbed a hand down her nose, talking straight to the horse and never even looking the men's way.

Before they could turn all the way around, Eldon spoke to the horse again. "Jacob, you have this man here take you by and see Miss Rose. She gonna skin Tremont alive if she finds out he come into town and didn't introduce you. Gonna be in trouble he brought you here first, anyways."

Lonesome Wolf chuckled. When they got back out into the street, he looked over at Red Eagle, waiting for an explanation.

"Miss Rose is really Mrs. Rose Eldon, Eldon's bride. She says if he wanted her to be called Mrs. then 'he shouldn't a oughta married a spinster who already had a name.'" Red Eagle cut Lonesome Wolf a look. Grinning, he said, "You might be getting a fairly accurate picture of Miss Rose."

Miss Rose owned and ran the town café, aptly named Miss Rose's. It was clean. And it smelled good. So good, in fact, that it had Lonesome Wolf wishing they had foregone the idea of a picnic so they could eat Miss Rose's cooking. His thoughts were cut off when a tall, broad woman came bustling out of the kitchen with two plates in her hands, hollering, "Hold yer horses, Alfred Holze. I'm a comin'."

"Now, I didn't say a word, Miss Rose," said a voice from somewhere near the back.

"You might notta said it within' yer mouth, but you said it with'n that tappin' hand."

Alfred Holze slid his tapping hand from the table and put it in his lap like a guilty schoolboy and gave Miss Rose a shamefaced smile. "If your cooking weren't so good, Miss Rose, I wouldn't be so impatient to get it."

"Oh, git on with you, you sweet talker, you." She plopped down his plate, heaped full of roast, potatoes, and carrots. When she turned to get the coffee pot from a stove in the corner, she saw the men.

"Well, I declare, if it ain't my favorite Injun! And you brought a Injun friend! Ain't you gonna introduce me?"

"I will if you give me a minute, Miss Rose. This here is Jacob. Jacob, meet Klein Creek's most famous resident, Miss Rose."

"Pshh. More like Klein Creek's loudest resident. Now get over here, Tremont, and give me a hug. I ain't seen you in a coon's age."

"I was here a month ago, Miss Rose."

Miss Rose leveled a look at Red Eagle. "Like I said, a coon's age."

Red Eagle was a big man, but he came close to being swallowed whole by Miss Rose's embrace. Lonesome Wolf decided right then that he liked Miss Rose very much.

He wasn't so sure how he felt when she swallowed him up, too, though.

He knew the entire town couldn't be as welcoming as the Eldons. He had ignored the hate-filled stares from hard, suspicious eyes of those inside the café. Alfred Holze was too busy eating to pay him any mind, but a few of the other men were watching him closely as if they expected him to try and count coup.

The worst experience he had, however, was with the blacksmith, Carl Schmidt. It was more like how he was used to being treated – with hatred borne of fear and ignorance.

He took the measure of the man in just a few moments by the way he treated both him and Red Eagle. He barely glanced at Red Eagle and ignored Lonesome Wolf altogether after a quick cut of the eyes. And when he finally spoke to Red Eagle, he spoke to him like he was speaking not to the white version named Tremont but to a lowly Indian named Red Eagle, his voice an odd mixture of disdain and caution. If Lonesome Wolf had to guess, he'd say that Red Eagle'd had to set this man straight a time or two. His suspicion was confirmed when he heard his friend say, "Now, I have it on good authority that you charged Richard Eldon three dollars and fifty cents just last week to have the same work done. I don't see no reason why you'd be charging me twiced that. Maybe you oughta rethink your price."

Lonesome Wolf's respect for Carl Schmidt dropped even further when he said aloud, "Fine, Tremont," but mumbled "thieving Indians," under his breath. It was all Lonesome Wolf could do to let it slide, but he minded Tremont's look that said, "Now is not the time to deal with this," which was probably a good idea. He guessed it wouldn't make a very good impression with the town if he picked a fight with the local blacksmith his first trip in.

Tremont was about to pay the blacksmith, so Lonesome Wolf decided it was a good time to head outside. He was just leaving the smith, almost tripping over three tow-headed, rambunctious boys, when Clara stepped inside. Carl's attitude changed instantly and visibly. He stood up straighter, met Clara in the eye, and smiled – actually smiled – at her.

Yes, Lonesome Wolf knew all hope of ever winning over the favor of the blacksmith was lost as soon as Clara walked in through the open doorway, looking for the men. It was clear that the blacksmith was carrying a torch for Clara. Not that the fact was surprising. Lonesome Wolf wondered if she knew it and how she felt about it. And then he wondered why he thought he had a right to care. He definitely had to curb this possessiveness he was feeling toward Clara and the boy. Protectiveness was one thing. Feeling protective made sense, made him a good man. Feeling *possessive* made him a fool.

His possessiveness only deepened when he heard good ole Carl ask Clara if he could come calling some time. *Calling!* Lonesome Wolf tried desperately to quell all thoughts of Carl kissing Clara and the quickly following thought of wrapping his hands around the man's throat. Fortunately, he heard Clara politely decline good ole Carl's request. Try as he might, he couldn't tamp down the surge of joy and relief he felt at her instant refusal. Carl, on the other hand, was irritated, frustrated, and just plain dissatisfied.

Thankfully, Red Eagle interrupted the moment when he stepped between them and asked to settle up his bill with the burly blacksmith, giving Clara a chance to escape. And escape she did, taking Lonesome Wolf with her. He didn't miss the suspicion on the blacksmith's face as Clara led him by the shirtsleeve back out into the sunshine of Klein Creek's streets.

When they were outside, he turned to her. "You know this won't be the last you hear from Carl."

Clara's lips parted as she blew out an exasperated sigh then murmured, "Not the last time, not the first."

"Clara –"

"Please," she stopped him with a grimace, "not now. We'll talk about it when we get home. Let's not spoil my day in town on that topic."

He, however, wanted to discuss this new discovery *right now*, but before he could question her about Carl the Blacksmith and his pursuit of Clara like Clara wanted to discuss... well, everything, Red Eagle came out of the smithy and the trio set out to the General Store to meet Deborah.

As they headed down the road, Lonesome Wolf resolutely ignored the cold stares.

Late in the evening, after a very long, unwelcoming day in town and a satisfying supper at Miss Rose's – ignoring the not-at-all furtive glances and whispers helped the food settle better – the party made their way home. Lonesome Wolf was happy to let the woman talk so he could think. The notion that Clara would be better off with a white man was an obvious one, one that he thought of on many occasions. So why, now, was the idea threatening to undo him? Was it because it had taken the shape of Clara and the blacksmith, an actual, breathing human man whom Lonesome Wolf had met and knew first hand wanted Clara for his own? Or was it because he had seen the life he wished to share with Clara mimicked in the life of the Tremonts, the *happy* and *successful* life of the Tremonts? Or was it that his feelings for Clara had grown deeper than he imagined they could, deeper than he had wanted, and there was suddenly, therefore, so much more at stake? Or was it...? He shook his head forcefully, trying to shake out the silly, romantic notions and leave only logic behind. It was no use, though, because the notions had crept up on him and become deep-seated before he fully realized they were there. He recognized that part of him *wanted* a life with Clara and the baby. He just wasn't sure he wanted to want it. He *shouldn't* want it. And most of their world would say he didn't deserve to want it. And there was the rub. How did a man choose to purposely and selfishly do anything to make life miserable for a woman like Clara.

Perhaps he should encourage her to accept the blacksmith's suit.

⌘

They didn't discuss Carl the Blacksmith when they got home. Lonesome Wolf was pretty sure Clara didn't really want to talk about him, and he wasn't sure he did anymore, either. And so the matter was altogether forgotten … well, dropped, at least.

The next evening, Clara suggested they read more in their book, but he declined, knowing that he wouldn't be able to concentrate on the plot. Instead, he went outside to chop down some trees, and Clara worked in her garden before they lost light.

They met back up after their work and took Nathanael to help gather the eggs. The baby loved to carry eggs back to the house… and now often made it successfully with both of the ones in his chubby little hands. Just as Lonesome Wolf was reaching to a bottom nest to gather the last egg, the cantankerous rooster flew at him. Having been lost in his thoughts, he was slow to move and the rooster flogged him. He jerked his hand and shook it out, keeping his words to himself. Too bad he hadn't kept the egg, too – it lay broken and oozing, a beacon of Lonesome Wolf's distraction, at the foot of a post.

They made it back inside with, surprisingly, all but the one egg. Nathanael proudly carried his two eggs into the cabin. He was quite pleased with himself and jabbered on about them, refusing to let Clara or Lonesome Wolf take them from him. Lonesome Wolf finally convinced him to put the eggs in their basket by making a show of putting the other eggs in. Nathanael watched him, his baby-eyes considering the situation. Finally, he decided being like Lonesome Wolf was more important than holding on to an egg or two. Last one in, he looked to Lonesome Wolf for approval of a job well done. When he received a wink and playful chuck beneath his chin, he released slobbery but more-beautiful-than-anything-else-the-world smile.

While Lonesome Wolf coaxed the baby to deposit his treasure, Clara reached in the cabinet to get a salve for Lonesome Wolf's bleeding hand. He reached to take it from her, but she held it out of his reach. "I'll do it for you. Give me your hand."

"I can do it, Clara. Just hand me the salve." He reached for the small pot again, but she refused to hand it over.

"It'll be easier for me to do with my two hands than with your one," she said as she uncorked the top and the potent smell of the salve filled the cabin.

All he could think about was how he'd felt when she had tended his scratches in those first days – and how excruciating it had been to endure her touch. When he reached for it again and she turned from him to get a kitchen towel, he glared at her back.

Apparently she could feel the ire firing from his eyes. "Don't be such a man. Sit down and let me help you.

He gritted his teeth against what he wanted to say and said simply, "I think I can manage."

She ignored him and gave a little laugh. "You're being silly."

"I don't want you to touch me!" The words bellowed out before he could muster the power to stop them.

Clara froze, a look of hurt, one so severe it made Lonesome Wolf feel as insensitive as he evidently was, blooming on her lovely face.

He drug a weary hand down his face and through his hair. "Look, I didn't mean it like that. I just meant that I'm not used to having a woman tend to me, and last time you... when you touched...I mean I can't... Oh, just tend the blasted thing!"

A confused Clara proceeded to *tend the blasted thing*.

⌘

The baby was so keyed up after playing with the chickens, that Clara decided to read aloud to him to calm him down. She went to the shelf and took down one of her five precious treasures. As soon as she went for the book, Nathanael began to settle. He loved to hear his mother read. She wondered if he knew what she was saying, if he could follow the story or understand some of the phrases. He listened so intently that, against her better sense, she imagined he comprehended it all. He watched her carefully from Lonesome Wolf's lap. Lonesome Wolf rocked the baby while they listened to the rhythmic cadence of Clara's voice telling the story of love and mystery. Soon, Nathanael was relaxed, with his fingers in his mouth and his head resting on the Indian's broad chest.

Lonesome Wolf heard the rise and fall of Clara's voice, allowing himself to fall into it like a feather bed on a cool autumn night. He completely lost track of the story, oblivious to the characters and their predicament. All he heard was a soft, clear voice, changing in pitch and tone in a way that produced its own kind of music – a beautiful music that sang a siren's song to him. He stopped his mind from going too far down that path, pushing away thoughts of fear or feelings, and sank into that song. Lost in it, he found himself alone with the voice. Deep within himself, his soul answered it in a silent promise, a realization that if he could hear only one voice forevermore on this earth, it would be Clara's that his heart chose.

And thoughts of allowing another man to claim her as his own fled as quickly as they had come the day before.

⌘

Trying not to be overly loud, Lonesome Wolf crept into the cabin to make coffee. He stopped when he saw Clara in the kitchen. In a low voice that suited the time of day, he asked "What are you doing up so early?"

"I couldn't sleep." She lazily covered a yawn as she handed him a cup of coffee. "A better question is where do you always go this early?"

He grinned broadly and grabbed her hand as he passed by, pulling her after him. "Come with me and I'll show you."

She followed him out of the kitchen door, down the porch steps, and around the cabin to the edge of the hill on the east side. She knew where they were going – she had seen him many mornings standing on the hill watching the sunrise. But he seemed so happy about showing her that she went obediently along, fully aware that he still held her hand. His hand around hers felt strong and protective. It made her want to step into his arms and just be held.

Lonesome Wolf interrupted her musings. "What is it? Why are you shaking your head?"

She hadn't even known she was doing it. "Oh, nothing. Just thinking." She desperately hoped that the morning was still new enough to hide the blush she felt coming on, and she was thankful when they reached the hilltop and came to a stop, facing the horizon that offered them first light.

They stood still, looking out onto the land, quiet settling around them, when Lonesome Wolf spoke. "I come here every morning. I love the sunrise. To me it's not only a gift of God's splendor but a reminder of the scripture that tells us that His mercies are new every morning. I find comfort in that scripture and also a challenge to myself to show mercy to others like God shows to me."

Clara thought the words beautiful, poetic, and as he watched the sunrise, Clara watched him.

⌘

As the sun relentlessly assaulted the landscape, he worked doggedly on preparations for building the corral, determined that he'd have the trees chopped down before the sun set that night and be done with it. It was work that would've been cathartic in the spring or autumn, but was nothing less than brutal in the meanness of summer. The heat was broken up some by the cool bucket of water Clara brought him after the baby went down for his nap. Lonesome Wolf was happy for the company she provided even if it slowed down his work.

They chatted about almost nothing for a short while before Clara made the comment, "I'm surprised there's so much Indian left about you, having left your village at such an early age." It was a simple observation that had Lonesome Wolf wondering in what ways she perceived him as "Indian." He didn't ask, though he did find himself answering her implied question. Talking to her made him feel free and, surprisingly, able to open up to her in a way he hadn't to too many people ever, and thus, before the morning had passed from early to mid, Lonesome Wolf found himself telling her about the closest thing he'd ever had to a friend.

"I rode with an old man, a Creek, for several years."

"Wait. Do you know a lot of the Creek language?"

"Yes... Why?" He almost hated to ask.

"Hmmph." She plunked her hands on her hips. "I should have asked for that."

"I think," he chuckled at her acting so... like her, "one difficult language at a time is enough. Don't you, Clara?"

"Yes, but Tremont is Creek. He knows Cherokee and," she waved a hand in the air, "other stuff because he used to be a scout. But I could've really impressed him if I had spoken in his own language."

She so amused him, but he thought it a good idea not to let on. "I think he was impressed enough, Clara Jane."

"What else do you speak?" She almost sounded accusatory.

Entertained by her, he answered. "Spanish. Some Apache. But I'm not teaching you those right now, either." He reached out and pulled on her hair then quickly withdrew his hand. "Now, do you want to hear this or not?"

She looked at him as if he weren't smart. "Of course I do. Go on."

"So I rode with this Creek. I think I've mentioned him before."

Clara shaded her eyes from the encroaching sun, and asked, "Franklin?"

He nodded, surprised she remembered the old man's name. "He continued my education on being a good Indian, so to speak. He was the best tracker I have ever met, and he was always talking in this low rumble of a voice he had, always teaching about the land and animals and tracking. And women." He grinned, remembering the outrageous things the old man had said. "I teased him to no end about all the advice he gave me on women. He was old enough to be my grandfather, and I thought him knowing anything about the creatures that so baffled me was ridiculous." Lonesome Wolf heard the wistful note in his voice as he spoke of his old friend.

"What happened to him?"

He laughed. "Well, it seems he knew more about women than I thought. He met a pretty senorita in a town down in Mexico." He paused. "He stayed. I left."

Something in the way he said those last words must have warned Clara off of asking more because she simply picked up her bucket and headed back to the house to check on the baby.

CHAPTER TEN

Clara needed more jars for putting up her vegetables. She had thought she had plenty, but her garden was going strong and steady despite the hot temperatures and she was coming up short on canning supplies. Of course, Lonesome Wolf wouldn't let her go to town alone, but after the welcome he received on his last visit, he wasn't too keen on escorting her around town either. For her sake, however, he'd suffer through it. He would just stop by the livery and talk to Eldon while she did her shopping.

When he dropped her off at the general store, he saw an older woman come bustling out.

"That's Miss Corabelle, the owner of the boarding house – well, it's just a couple extra rooms in her house, but she insists we call it the boarding house. She's a cranky old busybody. You'd best run and hide while you can." Lonesome Wolf chuckled, but took heed.

He saw Miss Corabelle wave a loud, "Howdy do?" to Clara, and as he walked away, he could hear her telling Clara to come by and visit before she left town. He wondered what the chances were of that happening.

Still chuckling, he walked up to the corral of the livery. Eldon happened to be training a young colt when

Lonesome Wolf got there. It was a beautiful horse, a dappled grey.

"Good looking colt there," he said by way of a greeting.

"Howdy there, Jacob." As was his wont, Eldon spoke but didn't look away from the horse.

Again, the name Jacob sounded almost foreign to him – and he felt a little guilty about trying to hide something that couldn't, and shouldn't, have to be hidden. So he made a decision. "Actually, Eldon, my given name is Lonesome Wolf. I go by Jacob when… well, I guess when it suits me, if you catch my drift."

Eldon considered that for a moment before answering. "I catch it. And it don't have to suit you here, Lonesome Wolf, so don't you worry none about that. Course you know soon as Miss Rose get wind of it, everyone in town and around these parts is gonna know, so you might wanna make that a once and for all decision one way or t'other."

Lonesome Wolf chucked. "Well, I guess I just did."

"Come on in here." Eldon nodded and motioned for him to come into the paddock, so Lonesome Wolf obliged. He was climbing through the slats when, Eldon said, "You look like a man that's tamed a few broncs in his day."

"One or two," he confirmed.

"You for breaking or gentling?" Eldon's voice was easy, but the question still sounded like a test.

Lonesome Wolf hesitated – he'd seen normally calm men come to blows over this particular question. He gave the only answer he could, what he felt was the truth. "I gentled mine. He'll come when I whistle. He'll stand ground-tied outside the cabin all day in a saddle ready to go in case I need him. And he follows me around like a dog.

But I've seen some horses that couldn't be gentled no matter how hard a man tried to do it, and had to be broke. I've broken a few, myself. Broken, not beat into submission, mind you."

Eldon nodded with approval. "Smart man. I knowed I liked you for a reason." His grin revealed a couple of missing teeth but held a lot of approval. "Had a few of them last kind of horses myself. I'd rather have this kind these days. This colt here is the calmest one I've ever seen. You see how he never moved when you stepped in? I've had him for only three days. It'll be an easy job."

"He yours?" Lonesome Wolf asked, making conversation, "or you training him for someone?"

"Training him for Mike Pesek, some new rancher out east a here. Nice enough feller, but he ain't got the sense God gave a gander. Not about horses. Fine by me, though. We both lucked out on this one, and I'll get paid just the same." Eldon grinned big and then began leading the colt around in laps inside the paddock, leaning gently into him with his hand on his back getting him ready for the weight of a saddle and eventually a rider.

Eldon spoke to the air, seemingly to no one in particular, when he said, "Seems to me, men are pert near the same as horses. Some come to reason real easy like, and others gots to be convinced a bit."

⌘

Clara stepped around the aisle into the back corner of the general store. She was looking at the new material Mrs. Keller had gotten in recently, thinking perhaps she could make Lonesome Wolf another shirt. He certainly needed a new one… or two.

She eyed a bolt of pretty, light blue cloth with a thin dark stripe through it, debating on whether Lonesome Wolf would look better in it or the dark green on the other side of the table. Nathanael reached over and patted the blue material like he was giving it his approval. Clara tended to agree with him and was smoothing her fingers over it softly, picturing Lonesome Wolf in it, when she overheard the name Jacob. Her ears perked up.

"Jacob. Like *that's* his real name. The man is full-blooded heathen, plain as day. Probably has some name like Quickly Running Deer Who Hunts in the Morning or something ridiculous like that." Clara was beginning to seethe. She knew that voice. It belonged to Missy Longbothom, and where Missy was so was Georgiana O'Toole. Clara peeked around the edge of the shelf just enough to see them. Yep, she was right. Missy and Georgiana. And, as usual, Missy was doing all the talking. "And he is *stayin'* at her house *with* her. Why, it isn't even *decent*. Besides *everyone* knows you can't trust Indians."

Oh, for heaven's sake. Enough was enough. "Why was it okay for Cletus to stay in my hand's bunk when he was helping me out, Missy? Because you had your eye on his son and didn't want anyone to think anything *indecent* was going on? Or because nothing indecent *was* going on? I fail to see the difference. And you don't even know Jacob. What business do you have saying he isn't trustworthy? Because of the color of his skin? Because all white men you know *are* trustyworthy and decent?"

Missy sucked in a quick breath, her mouth round with indignation. That remark might *have* gone a bit too far. Missy's Pa had run off with the one of Miss Rose's waitresses. Up and left her ma, Missy, and her four younger siblings. It was probably un-Christian-like to remind Missy of such a thing.

Heaving out a sigh, Clara took the high road. "I

apologize, Missy. That was wrong of me. But you are wrong, too. Lonesome Wolf – that's his ridiculous Indian name –" at this Nathanael stopped squirming and starting saying, "Oof, Oof," over and over. "–is a fine Christian man. And he doesn't deserve to be talked about. Especially when he isn't here to defend himself."

Missy got a gleam of nastiness in her eyes. "Well, he doesn't need to be here, now does he? Seems like you're doing just fine defending him by your little ole self."

"I certainly hope so," Clara retorted. "Now, if you'll excuse me, I need to get some fabric cut and pay for my purchases. Y'all have a nice rest of the day." She and Nathanael whipped around and fairly stomped up to the counter. With Nathanael repeating "Oof, Oof," getting more demanding each time he said it.

The two girls left the store without purchasing anything, which was fine by Clara. Her mind was still on their conversation when the clerk startled her back to the present. "I'm sorry," Clara apologized, "could you repeat that?"

"I said there's a letter come for you," he grumbled as he held out a cream envelope with her brother's rigid handwriting on the front.

She wasn't sure if she should be elated or petrified. It'd been months since she'd heard from her brother or his wife. The letter must carry big news, but surely the news must be good or she would've gotten a telegram. Right?

"Well, are you gonna take it?" the clerk grumbled.

She held a shaky hand out to grasp the letter, anticipation warred with worry, but the anticipation was winning out.

Clara was standing outside the store placing her

smaller purchases in the wagon when Lonesome Wolf walked up. He went to take the baby from Clara but she asked him instead to get the crate of jars she'd bought.

"Alright, but why didn't the clerk bring them out? He saw you had your hands full." When Clara just shrugged, Lonesome Wolf was afraid he knew why the clerk wasn't helping. And it had nothing to do with Clara other than the fact that she was associated with him. "Was he nice to you?"

"Nice enough. He's not real talkative."

Lonesome Wolf entered the store, and his suspicions were confirmed when the clerk pinched his mouth and raised up his nose. He didn't say a word, he just pointed to the crate by the counter and watched every move Lonesome Wolf made, like he was waiting to catch the Indian pocketing a little something extra on the way out. Lonesome Wolf thanked the clerk for his help, and the clerk just nodded.

As Lonesome Wolf placed the crate in the back of the wagon he eyed Clara, wondering if the clerk was, in fact, rude to her. "Cheerful fella. Full of friendliness that one."

Clara just giggled until she saw Carl heading toward the General Store. Ashamed with herself for the second time that day, she ducked behind Lonesome Wolf, whispered "Carl is heading this way," and then, pulling Lonesome Wolf along, escaped behind a wagon to cross the street and hopefully make it into Miss Rose's without being seen.

She ran the last few steps, practically leapt over the boardwalk, and tore open the door only to slam it shut as fast as she could. She frantically reached up to silence the bell Miss Rose used to alert her that a customer was coming in; Clara hoped it hadn't signaled Carl that a widow was running from him.

When she was safely inside the café, she checked the window to make sure she'd made it. She didn't see Carl, couldn't have seen him even if he was almost to the door. No, all she could see was an amused Indian staring back at her through the window, his hand on the other end of the doorknob that she currently had tightly clasped in one hand.

Sheepishly, she opened the door and let Lonesome inside. He was only half trying to hide the huge grin on his face. She smacked him on the arm and said, "Hush! I noticed you didn't turn around to go say howdy."

He just laughed at her until she glared hard enough to stop him, and then he made a show of looking around the café for Miss Rose. From the back room, she hollered, "Be out in a jiffy!"

As the amusement of the moment wore of and they waited on Miss Rose to come help them, Lonesome Wolf realized that Clara's face lacked her usual happiness. "Everything okay?"

She pulled the hair out of her eyes and sighed. "I got a letter from my brother, John. I haven't received a letter from him in months."

"Good news, I hope." He tried to sound unconcerned.

"I don't know. I haven't read it yet. Thought to wait until I got home."

"Clara!" Miss Rose cried from across the café. "So good to see you and that baby. Now, who's the heathen?"

"He's not a heathen, Miss Rose!" Clara looked horrified and more than a little mad at Miss Rose's insensitive question. Knowing good and well the boisterous woman remembered meeting him, Lonesome Wolf held in his laugh while Clara continued to school the woman.

"He's a good Christian, just like you and me."

"Huh. That so?" The old lady looked skeptical, overly so, Lonesome thought. "Reckon I never heared 'o no injun what was a Christian. Thought they had their own beliefs with them dances and all."

She hustled about the café, Clara following along behind her, her eyes starting to narrow and her voice stern when she said, "Miss Rose, you know Tremont. And you know he's not a heathen."

Miss Rose flicked away that reasoning with a jerk of her wrist. "Oh, ever'body knows Tremont's at least half white. He don't count." She gave Lonesome Wolf a thorough looking over and harrumphed again. When she saw he wasn't gong to be able to hold in his laughter much longer, she smiled a big smile and swatted Clara on the arm. "I'm just pullin' yer leg, Clara Jane. Miss Rose done met yer feller. Tremont brought him in to see me last time y'all was to town."

Lonesome Wolf, always alert to what was around him, especially while in town, checked out the other patrons of the café. Two men who had looked interested in the conversation were now speaking in low tones and casting glares at Lonesome Wolf. Miss Rose refilled their cups, but leaving their coffee untouched, they got up and left the café. One of them bumped into Clara on his way to the door. Lonesome Wolf's hand whipped out and grabbed the man's arm. There was a hard look in the man's eyes but Lonesome Wolf knew his was harder. "I believe a man normally apologizes for running into a lady. Especially when it was an *accident*."

"I ain't apolo – " At a tight squeeze from Lonesome

Wolf, the man reconsidered and bit out, "My apologies," as he jerked his arm away and stormed out the door.

Miss Rose, having missed the exchange, bustled over and settled Lonesome Wolf and Clara at a table by a window. "Well, let me get y'all some cool water. Actually, Jacob, you're gonna have t' git it. Somebody needs to tote another bucket up from the creek and I'm plumb tuckered."

When he returned from getting the water, Miss Rose was still talking up a storm. She saw he was back and turned her attention from the baby to him. "What you wearin' on yer legs there? That some new fangled Injun thing?"

"Uh.." LW looked down to check his clothes, trying to decipher just what about them looked *Injun*. "No ma'am, these here…" LW choked at his own language and cut a glance to see Clara trying to hold in her laughter. "I mean, these are called blue jeans. They're just trousers, but made out of new material called denim. A man by the name of Levi Strauss is selling them."

"A German, huh? Well, then I reckon they's alright. Those Germans are good cooks. I mean their food is kindly differnt, but it's good. I ain't seen any of 'em around here wearin' nothin' like them thangs you got on your legs, though."

"I got these in San Antone. You'll probably be seeing a lot more of them. A lot of cowboys've taken to wearing them because they're tough." Lonesome Wolg grinned. "Not quite as tough as buckskins, but tough enough for white man clothes."

He winked and Miss Rose chortled and looked at Clara. "I think maybe I like him." Then she turned her head to the other side of the room where a young family sat eating. She yelled like she was calling someone a mile away. "Bobby Don, get over here. You gotta a nasty nose. And one thing I can't stand is nastiness. Now get me that dishrag and let's wipe that nose." She wiped his nose then wiped her hand and threw the rag back on the work counter. "Third time I hadta wipe that boy's nose since they been here."

Clara turned a little green. She turned even greener when Miss Rose asked them to join her for lunch.

"I'm sorry –"

"Thank you so much, but we can't stay today –"

"I have to get back and do some canning –"

"We just came to town to get some more jars for Clara."

They were tripping all over each other, but neither one of them were willing to slow down long enough to untangle their words. For it was desperately necessary they did *not* stay for dinner.

⌘

Suppertime was coming up soon, so Clara put the chicken on to roast and prepared the biscuits. While she waited for them to rise she sat down with her letter. She slit the envelope and pulled out the crisp page. One page. And it was only half-filled. Typical John. When she read his missive, she turned pale. This couldn't be.

She had barely absorbed the news when Lonesome Wolf walked through the kitchen door.

He stopped as soon as he saw her, then rushed to her, covering the space in a few large strides. "Are you okay? What happened? Are you sick? Is Nathaniel all right? What's wrong?"

She grinned at him, or at least she hoped it looked like a grin. "If you'll stop long enough for me to answer, I'll tell you." While she spoke, he pulled her from her seat, led her to the rocking chair, and gently pushed down on her shoulders until she sat.

"I'm sorry. You scared me." He sat in the chair beside hers. "What is it?"

"It's the letter from my brother." She took a deep breath. "He sold the family estate to our uncle and is bringing his wife, Cynthia, out here." She folded the letter, creasing it over and over. "Uhm, my sister-in-law has weak lungs and her doctor recommended drier air, so they're settling around here." She could visibly see him tense and wondered why.

"When will they be here?" His voice was clearly agitated.

She felt some agitated herself. "They should be here in around a week, maybe less, maybe more. It'll depend on the weather, of course." She paused and took another breath. "Lonesome Wolf ..."

He held up a hand to stop her. "You don't have to say it. I'll get my things and leave tomorrow." His voice was laden with emotion and his eyes were full of pain.

Finally, she understood why he was troubled. "No!" She placed her hand on his arm to steady him, or her, or both. "You misunderstand. I don't want you to leave."

He looked deeply into her eyes with such caring and worry swimming in his own that, at that moment, she wouldn't have let him leave had he stormed out the door. "You don't?" The words were spoken quietly, as if had they been voiced too loudly Clara would change her mind.

"No. *No*," she repeated adamantly. "Why would you think that?"

"I thought ..." He looked away. "I thought you were upset at the idea of having your brother find a ... a heathen living in your home."

Clara looked at him for a second and then burst out with her rich, sparkling laughter. "I might be if I had one!" She reached up without thinking and cupped his chin with her hand, fingers gently lying on his cheek. She turned his head to face her. "You, Lonesome Wolf, are no heathen," her voice softened, "and I don't want you to leave." The sudden realization of her intimate touch made her flush. Slowly, reluctantly, she withdrew her hand.

He was looking at her intently. "Clara, have you thought about what your brother will say? Or how his wife will feel? Maybe I *should* go." He said the words as if he meant them, but his eyes pleaded with her to once again ask him to stay.

She was all too willing to do so. "You live here. They don't. If they don't like it, they can leave."

"Clara, he's your brother," he gently reminded her.

She sighed. "I know. And really I don't foresee a problem ..." Her conscience pricked. That wasn't an honest statement, no matter how much she wished it so. "Well, not one we can't conquer. At any rate, you can't leave. I'm not sure I could bear it." She willed him to read the sincerity in her eyes, to see in them all the things she couldn't say.

His words came out roughly when he responded, "I know that *I* couldn't."

They held each other with their eyes, the thoughts they couldn't voice caressing and speaking soft words like lovers. Clara was rendered almost without breath at what she saw in the dark eyes of the man who sat before her.

Nathaniel's cry drew them both back to the cabin room. Clara said, "I'm sure he's hungry," as if she should apologize.

Lonesome Wolf nodded and cleared his throat.

"You feed him and I'll finish supper." At the raise of Clara's right brow, he chuckled. "Yes, I can cook. How do you think I've survived the past eleven years?" He glanced with narrowed eyes at the stove against the wall. "True, I'm used to a campfire, but you've already done most of the work so maybe I won't spoil it too much." As he passed her on his way to the kitchen, he patted her shoulder, letting his hand slide slowly away. She allowed her eyes to follow him until Nathaniel's cry rose in volume.

As she fed the baby some leftovers from lunch, she replayed their discussion. He obviously didn't want to leave any more than she wanted him to go. And yet, he'd been willing to walk away to ensure peace between her and her brother. Once more she marveled at this man God had brought into her life. Until he said something about it, she hadn't considered her family's reaction to him. She didn't want to consider it now. She didn't want to see him hurt. And she surely didn't want him to leave.

⌘

While Clara was preparing for bed that night, she realized that her feelings about what had happened with John in the past hadn't softened over the years. And now, lying in the still quiet of her cabin in the Hill Country of Texas, so far away from her old life and so changed by the events of the past year and a half, she grudgingly sifted through her memories.

John had been an older brother that she adored … until their parents died. Then he'd become a boss, a taskmaster who tolerated little argument or input from his little sister. She mourned their lost relationship. From playmate and friend to authority versus the outranked.

With the thoughts of John came other memories, as they always did. She used to be so excited about the prospect of being courted. She had enjoyed the lovely dresses and the dances that allowed her to mingle with those around her age. Even now, she could almost smell the fresh scent of magnolia blossoms on the cool night air. And despite her claims that she hadn't been a good debutante, she was swallowed up by pleasant remembrances of waltzes and long walks in the dusk and giggling in the corner by the punch bowl over which boy was looking at which girl. Coy looks, flirting conversation ... it was indeed a distant life from the one she now led.

The change began when Father fell ill with the fever. Mother had nursed him for days until falling to the illness herself. Clara remembered the visit by the doctor when he'd said that all that could be done was to bathe them with cool cloths and administer laudanum if they became too restless. John had needed to give the laudanum to Father, who became delirious in his fevered state and thrashed about. She would never be able to rid herself of the memory of his haunting moans and raving screams. They never had to deliver the laudanum to Mother. She died peacefully only two days after becoming sick. Father had outlived her by a day, even though he'd fallen ill days earlier. Within little more than a week, Clara had gone from a carefree young woman and beloved daughter to a lost child, alone and frightened.

And then the fights with John had started. He began to dictate whom she could see, where she could go, and when she must come home. Their first real fight had come, however, when he had given Rob permission to court her. Of course, Rob was John's best friend. And, although Clara thought him handsome, she wasn't in the least bit interested in him romantically. She had wanted to marry for love, something her father had promised he'd allow her to do. And she didn't love Rob Henson. Rob, on the other hand, had professed to John his undying love and devotion to Clara. Within weeks he'd proposed … vicariously through John, who had accepted on Clara's behalf. Despite thousands of tears shed in John's presence and many a heated debate, Clara had, a few months later, found herself Mrs. Rob Henson. Two months after that, the newly married Hensons, accompanied by John Roth and his wife, Cynthia, were making their way from Louisiana to the western hills of Texas. John had stayed long enough to help Rob build the cabin and see the couple situated. Then, he had bid them farewell and ridden away, leaving Clara with a husband she… well, she *had* respected him.

Clara hadn't seen John in the long years since. They'd corresponded more when Rob was alive, but even then their letters were stilted and brief.

Thinking of their letters brought her back to the present. She would have to let Lonesome Wolf know about her past, about her relationship with her brother. After all, he deserved fair warning.

She fell asleep praying for her sweet sister-in-law.

To say that Clara's night wasn't restful was a vast understatement. She awoke with dark circles under her eyes and a heart filled with unease. She couldn't live like this, without God's peace she so cherished, any longer.

As they finished breakfast and rose to put their dishes in the dishpan, Clara took a deep breath and began to talk. "Lonesome Wolf, I want to tell you something. I was going to tell you yesterday, but we got off track …" their eyes met briefly, "and I didn't. But you should know the story before John and Cynthia get here."

"Here, let's sit." He led her to the sitting area with a

warm, gentle hand on the small of her back. "I'll rock Nathaniel and you relax and tell me." He smiled at her as he took the baby.

As soon as she was seated, she dove in. "Okay, this is about my brother, John … and also about me." Lonesome Wolf nodded an encouragement for her to continue. She closed her eyes, took a long breath, then nodding, opened her eyes and went on. "Our parents died when we were barely entering into adulthood. John, as the older, and male," she rolled her eyes so fast Lonesome Wolf barely caught it, "sibling, immediately took control of the estate… and me. It ruined what had been a very special friendship between us." She paused. "The loss feels raw despite the years we've come through since."

She huffed out a breath and continued on, "I think the responsibility weighed heavily on him, and I'm sure he really didn't know what to do with me. He was engaged to be married, and I'm pretty sure that the idea of his little sister living with him and his bride was not a pleasing thought to him." She smiled wryly but briefly before plunging on.

"Anyway, he had a best friend who was interested in me, and John, knowing how I felt, promised me to him. And I guess I was still so driven by grief that I allowed John to make plans for my future. Oh, we argued about it at first, but I just didn't have the strength to keep up the fight." Tears were welling up in Clara's eyes. Lonesome Wolf reached out and took her hand, and she gave him a grateful look and plowed onward. "So, John married Cynthia and, not long after, I married John's friend, Rob. Rob was obsessed with Texas and wanted to move here immediately after we wed. John stayed in Louisiana and continued life in our family home. And I was left in a land that felt quite foreign and wild… married to Rob." Clara sighed. "I don't mean to speak as if Rob was anything less than a good man. He treated me well, he loved the Lord, he was hard working, and he loved me. And I respected him, and I loved him as a friend, but … but not… not how I wanted to love my husband." She looked at Lonesome Wolf and something intimate passed between them. She forced herself to look away from his eyes and continue her story. "All that's to say that John is bound to mention Rob. I thought you should know the story because our relationship is strained and he's still mourning the loss of his friend. And I don't feel as though I can ask him not to talk about him.

"The other thing I want you to know is about Cynthia. She is the most gracious person you'll ever meet, and I love her dearly." Tears formed in Clara's eyes and she tried to blink them away. "She's very ill. You should know that."

Then she began to weep.

Lonesome Wolf coaxed her to stand and drew her into his arms, consoling her while she got control of herself. As he stood there holding her, he knew for certain that he considered her his, whether or not he had the right to do so.

When no more tears would come, Clara stepped back and looked at him with a rueful smile. "You must think I'm one weepy female."

"No, Clara. I think you're a strong woman who's entirely too hard on herself."

She grinned a tired grin. "I sure like your way of thinking better." She slapped her legs and gave a determined nod of her head. "All right. Right now, I'm going to start on some spring-cleaning, even though it's summer, because my sister-in-law keeps an impeccable house, and I don't want her forever scarred by having to stay in a filthy cabin."

"Are you sure you'll be okay?"

She nodded, seeming stronger and determined to meet the situation head on. "I'll be working on the corral, if you need me. Maybe I can finish it before they arrive."

Her eyes were soft and loving when she said, "Thank you, Lonesome Wolf, for everything."

He made himself walk away, heading out the door with the image of bright green eyes in his mind and the memory of the feel of Clara's body against his.

CHAPTER ELEVEN

Lonesome Wolf was consumed with thoughts of Clara. Not that he didn't think a lot about Clara on other days, but today ... he couldn't send his mind down any other track. Cutting the poles for the corral simply didn't take enough brainpower to focus his thinking on the work and off of her for very long at a time. But he cut them anyway. It needed to be done. Although it would've been better if it had already been done.

Marvin had escaped.

Lonesome Wolf did not want to have to give Clara the news of Marvin's breakout, especially in the state Clara was in. She'd grown attached to the cranky stallion. He wasn't happy about the ornery varmint's desertion either since he and Marvin had recently come to an understanding... or so Lonesome Wolf had thought. It had taken a while – a long, difficult while – but once Marvin came to trust Lonesome Wolf, the horse behaved beautifully, and a well-behaved stallion would be a great asset to Clara. Marvin being gone was a big loss. And Marvin *was* gone.

Lonesome Wolf had lost his trail that morning in a dried creek bed a good ways from the house. He might've taken the time to track and picked up the sign on the other side of that rock bed, if he'd had the time to spend searching every rock in Texas to find a blamed horse you knew would escape again as soon as he had the chance. No, as upset as Clara would be about losing Marvin, she would be more upset if her homestead didn't appear peaceful and well-cared for when her brother and his wife showed up. So, instead of spending more long hours in the heat of Texas looking for a bad-tempered creature, Lonesome Wolf was spending long hours in the heat of Texas working to finish Clara's corral.

Before he knew it, the day had come and gone and it was time for supper. He looked up at the sky and noticed that it was a late supper at that. As he brought in the last log, Clara leaned her head out the side door and yelled at him to clean up, that the food was all but ready.

Just as he finished washing up, Clara came outside saying, "I thought before supper I'd see how the corral was coming. I got supper on late, and by the time I'll be able to get out here after dishes it'll be too dark to see."

"Where's Nathanael?"

"Napping."

"Isn't it a little late for his nap?"

"Psshh. He sleeps when he chooses. Haven't you figured that out by now?"

"Okay, well come on and I'll show you where we are." They walked together over to the end of the barn where the corral started. He decided to put off telling her about Marvin and kept to the subject at hand. "I moved the barbed wire down there," he pointed down the hill a ways, "It takes a bit longer right now to turn the horses out and catch them again, but the fence line was in the way of the new corral." He pointed out the work he had finished. "You can see the posts I have in the ground. Today I finished cutting the railing down to size. Tomorrow, I'll get started putting them in. It shouldn't be a problem to finish before John gets here, depending on when that is, of course."

He looked down at Clara for approval. She nodded. "I like it."

She leaned back against the barn and looked up at him. She looked so beautiful, so… Clara. Then she tipped her lip up in a way that had his thoughts of her beauty turning to thoughts about other things. He smiled back, just a little, and asked her, "What's that look for?"

She just widened her smile and shook her head.

He stepped closer to her and asked again, "What is going on in that head of yours?"

Looking at him through her lashes, she shrugged. "I don't know." But she clearly did.

He moved right up to her, rested his forearm on the barn above her head, and leaned toward her until his face was very close to hers. "Oh, you have no idea, do you?"

Lips still grinning, and eyes sparkling with mischief, Clara shook her head slowly, purposefully. And Lonesome Wolf was completely done in by the gesture. Her nearness already had his insides on high alert, but at the look she shot him, heat passed right through him and he felt an overwhelming desire to kiss her.

Their faces were so close, just a few more inches and his lips could touch hers. She seemed to be aware of what he was thinking because she'd stopped smiling. But she made no effort to move. It was almost all the invitation he needed. He leaned down to kiss her, but just before his mouth covered hers, he realized what exactly it was he was doing.

He quickly pulled his head back. "I think we need

to be heading in for supper." He moved away from her and turned and strode up toward the cabin without looking back.

Clara didn't say anything, but she began walking back with him. Neither one spoke on the way to the house or while supper was dished out. As they were about to say grace, Nathanael started crying. "He probably smells the food," Clara spoke softly as she rose to get him.

"Sit down," he told her gently, "I'll get him."

Clara nodded. "I'll mash up some of these green beans and new potatoes so you can feed him."

A few minutes later, they were all eating… quietly. Not a word was spoken during the most awkward meal Lonesome Wolf had ever eaten – and he was an Indian, an outcast, in some people's mind a vicious killer or maybe only a *being* not human, less than man – yep, he had eaten plenty an awkward meal, and this was the worst by far.

Lonesome Wolf knew he had to say something. The longer they ignored the subject, the bigger it would grow. When his food was nearly gone, he broached the subject with an apology. "I am … I'm sorry, Clara, for … earlier. I don't know what I was thinking."

She quirked up an eyebrow.

Lonesome Wolf almost swallowed his spit wrong and had to cough out his reply. "Well, I know what I was thinking," *cough* "but I shouldn't have been thinking it." She just nodded. After staring at her – waiting for her to accept his apology or yell, cry, get him a drink of water, just respond *somehow* – he gave in and asked her, "Are you going to say anything?"

She sighed and set down her fork. "Lonesome Wolf, I mean, really. Why do you think I was smiling at you that way to begin with? Don't you think I feel what's between us? Don't you think I knew what you were about to do?" Well, *no*, he hadn't thought that. When he didn't answer, Clara pressed on, and if he wasn't mistaken, she was a wee bit irritated. "Well? I could have stopped you."

"That doesn't matter, Clara. It wasn't your place to stop things. It was mine." He took in a deep breath and let it out on a long sigh. He had to push it out, but what he said was right and true. "Clara, I don't think I should stay here any longer."

"What? Where are you planning on going? Are you leaving for good?"

"I can stay with Jim Kearney until I can think things through."

"With Jim?"

"Yes," he replied without looking at her, lest he lose his resolve, "I think it's best."

"And what about me?" He could tell she was about to get worked up and wasn't sure he had it in him to fight her.

"I can ask Jim to send Cletus over now and then, to help you out."

She stared at him for a moment. He felt her gaze on him so long that he finally raised his head and met her eyes. She didn't blink when she said, "I meant, what about what I think."

He stilled. "What you think? Clara, in a few days when your brother and sister-in-law get here, I'll probably have to leave anyway."

"Fine. Say that's true – which it *is not* – but let's say it is. You can go to Jim's then." She picked her fork up as if she had ended the conversation.

He couldn't miss the attitude in her words. It didn't surprise him. "Are you mad at me?"

"A little."

The tone sounded more like 'a lot,' but he wasn't about to point that out. He did ask, "Why?"

"Never mind," she answered, and she kept eating as if the conversation were pointless. "Just go."

He wanted to argue. He wanted *her* to argue. Desperately. Instead, he said, "I'll leave in the morning."

"No need to wait." Her fork clanged as it hit her plate. "Give me Nathanael and you can go now." She rose from her seat and took the baby from his arms.

Lonesome Wolf stood and looked at her, bewildered. He'd never seen her act this way before, and he didn't know what to do to calm her down. "Clara, please explain this to me. Tell me why it is you're so angry with me."

She stared at him a long moment before dropping her shoulders and answering, "I'm not really angry with you. I'm just … uuugghhh. Okay, I feel a little angry, but I don't know why." She began to pace the length of the cabin with Nathanael on her hip. "I just, I feel like you're always a hair's breadth away from saddling up your horse and riding away." She stopped pacing and faced him. "And I guess I feel you're your moving to Jim's is step one of distancing yourself from me, from us, Nathanael and me. And then step two, leaving for good, will be that much easier to take."

Lonesome Wolf didn't answer in words, but he knew the look of guilt on his face was answer enough. Suddenly, Clara looked terrified. "I don't want you to go."

His heart broke for her. For them. "Clara, I don't want to go either. I just feel like it's the right thing to do."

Her look of fear mixed with a resurging anger . "The right thing to do because you *almost* kissed me?"

"Well ... yes." What else could he say?

"What if you *had* kissed me? Would that have been so terrible?" She screamed the words. She had never screamed at him. Nathanael was very still with wide eyes staring at his mother. Apparently, the baby had never seen his mother this angry, either.

Lonesome Wolf blinked; he remembered she'd asked him a question, albeit one he wasn't about to answer. How could he answer it anyway? *Would* it have been so terrible to kiss her? Yes ... and no. How could a person want something so severely and yet not want it at the same time?

Clara spared him a response to her impertinent and pointless question. "Don't answer that. I don't even want to hear what you'd say to that." Her voice was shaking, and she put her free hand to her forehead and sighed. He could feel the distress coming off of her. He wanted to hold her, to draw her into his arms and murmur soft words of assurance to her, but he had just enough sense left to know *that* was a bad idea. "Look, Lonesome Wolf, we live on this place miles from our nearest neighbor. We spend the better part of each day together. And when we're not together, we're not far from each other. What are a few more nights going to do?"

He could tell that she was fighting her emotions, trying to rein them in. He just wasn't sure which emotions they were. A part of him hoped... He was getting sick to his stomach with the backs and forths of his thought, his emotions. He feared that he might be making a mistake, but he gave in anyway. "Okay, Clara. I'll wait until your brother gets here."

"You'll wait until my brother gets here to what?" Her voice was uncharacteristically small when she asked,

"Move to Jim's or leave us altogether?"
He hesitated.

She had to do something. She had to somehow make him see he was coming very close to making a mistake that neither of them would ever come back from. "Lonesome Wolf, what is it you're so afraid of?" The words were part question part despairing plea. And the impact on the man receiving them was immediate and made Clara wish she hadn't thrown them at him so recklessly. His face blanched. And he looked … well, stricken. He looked like she'd reached out and slapped him.

The air in the cabin stilled as if even it awaited whatever might happen next. In fact, Clara was certain that all the air had whooshed right out of the room and there was nothing for her to breathe in. Perhaps if she could breathe she could say something to make things better, to make time start up again, to heal the open wound in Lonesome Wolf's eyes.

Finally, at last, he spoke, his voice was rough and hushed. "I'm afraid, Clara, of losing another person in my life." He passed a hand over his face, through his hair, and back over his face again. "And even more so, I'm afraid of having harm come to someone I care about.
I am, as you so aptly pointed out the night we met, a lonesome wolf. Did you know, Clara, that a wolf will stalk its prey until the hunted falls and can be easily overwhelmed? A wolf is relentless in its pursuit. *That* is how I've stalked solitude, Clara, for eleven years. For more of my life than I was with either of my families. I've held on to being alone so that I didn't have to lose anyone again." He wanted to call the look on her face pity. It would make things easier. But he knew the look for the

love it was, and he felt unequipped to handle it.

"Lonesome. Wolf. Your name has become your curse."

"May be, but it beats grieving. You, of all people, Clara, should know that."

"You're right. I know about grief, but I completely disagree about being lonely. I've experienced a fair share of that since Rob died, and I can't say I'd purposely choose it. But apparently you would. Before, you suffered hardship and were alone because of circumstances you couldn't control. You *can* control this. You want to leave? Go. But know that if you do, you'll be lonesome by choice."

"That's the only way."

The room was quiet for a long while. Lonesome Wolf tried to place the strange new emotion swimming inside him. Suddenly, he understood. It was defeat. That's what he felt.

"Only way for what?"

"To survive."

Two words, two words that held such anguish. Quietly, she asked him, "Have you no faith?"

"Clara."

"What? Do you think I'm just going to let you contemplate walking out of our lives because of fear? Do you really want fear to rule over you? That's pretty arrogant if you ask me."

Lonesome Wolf stopped the argument about his faith from coming out of his mouth. He was too confused by the new direction of the conversation. Fear he got, but arrogance? "Arrogant?" It was both a genuine question and a challenge.

It seemed Clara was up for the challenge. She visibly steeled herself and met his eyes. "Yes. You must think that you're the only person in all the world who has fears that God can't overcome. Your worries are that powerful? That even the God of the universe, creator of all things, can't see you through?" Clara took a deep breath and softened her tone. "I know you're scared. And I know what it's like to be afraid to love because you're afraid to lose. I loved Rob only as a friend, but after he died, I was fearful of letting myself love even Nathanael, my own son. Afraid that I'd get attached to him and then something would take him from me and I wouldn't survive the loss."

Lonesome Wolf flinched. She was too close for his comfort to illustrating exactly how he felt. He needed to end this conversation before Clara talked him out of the only defense he had. "Look, Clara, I don't want to talk about this right now. I need to –"

"Well, too bad. We're going to talk about it and before you do something stupid."

Lonesome Wolf clenched his jaw shut on the sigh that wanted to escape. He desperately needed to storm out of this cabin and put some distance between himself and this woman. But his legs simple refused to answer his demands for self-preservation.

"Let me ask you this." She continued to press on. "After your parents died, didn't God see you through? Didn't He send someone to nurture you and love you and teach you truth and help you through your grief? And when that family was taken from you, weren't you better equipped to survive because of the strength God had been growing inside of you? Didn't you make it through that, as well? And when He sent you that old Creek that you rode with for all that time, wasn't that God's way of providing for a need you had? And when you left Franklin in Mexico, didn't you survive that? Don't you know that the faith you have in God in all other areas of your life springs from the same well that will bring forth the strength in you to *prevail* in this, even if you were to lose someone else you care for? Even if you lost me?"

"I know those things, Clara, with my mind. It's the practicing them that I have trouble doing." Lonesome Wolf sat back down at the table. He felt weary, but he also felt Clara's love and it washed over him like a soft spring rain. He would miss this, miss the way she cared for him, cared about him.

"Can I ask one more thing?"

Lonesome Wolf couldn't prevent his grin. "Why would I stop you now, Clara?"

Sitting across from him, she placed a hand over his. He turned his own over and clasped hers. He felt a gentle squeeze just before Clara went on. "Would it be harder to watch Nathanael grow up and be able to teach him things and see his laughter and his learning… would it be harder to have all of that with the possibility of maybe losing him at some undetermined point in the uncertain future than it would be to live knowing that you chose to deliberately turn your back on him and walk away?" He couldn't turn his eyes from hers, not even when her soft voice gutted him as she added, "Either way, you lose him."

Lonesome Wolf was glad he was sitting down because what Clara said... it would've taken his legs right out from under him.

He was silent for so long that Clara was beginning to think the conversation was over. Finally, he exhaled a deep breath and spoke so quietly she might have missed his words had she not been watching his lips move.

"Let me think about this, Clara." He met her eyes,

the look in his own so pained that Clara had to force her features to remain neutral. "Give me time to think."

Relief overwhelmed her, leaving her feeling weak. "Thank you, Lonesome Wolf." She cleared her throat, looking chagrined. "And, I'm sorry I acted so huffy. I was a wee bit irritated."

He lifted up one side of his mouth. "Yeah, I could tell. Remind me never to irritate you again."

She gave him a little laugh and handed him back Nathanael. "You get him settled on a pallet with some toys, and I'll start clearing away the dishes."

He did as asked, but he looked like he felt extremely rattled. So did Clara. After all, he still hadn't said he would stay.

CHAPTER TWELVE

He lay awake that night thinking back over what Clara had said and decided that she was right. He'd be losing much more by walking away than he would if he stayed. He felt like he'd been drug behind a horse for years and the rope holding him had just been cut clean through. In fact, he was so overcome with the rightness of the emotions flowing through him he thought maybe it was finally time he admitted to Clara the full extent of his feelings for her.

When she'd told him about her brother coming, the thought that she wanted him to leave had almost devastated him. Yet, when he'd realized how close they had become, an irrational need to escape had almost overpowered him. But the fact was, he couldn't see himself leaving, not now or ever. And the implications of that, and the reasons for it, were no longer things he could pretend to still be trying to figure out. He was in love with her, and that was that. He was in love with her.

And he wanted to marry her.

Of course, being free from his fear was all well-and-good, and well-and-good it was, but Clara was still white and he was still an Indian. He wasn't at all sure how

Klein Creek would react, much less how her brother would, at the idea of Clara and Lonesome Wolf together. The sensation of going from fear to disorientation to elation to rock solid doubt was dizzying. He needed to reconcile things in his own mind before he spoke to Clara about any of it. As he began to fall asleep, he thought of Red Eagle and his wife and the life they had created together. Tomorrow he would ride out and talk to the Tremonts. Surely Red Eagle would have some advice on how to handle navigating the road ahead of them.

⌘

Early morning found Lonesome Wolf in a strange mood. He was so distracted that even the sunrise almost slipped by without his notice. And he was paying breakfast very little heed. His emotions were still changing rapid fire from frustration to something akin to excitement to a terrible sense of foreboding. As he'd been carrying the milk pail up to the cabin, the feelings had dogged him. As he ate his breakfast without really tasting it, he repeatedly asked himself the same lone question that had woken him up that morning. If he loved her, how could he ask her to set herself, and any children they may have, up for the same prejudices, or ones worse than, he had endured?

He really needed to go have that talk with Red Eagle, who might not have a solution to his predicament but was someone who had the experience to help him figure it out. That reassurance alone was enough to send a wave of relief through him. A small grin escaped without his knowledge.

"Ahh, it's good to see your smile, Lonesome Wolf."

He looked up to find Clara's beautiful eyes trained on him. He could feel heat beginning to work its way up his neck and wondered what it was. Then he realized that he was blushing and hoped it wouldn't show on his darkened skin. He didn't remember ever blushing before he met Clara. Ever. He pulled himself together. "I'm sorry, Clara, I guess I've been a bit lost in thought this morning."

She shot him one of her looks. "I'd say so. I'm not sure that until now you even noticed another person was in the room with you. You haven't said word one. Besides, you just ate that whole stack of pancakes without butter or syrup."

Lonesome Wolf looked down at his plate where one slim wedge spoke of the previous existence of a stack of flapjacks. Sure enough, no sign of melted butter or of syrup could be seen. He grinned at Clara. "Okay, maybe I've been a *lot* lost in thought. I'm sorry."

"No need to apologize. I just hope everything is at least close to fine… and that if it weren't, you would talk to me about it." She spoke the latter rather pointedly, but her expression did not change one iota. He had the sense that she was thoroughly on to him.

"Nothing's wrong, just some things I'm trying to sort out. And if something were wrong, I'd share it with you." He smiled at her, allowing himself to look at her closely, freely through the eyes of love for the first time. She was an amazingly beautiful woman. Her outer beauty was matched only by the person she was on the inside, and in that it was far outshone.

"Have I lost you again?" Clara's voice pierced his thoughts.

He shrugged. "Maybe for a minute." He cleared his throat. "I'm sure breakfast was delicious, even if I don't remember eating it."

She laughed. "Well, there's an honest compliment."

Nathanael called from the next room, "Mama.

Mama. Oof. Oof."

They laughed and both rose to get the baby. Lonesome Wolf came up behind Clara as she pulled Nathanael from his crib. The baby reached up with pudgy hands and patted Clara's cheeks. He nodded his head, dark curls bobbing as he did so. His voice changed to a conversational tone and he said, "Mama." Clara and Lonesome Wolf laughed again. When Nathanael turned, looked at Lonesome Wolf, pointed, and proclaimed, "Oof," Lonesome Wolf put his arm around Clara's waist and leaned in to kiss Nathanael. It was an easy gesture that was made without forethought. Just as naturally, Clara responded, leaning her head into his chest. As they stood there, the three of them together, he was all at once suffocatingly overwrought with the wonderful emotions that came avalanching upon him. He could feel his throat constricting. Forcing himself to calm, he kissed the baby again and said, "I love you, Little One." He was rewarded with a huge baby grin. Suddenly, Lonesome Wolf couldn't stand there any longer. He kissed the top of Clara's head and then extricated himself from the embrace. "I have to go," he said, knowing it was abrupt.

Clara turned to him with a look that bordered on fear and demanded of him, "Where are you going?"

He smiled in spite of the tumult in his mind. "Clara, I'm coming back." She visibly relaxed. "Why're you so afraid that I'll leave without saying good-bye?"

"I don't know. It's just …a feeling? I don't know."

"I have no plans to leave, Clara. Not anymore. I'll be here for you if you need me. I can make it through your brother's visit, *we* can make it through, no matter how long he stays or how he acts. I've dealt with fear and prejudice before. It's of no consequence to me. I only hate it for you… but not enough to leave because of it." He made sure he held her eyes. "And I don't plan on leaving for any other reason, either."

Clara, gently bounced Nathanael and swayed in that way mothers do. She took her time in answering, watching Lonesome Wolf closely, probably looking for the reason for his change of mind. It was difficult to hold himself up under her scrutiny, he was so weak-kneed with love, anxiety, and a new kind of fear that she would now reject him, after last night. He could easily envision her weighing their situation. When she finally spoke, her words were soft in sound but fierce in meaning.

"Thank you. Thank you for that assurance. I needed it, after last night." Still, she stood there scrutinizing him, until she quietly chuckled out a laugh clearly directed at herself. "I'm sorry. I've been…anxious lately. I'm nervous about John's coming. He could be here any day or it could take a couple weeks. It's a little nerve-wracking, not knowing when he will step in and capsize our world, and if truth be told, I have no idea how he'll react to you."

"We'll face it, Clara. Whatever it is, we'll face it together." They were fine words. fine words he should be heeding.

"Okay," she said softly, then she squeezed Nathanael and kissed his head.

"I'm going to ride over to Tremont's. I should be back by dinner, but it could be later, so don't go to any trouble to fix me something. I'll eat leftovers or something when I get back. Okay?"

"If you can wait a little while, we could go with you."

"No," he couldn't get the word out quickly enough, "you should stay in case your brother comes today." He couldn't talk to Red Eagle with her there - besides, Clara's brother *could* show up any day. "I'm taking Fella. That way I can ride straight over instead of keeping to the roads. It won't take me nearly as long to get there, so I should be back soon. But if I'm not… don't worry." He kissed Nathanael one last time, endured the sloppy baby kisses with love swelling in his heart, drank in the beautiful smile the baby gave him, and couldn't resist the urge to kiss Clara goodbye. He leaned in and gently brushed his lips across hers. He wasn't sure who was more shocked, her or him. But he couldn't deny it felt … right. "I'll see you both later. When I get home, we need to talk." He paused at the door to her room and turned back around. He studied her for a moment and felt the words rising inside him. Deciding not to hold them in, he whispered, "I love you, Clara."

And then he left.

Clara stood by Nathanael's crib, holding the baby in her arms and staring dumbstruck after Lonesome Wolf. Nathanael finally insisted that she break out of her stupor and tend to him. All morning as she watched her child, washed the dishes, and cleaned an already clean cabin, the same thought repeated in her mind in a ceaseless refrain, "I love you." She could hear his voice, so familiar and comfortable to her now, speaking the phrase to her mind, which remained in a state akin to shock. And what about that ominous sounding proclamation about needing to talk? Despite trying to tamp it down, Clara could feel a tremor of anticipation working its way to the forefront of her heart. She could still feel his kiss and she couldn't help but smile at the thought of just what Lonesome Wolf wanted to talk about. She decided to put a roast on to cook, along with some carrots and potatoes. If tonight was going to be special, then she was going to do her part to help it.

⌘

He rode onto the Tremonts' place, thankful he'd finally made it. The ride seemed much longer than it actually had to have been. The emotions of the morning and the thoughts in a windstorm in his brain had churned into a thudding headache. He dismounted as Red Eagle came out of his cabin.

"Welcome! Wondered when you'd make it back over. Expected to see you sooner. You must be a stubborn one." Red Eagle grinned and slapped Lonesome Wolf on the back.

"What do you mean?"

"You came over to talk about you and Clara, right?"

Lonesome Wolf laughed, trying not to wince at the pain the action sent trouncing through his head. "I did. I guess now I don't have to worry about how to tactfully bring up the subject."

Red Eagle, still grinning, shook his head. "Tend to your horse and then come on in. I'll have Deborah fix you up some tea for your headache." The older man turned and went back inside his cabin.

Lonesome Wolf shook his head. He didn't even ask how the man knew he had a headache, but he was going to ask him why he assumed he would come to talk about Clara.

The relative dimness of the cabin was a soothing balm for his head. Even still, it continued to march a cadence so loudly he felt sure the Tremonts could hear it. Aside from the customary greetings, no one spoke much at first. When Mrs. Tremont brought him over some willow bark and chamomile tea, he gladly accepted it. After a while the dimness, the stillness, and the tea began to work, and the throbbing in his head began to subside.

When at last Lonesome Wolf let out a relieved sigh, Red Eagle started talking. "Feeling a little better? That tea might make you a bit tired, but it will sure knock a headache pain. We'll stay in here out of the bright sunlight a while and talk." He settled back into the rocker. "So what questions do you have for me about Clara?"

"And just what makes you so sure I came here to talk about Clara?"

Red Eagle grinned. "Well now, I might be a lot of things, but I ain't blind nor stupid. It doesn't take too discerning a man to see that, in many ways, you're already a family, an almighty complicated one." The older Indian settled back in his seat and prompted again, "So what, exactly, do you want to know?"

"I guess the first thing I need to know is ..." Lonesome Wolf sighed heavily and rubbed his temples, looking over at Red Eagle from under his hand. "Clara and I haven't discussed anything. I haven't even told her how I feel, not exactly. I mean I did, but..." He took a breath. "I haven't told her I want... Well, she hasn't exactly outright said anything to me, but I'm fairly certain she feels about me like I do about her." Lonesome Wolf leaned back in his chair, rubbing a hand through his unbound hair.

"Okay, let's say it's true. What, then, would you ask me?"

"Alright. The first thing I need to know is whether or not pursuing a relationship, a *marriage*, is the right thing to do, given the circumstances."

"And by circumstances you mean that you're Cherokee and she's white." Red Eagle crossed his arms over his chest and looked for all the world like a powerful

Indian chief.

"Yes, sir, that's what I mean."

"And you came to me because I married a white woman."

"Yeah. I don't mean to suggest that you made a mistake in your marriage. I only mean to ask... I want to find out..." Lonesome Wolf closed his eyes and leaned his head back to rest against the couch cushion. "I don't know what I mean to say."

"I think I do." The older man smiled reassuringly. "First, let me say this. Yes, we've met with our fair share of hardships. Yes, there are those who condemn me because of it, and there are those who condemn my wife. Frankly, there are those who condemn my children, as if our children had any say in the matter. Me, I would've faced prejudice regardless of my choice of wife because I'd still be a half-breed in a white man's world. And, my children would also have faced prejudice, maybe of a slightly different nature, but prejudice all the same, because my children would still be Indian no matter who their mother was. My wife, she's the one who's endured things she wouldn't have had to otherwise endure. So, it's really not me you should talk to. It's Deborah. What I'm saying is this, ultimately the decision is Clara's to make because she's the one who has to decide whether a life with you is worth the treatment she'll receive from ignorant people. Out here, today, in this land, it doesn't matter much. But in the future, it'll matter more. And *she* is the one who has to choose." At this, Red Eagle turned to Deborah and called her over.

She sat in the other rocking chair and smiled a knowing smile at Lonesome Wolf. "The main thing I have to say to you is that not one day has passed since I married

Red Eagle that I regretted our decision. Not one. We've
had some difficulties, but all marriages have their struggles.
Because some of ours are unique to our situation doesn't
make them any more difficult to endure than any other
couple's problems. Also – and please hear me when I say
this – if Tremont had walked away from me for my sake –
because I'm sure you've considered perhaps it'd be best for
Clara if you'd simply leave – well, if Tremont would've
left me, I would've been devastated. I love him with
everything in me, and it would've been a more difficult
road to live without him and struggle to forgive him for
abandoning me than the road we've walked down together.
That's what Red Eagle means when he says to you that the
choice is really Clara's to make. It's not fair for you to
make her decision for her." Deborah put a loving, motherly
hand on Lonesome Wolf's arm. She looked deeply into his
eyes as if she could reach in and sooth the pain in his soul.
"Lonesome Wolf, I know this is a struggle for you. But it
shouldn't be. You should pray and make sure that this is
what God has for you. If it is, then He'll see you through,
because He's all-powerful and He's a mighty, mighty God.
Don't take on His battles. Let Him fight them. Do you
understand what I'm saying?"

Lonesome nodded, he felt so relaxed and peaceful,
more so than he had in days. And it wasn't just the tea; this
peace went deeper. He'd been trying to fight for himself,
for Clara, and for God. No wonder he'd been so anxious
and agitated. No wonder his thoughts had been in chaos
since he'd ridden onto Clara's homestead. He had to give
up fighting battles that weren't his own. He rose and
hugged Mrs. Tremont. "Thank you, ma'am, for your
kindness in putting me in my place. I feel like a weight has
lifted that I shouldn't have been carrying. You're a good

woman. Too good for Tremont," he teased, trying to lighten the mood that had settled around them.

"That I am." Deborah winked. "Now, how is that head of yours? Do you need more tea?"

"No, ma'am, thank you. I think I should be getting back."

Red Eagle rose, smacked Deborah on the lips, and grabbed his well-worn cowboy hat off a peg by the door. The two men headed outside. They hadn't taken two steps out of the cabin when Red Eagle told him, "I'll ride with you partways. My boys are out that direction working cattle."

When both men were in the saddle and a few silent moments had gone by, Tremont looked over at Lonesome Wolf. "You know, when I first met Clara, she out and out refused to call me Red Eagle. For a short time I thought she had a problem with my heritage. Later, I figured out that her husband, Rob, didn't have a high opinion of Indians, and as long as Clara referred to me as Tremont and Rob never met me or my bunch, he had no idea I was Creek. Only Deborah went over to visit. And that way we were able to remain friends. In fact, it wasn't long until it became clear Clara had pretty well adopted us as family." His grin told Lonesome Wolf all he needed to know about this man's affection for Clara, but it was good to get the reassurance from Red Eagle when he said, "I felt like I had a grown child when that girl came along."

Red Eagle tightened up his reins and maneuvered around a fallen tree branch before he continued. "Anyways, I say all this because Deborah tells me Clara's brother is coming out to visit. I know he and Rob were good friends and," he cut Lonesome Wolf a look, "while that doesn't always mean their feelings are the same about such things,

I'd feel better if I could offer some advice."

Lonesome Wolf was more than willing to hear any wisdom Red Eagle wanted to impart. "We're worried about how John will react, too. Any advice you have to give, I'll gladly take."

Red Eagle tilted his hat, looked up at the sky, his eyes trailing a hawk as it made a pass across the Texas blue. It wasn't until the bird was out of sight that Red Eagle dropped his eyes, squinting from the sun, and said, "Just make sure you don't let any trouble he might make cause difficulty between you and Clara. She's not responsible for her brother's thoughts. And," he reined up, stopping his horse, and waited until Lonesome Wolf had also come to a standstill, "she'll probably try all she can to keep peace with him. You shouldn't take her acceptance of his words or behavior as her agreeing with them." Red Eagle squinted his eyes again, but this time it wasn't at the brightness of the sun. "You understand?"

Lonesome Wolf thought on the words for a moment. They were easier to understand than they would be to put into effect, he imagined. "I do hear what you're saying. And I thank you. But, to tell the truth, I'm not as worried about John driving a wedge between Clara and me as I am that she'll defend me too hotly to John and cause more problems in that relationship than are already there."

Red Eagle let a small laugh escape, his face full of the fondness Lonesome Wolf knew he felt for the little spitfire. "Yeah, that does sound more like our Clara." He quickly sobered. "But still, give me your word that you'll remember what I say?"

Lonesome Wolf made sure to steadily meet the man's eyes as he promised, "I'll remember."

The words had barely hit the wind when Red Eagle

nodded and kicked his horse into a gallop, leaving Lonesome Wolf alone with his vow still resonating in the air around him.

CHAPTER THIRTEEN

The ride back from Red Eagle's was much more relaxing than the ride out … that is, until he reached Clara's yard.

As Lonesome Wolf neared the barn, he spied the huge covered wagon in the drive. A man was helping a frail-looking woman down from the wagon, and another man stood off to the side with his hands in his pockets and a placid smile on his face. He appeared more as if he was welcoming company than he was the company himself.

John and his wife had arrived and apparently they brought a friend.

Lonesome Wolf sighed. What great timing they had. He wanted to speak with Clara, but that would have to be put off now. Instead, he would have to meet John. He slowed Fella to a walk and rode him into the front yard.

While Clara hugged one of the men – presumably John – and then the woman, Lonesome Wolf came up behind them and pulled Fella to a stop. Before he even dismounted, Nathanael was shouting, "Oof! Oof!" The little boy was bouncing excitedly and holding his hands. Lonesome Wolf walked over to Clara and, taking Nathanael, stood beside her. From the scowl on Clara's brother's face this reunion wasn't going to be a happy one.

The other man stepped forward. He was young and handsome, even a man could recognize that. He had a contented air about him Lonesome Wolf hoped was catchy, although he wasn't holding his breath on that one. John introduced the other man only as Reynolds and, looking at Lonesome Wolf instead of the man, added off-handedly that this Reynolds fellow was a preacher. Guess that accounted for the contentment.

Clara smiled brightly and extended a welcoming hand to the stranger. "Nice to meet you, and welcome to my home, Reverend Reynolds."

The preacher, with a slight bow over their clasped hands, happily presented himself. "Thank you, and it's just Reynolds, please. That's what everyone calls me."

"Okay, Reynolds it is, then," Clara lightly clapped her hands. "Now, let's –"

"Who's he?" John demanded, pointing an accusatory finger at Lonesome Wolf – who thought wryly about how he appeared: buckskin shirt, hair unbound and falling around his shoulder... holding John's nephew. After letting his stare harden and catch fire, Clara's brother demanded to be told what was going on. "And why are you letting him hold your baby? What's going on here?"

His wife's voice was soft but held a firm warning, "John."

Lonesome Wolf stood firm but determined to be friendly. Clara, though, she was ready for a fight. "His name is –"

"Jacob," Lonesome Wolf interjected, before Clara could make things more volatile.

She turned a frustrated glare on *Jacob*, who raised his eyebrows just enough to make her roll her eyes but not enough to stop her from confronting her brother. She leaned slightly forward, arms stiff and fists clenched, unknowingly giving Lonesome Wolf a peek of Clara-the-stubborn-little-sister. Her voice was low and mulish, and she fairly growled, "And why *wouldn't* I let him hold my baby? And John," she paused briefly, "be careful what you say."

Lonesome Wolf laid a hand on Clara's arm and spoke quietly. "It's okay, Clara."

John shot Lonesome Wolf a cold look. "I believe you should be calling my sister Mrs. Henson. Don't you?"

Clara's head whipped back to Lonesome Wolf, and she stared him down like... well, like a wolf challenging another alfa. In what could've been called a whisper except it was harsh and forced out through clenched teeth, "Don't you *dare* call me that." He swore he saw her praying for peace through the green of her eyes. She inhaled deeply and held it so long it was a marvel.

After calming a bit, and only a bit, she squared up against her brother. "I have given him leave to call me Clara. I do believe the leave is mine to give." She sounded every bit the debutante she professed not to be.

Her brother snorted with disgust, but after a breath of a glance toward his wife, he didn't pursue the matter. Instead, he turned his back to it and grabbed some items from the wagon, flinging them up and out as if they were the ones who had done him wrong. Clara started to say more – Lonesome Wolf could see the struggle playing out in her eyes before she reined herself in.

With clasped hands and bright voice, Cynthia attempted to ease the tension. "I have a wonderful idea." It was a ridiculous thing to say, considering the circumstance, but she went on, looking at one of them and then the other as if she were back at her plantation home addressing dinner guests – ill-disciplined, five-year-old dinner guests. "I am sure we are all very tired after our journey. I know I would love to go freshen up in the cabin. Why don't you men go down and clean off in the creek." Lonesome Wolf had never heard a voice so bright and yet so insistent. "You can bring our things in when you're done."

Barely giving her notice, John grumbled, "We can clean up later," as he hefted a traveling bag over the wagon's ledge.

"Oh, but I insist, *strongly*." That last word wasn't spoken, but everyone heard it. "As a lady, it *is* my privilege to insist upon such things. I will not have dirty, smelly men at the table with me. Now, run off and clean yourselves up," she opened her hands and lightly motioned them to scoot before clasping them again, "and then we can all settle in properly."

John paused a moment – an awfully short moment, Lonesome Wolf thought – but gave in. Clara let out an audible sigh of relief and ordered everyone to stay right where they were while she ran in and got some towels and soap. She returned almost before she left and shooed her brother and Reynolds down toward the creek.

As the men walked away, John shot Lonesome Wolf a cold look but Reynolds smiled and nodded an amicable greeting. He watched them as they passed by, worried thoughts swirling around his mind.

A light fragrance alerted him to Cynthia's presence beside him. He looked down on a face filled with a femininity he suspected belied a fierce spirit.

"I look forward to making your acquaintance…" she pointed a finger at his chest, "later."

Lonesome Wolf paused only a partial second more than John had then took the hint and carried Nathanael with him as he led Fella back to the barn.

As soon as the men were a good ways away, Clara turned to find Cynthia looking at her with an amused light in her eyes. Whatever opinion Cynthia held, Clara and God could deal with it. "Cynthia, I need to explain some things to you."

Cynthia smiled sweetly at Clara. "Oh, I don't think you do. I can very clearly see for myself exactly what is going on."

""I ... I'm not sure what you mean, Cynthia, but let me assure you ..."

Cynthia stopped her with a hand on her arm. "Let *me* assure *you* that I know what I see. I see, out here far from civilization, a wonderful Godly woman who would be alone with her child except for a strong and, may I be so bold as to add," she shrugged playfully and gave Clara an un-Cynthia-like saucy grin, "handsome man whom God sent to protect her... in a completely appropriate and *somewhat* innocent way." She giggled at Clara's open-mouthed reaction and added, "And who, I might also say, looks to be taking his job quite seriously." A slight question colored her words, but she didn't ask it.

Her lightheartedness faded. "I would also like to make clear to you the fact that I am aware my husband, along with all the wonderful qualities he has, also, unfortunately, harbors deep prejudices that probably will not allow him to see the situation as I see it." She paused and looked at Clara with raised brows. "What do you think?"

Clara pulled this woman whom she loved so dearly into a careful hug, wishing it could tell her how adored she was. "I think no other woman on earth has ever been so blessed as to have the sister-in-law I do. Thank you."

Cynthia squeezed her tightly before letting go. "Well, don't thank me until this whole thing is over and everything has been put to rights. For now, I'd best freshen up or we'll have a dirty, smelly *woman* at the table."

The two women leaned toward each other and laughed as they went inside the cabin. Just before the door shut behind them, Cynthia declared, "And as soon as I eat that last bite, I am going down to that creek and bathe for hours."

⌘

When everyone gathered around the table for a late lunch, the cabin air felt charged with an electricity something like a bad thunderstorm would usher in before it broke loose and played havoc.

Reynolds announced, sounding very much like the preacher he was, that it was time to say grace. Lonesome Wolf took Clara's hand in his. Her grip was awfully tight. He gave her a little squeeze then peeked at her and winked, trying his best to calm and encourage her.

Cynthia sat on his other side. He wondered if she would touch him, especially to take his hand in prayer, wondered if it were even a good idea to try. Before he decided, she extended her hand to his as if it were the most natural thing to do. He took it, offering her a thankful smile, which, much to his gratitude, she warmly returned.

He thought, perhaps, had John not been there, everyone would've had a fine time. As it were, very little conversation interrupted the meal. By the time dessert hit the table, Lonesome Wolf thought he had pushed his luck long enough and as soon as he set the spoon in his empty bowl of pudding, he excused himself and went to work on the corral.

Later, he would realize just how well lunch had gone.

⌘

That night, when Reynolds proclaimed "Amen" at supper, the bowls began to pass. John picked up the peas and grumbled something about "no serving spoon." When Clara, who had Nathanael in her lap, began to rise to get one, Lonesome Wolf reached out and softly put a hand on her shoulder. "You stay put, Clara. I'll get one." As he moved to the counter to grab the spoon, he let his hand slide away. When he turned back to the table, spoon in hand, he realized he had messed up. It was apparent that the comfortable gesture hadn't gone unnoticed by anyone in the room, certainly not Clara's red-faced and glaring brother.

Lonesome Wolf simply returned to his place at the table beside Clara and casually handed the spoon across to John. If he had hoped ignoring John's obvious anger would make it go away, he was sorely mistaken. John roughly grabbed the spoon out of Lonesome Wolf's hand and flung it across the cabin. He stood so abruptly his chair teetered and would have fallen to the floor had his wife not calmly put a hand out to it to keep it upright. John pointed his finger at Lonesome Wolf and demanded, "I want to know just what's going on here."

Lonesome Wolf had endured similar ridiculous and unfounded displays of rage in his life. He had met many men who hated the color of his skin and looked closely to find fault even when there was none to find. In the past, he'd had no use for men like that. But, this was Clara's brother. So, he took a breath to calm himself and replied as soothingly as he could, "There's nothing going on here but supper among friends."

"Oh, we are not friends. Make no mistake about that." Lonesome Wolf ignored John's remark and continued to fill his plate as if nothing had happened, but John was not about to let go of his anger. "I said I want to know what's going on here."

Lonesome Wolf lifted his head to meet John's livid, fiery eyes. His own held no hint of threat or challenge. He simply stated, "I don't understand to what you're referring, John."

"I am *referring* to the way you seem so *familiar*," he fairly spat the word, "with my sister." He crossed his arms in a way that told Lonesome Wolf he was used to being in charge. "I don't think it's right and proper. And I want to know just what you have been doing around here."

Lonesome Wolf stood. Slowly, but he stood. When he reached his full height, he made a pretty commanding presence in the room. He put his fists on the tabletop, knuckles clenched white as if they could hold in his rage, and leaned toward John. "Just what is it that you are implying?"

"I think you know," John sneered.

"I. Had. Better not. Know." Each word came out clear and hard. "You had better not be insinuating that the tiniest improper act has been committed between your sister and me. Because to suggest such a thing is to insult a woman with more strength and courage and goodness than you yourself possess. And just so you know, and listen carefully here, I *will not* stand idly by and allow you to insult Clara. So… I'm going to ask you one more time. Exactly what is it that you are implying?"

No one moved at the table. Even Nathanael was very quiet. Lonesome Wolf watched John closely, as he looked from Lonesome Wolf to Clara and back again. The full implication of what he had accused his sister of finally seemed to sink in to the man. He cleared his throat and said, "I would never insinuate that my sister is anything less than an honorable woman."

John made as if to go on, but Lonesome Wolf cut him off. "Good, then the matter's settled."

John stared hard as he slowly sat back down, and Lonesome Wolf glanced around the table. Reynolds was looking into his plate, but gave a clipped nod. Lonesome Wolf didn't know to whom or what he was nodding. Cynthia appeared to be doing her best to suppress a smile. Lonesome Wolf thought that he and Cynthia could get along just fine. Nathanael was happily tapping his spoon against Clara's plate. And Clara, poor Clara, looked tired. He wanted to take her in his arms and console her, but *that* surely would not go over well. He stepped away from the table and pushed his chair in. "I believe I'll take the rest of my meals in the barn." Clara started to protest, but he stopped her with a warning. Then he turned and left the cabin, without his supper plate.

He did not see Clara for the rest of that night.

⌘

Early the next morning, just as Lonesome Wolf finished milking the cow, Clara came into the barn with a full plate of breakfast in each hand. He carried the pail and set it down by the barn door then walked to Clara and took the plates. "Do you expect me to be extra hungry this morning?"

"I thought I'd eat with you. Is that okay?"

Her smile was almost shy.

His smile was definitely warm. "It's more than okay. It completely makes my day. Come on up to the hayloft. It smells better up there."

As they walked up the stairs leading to the hayloft, Clara apologized for not getting out to the barn to see him the night before. "Everything was just so tense. I felt like I needed to spend as much time with John as I can and try to salvage something of our relationship."

"Of course you do. I understand, Clara. It's important for the two of you to reconcile." He caught her eye. "Before that happens, though, you have to forgive him."

She blew out a breath. "Yes, I know. Easier said than done."

He offered her a seat on a small wooden stool and then handed her the plate. He took a seat near her leaning against the barn wall, and as they ate, he watched her. He did understand about her need to spend time with John, and he prayed that they would reconcile, but the truth of the matter was that he had missed her. One night in the barn away from her and he had missed her terribly.

"What is it?" Her sweet voice warmed him.

He smiled to smooth her worries. "Nothing. Just thinking."

"About?"

He studied her for a moment before deciding to be honest, after all, how could the move forward if he didn't start being more obliging in sharing his feelings. "I missed you last night."

He watched as a blush bloomed on her face. "I missed you, too. And I promise I'll make a special effort to spend as much time out here as I can tonight." Her words moved like warm honey through his veins.

He should've decided to be honest long, long ago.

⌘

Later that morning, Lonesome Wolf began laying

out the lumber for the front porch. He could finish the corral easily by himself, but maybe if he could make peace with John, the two of them and the good preacher could make fast work of Clara's porch. Just as he was rechecking his calculations, Cynthia slowly picked her way over the rocky ground to where he was working.

"Good morning, Lonesome Wolf."

"Good morning, Mrs. Roth. How are you this fine day?"

"I am grand as I can be," she proclaimed, "and please, call me Cynthia. I insist." She smiled a gentle and genuine smile. Lonesome Wolf had to wonder how a woman like this was married to a man like John.

"Thank you, Cynthia, I accept the honor."

She clasped her hands together primly. "Now, I see that you are busy, but I would really like to speak with you, if that is okay?"

"Of course it's fine with me. But I can't speak for how John would feel about it," he felt obligated to add.

Cynthia gave Lonesome Wolf a rueful look. "I know what John would say, but he's out fishing with Reynolds, thus he is not around to ask." At this she winked at him. "I would say that perhaps we speak somewhere not visible from their spot at the creek, if you would oblige."

Lonesome Wolf whispered conspiratorially. "I'd invite you into the hayloft, but if we were caught there we might cause an uproar."

Cynthia laughed a free yet gentile laugh and said in a perfect Southern Belle drawl, "Indeed, that would be a scandal beyond proportion."

Lonesome Wolf chuckled. The woman was a treasure. "Come, there's a gorgeous live oak on the other side of the house. We'll be out of the sun. We can pop in the cabin and get a blanket so we can sit a spell, if you'd like."

"That would be wonderful, thank you."

When they stepped inside and Nathanael saw Lonesome Wolf, the baby crawled over to him as fast as his arms and legs could get him there. He grabbed the leg of Lonesome Wolf's jeans and pulled up until he sat back onto his fat, little baby thighs. Rocking joyfully back and forth, he repeated, "Oof, Oof, Oof," and added his most recent word, "mine!" Lonesome Wolf reached down and swung the baby up and into his arms, giving him a big kiss on the neck. Nathanael giggled and Lonesome Wolf whispered into his ear, "I've missed you, Little One."

Clara handed Cynthia the blanket she requested and attempted to take the baby from Lonesome Wolf. The little boy kicked his legs and said, "No, no, no, no."

Clara and Lonesome Wolf looked at each other with wide eyes and then burst into laughter. She asked in wonder, "Where on earth did he learn that word?"

Lonesome Wolf shook his head. "Not from me. I certainly would never dream of telling you no to anything."

Clara laughed. "Well, he learned it from somewhere, and he learned it well."

Lonesome Wolf kissed the baby again. "I'll take him with me, if that's okay."

"Sure. Of course it is."

"Has he eaten recently?" Because if he hadn't, they would all be better off if they took a snack outside with them.

Clara nodded. "Yes, he should be fine for a while."

Lonesome Wolf turned to Cynthia. "Is it okay with you?"

"I do believe we would have a mutiny on our hands

if I did anything other than agree."

Laughing, they headed outside, Cynthia leaning heavily on Lonesome Wolf's arm as they walked out to the large oak that sat like a guardian over the cabin. Lonesome Wolf loved this place. The tree's branches reached out as if to wrap the home-place in its arms and safeguard it against evil. And the shade it provided was always a welcome respite. Cynthia spread out their blanket and they all sat down.

"He'll start learning new words every day. Soon he'll be talking in sentences," Cynthia said of Nathanael. "Speaking of new words," she looked slyly at Lonesome Wolf, "I do believe I've heard Clara saying words I don't quite understand. You wouldn't happen to understand them, would you?"

He knew it wasn't what she'd brought him out here to say, but he took the obvious ice-breaker for what it was and answered her. "I do. I taught her some Cherokee words," he added in answer to the unasked question he knew would be coming next.

"Cherokee?" she smiled and looked right in his eyes like she refused to make his heritage an issue. He respected her for that. "What was the first things you taught her? Tell me. Say it."

Lonesome Wolf grinned ruefully, appreciating the irony of having to share with Clara's sister-inlaw those first words. "Gvgeyuhi." At Cynthia's raised eyebrows, he laughed. "It means 'I love you.' Clara wanted to say it to Nathanael," he added, as if there might be some confusion.

Cynthia smiled like she knew a secret, and he began to get a little nervous. He decided to change the subject to something less awkward. "In case I don't get another opportunity to tell you, Clara's having a birthday in a few weeks. Some neighbors are coming over to give her a surprise party. One of her friends is bringing a cake. Some others are bringing food. It isn't necessary, but if you want to get her a gift, I can take you into town if you need. That is, if your husband wouldn't shoot me for it," he couldn't resist adding.

Cynthia's eyes filled with delight. "Oh, John has brought her a gift. He absolutely insisted on it. Our poor wagon team will be relieved to be rid of it."

"Oh?" He was surprised, given… well, given the way John treated Clara. He was also quite curious. "And are you going to tell me what it is?"

"No, sir, I am not." The words were harsh but they were said with eyes alight with joy. "It's a wonderful surprise!"

He was more than a little curious and wondered what in the world it could be, and why John would even go to the trouble.

He stretched out his legs, and Nathanael stood on them bouncing up and down in the safety of Lonesome Wolf's hands.

"That child certainly loves you."

Lonesome Wolf stilled Nathanael long enough to give him a kiss on the cheek. When the baby giggled, Lonesome Wolf smiled and told Cynthia, "The feeling is mutual, I assure you."

"Oh, I can see that. You love him as powerfully as if you were his father. Why, if I didn't know –" Cynthia stopped, likely seeing the look of agony he felt rushing to his face. "Why does that thought torment you so, Lonesome Wolf?"

He shook his head. "It isn't the thought of loving him that torments me. It's the thought of someday…" He shook his head again, unable to go on.

Cynthia regarded him closely for a moment then shook out her skirts and said, "Forgive my audacity at prying into your personal affairs, but here I go. It is obvious that you and Clara care for one another. Why any man would walk away from that, and from this child, would simply be a mystery to me."

He shook his head resolutely. "I wouldn't choose to walk away." Not anymore. Of that he was now certain.

"But you might leave if you felt it was the best thing for Clara? If you thought your staying would cause her harm or pain?" Cynthia sighed, something Lonesome Wolf was sure she was not in the habit of doing, and went on as if he had answered her in the affirmative. "And I suppose that my husband and his boorish ways could somehow cause something to happen that might make you consider leaving … for Clara's sake?"

The answer to that question he knew with certainty. "I would leave that decision up to Clara."

Cynthia looked surprised at his answer. Then a smile broke out across her face. "Well, I am most impressed. She would never forgive you for making a decision like that for her."

Lonesome Wolf gave a short laugh. "I was told the same thing recently by the wife of a good friend."

"Sounds like the wife is a good friend, too. Listen to us women, Lonesome Wolf. We know of what we speak." She immediately grew serious. "I want you to promise me one thing."

Nathanael was smacking Lonesome Wolf in the face and chortling gleefully. Lonesome Wolf gently reached up and held the baby's hands between his and kissed them then swung Nathanael around and sat him on the blanket. Baby settled, he turned to Cynthia. "What is it that you want me to promise?"

"Promise me, right now, that you will not be bothered by a single thing my husband says to you or tries to do to meddle into what is yours and Clara's business." When Lonesome Wolf hesitated, Cynthia plowed on. "Clara needs you to be patient with him. *I* need you to be patient with him. Do you understand what I'm saying?" Before he could answer, she continued, "I know you probably think him a horrible person. I assure you that he has shown only his worst side to you. Apart from the bitter prejudice, the man has many good qualities. And I am not sure that he will admit it, but he has been grieving the loss of Clara's friendship for almost seven years now. I know that coming here forces him to face what he did when he made Clara marry Robert. Guilt can be an awful thing, Lonesome Wolf, and it certainly cannot be helping his disposition any. Please, bear with him as he is working through this ugliness inside himself."

Lonesome Wolf thought for a long moment, wanting to be sure he was making no promise he couldn't uphold. He chose his words carefully. "All I can say is that I'll try. For Clara and for you, I'll try. I can't promise that my anger won't get the better of me sometimes. But I *will* try."

To his surprise, Cynthia leaned over and kissed his cheek. Then she patted his arm and said, "Thank you, sweetheart. You will never know what this means to me, and I suspect what it will one day mean to John." She stood then, this gentle yet powerful woman, pressing a great deal on Lonesome Wolf's shoulder to push herself up, and headed back to the cabin.

Lonesome Wolf lay on his side and propped himself

up on his elbow. Nathanael rubbed green eyes with tiny fists. Lonesome Wolf laid him on his tummy and patted his back until the little boy gave in and slept. For a long, long while, Lonesome Wolf lay there beneath the comforting shade of the large oak and watched Nathanael sleep.

When Clara came out carrying his lunch to him, he set aside his heavy thoughts and set himself to enjoying his time with her. As if he knew that food had arrived, Nathanael woke up, bright-eyed and raring to go. They had a short picnic, and then Lonesome Wolf went back to working on the materials for the porch. He thought that perhaps he should've spoken to Clara about the future at lunch. He hadn't, however. It just hadn't felt like the right time, maybe because he'd been focused on simply getting to enjoy her company, maybe because Nathanael had woken up rowdy, or maybe because he hadn't been able to shove out the worries about what John might do and what it would all mean for Clara.

CHAPTER FOURTEEN

Early morning a few days after Lonesome Wolf's conversation with Cynthia, Red Eagle showed up at Clara's wanting to head into town. Remembering his promise to Cynthia, he asked John and Reynolds along. Reynolds accepted for them both. The four men set out with very little talk amongst them. But Lonesome Wolf took it as a victory that John had even agreed to join him on the trip.

They weren't but a mile or so out from the ranch when John and Reynolds started lagging behind. On purpose, he was sure. Which was fine by him.

The ride was quiet most of the way. After listening to the wind and the birds for along while, Lonesome Wolf broke the silence, "Clara says the Creek are your people?"

"Were," was all Red Eagle replied at first. Then he shifted in his saddle and explained, "My mother was a white woman. She and my father met by chance and kept meeting afterwards on purpose. Her father was a hard, hard man from what little I ever heard of him. So, when her mother died, Mom came to live with Dad's tribe. The other women didn't like it. They didn't like *her*. She earned their respect, though, when our people migrated from Georgia to Fort Gibson. She took me and my brothers with her and walked the trip instead of riding in the keelboats like many of the other women and children. She walked it, but she was almost never the same after. Somewhere along the trail she lost a baby she didn't know she was carrying, and between the grief and the guilt, it started to eat away at her. The chief's wife came to her and gave her a talking to. Told her it was her place to serve her husband and to raise her boys, and if she couldn't force herself to do it then she should lay down and not get back up.

"Mom kept walking. She and that woman, Warrior's Woman –" he cut eyes sparkling with mischief to Lonesome Wolf, "also known as Martha, depending on who you asked."

"Not if you asked Clara."

"No, sir. Not Clara." Red Eagle raised his voice so he could be heard over their shared laughter at Clara's expense and coughed out, "I'm half-surprised that woman hadn't given *herself* an Indian name by now."

Once their laughter died down and the ride got quiet, Red Eagle picked up the thread of his story. "Anyhow, my mom and Warrior's woman, they became close friends. Mom never had much trouble with the other women after that." Red Eagle turned his head to the side and coughed out some trail dust. "Anyways, I was a mite headstrong growing up." He held out a hand and patted the air, "Now, now, I know that's hard to believe," he grinned broadly, "but it's true. Anyways, I was headstrong, and the Creek way of life was changing. Well, you know how it is. The Army needed scouts, and growing up around the fort I'd picked up several languages, so I signed on." Red Eagles spit in the dust of the road. "And if this ride weren't so blasted long, I wouldn't have to tell you no more."

Lonesome Wolf chuckled. "Well there isn't much better to do."

Red Eagle looked at him with orneriness in his eyes. "We could talk about you."

"No, sir. You already started this yarn, now finish it."

Red Eagle turned in the saddle and looked back behind them. Lonesome Wolf followed his glance. Reynolds and John couldn't be seen, but their dust was kicking up a couple of hills behind. Lonesome Wolf shook his head thinking this peace mission wasn't doing much good. Red Eagle must've read his thoughts. "Not one for mixing well with others, is he?"

"Not at all." He looked slyly at Red Eagle. "Although your reception was a lot better than mine."

Red Eagle grinned again. "Well, I ain't living with his sister. Plus, he thought I was Mexican. Guess that's a step up in his book."

The two men looked at each other, expressionless, just for a beat, and then they were off and laughing again. Lonesome Wolf gasped out. "When he said... When he said, 'Never heard... never heard of a Mexican name Tremont,' and you just..." He could barely get his words out over his own mirth "You just said, 'Me neither,'" it was all I could do not to laugh out loud right there in front of him."

"Did you see Clara leave the room?" Red Eagle nearly choked on his laughter. "Guess she doesn't have your restraint."

They laughed until Red Eagle was wiping his eyes. Poor John. He had ideas he needed to get over.

As their laughter dimmed, Lonesome Wolf prodded Red Eagle into telling the rest of his story.

"Fine," he relented. "If you want to gossip like a woman, I'll tell you." He adjusted in the saddle like was settling in to tell a long tale. "I met her dad first. He was a minister. I'd had a bad…" He blew out a breath before continuing, "a real bad experience on one of my scouting trips into New Mexico. First town I came to with a preacher, I went to him. I was shook up something fierce, and Deborah's dad? Well, he's about the calmest man you'll ever meet. Put me right to ease. Didn't care a lick that I was a half-breed. Didn't ask me what I believed. He invited me right into his house and then he just talked. We sat in the parlor and talked all morning, his wife served me lunch, and then we sat at the kitchen table and talked all afternoon. Mostly about nonsense, but he got the story out of me along the way. That's how he was. He let you get things out at your own pace, no worries about what else he might need to be doing.

"Anyhow, along about mid-afternoon the most beautiful creature I ever saw came traipsing in the back door. Long, soft brown hair, big ole eyes. My heart was pounding so hard in my chest I'm sure her dad could hear it. I thought to myself that, if my outside looked anything like my insides felt, I was about to find out just how much this man cared about a half-breed looking at his daughter like he'd just found his other half." He looked over with eyebrows raised and shrugged. "Turns out he didn't care a'tall whether I was a half-breed."

Red Eagle looked up the road to see the town coming into view. Then he turned to Lonesome Wolf. "Didn't matter anyways 'cause once she smiled at me I was gonna marry that gal whether her daddy cared or not." And with a rascally grin, he squeezed his knees, clucked to his horse, and took off at a trot, heading into town.

They pulled their horses up outside of Eldon's

livery and Lonesome Wolf dropped Fella's reins. Leaving Reynolds and John to their own devices, the pair headed into the mildly cooler air of the large barn and stopped to let their eyes adjust. Eldon came in from out back working the same yearling he'd been putting through the ropes before.

"How do?" Eldon asked as he waved them further into the livery. "Come on in and set."

Eldon and Red Eagle each grabbed a bucket and turned it over, while Lonesome Wolf leaned against a stall door. They were just settling in when Jim Kearney showed up and invited them all to a rodeo he was having in a few weeks.

The lot of them talked for quite some time about this and the other, and it dawned on Lonesome Wolf that he was experiencing what it was like to have friends. The four men weren't together because they had to be. They weren't working a drive together or on watch and bored. They weren't cowhands with bunks next to each other. They were all here, the four individually, because they wanted to be. He was so caught up in the idea and wondering how he felt about it that he almost missed it when Eldon said his name.

"…Wolf. Everybody in town knows that by now. Miss Rose saw to that. So's, Tremont, I was figurin' that you probably had one a them Injun names, too. Same as this one," he cocked a thumb over at Lonesome Wolf. "I asked Miss Rose what she thought and she said you prolly do a cuzzin' you's as good as half Indian yerself."

Red Eagle coughed into his hand to cover his laugh, and Lonesome Wolf had to turn his head to hide a smile. Jim didn't even try to hide his. These folks were something else.

"I am," Red Eagle coughed again, "as good as half Indian. And I do have an Indian name. It's Red Eagle."

Eldon laughed. "Well, that fits you just right! Being's as how yer hair is mostly red-like out in the sun. Course in here looks black as an Injun's. Meanin' no disrespect."

"None taken," Red Eagle and Lonesome Wolf answered together, and this time they didn't bother to hide their smiles.

After Jim Kearney left, they spent a good bit of time watching the colt's training and chatting with Eldon. Come close to noon, the liveryman closed up shop and the three men walked down to Miss Rose's for lunch. As they stepped in, they saw Reynolds and John paying. Lonesome Wolf introduced Eldon to the two men, noticing that the room was getting quieter and quieter. He settled his hand on his hip near his gun and scanned the area as Eldon shook hands with a sour looking John. That's when he saw Carl Schmidt rising to a slow stand in the back corner of the room. Lonesome Wolf slipped the thong off of his gun, relaxing his hand there and resting back on his heels. He didn't trust Carl Schmidt as far as he could throw him.

Reynolds had clued in that something was going on about the same time Lonesome Wolf had and his hand was slack down by the gun hanging low on his hip. Funny. He'd never thought much about the preacher wearing a gun. It just seemed to be a part of him. Lonesome Wolf cut his eye quickly back over to Carl who was spouting off loudly about the kind of people Miss Rose was serving, except he didn't use the word *people*. On the far side of the room from Carl, the poor waitress was trying to make herself part of the wall and was inching her way toward the kitchen door. By the time Miss Rose got herself into the room to see what the ruckus was about, Carl had his entire table and half the rest of the diners walking out of the café. Many of them hadn't even eaten their food and none of them paid. Reynolds went to step in front of Carl, but Lonesome Wolf gave him a subtle headshake. The men filed out of the restaurant, mouthing the entire way. And with Eldon mouthing back at them for being thieving cowards. Lonesome Wolf noticed that John had left, too. He sighed heavily. Getting along with John would be easier if John cared to get along back.

Miss Rose came over without her usual bluster. Instead, she was wringing her hands and looking at all the cleared tables. Lonesome Wolf gave a quick count of how many men had left and reached into his pocket for his money. "Here, Miss Rose. This should be enough to cover what those men owed."

"Now, now, that ain't yer fault." Eldon was having nothing to do with it. "That's all on them men. They'll pay double next time they come in or they won't get served. By Miss Rose or by me. That was downright unChristian of 'em."

"Eldon," Lonesome Wolf paused so his words would be heard, "it *was* my fault in a way. At least, it was because of me. And this is something I want to do for stirring up trouble." He handed the money to Miss Rose who hesitated in taking it. "You might never get the money back from everyone, but you'll get it from me." He closed her hands over the coins. "Take it. It'll make me feel better. Please."

"Well, don't go beggin', now," she grumbled as she pulled her hand away, and slipped the money into her apron pocket.

"What ya got to eat, woman?" Eldon asked, like nothing at all had happened. "Smells like chicken 'n dumplings."

"Tastes like 'em, too, you ornery man. Y'all grab you a place to set, and I'll be out with three bowls in a jiffy."

Lonesome Wolf hadn't seen little Bobby and his snotty nose around, so he figured it was safe to eat. They were the best dumplings he'd ever tasted, but he couldn't really enjoy them. He was mad and aggravated and feeling like he brought bad things to people he liked. And he liked Clara best of all. If the fine people of Klein Creek would walk out on Miss Rose, he could just imagine what they would do to Clara.

⌘

Red Eagle left town early to head home, so it was just the three men left to travel together. John took off without waiting for either of the others. After a short ways, Reynolds pulled up alongside Lonesome Wolf. "I wouldn't go to town without my gun if I were you. There's some of them I don't trust too much."

Lonesome Wolf was surprised by what felt like solidarity with the preacher. "I won't," he answered with conviction. "Apparently I can make an enemy of a man without even talking to him." They shared grim smiles.

A bit down the road, Reynolds spoke again. This time, he sounded almost hesitant. "I've got some news."

When he didn't continue, Lonesome Wolf prodded him. "Are you going to make me guess?"

Reynolds huffed out a laugh. "Nope. I'll tell you. Jim Kearney and George Keller approached me about being the town's preacher. Said they'd already had things set in motion for a church. Got some lumber ordered and everything. They said all it needs is the preacher, and they want that man to be me." He paused again. "I told them I'd think about it."

"Congratulations." Lonesome Wolf realized his response was genuine. "I know you'll do a good job."

"Thanks," Reynolds looked humbled, and Lonesome Wolf thought maybe the man wasn't much like the company he kept. "I guess I can count on you to come to the church raising?"

"I'll be there."

Neither said anything more the rest of the ride home.

⌘

Lonesome Wolf was cleaning a couple of Clara's cast iron skillets in a fire he'd built well before sunrise. A couple of hours in the flames and a good scrubbing, and they'd be good as new. He wished a good scrubbing would clear his mind as easily.

In the grey darkness of his sleep-filled mind last night, Lonesome Wolf had seen Clara stomping out of the café, a walking Nathanael going right behind her. He'd known it didn't seem right, Nathanael toddling along like that, but Clara walking away from him had fit just fine.

He knew what had prompted the dream. Wasn't hard to figure out between the to-do in the café the day before and the fact that he hadn't seen Clara once since. He wondered if not seeing her had anything at all to do with what had went on in town. Surely John had gladly told her about how Lonesome Wolf had cleared out half the diner just by stepping inside it. Shaking his head at the doubts, he quickly rejected the idea that Clara would judge him by others' actions.

The thought of John brought him around to how to

try and create some kind of friendship with Clara's brother, or at least acceptance of each other. He chewed on that situation as he pushed the skillets around in the fire, more for something to do than any effect it'd have on cleaning the pans. Getting along with John was one thing. Convincing *John* to get along with *him* was going to be a heck of a lot trickier. He knew it was important to Cynthia, but he was more concerned with how important it was to Clara.

He did have one idea. He still had lots of repairs to do around the place, and John wasn't doing much more than helping with the few heads of cattle and toting for the women. In fact, he spent a most of his time in the house with the women, which Lonesome Wolf found just plain odd. Maybe since work on the front porch was close to the cabin, John would help him work on it. He could ask, at least.

About that time, John came out of the house to get some water from the well. Lonesome Wolf left the pans in the fire and headed over to the man in question.

"Morning."

John looked at him and scowled.

"Just letting you know that I'll be working on the porch today and thought maybe you'd like to help." He was tempted to add, "If you aren't too busy," but thought that wouldn't quite be keeping in the spirit of getting along.

"Is that necessary? Cynthia doesn't need all that noise," John complained.

He wasn't quite sure how to respond to that because he wasn't sure why the noise was okay for Clara and the baby but not okay for Cynthia. Not that the noise would bother them today. "Clara said they were going berry picking today. So, they'll be out of the house. Should be a good time to get after it."

"If they're going out to pick berries, then I'm going with them. Women shouldn't be out there alone."

John was sure protective of his wife; Lonesome Wolf would give him that. But that was about all he could give him. He definitely couldn't give him the sense to know that the berries were within shouting distance of the house and that Clara was more than likely better with a gun than her brother was.

Later in the day, he was wishing John had taken him up on his offer to help with the porch. If John were there, Lonesome Wolf figured he'd put a stop to how much Reynolds was talking about Clara, because there was only so much a man could take hearing another man talk about his sister. He wondered if it was a shorter or a longer amount of time than a man could hear another man talk about the woman he loved.

He wiped sweat from his brow as Reynolds summed up his Ode to Clara. "What an amazing woman to have lived through what she has and stayed so strong, so at peace. To have stayed here and borne a child and raised him alone while taking care of this place. She's to be admired."

Interesting. Until then, Lonesome Wolf had been assured that talking about Clara to anyone would bring him joy. But, frankly, this entire conversation was beginning to fray his already frazzled nerves. He searched for some topic to derail the preacher, and he stumbled on one when the women's laughter from where they were berry-picking reminded him of why John wasn't there to help.

"Why is John so protective of Cynthia? I know she has weak lungs, but she seems okay."

"Seems it," Reynolds replied solemnly, "but she's not." The preacher stopped hammering and held Lonesome Wolf's eyes. "She's dying. And John knows it. She won't talk about it, but John said the doctor told him it was a miracle she has lived this long and that she wasn't strong enough to get through another bout of sickness. The drier air here is supposed to help hold that off from happening." Reynolds wiped his brow before he continued. "It took us over twice as long to get here as it could've. We stopped at practically every café and hotel we passed. Even with the slow going, it got rough. We took off every few days so Cynthia could rest up. Anyways, that's why he hovers over her, because he doesn't know how much longer he'll have her."

Lonesome Wolf's entire perspective of John had just been challenged.

CHAPTER FIFTEEN

A cool front had blown in during the night, and Lonesome Wolf was enjoying the crisp morning air. The sunrise had been beautiful, his hunt had been successful, and he could almost forget that Clara's brother had infiltrated their world.

"My, but haven't you been busy this morning," Clara called to him from the well where she was drawing water.

Lonesome Wolf dropped the doe on the ground at her feet to help her crank up the bucket. "The hunter returns home with his kill. Now it's his woman's job to dress it and tan the hide."

"Hmm... Well, I don't have any idea how to tan a hide, so I'm sure to let you down."

"It would take a lot more than an un-tanned hide for you to let me down." He looked at her, at her beauty, and hoped the time was right to tell her how he felt. "Do you know how much...." *I love you.* But he couldn't quite get the words out. He'd spoken them once. Once when they had come out without warning. Once when he had said the words and she hadn't said them back. Of course, he'd said them and then he'd run out the door. Now, even with the brisk morning air giving him courage, all he could say was,

"Do you know how much I care for you?"

He was about to say more – *what* exactly, he wasn't sure – when Clara – half accusingly, half in fright – grabbed his arm, fingernails biting into him, and demanded, "You aren't leaving, are you?"

She was obsessed with the thought of his leaving. And for the fear and sorrow he saw in her eyes at that possibility, he could've kissed he, not that it took much these days for him to want to kiss her. But, although he was glad she didn't want him gone, he did have to admit it wasn't a good sign that she hadn't acknowledged his confession. "No, Clara, I'm not leaving." He waited, but she still didn't say anything. "Is that all you have to say?" Clara merely looked at him as if she didn't know what he wanted from her. "Do you understand what I'm telling you?"

"You're saying that you care about us. We care about you, too. I –" They both turned at the slamming of the kitchen door and saw John coming toward them. Clara huffed out a sigh. "Maybe we should talk about this tonight."

Lonesome Wolf cut off a groan, reached down, grabbed the deer, and set off to take care of it – hating the fact that now that he had made up his mind about telling her how he felt, they had been interrupted. By John, of all people.

Their conversation would just have to wait.

Clara greeted her brother as she watched Lonesome Wolf walk away. Suddenly, what he'd been trying to say hit her with such clarity that she actually gasped.

"Is everything okay?" John asked her as he took turns looking at Clara and eyeing the man who had just walked off.

"Fine," Clara answered, not missing the hard glint in her brother's eyes as he watched the big Indian. She was going to have to talk to him about this whole matter, but not until after she herself had it better figured out, not until she and Lonesome Wolf finished their talk. She had been so distracted by the fear she couldn't shake of his leaving that what he was trying to say hadn't registered. He had wanted to tell her... again. He had wanted to tell her again that he loved her. She wanted to go after him, to chase him down and make him say the words again. But John was watching her like he thought maybe she would do just that.

She shook her head in frustration, forcing herself to continue on with the morning chores as usual when what she really wanted was to go after Lonesome Wolf.

But later, they would talk.

⌘

All day, Lonesome Wolf worked on the porch. Reynolds was splitting shingles, and he was finishing up the frame. But the work wasn't hard enough to get the conversation with Clara out of his head. He'd all but told her he loved her, and she had seemed clueless. Or maybe she'd realized what he was trying to say and had been gently letting him know where she stood on the matter. His heart didn't believe that was the case... No. He *couldn't* believe it.

It felt like his mind was being jerked first one way and then the other by a team of angry mules. As he drove the last corner post into the ground, he gave himself a good talking to. He needed to look at the situation logically. He tamped the earth back in around the porch post like he could stomp out all of his confusion.

And it was at that point that Clara appeared with a

glass of fresh lemonade. "I thought you men might like something to drink. This heat is so oppressive." The refreshing drink was a welcome sight in the heat of the day, but the thought of Clara's thinking of him was even better.

As he smiled and thanked Clara, he thought maybe he'd go ahead and tell her how he felt right then. No hesitation.

Just as he was about to speak, Reynolds rounded the corner of the cabin with an empty glass.

"Reynolds," Clara's voice sounded just as sweet and happy as it did saying *his* name, "you drank that down so fast, you must not have even taken a breath until the entire glass was emptied."

Frustrated they had again been interrupted, and certainly *not* because he was anything close to envious, Lonesome Wolf thrust his glass back in her hand. "Thanks for the lemonade, but I believe I'm due for a break now." He turned his back to her and headed to the oak on the side of the house, leaving a confused Clara behind. As he made it to the shade of the tree, he reminded himself that it wasn't her fault he hadn't yet worked up the nerve to tell her he was in love with her.

⌘

That evening after the supper dishes had been washed and put away, Reynolds approached Clara. He pulled her away from her brother and sister-in-law and spoke in a low voice, "Clara, would you like to take a walk?"

She hesitated. She had wanted to talk to Lonesome Wolf. It was a conversation, *the* conversation, she desperately wanted to have. However, Reynolds looked as if he had something on his mind. Masking her disappointment, she answered, "Sure, I think that'd be all right."

Reynolds escorted her to the side door. The night was a little chilly, so she grabbed a shawl, and they headed out the door and onto the side porch. She pulled her wrap closer to her body as she stepped out into the evening breeze. "My, it's certainly getting brisk out, isn't it? I love it when the evenings turn cool." Clara took in deep breaths and let them out as she walked, exhilarating in the cool night air. Finally, she couldn't contain herself any longer and put her arms out and twirled around. Laughing, she stopped and looked at Reynolds, her eyes shining with delight. "Isn't it great?"

Reynolds chuckled, obviously at her unexpected display. "I'm not sure I would call this *brisk* exactly, but it's certainly good to see you happy. You seem to be so solemn usually."

The observation surprised her. "I'm not usually solemn, at all. In fact, I'm normally quite contented." She closed her eyes in a pointless attempt to shut out her current situation. "You just happen to be here when things are a bit of a struggle." It was ridiculous to be anything but open about what was going on; she was sure it was every bit of obvious to all of them. So, she looked at him pointedly and shared, "I'm sure you've noticed John and I have a strained relationship." She dropped her shoulders and sighed weightily. "I worry about that."

Reynolds frowned. "I have noticed things were a bit tense between you. That's why I asked you to walk with me. To see if you wanted to talk about it. About you and John. I hope I'm not being too pushy, but I thought maybe I could help."

Clara took a moment to think. Maybe he *could* help. He was a preacher after all. He'd probably have Godly advice that part of her didn't want to have to listen to but the other part knew she needed. Yes, maybe he could help.

As they strolled around the property, she emptied her heart, spilling out her fears and misgivings about the entire situation. Reynolds proved both a listening ear and wise counsel, just as a pastor should be. Clara rubbed her arms a little against the slight chill of the evening and wondered vaguely if he would be willing to stay and preach in Klein Creek. She also found herself hoping he would give John some good advice like he'd given her. Approaching their issue from both sides certainly could do nothing but help things.

As they made their way back toward the house, he turned to her. "I'll pray for you, Clara."

"Thank you, Reynolds."

He placed his hand on the small of Clara's back and escorted her into the cabin. "I'm here any time you need."

She didn't talk to Lonesome Wolf that night.

Lonesome Wolf had stilled at the sound of laughter. A smile had crept across his face as he stood listening to the lilting sound. He would've recognized that laugh anywhere. It was the one that could most easily touch his heart. He'd braced himself, reminded his heart that she wasn't yet his, and then he'd stepped around the barn to meet Clara.

He had frozen, no longer sure that his heart was beating in his chest. There, in the waning light of the late summer sun, was the woman he loved sharing what appeared to be a private moment with another man.

He had watched as the couple took a walk in the pale light of dusk. After what seemed like forever, they had walked together back into the cabin. Reynolds had touched her. And she had seemed perfectly at ease with him and with his touch.

The mere thought of it all felt like a knife to Lonesome Wolf's gut, and he hated the doubts that jealousy brought – because, yes, he did recognize the feeling for the ugly thing it was.

⌘

Three nights in a row and Clara had visited him often. She had come every evening… and she had brought Reynolds with her every time. Tonight, he stared at the cabin door for quite a while hoping like crazy that Clara would come out of it and toward the barn to see him. Alone.

Only she didn't come alone. In fact, she didn't seem to go anywhere anymore without Reynolds.

After the pair left him, he headed to the barn and to his bed. He knew it was too early to turn in, but he suddenly felt like doing nothing else but lying down on his cot and staring up at the ceiling of his little room. He didn't understand what was happening. He couldn't see a reason why God would bring him here to fall in love with Clara only to take her from him.

Of course, if he let it happen, it would be his fault alone. It was his own fears that had held him back from telling her how he felt about her, from planning a future with her.

He recognized his cowardice now, which is why his inclination was to fight for her. If he didn't, then he might lose her altogether. However, he felt the Lord telling him that maybe he should go about dealing with this matter in a calmer way so he wouldn't add to Clara's worries. He wasn't sure if he was hearing right or not, wasn't sure calmer was the way to accomplish things or not – he didn't think he could just roll back his feelings for her to anything resembling calm – but he didn't want to be just one more thing that put stress on her, either.

And what about Clara? She could easily solve his problem with one word, one look. And yet she had not done so.

⌘

As Clara nestled in to sleep, she couldn't shake a feeling of unease. She knew she was struggling with forgiving John. Maybe that was all it was. Reynolds had been a big help in that area, but maybe she should talk to Lonesome Wolf about it, too. Perhaps he'd have some wisdom for her in dealing with her brother.

She wanted to talk to him anyway. They needed to finish their conversation from that morning at the well. She wondered if the unfinished conversation had anything to do with this feeling she had. She couldn't help but think that Lonesome Wolf had been trying to say to her the same thing she was feeling for him. Only, it didn't make sense that she'd be out of sorts over that. The thought of their growing relationship filled her soul with a cautious happiness. And yet, she couldn't overcome her sense of disquiet. She fell asleep praying that God would send His peace once again to her little cabin.

⌘

He hadn't slept well for the past couple nights. His brain had decided to stay awake all night trying to figure out some way to fix things with Clara without risking his heart. His brain succeeded only in tiring his body out.

One morning after a particularly beautiful sunrise, he was walking around the cabin to work on the front porch roof when Clara stepped outside with his breakfast. He stopped, wanting to turn around and hide but knowing he couldn't.

"Lonesome Wolf. Good timing. Here's your breakfast."

"Not hungry this morning. You can take it back inside."

She gave him a good, hard look but said only, "Okay, I'm sure John or Reynolds will eat it."

Lonesome Wolf made no reply to that.

She turned to take the uneaten plate inside, but quickly turned back around. "Oh! I wanted to tell you that one of Jim's hands came over while you were out riding yesterday. He came to tell us when the Kearneys' rodeo will be. They have it every year. It'll be a lot of fun..." At his continued lack of response, she faded away then changed topics. "Anyway, I need to get more canning done this morning, but I thought maybe we could all spend the afternoon down at the creek. You could come with us if you want."

How could he refuse such an invitation? "I don't think so, Clara."

She pinched the bridge of her nose and sighed. "You're right. It would probably be for the best."

Suddenly changing his mind about working on Clara's porch, he decided to get away for the day. "I'm going for a ride, maybe hunting. I'll probably be gone all day, so I'll be out of your way."

She looked at him with a mixture of confusion and frustration. "You aren't in the way, Lonesome Wolf."

It was a nice sentiment, but he knew it wasn't true. "Sure I am, but that's okay. Go spend time with your family."

He spun around on his boot heels and headed to saddle up Fella. Apparently finishing up the porch would have to wait until another day. One more thing he could blame on John. Or Reynolds. Or Clara. Or maybe just himself.

⌘

That evening, Lonesome Wolf came riding in on Fella after a day of aimlessly wandering about the countryside simply to keep himself away from home. No, not home – Clara's house. As he entered the yard and made his way to the barn, he saw Clara and Reynolds on another walk. She had Reynolds's coat wrapped around her shoulders. But that wasn't what bothered him most. Not that it didn't bother him on the most basic, possessive level of being a man. No, what bothered him most was that Clara was wiping tears off of her cheeks and smiling up at Reynolds like he'd just bestowed upon her a gift she'd always wanted. Maybe he had. The thought made Lonesome Wolf sick to his stomach. He turned away from them and went inside the barn to rub down Fella … and pray for mercy and strength.

⌘

The weather had turned warm again after the brief cool spell. Clara's family was still there, and she'd spent the last few nights walking with the handsome young preacher. So that morning, Lonesome Wolf found himself standing at the chopping block. Again. He knew that splitting logs for firewood wasn't a chore of first priority given the lingering warmth of the September Texas sun, especially considering the healthy pile of wood he'd already chopped. He had enough to shingle the porch roof and enough more split to do the smoke house he was going to build next. And still he chopped. It was a great way to clear away cobwebs and work out frustrations. Today he couldn't get rid of one simple thought – he should've told her earlier how he felt about her. Even so, if she wasn't his to have… He couldn't even bear to complete the thought. He looked at the growing woodpile – it was pretty high considering the current temperature. Soon, though, Clara would need the wood for more than just cooking, so he told himself he was just working to get a stack ready for winter.

As he walked to the well to get a drink, he shook his head, thinking about the breakfast that was again sitting, waiting for him on the table on the side porch. His appetite had fled to regions unknown. Even after the physical exertion of the morning, he didn't feel like eating.

⌘

The week passed in a blur of worry, work, and stress. Cynthia had been feeling very poorly and had taken to bed. Clara, along with John, and Reynolds had all worked endlessly to nurse her back to health. On the eighth day, Cynthia felt good enough to get up and around. She had even sat at the table and eaten supper with them.

Now that Clara could breath with relief, she would be able to spend more time with Lonesome Wolf. She was determined to talk to him. The few times she'd seen him lately, he had been distant and quiet, and he hadn't been eating well. The longer this nonsense went on, the more uncomfortable things would get. She only wished that she knew what exactly the nonsense was and what things needed to be fixed. The fact remained that even if she didn't know what was going on, something had to be done.

And she knew just where to find him. The telltale thud of ax on wood led her right to him. She set her pail down by the well and headed toward the chopping block. As soon as she caught sight of him, she stopped stock-still. He was chopping wood with no shirt on, and the strength of his corded, tan muscles brought unbidden images to Clara's mind. Not sure how long she stood there staring at him, she chastised herself thoroughly. She had no right to think of him that way, not yet. She swung back around and made a beeline for the well. She was grateful for the cool breeze, hoping it would fan the heat she could feel rising in her face. She'd have to talk to Lonesome Wolf later, when she recovered. She made a strict resolve absolutely not to approach him when he wore no shirt.

CHAPTER SIXTEEN

The moon was high in the sky, and the stillness of the night should've felt like a comforting blanket around him. Instead, as Lonesome Wolf abruptly awoke from his dream, he felt as if the night were suffocating him. The darkness served as the perfect backdrop for the barrage of images from his dream. Clara beneath the oak by the cabin in a beautiful dress. Clara standing beside Reynolds with his hand in hers. Clara kissing Reynolds as the words "I do" echoed in his mind. And Clara handing Nathanael to Reynolds while the couple smiled at each other.

Lonesome Wolf threw off his blanket and bolted from his room seeking air. He took off into the woods and walked until his willing mind couldn't force his weary legs to take one more step. He leaned himself against a tree and began praying.

If she were to be his, he didn't want to lose her. If she were to be another's, then he wanted the love in his heart, the desire that was in his blood, to be taken away. And he needed God to show him what to do because he was lost on his own.

It was some time before he returned to his room in the barn.

⌘

Clara was up before the sun the next morning. She set out to find Lonesome Wolf. Sure enough, he was standing on the hill east of the cabin, waiting for the sunrise. She walked to him, hugging her shawl tightly to ward off the damp morning chill from the light fog that had descending during the night.

Lonesome Wolf didn't turn to her as she approached. As the sun rose, she sighed contentedly at the beauty that God provided so faithfully. "It's beautiful every day, isn't it?"

"It is," was his short reply.

"I wanted to talk to you about something," she said after watching him for a while.

Lonesome Wolf shook his head.

"What? You don't want to talk to me?" She was teasing him, but when he shook his head again, she realized that he was *not* teasing her. "You're serious?" He didn't respond. "Lonesome Wolf, look at me," she demanded.

"Not now, Clara." He turned from the sunrise and away from Clara and began walking back toward the barn. She followed him.

"What's going on? What's wrong with you?"

"I just need some time to sort things out. I'm sorry." And with that he picked up his pace.

His stride was so much longer than hers that she would've had to run to keep up with him. At first she tried. She'd never seen him this way and was determined to fix whatever was wrong. "Lonesome Wolf, please talk to me. Does it have anything to do with what we were talking about the other morning?" His step faltered almost undetectably, but then he moved on. "Why are you acting this way?" The latter question had to be hollered after him, as he was leaving her behind. He kept walking. Finally,

---

Clara was shouting. "Speak to me this instant!"

He stopped. She had to know that if she weren't careful she'd have John out there, and she knew that Lonesome Wolf had had enough of her brother. She might be willing to risk that encounter, but he was certainly not up to it. With a heavy sigh he waited for her to catch up to him and, still facing forward, matched his pace to hers. "What is it, Clara?"

"Well, I'm not so sure I want to ask you now, but I do want to know what's wrong with you. Are you mad at me?" She was met with silence. She took it as a yes. "What did I do? Are you mad because I didn't come talk to you last night? I'm sorry about that but I was –"

He cut of her off. "Clara, your time is yours to spend as you want." He sounded as if he were weighing every word before he spoke it. "I'm sorry I was rude to you. I just need some time to think. Please."

She could see the tenseness of his jaw and knew that something was troubling him. It went against her nature, but she decided to let him be. "I'm going inside to fix breakfast. Your plate'll be ready in a bit. I'll bring it out to you."

"Just leave it on the table on the porch, and I'll get it."

She felt helpless, a feeling with which she was unfamiliar. "If that's what you want, I will. But I hope you know that I'm always here for you."

Lonesome Wolf turned to look at her for the first time that morning. Clara saw a deep pain in his eyes, and he spoke to her as if the words themselves hurt to say. "I can't talk to you about this, but thank you."

She nodded. Just as she moved to walk away, Lonesome Wolf called to her, "Clara?" She turned back to him, hopeful, but he only shook his head again and said softly, "Never mind."

A heavy burden filling her heart, she watched him disappear into the barn.

⌘

For days, Clara couldn't put the image of Lonesome Wolf's eyes out of her mind. The look in them disturbed her far more than his words. It was haunted, filled with desperation and betrayal. She sifted back through her memory, trying to find some clue as to what had happened to cause him to be so ... afflicted. She knew he had pain in his past, but she'd seen *that* pain in his eyes before. She knew that pain. This ... this was something altogether different. Something keener. Something more soul encompassing. And she felt powerless to do anything to ease it.

⌘

The next day, Clara went back on the deal she'd made with herself to stay away from a shirtless Lonesome Wolf when he, having eaten no breakfast and taken no break in what seemed like hours, was out chopping firewood... again. She forced herself to approach him without looking at his shirtless arms and chest. Standing several feet away, she waited for him to stop splitting wood so she could walk over to him. He didn't stop. She called out to him. He didn't respond. She practically yelled at him and still got no response. She ignored the flying wood chips and stomped closer to him, mindful of the weapon he held in his well-muscled arms, and she placed herself where he couldn't ignore her.

He stilled the ax mid-air and shot her an annoyed look, "What are you trying to do, hurt yourself?"

She popped her hand on her hips. "I'm trying to get

your attention so you'll speak to me."

"Can you wait until later, I'm in the middle of something."

"Yes, Lonesome Wolf, I can clearly see that you're in the middle of something very important. You're chopping wood … again. You've chopped wood an awful lot lately. In fact," she gestured to the ever-growing pile stacked beneath the lean-to, "you've got enough firewood to last us four winters. Are you expecting us to have several blizzards?" Picking up steam, she went on, "Are you operating on some special Indian weather sense and we're in for an uncharacteristically brutal winter? Or perhaps you were planning on going into business selling firewood to our neighbors. How many trees have you chopped into pieces, anyway?" Clara took in air. She wasn't sure, but she might've forgotten to stop to breathe during her little tirade.

Lonesome Wolf looked at her, and then he looked over at the mounting stack of firewood he'd chopped. The truth was, there had probably been enough wood to last the rest of the winter before he'd even started chopping that morning. He slammed the ax into the stump used as a chopping block and looked at Clara. "What do you want?"

"Oh, and so polite. Tell me, is all this cold weather making you testy?"

He just glared at her.

She ignored the off-putting look and softened her tone. "I want to talk to you." He didn't say anything, but he was still looking at her. Resolved, she lifted her head and spoke her challenge. "I want to know what's wrong. Something is bothering you, Lonesome Wolf. Your meals have barely been touched. Is that all you've eaten over the past several days?" He didn't respond but he didn't look away. "Lonesome Wolf, please, talk to me. I don't know what's happened. And I can't fix what I don't know is broken."

He stared into her eyes for a long moment. When at last he spoke, it was without emotion. "I'll talk to you, but don't ask me what's bothering me." Though his words were calm and even, his eyes implored her to give him what he asked. "I can't talk to you about this, Clara."

She put every bit of her frustration into her voice. "Yes, you've said that. Why? What does that even mean?"

"Clara, please." Those words ... those words held such emotion. And his eyes. The pain in them pierced Clara's heart. She moved toward him and placed her hands on his bare chest. She could see in his eyes now flashes of other, better emotions mixed with the pain. Those eyes spoke to her in a way no person could, and she wanted desperately to calm the hurt in them. She wanted to embrace the tenderness she saw hidden deep within them. It was to that tenderness that she spoke. "Have I done something to make you mad?"

His features softened the tiniest of bits. "No, Clara." He shook his head and lowered it as if he bore a heavy weight. His voice, when he finally spoke, was thick and strained. "It's a battle for me to fight. I'm giving it to God, Clara, but I cannot give it to you. Please, don't ask me to."

She stepped closer to him, ducked, and tilted her head to look up into his downcast face. Against everything she felt, she said, "Alright, Lonesome Wolf. I won't."

Suddenly he was very tired. He tore his gaze from hers, afraid he would lose all resolve in those green eyes that looked inside him and straight through his barriers. He had thought that if he were going to stay, he'd have to give a little.

He had been wrong.

He understood that now – he was going to have to give everything. He took a deep breath and forced out the words, "I've missed you, Clara. That's what's wrong with me. I miss you." Despite the fact that they were standing in the open where anyone looking out from the cabin could see them, he brushed a lock of hair away from her face and placed a kiss on her forehead. He held his lips close to her skin as he said words he thought he would never say to another human being. "I need you, Clara." Having said it gave him strength. "I need you, and I haven't had you, and I miss you." He softly stroked her cheek with the back of his fingers. "That is what's wrong. I need you."

His lungs filled with breath for what felt like the first time in days when Clara's eyes teared and she hoarsely replied, "I need you, too, Lonesome Wolf." She smiled at him and gently leaned into him. "I need you, too."

It wasn't exactly a declaration of romantic love on either's part. No, somehow it was more.

She dropped her hands from his chest as if suddenly realizing the intimacy of her touch. "How about I bring you out some breakfast. You must be starving."

He nodded and then gave a little laugh. "Yeah," he inclined his head toward the mountainous woodpile, "I think I might be finished here for a bit." He looked into the face of this beautiful woman that he loved, wanting to hold her, wanting *her*. "And I'm famished." He watched her walk toward the cabin to get his breakfast, relieved at the peace he'd made with her but burning with the memory of her touch on his chest and the feel of her soft skin beneath his fingers.

He went to the well and pulled up a bucket of fresh

water, dunked his handkerchief in it, and washed himself off before putting his blue shirt, the shirt she had sewn him, back on. He thought of the hours she'd spent on making the shirt, of the look he knew he'd seen in her eyes when she gave it to him, of the many times since then he had seen that same look.

And he decided right then that he was going to fight for his woman.

CHAPTER SEVENTEEN

Reynolds showed up shortly after breakfast to help Lonesome Wolf with Clara's smokehouse. It was entirely awkward knowing they both wanted the same woman, and though Lonesome Wolf was happy for the help, he wasn't altogether relaxed around the friendly preacher.

As they were finishing up before a lunch break, laying aside materials and tools, Reynolds closely regarded him and said, "I'm worried about you." Lonesome Wolf eyed him warily, not sure where he was going with that comment. "You seem to be much more distant and unhappy than when we first came here. I can't help but wonder if John has something to do with that. It'd be a shame for Clara to lose a friendship because her friend blamed her brother's prejudice on her."

Lonesome Wolf straightened to his full height – silently reminded himself that God had told him to act calmly – and looked Reynolds square in the eye where there would be no confusion. "If you think for one second that I would blame Clara for something her brother thinks or does, then you don't know me at all." His head cocked to the right. "Then again, you really don't know me, do you?" His head leaned as closely in as it could and still remain calm. "Well, know this. I would never do such an ignorant thing. Ever. Especially not where Clara's concerned." It wouldn't serve well to put his feelings for Clara up for conversation, so he decided to switch to another tack and straightened back to his full height. "John is responsible for his own insufferable behavior."

Later, Lonesome Wolf would remember thinking that Reynolds had the whole be-calm act down. He simply took his time and studied Lonesome Wolf carefully. When he did speak, he said, "It would be good for everyone if that hurt could be healed." The first words out sounded to Lonesome Wolf like Reynolds was trying to push his calm on everybody else.

It didn't work.

Lonesome Wolf all but lost his and talked right over the preacher. "Now let me tell you something you need to know. You need to know that my relationship with Clara is between Clara and me. It does *not* involve you. And it would be a good idea if, in the future, you kept any further thoughts you had about Clara and me between you and the Almighty."

Reynolds had grown very still. Lonesome Wolf held his gaze steadily. After an uncomfortable moment, the preacher cleared his throat. "I didn't mean to offend you. I just wanted to make sure that your friendship with Clara isn't suffering because of the way things are with John."

Lonesome Wolf bristled at the word friendship. He felt his jaw clamp together. He took a deep breath in through his nose and forced his jaw open enough to speak. "I am more concerned about other things in my life than Clara's relationship with her brother."

Reynolds eyed him closely and it was making Lonesome Wolf feel like he had something to hide. Well, maybe he did at that. Finally, the preacher's assessing look relented. "Like I said, I'm sorry. It's just that Clara's worried about you. She says you aren't eating right, and I can see for myself that you look haggard. If there's anything you want to talk about, I'd be happy to be a listening ear."

If only the man knew. Somewhere in the Good Book it says that a soft word turns away wrath, and although Lonesome Wolf didn't want to like this man, Reynolds's unruffled, preacher-ly-ness was making it impossible to dislike him. Oh, the closeness Reynolds shared with Clara still rankled, but Lonesome Wolf just couldn't seem to hold on to the anger toward the man himself. And so, he cleared his throat and told himself to... well, to be calm. "Thanks, Reynolds, I appreciate your offer. Clara and I have already talked things through, but I thank you for your concern."

"Well, I'm glad then." The young man appeared to be searching for a graceful end to the conversation. At last, he humbly said, "May God grant you the desires of your heart," and turned and left.

It was a good thing that Reynolds disappeared inside the cabin, because Lonesome Wolf didn't want the young, handsome preacher who appeared to be courting the desire of Lonesome Wolf's heart to see the reaction his parting words created.

⌘

That night, when Cynthia stepped outside to put his supper plate on the small porch table, Lonesome Wolf caught the door and held it open. Cynthia sat back down at the kitchen table and Lonesome Wolf took one step inside. He motioned to Clara. "Get your plate. I'm tired of eating my supper alone."

Clearly not liking Lonesome Wolf's proprietary

tone, John made to get up, but Cynthia stopped him with a hand on his arm.

Not the least bothered by the bossy edge to his words, Clara grinned and grabbed her plate, following Lonesome Wolf out the door and to the barn.

And so that's how it went. She, and usually Nathanael, had breakfast and supper with Lonesome Wolf... and she shared lunch and after supper walks with Reynolds. It was an odd way to court a woman, but that's what he was doing. And he was giving her the gifts he thought she'd most want to have – his words. Every time they met, he told her a little more about himself, about his past. He only hoped she would understand the significance of what he was doing.

⌘

It seemed like Reynolds was hanging around Lonesome Wolf an awful lot. Each afternoon for the past three days, the preacher had come to help him work on his projects. Lonesome Wolf was determined to be friendly. The way he figured it, if he looked happy, then Reynolds would be less likely to ask him more questions about what was troubling him. If nothing else, Reynolds's help sure was bringing the project of the smokehouse around quickly.

In an effort to keep Reynolds far away from the topic of Lonesome Wolf's feelings, he decided to steer their conversations toward Reynolds. He'd asked about where he was from, his family, and why he became a preacher. He was getting answers like he himself would've given – short and without much meat to them. He was beginning to run out of topics to ask about, so at the risk of being rude he asked the one question that had been dogging him about the preacher. Straightening from nailing down another of the shingles, but without meeting Reynolds's eyes, he asked, as offhandedly as possible, "So, why'd you leave your church and set out across Texas with John and Cynthia?"

Reynolds was quiet for so long that Lonesome Wolf regretted his question. "I apologize, Reynolds. I'm not about to share my past with you. I have no right to ask you to share your past with me. Forget I asked."

He was just about to begin hammering again, when Reynolds threw down a shingle. "No, no. It's all right." He wiped sweat off his face with the back of his wrist. "I knew somebody would ask sooner or later. I'm just thinking how to word it." He thought another moment before he shrugged. "The bottom line is that I left because of a woman." He chuckled like it wasn't funny at all. "Or two women if the truth be known."

At Lonesome Wolf's raised eyebrows, Reynolds raised his hands to hold off questions and explained, "There was a young woman in my congregation. Her mother was somewhat anxious to see her married off. I think maybe the young men around were scared off by her rather... formidable personality. Anyway, for whatever reason, the young woman set her sights on me."

"Must've been a lack of other prospects," Lonesome Wolf slid in without looking up.

Reynolds grinned and agreed, "Must've been. At any rate, she could be quite determined when she put her mind to something, and she'd put her mind to having me for a husband." He raised his eyes to Lonesome Wolf and said flatly, "I did not return the sentiment. Things got ... prickly. In fact, the young lady tried to force me into a compromising situation where I'd feel honor bound to marry her." Reynolds looked off across Clara's land like he was seeing past events. "I thank God that He was watching out for me.

"So happened, John was bringing a book over to the parsonage for me at the same time the girl came into my home, uninvited. Then her mother showed up at what would have been just in time to 'catch' us alone." Reynolds shook his head. "The girl actually had the gumption to march right into my bedroom. She didn't know, of course, that John was in the house. It didn't matter that I was standing in the hallway ordering her out of my home. If her mother came in and found her in my bedroom and us alone in the house, it would've been trouble for sure. But John *was* there, *and* he'd brought Cynthia along with him. So, when the mother stormed in," Reynolds mumbled under his breath, "*on cue*," and then continued, "the young lady's story didn't hold any water since she was alone in my bedroom while I was in the hallway with both John and Cynthia who'd seen the entire encounter." Reynolds shuddered. "Praise God."

He paused a moment before continuing. "John was more than willing to help me." The preacher found something to keep his hands busy as he finished his story. "He was sympathetic considering that the young lady at one time had a bit of a … er … crush on John."

Lonesome Wolf raised his brows and couldn't help asking, "Was he married at the time?"

Reynolds eyed him with what could only be called a preacher look. "Yep. Unfortunately, the young woman is … well, let's just say she's *forward*. When her little ploy to catch me didn't have the intended result, her mother began to spread gossip about me in some strange attempt to somehow force me into marrying the girl." Reynolds started beating away at a shingle like he could see the old woman's face on it. After a few minutes he whacked one last blow and went back to his story. "Then, I don't know how, but she found out about… my past, which is interesting in itself since I'm from out West. Needless to say, I wasn't looking forward to the young lady's next trick or her mother's next lie." He paused and pointed his hammer at Lonesome Wolf. "I know we're not supposed to worry, but I admit freely that I was worried.

"John rescued me. He suggested I accompany them on their trip. I had lived off a pastor's salary for the last couple of years, so I didn't have much money to contribute to the supplies and food, but John said that my lack of money was inconsequential," Reynolds set his hammer down and kept constant eye contact with Lonesome Wolf, like if he didn't look away, Lonesome Wolf would be forced to see the good in John, "that's the word he used – *inconsequential*. And he said my company would be worth the added expense of my coming along. I'm afraid leaving so abruptly made me look either guilty, which I most definitely *was not*, or like I was running scared, which," he grinned, "I most definitely *was*. At any rate, I resigned effective immediately, and here I am."

Reynolds picked up his hammer again and began nailing the next shingle in place, ending the conversation.

By evening the smokehouse was done. Lonesome Wolf was thankful for the help Reynolds had given. He couldn't have finished so quickly without the man. And he'd even kind of enjoyed the company while they worked. In fact, he could even admit to himself that he liked Reynolds … even if he did think Clara spent too much time with the man. He could almost convince himself that if Reynolds made Clara happy, then Lonesome Wolf could be happy for her. Almost. But it wasn't true. Not even in the tiniest way possible was it true.

He wanted to be the one to make Clara happy. And he was determined to do everything he could to make it so.

⌘

The next morning, Lonesome Wolf asked Cynthia to keep Nathanael inside with her. She seemed to have a soft spot for Lonesome Wolf, and he was going to use it to his advantage because he needed all the help he could get. After he shared breakfast with Clara, he set their plates aside and pulled her along behind him as he went out the barn door and over to where Fella stood obediently by the barn. Without even asking her permission, Lonesome Wolf hoisted Clara up onto Fella and climbed up after her.

They were going for a ride.

He turned Fella toward the creek, and they splashed across to the other side, up the embankment, and across the rolling hills. He gave the horse his head and just relaxed, enjoying the closeness to Clara. They didn't speak. She just laid her head back on his shoulder and he nuzzled her hair with his chin. He could get used to having this woman in his arms.

After a good long while, he grudgingly turned Fella back toward the homestead. He did not want John out hunting him with a shotgun. And Cynthia could only hold John off for so long and mind the baby, too. He smiled at the thought. Cynthia could certainly control that man with just a soft touch from her pale hand. Lonesome Wolf might not be in the cabin with them, but he watched them when they were outside, and it was plain as day that John doted on Cynthia, made sure she didn't overdo, did for her. It was a beautiful picture, the way he cared for his wife.

Lonesome Wolf thought he could really like Clara's

brother if the man didn't have such a problem with color of an Indian's skin..

CHAPTER EIGHTEEN

The next few days crawled by, and Lonesome Wolf endured them as best he could. Clara was still going on her walks with the preacher. However, Lonesome Wolf made sure that he got time with her, as well, and they were becoming closer. He read to her and the baby underneath the oak by the house, took them down to the creek for a picnic lunch, and put them both up on a horse he led around the new paddock. Nathanael loved that the best. Lonesome Wolf had enjoyed it quite a bit himself.

On an afternoon that was almost cool, he decided to put a railing on the front porch as a surprise for Clara. It wouldn't take long, and he wanted to have it finished before the day of her birthday party.

As he came around the side of the cabin, he heard John's voice and hesitated. It certainly wasn't worth a confrontation with Clara's surly brother to get some time in on the new porch. As he was turning to head back to the barn, he caught a snippet of the conversation, and it stopped him before he could take another step.

He very clearly heard John say, "talking about Clara's future here."

Lonesome Wolf had never been one to indulge in eavesdropping, but he was in such a state over his relationship with Clara that he considered himself on the verge of not being responsible for his own actions. So, like a mischievous little boy, he crept up on the side porch as close as he could get to the corner of the cabin and listened.

John was speaking to his wife. "Cynthia, you don't have the responsibility of taking care of Clara."

"Neither do you. She is a grown woman. She was married for years, John, and she has a child. She has lived out here by herself for over a year and a half. I believe she is big enough to take care of herself. Besides, haven't you seen the way—"

Lonesome Wolf really wanted to hear how that question ended, but John interrupted, saying, "Cynthia, I don't want to argue with you about this. Clara is going to marry Reynolds, and you will just have to get used to it. It's for the best. She'll marry Reynolds and then she and Nathanael will be taken care of when we move to town. You should be happy about that."

Lonesome Wolf turned and stumbled down the porch steps, not wanting to stay to hear the rest of the conversation. He righted his footing and then stood still, trying to absorb what he'd just heard.

Clara, *his* Clara, was going to be married to another man.

Suddenly, he was furious.

He was mad at John, he was mad at Reynolds, he was mad at Clara. And, he admitted, he was mad mostly at God. God had told him to stay, to be calm, and for what? To experience a pain keener than any he'd ever felt? To live a life pretending to be friends with the woman he loved while she was married to another man? His heart simply couldn't bear it.

He made a quick and desperate decision, and tore

off for the barn to get his things.

On her way in from the garden, Clara saw
Lonesome Wolf storming out to the barn. At first she
simply wondered what her brother had done to anger him.
She would have to say something to John and soon, despite
her pact to try and keep peace with her brother.

A piercing whistle cut off her thoughts. She looked
out toward the corral to confirm what she thought she'd
heard. Sure enough, Fella was galloping toward the back
barn door. A feeling washed over her that she needed to get
to Lonesome Wolf and fast. She set down her bucket and
jogged out to the barn, stepping just inside and then
pausing to let her eyes adjust to the relative dimness. She
heard Lonesome Wolf before she saw him. He was
descending the stairs from the hayloft. The ladder shook,
but less with the weight of the man and more with the
intensity of his steps. For a man who could tread almost
without sound, he sure was making a lot of noise.

When he came into view, Clara's concern became
alarm. He looked worse than she'd seen him in days. In his
hand, he had the Bible he usually kept in the loft where he
often studied. He strode purposefully to where his
saddlebags were draped over one of the stall doors and
stuffed the Bible inside. That's when she noticed he had his
bedroll with him. She stepped toward him. "What're you
doing?" It came out like an accusation. And maybe it was.

He walked past her to the back door to let in Fella.
He reached up and grabbed his saddle. Clara could feel the
panic rise up in her. She crossed to where he was and
demanded again, "What are you doing?"

He answered in an even, emotionless tone, "I'm
leaving."

"And when will you be back? In time for supper?"

"No, Clara. I won' be back." He didn't even look at her as he spoke.

Clara's face went ashen as her particular fear was realized, and her voice came out as less than a whisper. "Why?"

"Because I have to."

She felt a flash of anger, and without giving him a chance to explain, she flung at him, "I knew you would leave!"

"Clara, I think we both knew deep inside that I couldn't stay forever."

Her anger fled as quickly as it had washed over her, and her fear accelerated. "Lonesome Wolf, I don't want you to go."

His hands stilled. For a moment she thought he would stop his nonsense, but he simply returned to his work, saying, "Clara, it's right that I go."

"*Right*? What's that supposed to mean?" When he didn't answer her, she tried again. "I don't understand. Tell me what happened." She marveled that he could keep his face so impassive at a time like this.

When she started to ask him another question, he stopped working and turned to her. He was not impassive any longer. She was struck by the fierceness and range of emotions that tumbled through his dark eyes – love, regret, respect, sorrow. She'd never seen such sorrow there before. The passion that had sometimes haunted her nights flashed intensely and was then replaced by … was that rage? She almost didn't recognize it in this man's eyes. And she surely didn't understand it.

For a long while they stood there looking at each other. It seemed as if he were trying to memorize every aspect of her face. At length, he tore his eyes from her and went back to saddling his horse. Twice he stopped and looked at her as if to speak, but finally he grabbed Fella's reins and walked him from the barn without saying another word.

Once outside, he swung up on the horse and rode slowly past the cabin.

Clara strode purposefully after him calling his name, but he ignored her and walked on. Out of the corner of her eye she saw John and Cynthia. They had stopped whatever they'd been doing and were watching Lonesome Wolf leave. Clara thought perhaps she might actually faint. Her mind was roiling. Her vision was fading. She simply couldn't let this man calmly ride out of her life forever. Suddenly, she cried out to him, "Gvgeyuhi!"

Immediately his horse stopped. She watched as Lonesome Wolf bowed his head. But he made no move to turn around.

She drew closer to him and pressed on. "Stay. I don't want you to go. Please. Don't go."

Slowly, he slid from his mount. He turned to face her with eyes so filled with emotion that she was sure she couldn't endure it. She quietly repeated, "I love you," as if perhaps he hadn't heard.

He drew in a ragged breath and, letting his eyes move off to stare into the distance, he answered softly, "I love you, too Clara. But it's not enough, is it?"

She felt a sob building in her chest. Aware that her brother and Cynthia were watching them, and probably listening to all they could strain to hear, she spoke softly. "How..." A sob worked its way out and interrupted her. "How can you say that? I don't understand." He didn't answer right away. Still he looked away from her. He held his jaw tight, the muscles in his face taut with emotion.

Finally he spoke. "I do love you. I can't imagine that a man ever loved a woman more. But you ask too much. I can't stay here and watch you marry another man. I can't watch Nathanael be raised by someone else." He turned to her then, eyes filled with anguish. "I can't watch you give to another what I want for myself. I ... I just can't. Don't ask me to, Clara."

Clara fought to make her mind function, to comprehend. "Lonesome Wolf, I ... I don't understand. What other man? What do you mean marry –" Realization hit her. She fought to breathe. For a moment she feared she would suffocate before she could put her thoughts into words. She forced herself to take in breath, to let it out. What she had to say to her brother could wait until she'd set things right with Lonesome Wolf, so she made herself continue to speak but no longer worked to keep her volume down. She was so worked up that the words might not have all come out just right, but what she lacked in vocabulary she made up for in intensity. The words came out fast and they came out loud. "Just what do you think is going on here? Do you really think I would marry another man?" She smacked him in his chest. "You had to know I love you! You aren't blind! You know how I felt about marrying Robert. But I've changed. Things have changed. How can you think that I would love you and marry someone else? How could you love the person that would do that to you?" She was breathing hard and trying her best to stave off all emotion save determination to uncoil this twisted mess.

Lonesome Wolf's expression had gone from sorrow to relief to shock and confusion as he listened to her outburst. She might've found his reaction comical had she not been so furious with him. She knew she must look like her senses had fled.

She wasn't sure what she'd expected him to do, but she was stunned when his response met hers for fierceness and volume both. "What did you expect me to think? You've taken walks with him every evening lately. Time you used to spend with me, time you *promised* to spend with me, you spent with him. And, I told you I loved you, but you never said a word about it. All you could say was how great of friends we were. You kept saying it over and over until I wanted to scream. And I've seen the touches. His hand on your back, your hand on his arm. What did you expect me to think, Clara Jane?"

At this point John was right beside them, glowering. "You need to watch the way you talk to my sister."

Clara momentarily turned her ferocity on John. "Shut up, John! If you value any relationship you and I have left you will back away and not open your mouth until I ask you to speak!" Without waiting for a response, she turned back to Lonesome Wolf. "What exactly is it you're accusing me of?"

"I'm not accusing you of anything! I'm just trying to understand what's happened! I thought you … I thought maybe you … I thought you were beginning to feel something for me and then you turned all your attentions on *him*!" He gestured to the cabin where Reynolds had been reading but was now probably listening to them shout. "If you don't care for him, why didn't you tell me? You saw how hurt I was. You *knew*. Why wouldn't you tell me what was going on? Why didn't you ever say how you felt? I *told* you, days ago, and you haven't said a thing since."

"Why didn't *I* say something to *you*? Before this

past week, you'd pulled yourself away from me! You wouldn't even come in the house! If you hadn't turned your back on me when I needed you to lean on, then maybe you would've known what was happening!"

Lonesome Wolf opened his mouth, ready to shout, but stopped short. He saw the truth in her words. He knew her history with her brother, but he'd let his insecurity and jealousy keep him from being there for the woman he loved when she needed him. Abruptly, his other feelings fled and he was filled with remorse. And shame. His voice gentled and he let all the good feelings he had for her flow out of him through it. "You're right. I'm so sorry. Clara, forgive me." He took her hand and moved to pull her into his embrace.

"Keep your hands off her!" John reached out to yank Clara away, but when she turned on him with eyes of fury he let her go.

Through gritted teeth Clara addressed her brother. "I think it best you take your wife and go inside." He hesitated. "Now, John." Reluctantly he turned and stalked back toward the cabin, leading Cynthia in front of him. Clara waited until the couple was inside and the door slammed shut before she turned back to Lonesome Wolf.

He appraised her with a raised eyebrow. She shook her head. "We'll talk about that later. I believe you and I were in the middle of something."

He grinned. "Yes, we were." And he pulled her up against him. She put her arms around his waist and he laid his cheek against her head. They stood, enjoying the closeness of each other, until Lonesome Wolf *had* to speak. "I'm sorry. I know I don't have a good excuse, but you have to know that I'm sorry. At first, I thought I was doing what was best for you and your family by giving you the time you needed to heal things with John. And then I didn't know what to do when it looked like Reynolds was courting you. When I heard John say that you were going to marry Reynolds… well, that was more than I could stay here and watch."

He felt Clara stiffen in his arms. She leaned back and looked up at him through slitted eyes. "I almost forgot about that part."

He shook his head. "Clara, he's your brother."

She didn't reply. She whipped around and tromped off to the house. Lonesome Wolf trotted after her. He gently grabbed her arm and turned her to face him. "Clara, I'm not going to stop you from talking to John. In fact, I think you and your brother need to hash things out. I just want to ask you to do two things."

He waited for her nod before continuing, "I want you to wait for me to take Fella and let him loose in the corral, and I want you to take some deep breaths and pray before you go in there. Can you do those things for me?" Again she nodded, albeit more reluctantly this time. "Okay. Come with me and I'll walk back in there with you after we take care of Fella. I'll be right beside you. The time for hiding out in the barn has long since passed."

He took her hand in his and held her body close to him as they walked back to the horse. Clara leaned her head on his shoulder. He looked down at her and felt the rightness of her in his arms, felt his heart settle in his chest.

As they made their way to the barn, in a voice laden with betrayal and defeat, Clara spoke. "I just can't believe he did it again. How could he? He knows full well all that last time cost him, cost us, and now he goes and does the same thing. How could he?"

"Clara, honey, I think that's a good question to ask him. He has to have some reason. You might not like it, but you should hear it, at least."

"I know, I know. I will. I have no choice if we're ever going to make up." Reluctance was nearly a physical presence around her. "It's harder than it sounds, you know."

Lonesome Wolf chuckled at her, and Clara halfheartedly smiled back.

When they reached the paddock, Lonesome Wolf laid his belongings on the ground, took off the saddle, set it on the corral fence, and then opened the gate and led Fella inside. As he did so, he thanked God for stopping him from making the biggest mistake of his life.

The enormity of what he had almost done in a fit of temper and lack of faith suddenly hit him. He reached for Clara and wrapped her in his arms tightly. "I'm so sorry, Clara. I almost left. How could I have almost left you and Nathanael? What would've happened if you hadn't stopped me?"

He pulled back from her and, taking her face in his hands, looked into her eyes, seeing no condemnation, only love. He pulled her close again; the softness of Clara next to him was like a healing balm. She didn't speak, she just allowed him to hold her, to soak up her love, her forgiveness.

He held her for a long while until he could feel his heartbeat return to normal. Then, kissing her temple and releasing her, he smiled, truly smiled, for the first time in what seemed like a lifetime. "We need to work on communication."

Clara chuckled, then she giggled, then they were

LANNA WEBB

both outright laughing.
And it felt so good.

When his things were put away, he swiped a hand
through his hair and took a quick glance around the barn.
"This isn't at all how I would've chosen to do this, but I
reckon we should get something clear before we go inside."
He led Clara to a hay bale and sat beside her, taking
her hand and almost getting lost in the feel of it. He set her
hand back down and cleared his throat, and his mind.

"Clara, I love you. And I love Nathanael. Already,
y'all are my family." He could hear the steadiness slipping
away from his voice but didn't care. "I want to be here to
take care of you and love you both. I want to be a father to
Nathanael. I want to take care of you because I'm your
husband and it's my job. And," his voice softened but his
eyes darkened with the passion she had so missed seeing in
them, "I want to be with you as a husband is his wife,
Clara. Will you have me?"

Smiling at him in a way that told him she'd
momentarily forgotten the others were inside the cabin
waiting for them to come back, she leaned closer to him
and whispered, "I most certainly will have you… and
consider myself blessed."
He wanted badly to kiss her, but *he* did remember
what awaited them in the house and didn't want to rush or
be distracted through their first kiss. And he didn't want to
make things worse with her brother by not returning her
back inside before the man's slight patience wore
completely out. Besides, he could only imagine what John
would say if he came looking for them and found them

kissing. So, with great effort, he restrained himself and instead of giving her the kiss he so desperately longed for and was pretty sure she wanted too, he settled for taking her hand, entwining her fingers in his. "Let's go talk to that brother of yours."

Just as they were exiting through the barn doors, she stopped. He waited for her to work through whatever was tugging at her. Either she would push through it on her own or she, hopefully, would share it with him. This holding things inside wasn't working too well for them. If they were going to make it, they both had to learn to share their troubles.

Finally, she shook her head and grumbled, "I don't know if I'm more angry or hurt."

Lonesome Wolf moved his hand to her back and rubbed. Without warning, she dropped against him like a dead weight. He wrapped his arms around her and held her, wishing he could protect her from what was coming.

The barn cat rustled as it snuggled into a hay pile in the corner, and a horse whickered happily just outside the barn. The sounds felt like home, like peace. He whispered into her hair, "I know you're angry and I know you're hurt. And I hate that I haven't been here for you like I should've been to help you go through this. But I intend to make that up to you. I'm here now, and I promise I'm going nowhere." He squeezed her gently, kissed her head, and repeated, "I'm going nowhere."

Rubbing her back in slow circles, he waited for her tension to ease, if only a portion. "Let me pray with you before we go in there." He felt her nod against his chest. So he prayed. When he was done, he kissed the top of her head again and asked, "Ready?"

She closed her eyes and breathed deeply, then straightened. "I reckon I have to be."

They could hear the shouting before they made it even halfway to the cabin door.

Angry bursts were followed by short periods of silence they could only presume was Cynthia trying to quiet John. Lonesome Wolf shook his head. "I'd hoped he wouldn't still be hollering like that. Maybe you should get some of the things that'll make him angriest out of the way now. And then after he's gone through the shock of hearing that, maybe later tonight or tomorrow," he winked at her, "the two of you can speak peacefully," and opened the door.

At first, John didn't even hear them come in. The sound hadn't made it over his ranting. Lonesome Wolf couldn't catch everything he was saying, but he understood enough to know that John was livid with Clara. Well, that was fine. Or at least he thought it was fine until John turned half-crazed eyes on his sister and started yelling.

"Clara Jane, just where've you been? And how dare you send me inside like I'm a child for you to order around. Need I remind you, I am the elder sibling here? As so, I want some answers and I want them this instant!"

"*You* want some answers? *You* want some answers?" Clara cleared the space between them and stood just inside the living area facing off nose to nose with John. "I think that I'm the one who deserves some answers."

John's confusion momentarily brought down his volume. "What do *you* want answers about?"

"Did you tell Reynolds I would marry him?"

Reynolds's eyes went wide at the question. Lonesome Wolf saw the reaction and had to wonder what exactly was going on.

John stood up straight and stared right into Clara's eyes. "As a matter of fact, I did not."

Before Lonesome Wolf could say anything about what he had heard, Cynthia spoke up. "But, John, that's what you told me you intended."

"Shut up, Cynthia." John hadn't even turned to her as he spoke.

Reynolds stepped forward. "Now listen here, John. I don't care if she is your wife, you won't speak to her that way in my presence. Besides, I think you owe all of us an explanation. Why would you tell Cynthia that Clara and I were going to be married?"

"Well, you've practically been courting her," John threw back at him.

Lonesome Wolf felt like adding his "here, here," but thought he had best stay out of matters.

Reynolds looked at John as if he were daft. "I most certainly have not. I've been counseling her," and for added emphasis lest everyone had forgotten, "as a *pastor*."

"What?" This came from Cynthia, John, and Lonesome Wolf.

"Yes, John, you yourself told me that first night I took her walking that she needed to speak with me about something."

Clara turned to John. "You did what?"

At first John looked like he was going to go off on a screaming spree again, but finally he just sighed. "I was hoping you two would get along. I told him that you wanted to talk. I figured if we could stay here long enough then you'd at least like each other. And then I could... convince you that... the two of you... that at least enough... was *there* for the two of you to... get married."

Having at last gotten through the admission, his confidence returned. "Then you'd be taken care of, Clara, when Cynthia and I move out."

"John! You deceived a preacher!" His wife was obviously horrified.

Reynolds was, too. "I can't believe that you would try to manipulate two people's lives like that, John."

Clara wasn't at all surprised, "Why not? It wouldn't be the first time he arranged for his sister to marry a man she wasn't in love with." Realizing how her words might sound to Reynolds, and without changing her inflection or interrupting her stare at John, she added, "Sorry, Reynolds. I meant no offense."

Lonesome Wolf would have laughed at the ridiculousness of it all had it not been so infuriating.

"Oh, please!" John planted his hands on his hips. "I cannot believe that you're bringing this up again, Clara. It has been seven years."

"Yes, John, and it was five years of my life that you made into something I didn't want. And now, here you are, trying to do it again."

"You don't know how it is to feel so accountable for someone else's life all of a sudden and not know what to do!" He was shouting again, but the words themselves were the first sign of vulnerability he'd shown, and John heard it, too. Hands on hips, he stared at the empty fireplace. Just when those in the room thought he wasn't going to speak, he ran a hand over his face and sank into one of the chairs. "I just feel a great responsibility for you, Clara."

Clara pulled a chair up beside him and laid a hand on his arm. "I understand that, John. But to marry me off when you knew I didn't want it?"

"Clara, I almost went crazy with the weight of everything I was suddenly in charge of when our parents died. I know I was wrong. Believe me, when Cynthia found out what I had done, I almost lost her, too. And I did lose you."

Clara reached out and hugged her brother. Lonesome Wolf saw Cynthia wipe tears from her eyes. He was happy, too, to see the beginnings of reconciliation, but he knew that matters were far from settled. He stood back and waited for the next wave to hit. He didn't have to wait long.

Clara stood up as if suddenly remembering recent events, and firmly informed her brother, "I forgive you about what you did back then. It was as much my own fault for going through with it. But, what about this time?"

"I wasn't going to *make* you marry anybody, Clara." John was back up on his feet with defensiveness in his voice. "I just worry about you out here all alone, and I thought I could kind of help you two along."

"Well, I don't need your help. And I'm not out here all alone."

"Well, yeah, but I hardly think Nathanael is old enough to help out around the place."

At this point, Lonesome Wolf knew things were going to get sticky. He decided it would be best to simply say what needed saying, so he stepped forward and cleared his throat. "Excuse me." Everyone turned and looked at him. "What Clara means, John, is *I'll* be here to take care of Clara, as her husband." He reached and took her hand; then, looking at her only, he said, "We're getting married."

There was a moment suspended in time when no one spoke or moved.

Then John snorted. "Married?!" He laughed, but it came out sounding hate-filled. "Married! Oh, that is rich. And just what preacher in all the world would marry the two of you?"

Without hesitation, Reynolds stepped forward and calmly stated, "I will."

John looked at him, hard, but the preacher simply repeated, "I will. Clara and I ..." He hesitated and looked at Clara who nodded vigorously to him. "Clara and I have discussed this at length. I mean, really, John, haven't you seen the two of them together? At any rate, they're in love, and I find absolutely no reason," he looked pointedly at John and slid into his preacher tone, "biblical or any otherwise, that the two shouldn't be married." He quickly added, "And soon, because they can't go on living so close to each other any longer."

If Clara's face hadn't already been flushed with anger at John, it would've been so at the matter-of-fact way Reynolds spoke of her relationship with Lonesome Wolf. Lonesome Wolf, however, was grinning ... at Reynolds ... who was grinning back. Men! If she weren't sure she'd be eternally grateful to Reynolds for what he was doing, she might raise a reproving eyebrow to him. Hmmm. She decided to so anyway. He just grinned bigger. Pffft. Men.

She turned her attention to John to see his reaction to the preacher's news. He looked as if he would explode with fury. He pushed the newly betrothed couple aside, stomped out the door, and slammed it shut behind him.

When Cynthia made as if to get up and follow him, Reynolds put a gentle hand on her arm. "Let him be for now. He's going to have to cool down before he'll hear what anyone has to say, even you."

Cynthia nodded but stood. At a look from

Reynolds, she nodded again. "I know. I'm not going out there right now. But it's time to get lunch on, so I am going to the kitchen." She handed Nathanael off to Lonesome Wolf, and she and Clara began to fix lunch... not that anyone was hungry.

CHAPTER NINETEEN

It was decided that Clara and Lonesome Wolf would marry in a little over two weeks' time. It would be busy, with the rodeo coming up on the first Saturday, the church raising the next, and Clara's birthday in between. However, as Reynolds pointed out, sooner was better.

In the meantime, Clara was no longer spending her evenings after supper walking with Reynolds.

That first night, she showed up in the barn while Lonesome Wolf was finishing evening chores. As soon as the barn door closed, he looked at her and, for the first time, made no attempt to prevent his thoughts and emotions from showing through his eyes. He looked her over and then raised his brows and said, "I believe you told me something important earlier. I wish to hear it again. Privately."

"I see." Her smile was a wondrous thing. "Well, perhaps I'd like to hear it first."

Dropping all teasing from his voice, he looked intently into her eyes and told her, "I love you, Clara."

"And I love you, Lonesome Wolf." She took a step toward him. "Are you going to kiss me now?"

"Excuse me?" He was trying not to smile, but he was way too happy to conceal it very well.

"Are you going to kiss me? We're going to be married in a couple of weeks. You now have the right to kiss me."

"Clara!" He was giving his best effort to appear scandalized, though he knew he failed.

"What? Don't you want to?" She gave him a thoroughly coquettish look and took another step toward him.

He shook his head at her. "You know I do."

"And have you not desired to for a while now?" She stepped closer.

His voice dropped to a low timbre. "I have."

"As have I." Lonesome Wolf raised his eyebrows at this, but Clara just gave him an impish grin and took one more step, a step that put her directly in front of him, so close, in fact, that if he took a deep breath, they would be touching. "Well ... how long does a girl have to wait?"

"One chaste kiss?"

She nodded, her green eyes sparkling with delight and some other emotion he had best wait to identify until after the wedding. With a hand around her waist, he drew her more closely to himself then lifted his other hand and placed it on her neck, fingers engulfed in her thick auburn hair and thumb lightly stroking her cheek. Looking into her eyes, thankful that now, if she read everything within his soul and spirit, every thought he was at this moment thinking, it would be okay, he slowly moved his head toward her and gently placed his lips against hers. The simple, tender act seemed to open a floodgate of emotions in his mind and feelings inside him that he'd been unaware were hidden there. She parted her lips, and he pressed his against hers with a bit more passion, allowing himself to absorb the thoughts that washed over him and to enjoy them without guilt or dishonor or fear. Feeling her arms around his neck, he pulled her closer still, kissing her again, enjoying the feel of her lips touching his but knowing that he had to stop before they drowned together under the weight of these new desires. He pulled away slightly, resting his forehead against hers. His breathing finally settled down enough for him to speak. "I love you, Clara."

"I love you, Lonesome Wolf." Both her reply and the way it came out almost breathlessly sent a pleasant surge through him.

He placed a soft kiss on her forehead and then stepped back enough to put some space between them but not so much that he would have to forfeit his hold on her. A strand of hair had fallen across her face. He pushed it back then traced her jaw and lips with his finger. "I thank God that, even though He told me to stay and I rebelliously tried to leave, He sent you to stop me. I can't even think what my life would've been had God allowed me to leave and live with the consequences of my disobedience."

Clara's eyes misted over, but she did not reply.

Reluctantly, Lonesome Wolf let go of her. "You should probably go inside before your brother comes out here to get you."

She sighed and rolled her eyes. "My brother. Please pray for him … and for me. I want things to be right between us before he leaves. I'm ready, but he's not. I need wisdom for what to say or not say, what to do or not do." She blew a strand of hair out of her eyes. "Pray, please."

"I will. We will."

She nodded and turned to go. Lonesome Wolf reached out and grabbed her wrist. He pulled her close again and gave her a quick kiss. "Goodnight."

As she walked away, she smiled at him over her shoulder. "Until morning."

When she left the barn, Lonesome Wolf sighed and thought to himself that two weeks had never seemed so long a time before.

⌘

The following morning, Clara met Lonesome Wolf to watch the sunrise. She walked up to him, pleased with the smile on his face at seeing her, and gladly let him take her hand. She felt an overwhelming sense of gratitude at the simple freedom of being able to stand here with this man and hold his hand while they watched the sun break over the horizon. An awful lot of people compared the sun coming up with new beginnings. She'd heard people commenting on it in church services, read the metaphor in many books and poems. Well, it was no wonder so many authors used the notion. It was true. She felt as if she were standing on the threshold of a new horizon, a new life with Lonesome Wolf.

Once the sun had risen, he smiled down at her, and she looked at him as if deciding whether or not to share something. He could tell by the spark in her eye that she would tell it or burst trying. He pretended not to notice. "Well, I have a lot to do today, so I had best…"

"Wait. Not so fast, mister. You've been lean on words with me lately and you're about to start making it up to me."

He could no longer pretend indifference. He laughed. It felt so good to laugh with Clara again. For a time yesterday he felt his world would no longer contain laughter, and here he was, watching the sunrise with the woman who would soon be his bride. "And what, my dear, would you like to talk about?"

"Last night."

He laughed again. "And why am I not surprised by that?"

"Probably because you know me so well." She smiled her breath-taking smile.

"And what is it that you wish to say?"

"I wish to say," she dropped her voice a little and let her eyes dance as if she knew how to set them in motion and what it did to Lonesome Wolf's heart, "that was the most amazing kiss I've ever had."

"I should apologize for that." She gave him a confused look and he grinned, "I promised to give you one chaste kiss, and I'm afraid I failed on both counts."

To her credit she did now have the grace to blush, which only made her more attractive. "I would say you did."

"Which is why it isn't going to happen again until after we're married."

She looked like he had refused to marry her. Her hands were planted on a hip apiece. "I'm sorry, what? What did you say?"

He simply shrugged.

"For the next two weeks you won't kiss me?" She stared him down and looked so cute doing it that, if he hadn't known for certain it was the smart thing to do, she could've changed his mind.

But it was, the smart thing to do, so he replied, "Not like that."

She studied him closely to see if he was kidding. He didn't seem to be. Well, she could wait. For that, she could wait. It wouldn't be easy, but it would be worth it. And she wasn't about to let him forget just how worth it. She slipped her hand back in his, and as they walked toward the cabin, she decreed, "I forgive you. But only if you'll have breakfast with us." For good measure, she added, "inside, at the table."

Lonesome Wolf pulled her to a stop and looked down at her with more than a touch of concern in his eyes. "Clara, do you think that's a good idea? I don't think your brother will take kindly to it."

"Maybe not. But, we've let his anger rule us for far too long. No one else here agrees with your eating in the barn like part of the livestock. John can just get over it." Lonesome Wolf shot her a disapproving look, but she forged on. "I also think he needs to be around you more, to get to know you. Besides, he and Cynthia were up half the night talking and again early this morning. I can only imagine that they were talking about you. I have an idea that Cynthia will be able to make him behave at least for a while."

"I see. And after we get married will you be in charge of my behavior?"

Clara grinned. "Most certainly."

Squinting his eyes playfully at her, he asked, "And who, pray tell, will be in charge of yours?"

"Why, I will!" At the look on his face, Clara amended her statement. "Unless I need help, and then you will. We'll help each other, you see?"

Lonesome Wolf chuckled. "Yes, I think I do see. That's what has me worried."

Just outside the door to the kitchen, Lonesome Wolf touched Clara on the arm, stopping her before she went inside. He looked carefully at her, wanting to see it in her eyes if she had any misgivings. "Are you sure I should do this?"

"I am sure. Please, come in."

The tension in the room could be felt as soon as he set foot in it. The only good news was that John didn't jump to his feet and demand Lonesome Wolf out of the house. Clara offered a cup of coffee while breakfast was being made and pointed to a chair across the table from John. Lonesome Wolf sat down, thankful that Reynolds was also at the table. The whole time the women fixed breakfast, John sat without speaking. Reynolds conversed pleasantly with Lonesome Wolf, who had a growing respect for the preacher. Soon, the food was on the table and breakfast was under way.

They made it through the meal without an incident.

They made it through lunch, as well.

They did not make it through supper.

Cynthia made the mistake of asking Lonesome Wolf how long he'd known Clara. Lonesome Wolf made the mistake of telling her that he'd ridden in almost four months ago and had stayed because God told him to do so. Clara then made the mistake of saying that God had told *her* to *ask* Lonesome Wolf to stay. Reynolds, bless his preacher heart, made the mistake of commenting on the wonder of how God does marvelous works.

John begged to differ. "How can you all sit around here and act like God had anything to do with putting these two together? I don't for one second think that God has anything to do with my sister thinking she's in love with an Indian!"

Lonesome Wolf pushed his chair back to leave, but Clara reached out and clasped his hand with such a fierceness that he remained where he was. Instead, she turned to John and in a clear, firm voice said, "Leave."

John just looked at her, scoffed, and continued eating. Clara slammed her fist down on the table so hard that the dishes jumped and clattered. She said again, more loudly this time, "Leave!"

John looked at her incredulously. "What do you mean *leave*? Where do want me to go?"

"I don't care. Get your things and go sleep outside or leave and go to town, but you will get out of my house. In fact, you should know this. As far as I am concerned this is just as much Lonesome Wolf's house as it is mine. And I won't allow you to continue to insult him in his own home, in *our* home. So get out. When you've come to your senses and decide you can treat us like you were raised to treat people, then maybe you'll be welcome to be a guest in our home again."

John stared at her with anger and hate tinting his eyes. He slowly rose from the table and turned to Cynthia. "Get your things together. We are no longer welcome here."

Cynthia remained seated. She calmly met John's rabid eyes. "John, I believe you have misunderstood your sister. *You* are currently not welcome here. *I* am still welcome as a guest in their home. And I don't intend to sleep out under the stars when I have a perfectly good feather bed to use here." Then she picked up her fork and continued eating.

John grabbed his water glass and threw it hard against the far kitchen wall. Glass and water exploded into a thousand pieces. No one moved. Cynthia took a slow, deep breath and faced her husband. Lonesome Wolf marveled at her self-control. She spoke evenly, as if he were a wayward child who needed to be guided gently back to obedience. "John, listen to me carefully and hear what I say. I will not leave this place until you have asked God's mercy on you, reconciled with Clara, and begged Lonesome Wolf's forgiveness. If you leave now, in this way, you will leave without me." Lonesome Wolf watched as the words flowed out before she could reach them and pull them back. Seconds later, what Cynthia had said hit her. But it had already been said. Maybe it needed to be said. For pity's sake, something needed to be done. They all watched John carefully. Lonesome Wolf could see in his eyes that he was wavering. Chances were he already knew he was wrong and was too stubborn to admit it.

Finally, he yielded to his wife's threat. "Fine. Have it your way. We'll stay. I'll sleep outside. But we might grow old here before I approve of this mess." And with that, he stomped out the door.

As soon as he left, everyone in the room let out a sigh as if they'd been holding a collective breath. Cynthia tried to apologize for John's behavior. Nobody held her responsible. Reynolds tried to apologize for setting John off on his tear. No one felt he was to blame. Clara tried to apologize for getting others involved in her family troubles. Not one person felt it was her fault. Lonesome Wolf looked around finally and said, "Well, I guess I could apologize for being an Indian." Everyone laughed – that hearty, nervous laughter that is infectious and uncontrollable and often at nothing at all, that almost hysterical laughter that one falls into in order to keep from crying.

As the laughter settled down, they set about the tasks at hand. Lonesome Wolf took Nathanael to his crib while Clara cleaned up the broken water glass. Cynthia's laughing fit had brought on a coughing fit, but she acted as if she hardly noticed. Instead, she went and gathered some of John's things and placed them neatly in a stack on the side porch. When she finished, she put away the leftovers while Reynolds cleared the table and Lonesome Wolf and Clara washed the supper dishes.

CHAPTER TWENTY

It was on a beautiful morning mid-October when the entire group made their way to the Kearneys' to help Jim and Lydia get ready for the rodeo. Clara, Cynthia, and Nathanael rode in in the covered wagon John drove, while Lonesome Wolf and Reynolds rode their mounts alongside. Now that he knew Reynolds had never had his sights set on Clara, it was a lot easier for Lonesome Wolf to admit he liked the young preacher. Of course, even if he hadn't liked him, it would've been preferable to ride on the trip to the Kearney Ranch on the other side of town with him than in the wagon with John.

They passed the trip amiably and were almost to the ranch when a rider came out to greet them. It was an older man, much older, and he was moving slow in the saddle. "How do?" the man said.

Lonesome Wolf leaned over to shake his hand. "Lonesome Wolf. I do great, and you?"

"Oh, I do right nicely, right nicely." The fellow moved his hat back to scratch his head, and Lonesome Wolf saw skin wrinkled from the sun and hair worn grey with age. "And what's your name, there, young man?" he asked, eyeing Reynolds. Or maybe he was eyeing the gun slung low on Reynolds's hip. Lonesome Wolf wore a gun, too, but not quite the way Reynolds wore his. It made the preacher look more like a gunslinger.

"I'm Reynolds. I'm the new preacher in Klein Creek."

"Preacher?" The old man acted like it was the most surprising thing he'd heard in all his life. His face turned thoughtful. "Well, I guess we need one about as bad as anyone else. Welcome to town."

Lonesome Wolf found himself liking this old man. There was something about him that just made a body feel good, at ease, even happy. Or maybe he was just happy because in a couple weeks he was going to marry Clara.

"...your name?" He heard Reynolds asking the old man.

"Oh, most folks just call me Cletus."

Cletus! This was Cletus?! Lonesome Wolf stared for one long moment and then burst out laughing. *This* was Cletus, the same Cletus who Lonesome Wolf had been jealous of when Clara spoke of him with such warmth. The realization that Cletus wasn't young and good-looking made Lonesome Wolf even more ridiculously happy than he already was.

Clara was so glad they had come over to help the day before and spent the night. The morning of the rodeo had dawned bright and beautiful... and there was no long ride ahead of them before the fun could begin.

She helped Lydia prepare breakfast for their combined families, thankful that the Kearneys had a cook for the boys in the bunkhouse because she'd seen them eat the night before and they could sure put away food. Making enough for seven adults and four kids was enough of a chore for her.

She set up a washtub so that they could do up the dishes as they dirtied them. No sense in having all of them to wash and dry at once.

"So, Clara Jane," Lydia started none-too-subtly, "you sure have a fine-looking gentleman with you this trip."

Clara smiled her happiest smile. "He is awfully handsome, isn't he?"

Lydia responded with a hearty, "Yes, he is. And a preacher, to boot."

Clara dropped a stack of tin cups. They clanged on the hardwood floor as they bounced up and down. She was thankful it had been tin cups and not one of Lydia's pretty china teacups. She knelt to pick up her mess, and when she stood again, she was looking straight into Lydia's shocked eyes.

"I was talking about Reynolds," Lydia said needlessly.

Clara tried to laugh. "Well, he *is* the preacher, Lydia. That does tell me who you meant."

Lydia's eyebrows rose higher. "*After*. You knew who I meant *after* I said preacher. Before that you thought I was talking about Lonesome Wolf! Oh, Clara!"

"Don't 'Oh, Clara,' me. He *is* awfully handsome and you're a liar if you don't admit it." Clara teased. She was too happy for Lydia's scandalized reaction to ruin her mood.

Lydia blinked big owl eyes. "Clara, honey..." She sat hard in a chair. More like fell into it, if Clara were being honest. "It won't be easy on you," she breathed out.

"How did Robert make life easy on me?" Clara clapped her hand over her mouth. She couldn't believe those words had come out. She had loved her husband in her own way. She had loved him. But being in love was a totally different emotion. One that made you do and say crazy things, apparently.

She looked at Lydia, trying to gauge what her friend was thinking. "I shouldn't have said that, Lydia. Robert was never unkind to me. But there is loving someone because he's a nice man and there is being in love with someone who adores you and would, in a quite literal sense, take on the world for you."

"Don't you mean that *you* would take on the world for *him*?" Lydia's question was as soft as the first rays of sun dancing in the dust of the room.

Clara sobered. "I mean that, too, Lydia. I do. I would. I *will* if necessary. And if I have to start with family and friends, if that is the way it has to be, then that is the way it'll be. But I am not going to throw the wonderful gift God has given me back in His face because people have small minds or even because people love me too much to ever want to see me struggle." Clara sat beside Lydia and gently laid her hand on her arm. "Sweetie, you know what I've gone through, you more than anyone know what it was like for me. Don't you want me to be happy? And don't you think that I'm strong enough to make that happiness happen? Don't you?"

"I do, Clara. I do." She patted Clara's hand where it still rested on her arm. "I just wish it weren't the way of things."

"It's always the way of things, Lydia."

⌘

Everyone else arrived after breakfast for the rodeo. People were milling around in the Kearneys' barnyard waiting for the troops to gather and unloading goods for lunch. Lonesome Wolf was glad to see John doting on

Cynthia, not letting her do anything but sit in a wagon. Cynthia might have sent him to sleep outside, but while she wasn't sleeping out there with him, she was taking her meals and spending good chunks of the day with him. And even though John hadn't apologized to Lonesome Wolf, he hadn't made any new remarks either.

Looking around, Lonesome Wolf saw that it was just about time to move out. The first events of the day were shooting competitions, a rifle contest and a pistol shot, and everyone was going to ride in wagons out to the shooting site, far enough away that the horses for the rodeo weren't all half-spooked after lunch when the riding began.

Once out where the shooting would commence, everyone gathered his or her gear from the wagons. There were two contests – distance shooting and a trick shot. First up was the distance shooting. Mason jars were set way off in the distance. Each man, or woman, got one shot. Those who made it, got a second shot at a target farther away, and so on until only one person made his shot. This event had the most people, several of whom were women. The last ones left were Cletus, Lonesome Wolf, Red Eagle, and Clara. Several of the men were not happy to have been beaten by an Indian. Or a woman – but with her Spencer rifle and her experience borne of desperation in the months since Robert died, Clara was sighting in and making every shot she took.

Cletus missed his next shot. "Eyes aren't what they used to be," he grumbled as he joined the others who had shot and missed.

Red Eagle missed his shot, too, claiming the same affliction and getting a chuckle out of the crowd.

That left Lonesome Wolf and Clara pitted against each other. The sun winked off the jars, almost obscuring the targets. Clara made her shot. If Lonesome Wolf made his, they'd have to shoot yet again. If not, then Clara would win the prize money.

She turned to him with a hard glint in her eye. "Don't you *dare* let me win, or I'll put salt in your coffee for three weeks running."

He laughed and put his arm around her neck, pulling her close to him for just a moment. "I'd never let you win, Clara Jane. And especially not if you're gonna mess with my coffee."

When their laughter died down, they noticed that the group had gone awfully quiet. Clara turned to them, looking from one person to another with confusion. Finally, she asked, "What? What happened?"

Lydia stepped forward. "Clara, honey, uhmm… well, everyone here hasn't heard your good news, and Lonesome Wolf was, well… touching you?"

"Are you telling me or asking me?" Clara laughed. Then she turned to the guests, her rifle resting over her shoulder, right hand on the stock and left on the barrel. "Lonesome Wolf and I are getting married. If any of you take offense to that notion, then you can deal with me right now."

Lonesome Wolf sputtered behind her.

It was Reynolds who saved the day. "Man, are you going to have your hands full with that one. You'd better win this contest because you'll never win another one the rest of your lives."

The laughter started slowly and then built through most of the crowd until the discomfort had passed. There were surely some there who disapproved, Clara's brother being chief among them, but with the preacher publicly giving his blessing, there wasn't much anyone wanted to say about it at the time.

Lonesome Wolf did not let Clara win.

But she did anyway.

Last up for the shooting games was the trick shot. This year's challenge was a chicken suspended from a tree branch about forty yards away. With the weapon of his choice, each participant had one shot. The person to sever the rope holding up the chicken got to take it home.

Men pulled out their rifles and took their shots. And missed. When it was Lonesome Wolf's turn, he pulled out the Apache bow and arrow. The dark-haired cowboy, the one who had visited Clara's for a short time the day Lonesome Wolf met the Kearneys, the one who had gotten sent home by Jim for being unsociable, *that* cowboy, loudly complained, "Now, this is a sorry state. These here ain't Indian games." One of the others hushed him saying, "Won't make no nevermind, Lowell. He ain't gonna make it. If'n he's fool enough to try to shoot a rope in half at 50 paces with a bow and arrow, then let him try it."

Lonesome Wolf ignored them, staring hard at the rope which was swaying slightly with the light breeze. Finally, he drew, raised, and shot in one motion. The chicken spun around as the arrow nicked the rope. The cowboys who had spoken up before were very quiet, and the dark-headed one named Lowell had something akin to dark and mean in his eyes. And he was watching Lonesome Wolf closely, looking away only to spit. Lonesome Wolf met his gaze boldness for boldness, then purposely turned his back on him to watch the rest of the competition.

Last up was Reynolds. When he toed the line without his rifle, Jim said, "I think you forgot your gun, there."

Light laughter skittered around the group, but it died when Reynolds dropped his hand down by his Peacemaker.

The two fellows who mocked Lonesome Wolf looked like they had a powerful urge to say something again, but they refrained. It was a good thing for them, too, because before anyone was even ready for the shot, Reynolds's hands flew. His left hand slapped the hammer at practically the same time his right one pulled the trigger, and the chicken dropped the few inches to the ground.

One shot straight through the knot.

At first, no one said a word. Then the place erupted. Lonesome Wolf slapped Reynolds on the back and raised his brows but didn't comment. There were plenty of others who weren't so smart.

Reynolds ignored them all.

On the way back to the house for lunch, all Reynolds said was, "I'm not wanted, if that's what you're wondering."

Lonesome Wolf responded with the truth. "I wasn't."

⌘

The afternoon rodeo was moving along smoothly with a short race around some obstacles, a long race around a part of the pasture, and roping and such. Cletus and his cow pony won the cutting contest, but it was a close win, with the dark-haired Lowell coming in a near second. Lonesome Wolf enjoyed seeing all the horses perform what it didn't seem a man and horse should be able to accomplish, especially since the horse did most of the work. Or maybe that's why it worked as well as it did.

At any rate, the bronc riding was up next and in the corral was one of the orneriest horses Lonesome Wolf had ever seen. If this had been a betting party, and if he'd been a betting man, he would've bet all the money he had on him that not one of the ranchers or the hands was going to ride that horse.

He let the other men go ahead of him. The ones talking the biggest always went first. So, he let them talk and he let them go. And he watched them fall. Some of them fell before they even had both hands on the horse.

When it had been well established that the stallion would not be easily ridden, Lonesome Wolf stepped forward. "Men. I have figured out the problem with this here horse."

A chorus of "Oh, really?" and "Is that so?" went up around the corral.

Lonesome Wolf nodded sagely.

It was Cletus that asked what they all wanted to know. "Well, what is it? If'n you know, then tell us."

"That horse right there ain't no white man's horse." He looked over and caught Red Eagle's eye and gave him a small wink. "That right there, gentlemen, is a bonafide Indian pony."

This time the chorus was made up of "aw" and "oh, shoo."

"I thought you was gonna tell us something for real," Cletus accused as he waved him off with his hand.

"I *am* telling you something real. That right there is an Indian horse. And he ain't gonna let nobody ride him but an Indian." He looked over at Red Eagle again and raised his right eyebrow. Red Eagle took the cue.

"Alright, then. If he's an Indian horse, I'll ride him," and he made like he was going into the corral.

Lonesome Wolf stopped him with a, "Now, now, *Tremont*, that ain't no half-breed's horse." The men around roared with laughter. "I said that was an *Indian's* horse, and it's gonna take a full-blooded Indian to ride him."

Laughing, Red Eagle bowed with an arm out for Lonesome Wolf to take his try. And he did. He made a big show about walking in a huge circle around the edges of the corral and then slightly smaller circles closing in on the stallion. "You've got to approach this horse like an Indian if you want to ride him," he explained. By now, everyone on the ranch was paying attention. He saw the laughter in Clara's eyes, but quickly looked away before he joined her. Everyone was watching him. No one was talking. The shuffle of a boot here and there was the only sound. As he closed in on the horse, he spoke in a loud whisper into the quiet, "And you've got to talk to him like an Indian, too, if you want to ride him." And with that pronouncement, he began to chant low, nonsensical words at the horse. Then he walked right up to him and started whispering in his ear. The horse just stood there and let him. The men stood around in jaw-slackened amazement. Lonesome Wolf finally put his hand around, grabbed a handful of hair, and vaulted onto the horse's back. The horse just stood there, stock-still.

A murmuring started in the crowd. It grew louder when Lonesome Wolf clicked his tongue and the horse calmly sauntered over to the fence, stretched its neck out, and nuzzled Clara as if she were an old friend.

"Well, I'll be."

"I ain't never seen nothing like that in my life!"

"Did you see that, Cletus?"

"Don't that beat all."

"How did he *know* it was an Indian's horse?"

Clara tried to hide her grin by leaning in to rub the horse's nose. Without looking at Lonesome Wolf, she murmured, "You gonna tell them?"

He didn't even try to hide his own smile. "I already told them. This *is* an Indian's horse."

Clara started giggling and before long the sound rose above the astonished voices around them. Several men turned their heads to watch her – her laughter was just like that – it made an already beautiful woman stunning. "I'll tell Jim later on," he said. "Let them wonder for a bit first. It'll make for a good story."

Lonesome Wolf winked at Clara then set off for the barn seated calmly on Marvin, the beautiful bay stallion who had escaped his corral several weeks earlier.

CHAPTER TWENTY-ONE

Lonesome Wolf sat upright on his cot in the bunkroom so fast his head swam. His heart was racing and he was trying to determine what had woken him so suddenly. A loud crack of thunder cut through the fog of leftover sleep, and he realized that it was only a storm that had roused him from his sleep.

Just as he was settling back in for the remainder of the night, he heard a crash from beside the barn, from the same place where John was sleeping in his wagon. Lonesome Wolf hurried into his boots and creaked open the barn door. Just as he was about to dash out and check on John, John came running into his room carrying a crate from the wagon.

"The wind knocked down a huge limb. Missed me by about a foot but got my wagon good. Brought down the cover right off it," John huffed out as he set the crate down in a corner of the room. "Everything inside, including me, was getting drenched. There are a couple more crates I'd really like to save if I can get to them." He shot Lonesome Wolf a look that imparted just how important the contents of those crates were and then ran back outside.

Lonesome Wolf answered John's unspoken request for help and followed him into the blowing wind and rain.

Together they brought John and Cynthia's belongings into the bunkroom. When they were finished, both men were soaked through. Lonesome Wolf offered John a towel and a fresh set of clothes, which left him with only his buckskins to wear. If John were offended before when Lonesome Wolf made sure to dress like a white man, this decidedly Indian look ought to go over right well.

He could feel John's eyes on him, but when the other man spoke, it wasn't what Lonesome Wolf was expecting to hear. "I look like a kid playing dress up in his daddy's clothes."

Lonesome Wolf looked to see what John meant and tried without success to hold back a bark of laughter. Luckily, John could see the humor in the situation, too, and smiled and shook his head. There he stood in a shirt with sleeves that hung down over his hands and pants that, while they were a good length, were so big around the waist he had to hold them up. "I never realized how big you are. Guess I should be a little nicer to you, or I might find myself in a heap of hurt."

Lonesome Wolf laughed again. "I wouldn't fight you, John. If I did, Clara would hurt me more than I could ever think about hurting you."

The two men shared a grin and Lonesome Wolf felt hope for the situation for the first time since John's arrival.

⌘

After spending the remainder of the night in the bunkroom with Lonesome Wolf, John was let back into the house with his promise to "try and behave" himself.

⌘

As they were having breakfast the next morning, Cynthia suggested that the men all go to town together to get supplies to fix the wagon. For some reason that quiet, frail woman with her soft voice and firm eyes was the hardest person to say no to. So, Lonesome Wolf, Reynolds, and John all mounted up and headed into town in the mud.

It was a far less uncomfortable trip to town than the last one Lonesome Wolf had taken with John. It wasn't exactly warm and friendly, but John did at least ride beside him this time. They even talked a bit.

And it was John that started the conversation. "Two of those big heavy crates you helped me with last night? They're for Clara." He shook his head. "Her birthday present made it all the way through our trip then almost got ruined right before her birthday."

"What is it? Whatever it is, it was sure heavy." There. They were having an actual conversation.

John looked around at the hills and said, "Books."

"You brought Clara's books?" He couldn't keep the shock from his voice.

John looked sheepish. "I know it's kind of silly giving somebody their own stuff for their birthday. But..." He shrugged like he didn't really have an excuse for his choice.

Lonesome Wolf knew he wouldn't need one. "John, there isn't a present you could've made or bought that would be worth more or mean more to Clara than those books."

John shrugged again. "I should have let her take them when she left. Robert didn't want them weighing down the wagon or taking up the room, so I told her she could only take a few." He shook his head. "I should've let her take as many as she could pack."

"She said your library was one of her favorite places."

"It was." John actually grinned at Lonesome Wolf.

"If she wasn't off getting into trouble, then she was in there reading, pretending she was getting into trouble." "I wish I could've brought them all, but I packed as many as we could carry. I remembered some of her favorites, and Cynthia helped me choose the others. I hope she likes the surprise."

"She will. She will *love* the surprise, John, no doubt about it. Makes my present kind of small in comparison."

Reynolds weighed in on that comment. "Better than what I got her, which is nothing." He was thoughtful for a brief moment then told them, "Remind me to pick something up when we get to town; I can't be the only one without a present. Y'all'll have to help me come up with what, though."

Lonesome Wolf had an idea already because he would've gotten them if he hadn't already had a present. "How about some hair combs? She can use them to hold her hair back out of the way but keep it down like she likes."

"Like you like, you mean," Reynolds teased.

Lonesome Wolf laughed. John scowled.

Whatever headway they'd made, and they certainly had made some, it wasn't a total victory yet.

They stopped by Keller's General Store first, to see about the combs for Clara but also to get out of the streets. As soon as they rode in, everything got quiet. Apparently news of the upcoming wedding had made it to town. Lonesome Wolf reached down slowly and slipped the thong off his gun. He saw Reynolds do the same. Not John. John seemed clueless as to just how badly this could go. And Lonesome Wolf didn't know enough people in town yet to know who might cause big trouble.

Other than Carl.

And they needed to get nails for the wagon, which meant a trip to the blacksmith. After they got Clara's gift at the General Store.

So, there they were. Reynolds kept one eye on the door and the street outside, and one looking at the women's pretties, discussing which comb set was the best for Clara.

Lonesome Wolf groaned to himself when he saw the new clerk was working and Mrs. Keller was nowhere to be found. Not only was the man rude, but he wouldn't be any help at all in picking out women's combs.

They were looking a good long while, until Lonesome Wolf saw the set that had to be Clara's. They were a bright silver that would shine in her hair and had some green stone that winked in the sunlight coming in through the window. The green would match her eyes. He didn't know how much they cost, but he knew that if Reynolds didn't buy them, he would. He could always give them to her as a wedding present.

That's when he remembered he needed to get Clara a wedding ring. He glanced over at John, who looked like the only reason he was there was because his wife made him come – which she had, of course. He certainly hadn't come to help Lonesome Wolf pick out a ring for Clara.

This trip to town took on a whole new kind of stress. Staying out of trouble with Carl. Getting just the right gift for Clara. Staying out of trouble with John. Not causing a ruckus because of Carl. Staying out of trouble with John. Getting just the right wedding ring for Clara. Practically shouting a reminder to the whole town that he was marrying Clara. Dealing with John. Dealing with Carl. John Carl. Carl. Clara. John.

"I see you eyeing them combs." Reynolds's

observation stopped Lonesome Wolf just short of a tailspin. Taking in a deep relaxing breath, he turned to Reynolds then realized the relaxation hadn't hit his eyes yet. Reynolds raised his eyebrows with a mixture of concern and not-well-hidden amusement, but he didn't say a word about Lonesome Wolf's wild eyes. He just went on talking about the combs. "I think *you* ought to get them for her. I'll get her some fancy hand cream or something. I think it best if you give such a personal item to her – especially since you have a look in your eye like you're seeing her hair and not what's in that case."

Lonesome Wolf grinned, knowing he looked silly in love and not caring. "They sure will look good in that pretty hair. Don't you think?"

John groaned and rolled his eyes, and Reynolds laughingly said, "I don't think anything about that hair. But I do see a ring that matches." He pointed it out, and it was sold whether the missing clerk knew it or not, if he returned that was.

John must've had a similar thought because he asked where the clerk had gone to. No sooner was the question out when the raised voices started from the back room.

"I didn't hire you to judge who needs what, Mr. Sykes. I hired you to sell my wares."

"Well, I ain't selling a wedding ring so's a white woman can marry no Indian," came the overly loud response.

"You are speaking about my friends, Mr. Sykes." Mrs. Keller's voice was stern and hard.

Mr. Sykes's terse reply of, "I don't care," was not well received.

The men out front could barely hear Mrs. Keller

when she bit out, "Then I'm afraid you have found yourself out of a job."

Lonesome Wolf walked to the back of the store and stepped in. "Mrs. Keller, I don't want to cost a man his job." He glanced at the man whose job he was trying to save. "If you don't mind me offering a solution, ma'am," he paused until she nodded, "*You* sell me the ring, Mrs. Keller, and he can stand by his…" – *ignorant, prejudice* – "beliefs and keep his job at the same time." He got what he was fairly certain was the same kind of look this Mr. Sykes fellow was getting. She took so long to speak that Lonesome Wolf began to wonder just what it was Mrs. Keller was thinking and not saying. Her silence was making him a little nervous, so he added, "And, Mrs. Keller, this man," he looked expectantly at the man, who provided his name – *Sykes-* in a shaky voice and then continued his sentence, "Mr. Sykes here, has always given me service before today." He didn't say how good of service, thought it might not help current matters. "And besides, Mrs. Keller, if folks around here found out I cost a white man his job – and you know they'll find out, and fast – well, it sure wouldn't do anything to help my welcome to town." Mrs. Keller pursed her lips and stared hard back and forth between the two men. Lonesome Wolf couldn't help but add, "I respectfully ask if you take that into consideration, ma-am," then wondered if he had tipped the barrel just a little too much.

Mrs. Keller folded her hands together primly, raised her right eyebrow at Lonesome Wolf in a challenge-me-if-you-want-to way, and without a look towards the clerk, stated, "I'm not so sure I want someone with his *beliefs* running my shop, especially when I'm not here."

The backroom of the store was taut with silence.

Lonesome Wolf decided he had talked enough, at the very least. He was so busy watching Mrs. Keller, waiting for her answer, that he jumped a little when the tension in the air was suddenly burst by Mr. Sykes, the clerk, shouting, "Fine, I'll sell him the stupid ring!"

The words were rude, but there was a glimmer of respect for Lonesome Wolf in the man's eyes – and more than a glimmer of triumph in Mrs. Keller's.

As Lonesome turned to head back to the counter, he noticed Reynolds was staring hard out the shop window. Lonesome Wolf followed his gaze to a small group of men gathered on the barbershop steps. They hadn't been there earlier. He tensed, relaxed, and shifted his right hand so that it was down by his side. While he paid and thanked the clerk – because it was the right thing to do and not because the particularly wanted to – Lonesome Wolf glanced back to check the window so many times the clerk stretched his neck to see what was so interesting. His eyes widened a bit, he shot a look at Lonesome Wolf, hurriedly wrapped the jewelry, put it in a bag, handed it over, and then turned swiftly to go. Lonesome Wolf Had to call him back and remind him to take the money.

Their purchases made, the trio readied to leave the store when Reynolds put his hand out to stop them. "The blacksmith is making his way over here."

Lonesome Wolf forced himself to relax, and they all stepped out into the street in time to meet Carl out front of the General Store.

He had a few friends with him. Lonesome Wolf recognized a couple of them from the café the day Carl had walked out without paying. The cowpuncher from Jim

Kearney's rodeo – Lowell, if Lonesome Wolf remembered the name correctly – was also a part of this group. Good. They could all hash this out at once. And Lowell the Cowpuncher knew not to mess with Reynolds's gun.

Instead of the snide remarks he expected from Carl, Lonesome Wolf had to listen to an accusation he didn't want to think too deeply about. The blacksmith, legs apart, hands on hips, and blame in his voice, asked Lonesome Wolf the one question that had haunted him... well, apparently both of them, for months: "How could you do this to Clara? Do you know what this is going to mean for her? Do you care only about yourself? Did you even think..."

Lonesome Wolf heard his tirade continue, but he was more concerned with what he saw playing out behind Carl and his small pack. A rider was coming into town, horse kicking up a dust storm, hooves drumming a fast beat when they hit the packed dirt of the road. The rider was not checking where he was heading and he wasn't slowing down. And Carl's youngest son was running across the street toward his dad.

Lonesome Wolf took off, almost knocking into Carl in an all out run. He scooped up the kid just as horse and rider would have barreled into him.

The rider pulled to a hard stop, almost hitting the hitching post, in front of the saloon, not sparing even a glance in their direction. Lonesome Wolf handed off the small boy to a white-faced Carl and went after the rider. Reynolds, usually the voice of reason, stepped back to let him pass. Long strides and hot determination carried Lonesome Wolf across town to where the rider was tying off his slathered horse. The man had one hand on the swinging doors, making to enter the saloon. Lonesome

Wolf didn't hesitate a second as he intercepted the man, pulled him back by the shirt collar, and punched him right in the jaw, dropping him to the boardwalk. Then he turned without another look at the rider and walked calmly back to where a silent group of men stood.

Lonesome Wolf got his nails at no charge.

On the ride home, when John lagged a short distance behind, Reynolds pulled in close to Lonesome Wolf. "That man, the dark-haired one who was with Carl?"

Lonesome Wolf nodded. "Lowell. He's one of Jim Kearney's hands. Cletus had a few words to say about him." He adjusted in the saddle and looked at Reynolds. "No love lost between those two."

"I can imagine. Cletus seemed like a decent fella." Reynolds was quiet for a while then he shook his head. "You might have made a friend in Carl, but you haven't heard the last from this Lowell." He cut his eyes to Lonesome Wolf. "I'm figuring you already knew that, though."

"I have met my share of men like him. Well, somewhat like him. Most folks I've had trouble with just don't want me around or they like to start trouble. That one there, though…"

"Yeah," Reynolds turned in the saddle to check on John's progress, "he's got something else in his eyes, and I don't like it one bit."

"You and me, both, my friend. You and me, both."

⌘

At supper that night, the harrowing rescue was all anyone would talk about, asking questions and making exclamations. Finally, Lonesome Wolf had had enough.

He pointed at Reynolds and practically accused,

"You would have done the same thing. Tell me you wouldn't have."

Reynolds nodded. "Yep, I would've. If I'd seen it. I was too busy watching that cowpoke's hand, making sure he wasn't gonna go for his gun."

Lonesome Wolf turned on John with pointed finger. "What about you? You'd have done it, too."

"Yeah, I would have." John nodded, smirking. "But I didn't see it, either, because I was too busy watching Carl's face turn purple."

"Then if we all would've done it, *why* do we have to keep rehashing it?"

Clara grinned, "Well, now we *have* to because we know you hate it."

Everybody laughed. Even a reluctant Lonesome Wolf.

⌘

Afternoons were back to being hot as all get out. Lonesome Wolf toted the pail of well water into the barn and proceeded to peel off his sweat-soaked shirt. He dunked a towel into the water and, without even ringing it out, sloshed it over his head and face and neck and chest. It felt just good enough to make him want to go dunk himself in the deep part of the creek. He cocked his head to one side considering the possibility. He and Reynolds had already knocked off of working on barn loft repairs for the afternoon, and it would be a while before Clara's birthday supper, so he should have time. He decided to give in to the call of the cold creek water and headed to the bunkroom to get clean clothes. Just as he turned to go, the barn door swung open, and sunlight imposed itself on the blessed dimness.

When the door shut again, warding off the

unwanted advances of the sun, he saw Clara looking at him smiling. It was one of those smiles that warned him to run, but he knew these days he was in no shape to run from her. At any cost.

The glimmer in her eye could be seen even in the shadows of the barn.

Hesitantly, he said, "Good afternoon, Clara."

"Good afternoon." She smiled cheekily. "I see I came at just the right time."

He sent her a questioning look, but he had only to watch her eyes to see what she meant. It was the first time in her presence that he had ever felt as if he needed to grab something to cover his chest. The woman was going to drive him crazy.

"Clara Jane! You are a brazen hussy."

Clara tried to look indignant. "I cannot believe you called me that!" And she would have sounded truly offended, but for her laughter. If he were a blind man, he would've known her beauty through that laugh, and especially so now, when her happiness and her love sang through it.

He could do nothing but laugh back. "Oh, you can, too. You've suddenly become the most forward female alive." He raised both eyebrows, looked down on her, and lied, "Frankly, I'm surprised at such behavior."

His teasing was once again rewarded with her laughter, as she shoved him in the shoulder and shamelessly spoke the truth. "You like it."

"I might at that." He felt more playful words dancing in his head and almost spoke them. But, he knew the flirting had gone on long enough. Clara might be adorable, and beautiful… and, yes, brazen, but she was *not* his wife. He gently reminded her of that fact. "But I'll like it better *after* we're married."

Clara still smiled, but it was the pouty-est smile he had ever seen. He was surprised to hear nervousness in her voice. "I'm just trying to make sure you are sufficiently anticipating it."

"Oh, I am," he reassured her. "Believe me, at times – like now, seeing you with that look in your eyes – I have to wonder why we're waiting until Saturday after next." It was true, and saying that much aloud to her opened the gate to the impatience he had been keeping to himself. So, he let it out. " Clara, why are we doing this to ourselves? We have a preacher living in our house. We could go get him and get married right this instant."

"We could, but we would miss out on the courting, and the joy of anticipating it, and the…"

"Agony?"

The word hung in the air of the otherwise silent barn until Clara, a slow smile dawning on her lovely face, stated simply, "I love you, Lonesome Wolf."

"I love *you*, Clara Jane."

Lonesome Wolf pulled her gently into his arms and breathed her in. She placed her hands on his chest and was lowering her head to rest against his shoulder when, without warning, she slammed her fists into him.

His eyes flew open wide. "*Why* did you do that?"

"Your chest … it feels like a rock. Are the rest of your muscles like that?" She placed her palms against him, running her hands over his chest and upper arms, smacking his muscles.

He reached up and took both of her hands in his to stop their explorations. "Clara, if you love me at all, you will not do that."

The innocent look she gave him only made him

want to kiss her more. She asked, with no hint that she was anything but sincere, "What do you mean?"

"We still have ten days until we're married, correct?" She nodded. "And we want to honor God in all we do, right?" Another nod. "When you touch me like that …" He struggled with what exactly to say. Pretty soon he would have to get comfortable talking to his wife about… *things* like this, but she wasn't his wife, yet. Thankfully a light dawned in her eyes and he was saved from trying to explain. "Do you understand now?" Again she nodded, this time with her lips planted firmly between her teeth and the corners of her mouth trying desperately not to curl upward. "You think this is funny?" She shook her head no, but her smiling eyes disagreed.

He kissed her on her nose and released her hands. "I am so glad you're enjoying this." When he heard her giggle break free, he grabbed her and, wrapping her back in his arms, leaned in and kissed Clara lightly just below her ear. Once.

She leaned into him.

Twice.

She stilled.

A third time, more firmly.

She did not move.

He slowly pushed her away from him and, with a gentle finger, lifted her chin. He looked into her eyes. They were no longer smiling. "Still think this is funny?" Eyes wide, she shook her head. "Perhaps you should go back inside now." Clara nodded vigorously and then turned and fled the barn.

By the time Lonesome Wolf made it back up to the cabin from his bath, it was all but time for the guests to arrive. He walked in the side door and laughed at the sight before him. Clara was having a stand off with Cynthia, who he was glad had an inner strength that far surpassed her physical one. She was resolutely refusing to let Clara help with the supper preparations. Apparently John had kept Clara busy outside so Cynthia could get started, and now they'd been found out.

"Cynthia, I let you put the roast on earlier today because you said you were bored, but you can't be so bored that you won't let me help with getting things finished up. At least let me set the table."

"I told you I had it. Now, you wouldn't want to upset me, would you?" Cynthia asked like she wasn't being manipulative at all.

Clara called her on it. "Upset you by helping you get food on the table in my own house?"

Cynthia looked to John who looked at a loss, so Lonesome Wolf decided it was time to step in. They all knew that if Clara found out just how much meat was actually cooking in the oven, the surprise would be over, so he pulled her by the hand toward the door. "Come on, you contrary woman, you, and walk with me and the baby out to the corral and let Cynthia be."

He had to tug a reluctant Clara away from the stove, push her out the door, shut it in her face, and then rush and scoop up Nathanael from where he was playing in the living room before Clara came back inside and started more trouble.

When he opened the door, she was glaring at him. She blew her hair away from her face. "I swear I don't know what is wrong with everyone around here. I think you've all taken a leave of your senses." When Nathanael gurgled to her in his yammering baby talk, interspersing a few actual words here and there, Clara laughed. "Are you agreeing with me, my son?"

"No, he is not. He's telling you to leave people alone and let them do for you sometimes. And to show him the horses."

Following their rather lengthy trip to the barn, they returned to the cabin and hadn't made it all the way through the kitchen door when Clara saw the sawhorse and planks set up in her living room and a stack of plates enough for three times as many people as lived at the cabin.

That's when she remembered that it was her birthday.

Her exclamations were cut short by the arrival of the Tremonts, followed closely by the Kearneys. As they sat around the makeshift table and shared a meal, Clara thanked God for her family and friends.

She was so happy that the gifts almost overwhelmed her. She cried when Lonesome Wolf handed her a small package marked "Love, Nathanael" and filled with the most amazingly beautiful hair combs. She cried, this time in delight, when Lonesome Wolf presented her with a deerskin carrier so that she could hold the baby and have her hands free to ride her horse. The hours that he must have worked on that… and just for her.

What truly took her breath away, however, was the last gift. John had abruptly stood up, said "don't move" rather bossily, declared the cryptic statement "let's go, men" to the room, and left without a goodbye, or a "we'll be right back," or even a nod of farewell. When she turned to the women in the room, they all shrugged… in unison… as if rehearsed.

When men were gone from the cabin for only a

short time and returned with several crates – heavy crates, if judged by the way they were carried - curiosity sparked within Clara. It was drastically heightened when the men all backed away, sitting or leaning against a chair or wall, leaving John standing alone in the center of the room. Looking nervous.

He took a breath, looked at Clara, then quickly glanced away to turn pleading eyes on Cynthia, who merely smiled in a way that said she was on his side but wasn't about to help him. His faced flushed with nerves, he looked back at Clara and steeled himself as if ready to recite a memorized verse or give a lengthy speech. Instead, he blurted out, "Those are your birthday present from me," and moved out of the way to reveal the stack of crates.

Clara slowly rose, scanned the room as if to ask if anyone knew what was going on – most of them looked suspiciously innocent. Lonesome Wolf suddenly found great interest in the window frame next to him, and Cynthia gave her the exact look she had just given John.

Clara burst into laughter. It was all completely absurd. "Y'all are being ridiculous! Are these crates chockfull of gold?"

Feeling silly with mirth, Clarawent to the closest crate and dramatically whisked off the top as if she were revealing a treasure trove. Lid in midair, Clara froze. Gold treasure indeed! Her amusement turned seamlessly into awe.

Her books! The crates were packed with her beloved books!

She tried to look at John, but her eyes were blurry with tears. No wonder he had been so uncomfortable. Oh, the conflicts and confrontations they'd had over these books. That her brother even thought to salvage them before he sold the estate to their uncle made all the trouble he had caused simply disappear. The thought of him traveling miles upon miles with the weight of these books slowing them down made Clara afraid she might fall into a sobbing mess on the ground.

John's precious gift, so much more than the physical books themselves, reminded Clara what a thoughtful, kind man her brother was when he wasn't being pigheaded.

CHAPTER TWENTY-TWO

When Lonesome Wolf came in for supper, Nathanael was asleep. He slept through the whole meal of chicken and dumplings and through the berry cobbler dessert. He slept through cleanup. And he slept while the adults gathered in the living room to visit. When he whimpered from the other room, Lonesome Wolf rose to get him. A moment after he entered the baby's room, he bolted out of it, pulling Nathanael's clothes off as he ran to the kitchen where the pail of fresh water was kept.

Clara dropped her sewing and ran up behind them. "What is it?"

"He's burning up." Lonesome Wolf drenched a towel and placed the cool, wet cloth to Nathanael's body. "Reynolds, can you take a lantern down to the creek and get a pail of water?"

With a hasty, "Of course," Reynolds grabbed a lantern and headed out of the cabin.

"Is there anything I can do?" Cynthia walked over, concern filling her voice.

"Yes, please. If you could put on some water to heat. Willow bark tea should help bring down his fever." Lonesome Wolf then turned to a worried Clara and asked if she had seen any other symptoms.

Fear clouding her words, she said, "He didn't sleep very well last night. In fact, he kept me up most of the night. He seemed fine today, though." She scrunched her forehead as she thought back. "Well, he didn't eat very well, now that you mention it."

As he took the baby, now wrapped in the cool but already warming towel, back into the bedroom, Clara followed so closely she almost bumped into Lonesome Wolf when he laid Nathanael on the bed. Clara reached down to wipe the baby's hair from his face and felt his fever for the first time. She drew her hand back quickly and gasped. "He's burning up!"

"I know, Clara. We're taking care of him."

"You said he had a fever, but you didn't say he was on fire." Clara's voice sounded airy with panic and her face had lost its color. She picked up the baby and began pacing wildly back and forth in the small space beside the bed.

John came into the bedroom and looked worriedly between mother and child.   Lonesome Wolf stopped Clara's pacing with a gentle touch to her arm and reached up and ran the back of his hand down her cheek, trying to calm her. He could see in her eyes the exhaustion from a sleepless night. "Sit down, sweetheart." Lonesome Wolf stopped her before she could pace out of range again, coaxed her over to the bed, and told her again with a bit more sternness, "Sit down, Clara Jane." She slowly obeyed. He took Nathanael from her and tried again to calm her nerves. "It'll be alright. We'll tend to him and we'll pray. And it'll be all right. Okay?" She nodded. He could see the tears coming – he'd never seen this strong, confident woman so upset. He reached out a hand to her and one of hers engulfed it immediately, and she buried her face in his shoulder. He could feel her shaking with sobs and was torn between comforting her and caring for Nathanael.

Cynthia made to come over but was stopped at the door with a slight shake of John's head that said he didn't want her too near the sick child. From the doorway, she called to Clara in a low yet clear voice. When the worried mother didn't answer, Cynthia did not raise her voice but spoke with the quiet authority Lonesome Wolf had heard her use with John. "Clara." When Clara's eyes reluctantly left the baby and landed on her sister-in-law, Cynthia continued, "dear heart, has Nathanael never been sick before?"

Clara shook her head. "Not a day in his life. Well, he got fussy when he was teething and he's had a runny nose, but not sick, not a fever."

"Children sometimes get a fever." Cynthia, in that calming way she had, tried her best to reassure Clara. "Let's not borrow trouble, okay? We're taking care of him the best we know how, and we're trusting in the Lord."

Reynolds returned with the creek water. After he set it on the floor by the bed, he put one hand on Nathanael's shoulder and one hand on Clara's and began to pray.

Lonesome Wolf could feel the peace descend, like a physical presence in the room. The cabin generally felt like peace itself, but this was thicker, heavier. When he looked over at Clara's face, however, he wasn't sure that she had released her fear enough to feel the change.

After the short prayer, Cynthia left to ready the tea, taking Reynolds and John with her with a simple tilt of her head. When they had cleared the room, Lonesome Wolf squeezed Clara's hand. "Are you all right?" She nodded almost imperceptibly. "Can you bring me a bowl for the water and ask Cynthia to reheat some broth from the dumplings? Just until it's barely warm." She hesitated to leave the baby, but at Lonesome Wolf's insistence, she nodded again, this time more noticeably, and rose. He could have gone himself, but he felt like she needed to do *something*.

Alone in the room with a listless Nathanael, Lonesome Wolf bent down and whispered in the child's ear, "You need to get better quickly, Little One. Your mama and I don't like to see you sick." He kissed Nathanael on his pudgy, fever-pinked cheek. The baby felt terribly hot.

A few minutes later, Clara and John re-entered the room together and set the tea and broth on the bedside table. Lonesome Wolf held Nathanael while Clara tried to spoon the tea into his mouth. The child wasn't very responsive, and Lonesome Wolf was worried that he might not swallow. Clara certainly didn't need to have the baby choke while she attempted to spoon-feed him. Thankfully, Nathanael slurped a tiny bit of the tea off the spoon. The horrible look on his face in reaction to the taste would have been humorous in different circumstances. M*uch* different circumstances.

After a couple more small sips of the broth, Clara gave him some cool water, and then Lonesome Wolf lay him on the bed and put on fresh cloths soaked in the cool creek water. They warmed alarmingly fast.

Thirty minutes later and the fever was still high. Lonesome Wolf rose from his seat and spoke quietly into Clara's ear. "It's important for him to have plenty to drink. Can you see if you can get him to nurse? That'll be much easier and faster than feeding him water or broth off a spoon. I'll go and get a tub to give him a cool bath. I'll be right back in." Clara nodded. Her eyes were red and swollen, but for now the tears had stopped. Lonesome Wolf lifted her chin until she met his eyes and then smiled reassuringly at her. She did her best to smile back. He kissed her forehead, holding her to him for just a moment, then left to get a washtub and some peppermint.

When he came back in, Clara was modestly covered with a baby blanket and clinging to Nathanael as if he were a precious treasure she was afraid of losing. The scene bit into Lonesome Wolf's heart. She looked up at him hopefully. "He's nursing. He acts like he's still asleep, though, and he's awful hot."

"When he finishes nursing we'll give him a cool bath." He ran his hands through her hair then kissed her forehead again. "Right now, I'm going to put this poultice of ground peppermint leaves on his feet. It should help bring down his fever."

Poultice applied, he sat on the bed next to her and put an arm around her. She drooped her head down against his chest. "It'll be alright, Clara." He prayed that she wouldn't worry herself so much that she took sick, too. She needed to sleep that night as much as she could. He could stay up with Nathanael and awaken her if she was needed.

Cynthia came yet again to stand in the doorway and check on the baby. John and Reynolds stood anxiously behind her.

After what seemed like a long while, the cool bath and peppermint did their jobs. The fever didn't go away completely, but Nathanael was considerably less warm. As they looked down upon a sleeping Nathanael who was no longer whimpering, Lonesome Wolf took Clara's hand. Again, she lay against him, and he knew she was leaning on him for more than physical rest but for emotional strength and spiritual peace, as well.

Lonesome Wolf knew she was in all ways weary and insisted she lie down beside Nathanael and get some sleep, but she shook her head. He moved from the bed to kneel in front of her. "Clara," he turned her face to him with a gentle hand, "I need you to listen to me. You're exhausted and you need rest. I won't allow you to make yourself sick with worry. Understood?" He waited for her nod and then continued, "You will lie down next to Nathanael and get some rest. I'll tend to him. I promise to wake you if he gets worse or if he needs you. Yes?" Clara nodded again. Slowly, but she nodded and, fully dressed and in front of the crowded room, climbed into the bed next to Nathanael and closed her eyes.

Reynolds made a quiet suggestion, "I think we should all try to get some rest, though maybe one of us should stay up with Lonesome Wolf in case he needs someone to fetch water from the creek or make tea or… anything else. I can take first shift."

"No." It was John who spoke, and Lonesome Wolf steeled himself for a scene. He was stunned when John simply offered, "Let me do it. You've all helped. Y'all go rest, and I'll stay up with Lonesome Wolf."

For a full minute, no one moved or spoke. Lonesome Wolf glanced at Clara and saw that she'd already succumbed to sleep. He nodded to Clara's brother. "I'd be much obliged, John. Thank you." Reynolds went out to the bunkhouse so that Cynthia could have his and John's room. Lonesome Wolf picked up Nathanael, and he and John moved into the living room so they wouldn't disturb Clara. As John pulled a book from the shelf and sat with it in silent watch, Lonesome Wolf went back to bathing Nathanael with cool rags.

About thirty minutes into John's shift, Nathanael

began to stir and whimper again. The slight noises from the baby tore at Lonesome Wolf, but he much preferred them to the lethargy Nathanael had fallen into during the high fever. He picked up the baby and placed him over one broad shoulder. Tenderly stroking his back, he murmured softly into his ear how much he loved him, and began singing a soft lullaby, rocking him slowly.

Lonesome Wolf could feel eyes on him. He looked up and saw John intently watching the scene. John met his gaze briefly, revealing no thoughts or emotions, and then went back to reading. As the lullaby came to an end and Lonesome Wolf paused for breath before beginning another, Nathanael lifted his head slightly, looked at the big man, and said, "Oof," in a tired baby voice filled with love and trust. Lonesome Wolf smiled, a smile that united with the look in his eyes and spoke of his deep love. Nathanael then put his head back on Lonesome Wolf's shoulders and went to sleep to another soft refrain.

Lonesome Wolf gently laid the baby on the couch and watched him sleep. Still, John silently sat by, observing. Periodically, Lonesome Wolf leaned over and felt the boy's forehead and body for fever. For a time, it seemed held at bay.

At one point, when Lonesome Wolf was making another peppermint poultice just in case the fever returned, Nathanael whimpered and John rose. He gently, almost awkwardly, held the boy, kissing Nathanael on his cheek and stroking the baby's head softly. Lonesome Wolf watched the exchange with interest. This was the loving John that Cynthia had assured him did exist. He'd seen other signs, as well, of course. The first one that came to mind was the books that John had insisted his poor wagon team haul for hundreds of miles because he knew Clara would want them. Lonesome Wolf would long remember the joy on John's face as Clara cried happy tears over the gift. He realized how guilty he was of judging John based on what was probably the man's worst behavior. *He* surely didn't want to be judged by *his* worst moments. Lonesome Wolf decided to see John through eyes unclouded by their own set of prejudices and was determined to make a concerted effort to get to know Clara's brother better.

Shortly, Nathanael began to stir. He whined and sat up, rubbing his little eyes. "Oof. Oof." Lonesome Wolf reached over and picked him up, cuddling him close to his body, not surprised to find he felt warm with fever again. Sickness always seemed to get worse in the hours after midnight.

Speaking in low tones so as not to wake Clara or Cynthia, Lonesome Wolf said, "John, Nathanael is running fever again. Would you mind heating some of the broth that's on the stove? We can use that to make the tea. We need to keep fluids in him."

John acknowledged him with a nod. "Is the fever bad? Should I head to the creek and get some fresh water?"

"That might be a good idea."

Stretching, John set aside his book and got up. "I'll set broth to heat and then head down there."

Lonesome Wolf paced around the main room of the cabin with Nathanael, who was crying faintly. When John returned, Lonesome Wolf settled into the rocker with Nathanael in his lap. He first gave him a couple of teaspoons of the tea. The baby didn't want much to do with it, but Lonesome Wolf thought he got enough down to help. John poured some fresh water into a cup, and Nathanael messily drank down about half of it before falling wearily back against Lonesome Wolf's chest.

The two men worked together to bathe the boy. Nathanael smiled lazily as the cool cloths touched his face, and Lonesome Wolf crooned, "That feels good doesn't it, Little One? It's helping you get well."

When they had the baby cooled down considerably, Lonesome Wolf pulled him up to his shoulder and began rocking him back to sleep. Nathanael snuggled in against him and patted his chest, saying, "Oof, Oof. Mine." Lonesome Wolf chuckled softly, a low rumble in his chest that made Nathanael smile. It was very good to see the baby smile.

After a while, John spoke. "You care for him as if you were his father."

Lonesome Wolf, who wasn't sure if the comment was an accusation or an observation or a compliment, answered the best way he could think – honestly. "I couldn't love Nathanael more if he were my own child."

"I know. I see it in your eyes." John paused for a moment. "He loves you, too."

Again, Lonesome Wolf was careful with his reply. "It's an honor to me."

"His father was my best friend."

If one didn't know the situation, the comment would have seemed to come out of nowhere. But Lonesome Wolf knew why John said it. He willed his body to remain relaxed so he didn't disturb Nathanael, but he was getting more and more nervous with the line of this conversation. He had to admit, however, that nothing in John's voice indicated anger. In fact, there was still no emotion in his voice, at all. Lonesome Wolf responded in an easy manner. "Yes, Clara speaks very highly of your friend." He hesitated, but decided it needed to be said, so he told John, "Nathanael will grow up to know that his father was a good man."

Lonesome Wolf had long thought the conversation ended when the stillness and quiet of the cabin was broken. "Thank you."

It was a simple statement, but in it Lonesome Wolf felt an offer of truce. It was a risk, he knew, but he turned to John and faced him, making sure that the man was looking directly into his eyes when he said, "I love your sister, John. And I'll take good care of her. I give you my word."

John nodded and looked off across the room. "I know you love her. I can see it in the way you care for her, look out for her. And I know she loves you, trusts you." John heaved out a heavy sigh as if it were a weight he'd carried for too many miles. "I just don't want Clara's life to be hard, and with you..." He let the thought drop and said instead, "Tonight, the way you took charge when Nathanael got sick... Clara let you take over. She let you take care of her child when he was sick." He huffed out a small laugh. "She even went to sleep." John cast a cautious glance back at Lonesome Wolf as if to gauge his reaction to what he was about to say. "It's plain to see her trust is well-founded." John seemed nothing but genuine.

Lonesome Wolf was stunned. "Thank you, John." His voice cracked and he had to clear his throat to fix it. "You have no idea how much that means to me."

"How did you know, anyway?" John's obvious curiosity ended the tense moment. "What to do?"

Lonesome Wolf shifted Nathanael away from his voice and explained. "My friend Franklin married this young Mexican woman. She lived with her sister and her sister's passel of kids. I was there with them for... almost a year, I guess. One cold November night, they all took sick. The sister and I were the only ones who were spared whatever it was that hit. She taught me how to help out. How to bring down fever, ease pain." He dropped his head back against the chair and stared at the ceiling, trying to push away the memories, that one and others that tried to follow. "Only four of the kids made it," he murmured into the emptiness of the room.

John didn't say anything until Lonesome Wolf sighed and looked over at him. When he did speak, his eyes were solemn and considering. "That sounds... It must've been tough."

"Yeah," he answered, not wanting to think back about just how tough, not wanting to remember. "It was."

They were quiet for a good long while before John broke the silence again. "I have a lot of mending to do."

With a shake of his head, Lonesome Wolf assured John, "A simple *I'm sorry* will suffice for Clara. She longs to have your relationship restored."

"Maybe so." John looked pensive for a moment. "But I owe her more than an *I'm sorry*."

Lonesome Wolf shrugged. "People don't always demand what they're owed."

"And what about you?" John asked hesitantly. "What will you demand for your forgiveness?"

The answer was a simple one. "You already have my forgiveness."

John grimaced. "I'm not sure I deserve it."

Lonesome Wolf grinned ruefully. "Well, thank the Good Lord we don't all get what we deserve."

John gave a short laugh. "Yes, thank the Lord for that." He sat silently for a couple minutes longer and then spoke again, this time with a lightness in his voice that

Lonesome Wolf had never heard there before. "How is our boy?"

Lonesome Wolf looked down at the resting baby. "Better." He touched his lips to Nathanael's cheeks and forehead. "Much better. Fever seems to be all but gone."

John set his book on the couch and stood, blowing out a relieved breath. "Want me to fix us some coffee?"

Lonesome Wolf eyed John carefully as his soon to be brother-in-law made his way across the room. Thinking on deeper things, he said, "Sounds good, thanks."

Lonesome Wolf jerked his head up. He'd fallen asleep in the rocking chair with Nathanael, but a soft noise woke him. He looked over to see Clara standing in the doorway of her room, watching him. He smiled at her and was rewarded with a smile back. Her smiles caused a deep wanting ache in his heart, and he had to remind himself that he didn't have to feel that ache of loneliness anymore because he was staying, here with her, and she would soon be his.

"How is my baby boy?" she whispered to him as she tiptoed across the room.

"He's well. His fever is gone for now. It broke early this morning. We just need to make sure we watch him closely today." As he saw worry creeping back into her face, he rushed to add, "He'll be fine."

Clara stroked Nathanael's head with her hand and leaned in to kiss him. She looked with love at Lonesome Wolf. "And what about you? How are you doing?"

"I'm fine. I took a little catnap."

Clara knelt beside the rocking chair and took his hand. "I'm so thankful for you. I don't know what happened to me. I just, I don't know, I went hysterical practically."

He cupped her face in his hand and lifted it so that he could look right into her eyes and she could see his. "You aren't alone anymore."

She leaned up, kissed him softly on the lips, and smiled. "And aren't I thankful for that."

CHAPTER TWENTY-THREE

As they gathered together for supper on the eve of the church raising, Reynolds stood and asked for everyone's attention. Clearing his throat, he made an announcement. "With the church going up tomorrow and, of course," he looked at Lonesome Wolf and Clara, "y'all getting hitched, I believe it's time I moved into town and began my ministry there. Corabelle has a room at the boarding house." He paused with a raise of an eyebrow. "She said she wasn't going to rent to me if I performed the wedding, but when I said that was just fine, I'd rent out a room with the Eldons, she changed her tune right fast." They all chuckled at the woman's expense. "At any rate, I'll stay there until a more permanent solution can be had. I want to thank you..." His eyes moved over the people assembled at the table, and Lonesome Wolf realized he'd begun to consider him family. "I wanted to thank all of you for your hospitality and your care and your help. May the Lord bless your lives richly."

No one spoke for a few minutes until Nathanael screeched out a long line of gibberish accompanied by the banging of his spoon on the table. Lonesome Wolf laughed and said, "I think Nathanael has the right idea. To Reynolds!" and he banged his cup on the table. The others joined in with blessings and bangings until the whole assembly fell apart into giggles and laughter that felt so good, like those times in life when all is right even if it is bittersweet.

⌘

Clara was amazed at how many people turned out at the church raising. She had no idea there were so many people living near enough to Klein Creek to gather such a crowd. Several families that she hadn't even seen before were present. It seemed the sleepy little town was not so small as she'd thought. As she looked around at the tables laden with food, the children running around meeting new playmates and playing with old ones, and the groups of men working on their given tasks, she was filled with a new sense of pride in her little town and a hope for the future of it, a hope that included the futures of her own children.

Her eyes scanned the crowd for Lonesome Wolf. There he was, the man she loved, her soon-to-be husband, in a group with Carl. The big burly blacksmith was introducing Lonesome Wolf, Jacob as most of the town knew him, to the other men as if he were presenting to them an old friend or, Clara hid a smile as she turned away, a hero. As a nod to the happiness she was feeling, she refused to acknowledge the men who walked away without shaking Lonesome Wolf's hand or to let the stares and whispers of many of the other townspeople ruin her day. Her little town was getting a church! It was too good, too perfect, something that could have been orchestrated only by a loving God.

And then disaster struck.

Tired from the work of the afternoon, Clara decided

to join Cynthia and Nathanael, who were resting away from the teeming people and loudest part of the building. She was walking around to the back of the wagons to sit with them for a moment under a shade tree when she was grabbed roughly by the arm. Her first instinct was to give a dressing down to whoever it was who was treating her so roughly, but when her arm was twisted up behind her so she couldn't turn around, she knew true fear.

She opened her mouth to scream, hoping someone would hear her over the hammering and shouts, but she barely got out a sound before a dirty hand covered her mouth.

She belatedly thought she should have told someone where she was going, but she never would have dreamed that she would be attacked at a church raising. She began to scream and kick and thrash about with all her might.

If her captor's words were to be used as measure, all she succeeded in doing was making him angry. She certainly hadn't loosened his grasp on her. Just when she thought no rescue would come, she heard a loud grunt and was thrown free of the man's grasp. Before she could rise from the ground, she found herself looking down the barrel of a gun.

Lonesome Wolf had seen the cowhand named Lowell walking purposely after Clara as she headed away from the building site. When they both disappeared from view, Lonesome Wolf had been filled with an urgency to get to her. He'd called to Reynolds and John as he ran toward the back of the wagon lot. Several other people followed to see what the commotion was about. By the time Lonesome Wolf got to Clara, Lowell was dragging her farther away from the crowd, easily overcoming her, though she kicked and threw herself around.

Without pause, Lonesome Wolf kept running and plowed right into Lowell, knocking him away from Clara and Clara off balance. Working to steady himself, Lonesome Wolf turned back to the scene. What happened next played out slowly, through a sort of quiet fog.

Lowell righted himself.

Someone grabbed Lonesome Wolf, locking his arms behind him.

Lowell reached for his gun.

Lonesome Wolf stilled as a blurry thought of dying washed through his mind.

Lowell's arm raised, but instead of aiming at Lonesome Wolf, he was turning his gun on Clara.

Lonesome Wolf shouted and thrashed to get free and put himself between Clara and the gun.

Lowell sneered at Clara and spat on the ground in front of her.

Lonesome Wolf screamed Clara's name.

Then the air cracked open with a gunshot.

It was the only sound Lonesome Wolf could hear save his blood pumping through his veins like a locomotive. He could smell the gunpowder in the air. He could see a hazy picture of disbelief from the crowd that had gathered. He could feel what had been a nice cool breeze but now was an icy chill. But his brain had a hard time making sense of the scene.

Lonesome Wolf searched for Clara amongst the marred details of the scene before him. Through eyes stinging from gunpowder, he saw her, waited for the blood to begin seeping through her dress, waited for her to stumble and fall to the ground. Instead, he saw her stand firm, unwounded and being held by Lydia.

Mind overcome by the reverberating sound of the gunshot, Lonesome Wolf struggled to comprehend... until his eyes focused several feet away on Lowell's gun lying in the dirt.

The sound of the gunshot ricocheted faster, echoing through his senses, until suddenly everything was at full speed again.

Lowell stood staring at his hand. Slowly his gaze slid over to his gun lying in the dirt. His eyes trailed over the crowd until they lit on Reynolds, who had drawn and shot before the cowhand could finish his aim. A long moment later, Lowell's face contorted in pain and he grabbed his bloodied hand, letting out a bellow that seemed to give everyone permission to speak.

They could express their opinions about the series of events all they cared to; Lonesome Wolf just wanted to get to Clara. Unfortunately, he was being held firmly from behind. He had almost forgotten the tight grip on his crossed wrists. Thinking someone meant to keep him from getting in the way of Lowell's gun, Lonesome Wolf turned his head to the side and said, "You can let go now."

He heard a dark chuckle, and then a cultured voice drawled out, "Oh, I can, can I? Hmmm... I suppose that's true enough. But that doesn't mean I shall." The gripped tightened and pulled outward, crossing Lonesome Wolf's arms almost at the elbows, and the voice lost all hint of culture, turning itself just short of a growl. "What exactly are you doing here, Injun? Huh?" The man yanked Lonesome Wolf, pulling him roughly backward. "And what part did you have to play in this little to-do? Thought you'd kidnap yourself a squaw?"

Instinctively, Lonesome Wolf's eyes sought Clara.

Someone had brought her a chair. She sat still, eyes staring to an unknown somewhere up ahead, while John comforted her. That was *his* job. That's where he should be, taking care of her, not listening to some man's ignorance talking.

He decided he had no more time for this nonsense.

He canted his head back to make sure whoever it was that stood behind him, and thus between him and Clara, heard what he was about to say. "I'm not sure who you are," his voice was harder than he had ever heard it before, "but I'm guessing you're new to town. The woman that man was after will be my wife this time next week. If you'd been in town any time at all, you would know that." He paused a beat. "We've kind of caused a stir." His tone turned cold as he gave the man his options. "Now, you can let me go so I can get to her, or you can get hurt." His upper body muscles, recently strengthened by a steady exercise of wood-chopping, flexed, and he pulled outward so that his arms quite nearly met his sides. With just a bit of a smile, he offered, "Your choice."

As soon as the man loosened his hold enough, Lonesome Wolf wrenched free. He ran to Clara without even looking behind him to see who the man was.

When he reached her, Clara was repeating, "I'm alright, I'm alright. It's okay. I'm alright."

Well, *she* might be alright, but it would be a good long while before *he* was.

⌘

Miss Rose was beside herself. She couldn't stop talking about the incident with Lowell, but Lonesome Wolf didn't care to relive the event over and over. In fact, he could go the rest of his life never hearing or thinking a word about it. Especially considering Lowell had lit out of town.

Lonesome Wolf prayed all night that the man wouldn't be stupid enough to come back. He couldn't sleep for thinking of what could happen if Lowell doubled back around and came to the Eldons' for Clara while everyone slept. He sat up outside her room, pistol in his lap, the entire night... just in case.

The other men sat up with him for a good while. They were all too keyed up to sleep, anyway.

After a particularly long but not restful silence, Eldon drawled out, going on as if Lonesome Wolf had spoken his worry aloud. "I don't think you have a whit to worry about. That feller, he ain't comin' back here no time soon. Heck, pert near the whole town saw what he did. He wouldn't get two steps in afore somebody raised a ruckus."

It was a comforting thought. And most likely a true one. But, as Reynolds had said during their trip to town the week before, he wasn't sure they'd heard the last from Lowell. He would have to do a lot of praying in the future before he felt safe from that threat.

His thoughts were pulled away when John asked, "Who was that man that had a hold of you, Lonesome Wolf? What was going on there?" With all his thoughts swirling around Clara's safety, he had all but forgotten about the man.

"I know who he was," Eldon said before Lonesome Wolf had the chance to finish shrugging. "He's a new rancher out east of town. Goes by the name a Miller. Just settled in. Hadn't seen him but onced or twiced in town. Real uppity feller. Thinks he's something else beings as how he comes from money. Well, money don't trump good sense around here." Eldon spit into a spittoon on the floor between his feet. "I don't look for him to stick around." He raised a brow to Lonesome Wolf. "He ain't made too many friends around here. And I don't look for him to."

He certainly hadn't made a friend of Lonesome Wolf – especially considering how the man had held on to *him* but let Lowell get away.

That thought, of Lowell getting away, would not disappear from his mind, and he wondered aloud, "Why does this town not have a marshal?"

They all looked to Eldon for the answer.

"Well, up 'til now we didn't need one." He spat again and scratched the back of his head. "Sure woulda been good to have one today. Maybe that sidewinder wouldn'ta got away. Anyhow, that's somethin' we need to talk about tomorrow morning at our Sunday meeting. Everybody's gonna be talkin' about what happened today. We might as well git some good out of it. Make us a decision to get us a lawman."

Eldon spit once more, the opened up his pouch and pinched off another chaw. He didn't even wait to finish shoving it in his mouth before he started speaking again. He just talked around his fingers. "If'n you ask me, I'd say Jim Kearney and George Keller oughta be the ones to find somebody." Lonesome Wolf thought what a nasty habit chewing tobacco was when Eldon used his shirtsleeve to swipe a dark spot of spit off his chin. "They kinda act as a joint mayor in these parts as it is." He paused to scratch the back of his head and nodded. "Ayup." Spit. "That's what we oughta do."

Lonesome Wolf whole-heartedly agreed.

In the early hours of the morning, long after the others had gone to bed, Lonesome Wolf sat in the hall outside Clara's door thinking about her socializing at the church raising. Watching her laugh at the kids playing in the churchyard, watching her be a part of that camaraderie she had with her friends only served to underline the pain of the truth, a truth that had been blatantly expressed yet again in what had happened to Clara. Lonesome Wolf did not belong in Clara's world.

He had no right to take the place of another man, a *white* man, giving her a marriage and more children, things he had thought that maybe he could give her. But he had no right to dream that dream. He had no right to feel so protective and possessive of her. But most of all, he had no right to love her. No right at all. And yet, all these things were true.

He thought of Nathanael at the picnic with his cheeks messy from the meal and his chubby hands clapping at some antics of the Kearney children. He could easily include many things about the little boy in a growing list of things he had no right to do or feel or think.

Some part of his mind told him that the smart thing to do would be to pack up as soon as they returned home, as soon as they returned back to *Clara's* home, and ride out. Not even wait until first light but set out as soon as he could gather his meager belongings and a few food supplies for the trail. He should protect the tiny sliver of his heart that might could possibly still be alive after all this was over, that might possibly survive the reaching in and ripping out that leaving Clara would be. He should go ... now. But he knew he wasn't strong enough to leave.

Or, maybe he was strong enough to stay.

About three in the morning, Lonesome Wolf heard coughing coming from inside the ladies' bedroom. Cynthia's cough had gotten worse in the past several days. He felt for the poor woman who had such strength in all things but the physical.

There was a murmuring of voices, and then Clara opened the door, face ashen.

His heart shuddered in his chest. "Are you okay?"

"It's Cynthia. She's sick. Get John."

Lonesome Wolf took off to the Eldons' living room where John and Reynolds had bedded down. "John. John!"

Reynolds shot up, instantly alert, gun in hand. Lonesome Wolf shook his head at the gun-toting preacher. He was sure there was a story there, but it wasn't the time nor his business to find out what it was. He crouched down and shook John until he sat up from his pallet, bleary eyed and looking like Lonesome Wolf felt. And he was about to make the man's night any better. "John." Lonesome Wolf waited impatiently until John focused his eyes and scowled. He started to grumble, but Lonesome Wolf talked over him. "John, it's Cynthia. She's–"

John didn't wait to hear anymore. He jumped to his feet and bolted to the women's room, Lonesome Wolf and Reynolds following closely behind him.

"Cynthia, honey, you're burning up." His words were soft and low as he spoke to his wife. But when he turned to speak to the rest of them, his voice was raised and anxious. "Someone do something for her. Her skin is putting off heat like a furnace." Wild eyes turned to Lonesome Wolf. "You helped Nathanael. You know what to do. You helped him. You know what to do. Help Cynthia." John's words came at rapid-fire pace, his voice stretching out until it was thin with fear.

"I will, John" Lonesome Wolf said gently trying to put some calm into the chaos. "We'll all work together. I'll be right back with whatever I can find to help." Reynolds went with him to wake the Eldons to see what they had on hand. When he returned with willow bark tea, John and Cynthia were having a fierce discussion.

"That is not a good idea, sweetheart. I don't think you're thinking clearly." How John could sound so aggravated and so tender was a mystery.

"I am thinking as clearly as ever, John Roth. Now, hitch up –" Cynthia's vicious cough interrupted her, "hitch up the wagon and take me to Clara's." Her voice was weak, but there was strength in her words. And Lonesome Wolf had seen the couple interact enough to know that John was going to lose this battle. Still, John looked like he hadn't figured that out. And then Cynthia, her hand shaking as she removed it from under the blanket, reached out and touched John on the arm. "I don't want to die in the home of strangers, John."

Clara left the room, whispering to Lonesome Wolf on the way out the door, "I'm going to get Miss Rose to help me make up a pallet in the back of the wagon."

He nodded and turned to look at Reynolds, who nodded back and left to hitch up the team. Taking a moment to admire the remarkable strength of the woman who, but for her one source of weakness, would've made an almighty good frontier wife, Lonesome Wolf quietly set the tea on the bedside table and followed Reynolds out into the cool night to saddle their horses.

It looked like they were going home.

By the time Cynthia finished her tea, John had relented, somberly carrying his wan looking wife out to the waiting wagon.

Cynthia's cough was much worse by the time the wagon made it to Clara's. Her breaths were ragged and wheezy, and the tea she had been given had done little to bring down her fever.

John carried her inside and refused to let anyone else tend her. He accepted more willow bark tea from Reynolds, he grabbed the peppermint poultice from Lonesome Wolf, he took the broth from Clara, but he was the one to give them to Cynthia. She allowed John to apply the poultice, but took very little of the broth or the tea. John coaxed and she tried to comply, but she was rapidly worsening – and they all could see it.

Lonesome Wolf fixed himself a pallet on the living room floor in case he was needed. As he was settling in for the night, he listened to Cynthia's coughing in the other room. It seemed to go on for much too long. He rose and put some water on to heat and gathered the tea and honey. He also grabbed the medicinal whiskey Clara kept in the back of the upper cabinet. Once he had everything set out and was waiting for the water to boil, he went to the doorway of Cynthia's room. John looked haggard, and a haunted look resided in the man's normally sharp eyes.

On the third day… the third day of John's vigil, of John sitting by Cynthia's bedside and refusing to leave, to eat, to sleep… on the third day, Clara confronted him. "John, you're going to make yourself sick if you don't get some rest."

"So what?" John's words might've sounded harsh if they hadn't been so fraught with weariness. "*I* can handle sick, Clara, but *Cynthia* can't. *I'll* be fine. If you feel the need to worry, worry about Cynthia not me." He immediately apologized for being rude, but no one would have held it against him if he hadn't.

By the fourth day it was obvious that Cynthia was getting worse and not likely to get better. John had lain down with her and was holding her in his arms. At dusk, everyone crowded into the little room and held each other as they watched Cynthia struggle to breathe. It was a little over an hour later when she breathed out and didn't draw in another breath. The room stilled of all activity. For some time they stood riveted to her, willing her to breathe. It was John who pulled them out of their useless watch. "I'm really tired. I haven't slept much the last few days. I'm going to rest, and then we'll see to my wife." He pulled his arms out from around Cynthia, flattened his hands and put them under his head, and closed his eyes.

They could already hear the gentle even breath of sleep as they filed out of the bedroom.

CHAPTER TWENTY-FOUR

While Lonesome Wolf and Reynolds were out spreading the word of Cynthia's death to their friends, Clara stayed with John to get Cynthia's body ready for burial. When they finished, Clara led John to the table and fixed him a stout cup of coffee and some toast and eggs. If he would just eat, it would be one less weight on her mind.

But John ate only a few small bites, and then he set down his fork and bread and looked at Clara.

"I hate that your friends are coming." When Clara's eyes went large, he held up a staying hand. "It isn't that I don't want them here, Clara. They've all been helpful to you over the years, and that fact would make them friends of mine even if I hadn't come to know them over the last few weeks. I know that Cynthia certainly respects ... *respected* the Tremonts and the Kearneys. It's only that I know how hard everyone works around here, and I hate that they're being called away from their homes today and will have to come again Saturday for the wedding."

"Oh, John!" Clara dropped the wet dishrag into the soapy water and turned to him, incredulous. "You couldn't possibly think that Lonesome Wolf and I still plan on getting married Saturday! It wouldn't be right. I wouldn't *feel* right."

John gave her a rueful look. "Not only do I think you should go on with the wedding, I'm willing to beg you to do so." At Clara's lack of agreement, John smiled sadly. "Clara, Cynthia was so excited about your upcoming marriage, and I know …" his voice broke and he closed his eyes, gathering himself before continuing, "I know that she wanted so much to be here. It would've meant a lot to her, and it would really mean a lot to *me* if you'd go on with your plans."

"John –"

John held up his hand and silenced her protests with a pleading look.

Clara didn't speak. She didn't know what to say and probably couldn't have spoken over the tightness in her throat anyway. So, with tears freely falling, she simply nodded. And then she threw her arms, wet and soapy hands and all, around John and hugged him tightly while they both cried.

⌘

The neighbors began trickling into the cabin. The Kearneys were the last to arrive, running, laden with bags and children, through the heavy rain that had descended at some point during the day – Clara couldn't recall exactly when. Lydia handed off baby Mae to Lonesome Wolf, kissed John on the head as she passed by the chair he sat in with a sleeping Nathanael, and took Clara aside. "Sweetie, I'm going to tell you what I have planned, and then you're going to tell me you like the idea. You hear?"

Clara couldn't help a small smile. She handed Lydia a kitchen towel so the bossy woman could wipe the rain off and dutifully replied, "I hear."

"All right, then, you listen hard. We brought our things to stay a couple nights. I'm going to help you, and

Jim is going to help with what all we can find him to do that'll keep him outta my hair." Winking, Lydia finished wiping down her arms then set down the towel to put her hand on Clara's arm. "First, I'll fix supper. Then, tomorrow we'll finish your wedding dress. On Saturday, I'm going to help you get ready for your wedding day." When Clara opened her mouth to protest, Lydia glared at her, picked the towel back up, and lightly swatted Clara with it. Clara closed her mouth without uttering a sound and let Lydia say what she was determined to say. "I'm going to cook a nice brunch for your wedding guests, and then I'm going to clean up afterwards. And then," she grinned mischievously, "I'm going to gather my family as fast as I can, and we're going to hightail it out of here. And we're taking Nathanael with us." Lydia pointed a finger at her to stop her objection. "He'll stay for three nights, and then we'll bring him back." She raised her eyebrows in a challenging look and waited for Clara to submissively agree.

Clara hesitated. Before she could voice her protest, Lydia nodded her head emphatically. "Good, I am glad you like the idea. I knew you would." And then she swung around and crossed the room to offer her condolences to John.

⌘

The day of the funeral was clear and beautiful, as if God had designed it as a fitting tribute to the woman whose body was being laid to rest in the rain-soaked ground and whose spirit was rejoicing in being home. As Reynolds prayed, Lonesome Wolf stood at Cynthia's grave mourning the woman who was so strong and yet so frail. He would miss his friend's gentle strength and wise counsel.

Next to him, John stood staring, with open eyes not seeing the scene at the gravesite. Lonesome Wolf wondered if he was even hearing the small crowd singing "Amazing Grace." Were he in John's place, his thoughts would be on all he had lost and not on the funeral itself. He kissed Clara's head as she leaned in to him in her grief. He thanked God for her and felt guilty in being so thankful that he had her when John had just lost the woman he obviously loved so much.

Before the last note of the hymn was sung, Lonesome Wolf saw John turn and leave, walking toward the copse of trees down by the creek.

When John still hadn't returned in time for supper, Clara began to worry in earnest. Lonesome Wolf had tried to assure her that he would make certain her brother was all right, or as all right as a man could be when his world had just been turned downside up. However, Clara was worried, so he found himself searching the growing twilight for John.

Walking down toward the creek, Lonesome Wolf breathed in the brisk night air with the smell of impending fall and the faint tinge of the smoke from Clara's stovepipe. He let the evening wrap itself around him, comforting him as it softly caressed his face. He prayed that John would find similar solace in the subtle but powerful gifts that God provided.

He was about to turn back toward the cabin when he saw, in the cottonwoods down by the creek-bank, a shadow moving counter to the slight winds. He walked toward the trees making no effort to conceal his approach. John didn't turn to look at him as Lonesome Wolf grew near to him, but Lonesome Wolf knew he was aware of his presence. He leaned against the trunk of a tree near John and waited for the other man to … speak, acknowledge him, cry out, do whatever was necessary for him to do to help ease his grief if only for a moment.

When at last John did turn to him, he did so with a stark admission. "I don't know how I'll live without her." And that's when Lonesome Wolf recognized the look in John's eyes. Terror. The man was scared to death.

Lonesome Wolf was trying to think of something he could offer up as words of comfort when John continued, his voice hollow and soft, "Cynthia always swept aside my bad qualities and brought out in their stead features of an honorable man." His eyes lost focus somewhere over Lonesome Wolf's shoulder in the depths of the shadows of the cottonwoods. After some time, John released a burden-laden sigh and confessed, "I'm afraid of what I'll be without her."

As if the admission freed him from his need to be alone, John moved quietly away from the shelter of the trees and headed back up the hill to the cabin.

Lonesome Wolf let him go, following quietly along behind him. He wished he had words of wisdom but no words of wisdom came. Instead, he prayed.

Clara's eyes traced her brother as he entered the cabin and headed to his room. As if he could feel her concern, he stopped on his way through the kitchen and pressed a kiss to her forehead, whispering, "I'll be okay, Clara. In time, I'll be okay." It was a much prettier picture that John painted for Clara than the one he had shown to Lonesome Wolf.

When John's door was firmly shut, Clara came and put her hand in Lonesome Wolf's and tilted her head toward the front porch. He willingly followed her, knowing that John's return to the cabin did only a little to calm

Clara's concerns for her brother.

Before the door was firmly shut behind them, she was peppering him with questions in true Clara fashion. "Is he really okay? What did he say to you? Where did you find him?"

"Clara, sweetheart," – he took her face between his hands to quiet her – "slow down. Take a breath. John will deal with Cynthia's death the best way he can. If he needs time alone, then we need to give it to him." He cradled her in his arms and touched his lips to her forehead. "I love you, you know that?"

"I do. And I love you." They held onto each other. "And thank you for going after him. I was worried." She pulled back a little and cocked her head to the side, studying him for a long moment. "And you? How are you doing with all of this?"

He softly smiled to reassure her. "I'm making it." Curling a piece of her hair around and around his finger, he confessed, "I miss her already, but I'm not feeling the need to ride out at dawn like I would've thought a few weeks ago. I…" He paused, tucked her head under his chin and tried to put his thoughts into words.

He decided to give up deciding what he felt and just let the words come as they may. "This morning, John told me that he would always have Cynthia in the memories she left behind. I thought that was beautiful. And I couldn't get it out of my head. He said that having them made losing her bearable. Then… something just… settled in me when I was watching him today. Only a short while ago, I wanted to run from you, and now I can't even imagine walking away.

"I understand what you were telling me about losing you or Nathanael. I'd much rather have you for as long as the good Lord lets me than not to have had the two of you at all. Now that I've decided to let myself have you and Nathanael? Now that I've let go of the fear? That bone-deep desire to run is gone, too."

She looked up at him, and her smile was so beautiful that he couldn't help but kiss it.

Afterward, she scrunched up her nose. "That's all I get? Just a little peck? I hope you can do better tomorrow."

He laughed. He wouldn't have thought he had the ability to laugh in him at that moment, but sometimes the woman's sassiness caught him off guard. The look on her face portrayed utter innocence. But he knew better.

He was in so much trouble. And it felt so good.

⌘

The next morning after breakfast, Lonesome Wolf sat in a room filled with friends, listening to the rain bounce off the roof. The Kearney's two older children were putting on a show, entertaining the babies and adults alike. Mae was clapping her hands and Nathanael was laughing full belly giggles. The adults couldn't help themselves but laugh with them.

As Lonesome Wolf looked around the room, he missed Cynthia's presence, knowing that she would so enjoy watching the children's silliness. A wave of grief poured through him – and yet, one look at Clara and the joy of marrying her the next day was almost overwhelming. How did one manage to feel both immense grief and amazing joy at the same time? And which did one give in to? Should he give in to the grief and purge it from himself? Or should he grasp the joy that he knew for a fact was a fleeting thing in one's life?

A look at John's face answered his question. There John sat, holding a giggling Nathanael. And John was smiling. His eyes held a heavy shadow of grief, but his face held joy, too. And Lonesome Wolf knew that it was right to feel both at the same time.

⌘

In the hours after supper, Clara and Lydia worked to finish up Clara's wedding dress while Jim and Reynolds played a game of checkers. When Lonesome Wolf rose to put a sleeping Nathanael in his crib, Clara set down her sewing and stood to embrace them both. She put her hand on the back of Lonesome Wolf's head and pulled him down into a kiss.

Her lips felt soft and warm on his. It was a simple act and yet stirred such deep feelings within him. Just when he was about to forget his promise about not kissing her until the wedding, John cleared his throat loudly. "Ahem, y'all can at least wait until tomorrow." His voice was loud but laced with a bit of teasing, and not a little disgust. "I can't stand to watch that.'

Clara's eyes flew open and she obediently took a step away from Lonesome Wolf. The two men laughed. Lonesome Wolf leaned down and whispered in her ear, "He's teasing." He kissed her lightly on the cheek and went to put Nathanael in his bed.

On the way back through the living room, he caught Clara's hand and pulled her outside where they could walk out to the corral to watch the horses.

Arms resting on the top fence rail, he looked closely at her for a long while, wanting to talk but hesitant to do so. "Do you remember when you said my name was a curse? Do you still feel that way?"

Clara nestled closely into him, arms around his waist, head on his chest. "I don't feel that way. Not at all." Minutes later, letting go of him, she turned and leaned against the fence. "I think the curse has been broken. I think your name is a reminder of all you've come through and all you have."

Once the tightness in his throat passed, he said, "And I do have so much. I've never been less lonesome in all my life." She smiled up at him that beautiful, coy smile that made her look so desirable. One more day to go. It was exquisite torture. "Waiting for you has been a difficult thing, Clara Jane."

She laughed her light, clear laugh. "You only had to wait a little over two weeks."

"That's where you're wrong. I've waited for you since the first day I road in here and you reached in and touched my heart with those bewitching green eyes of yours." He adjusted his foot on the corral fence and shook his head, running a hand through his hair. "For a long time I prayed for God to take away my thoughts and feelings. I fought it harder than I've fought anything else in my life. But still, a part of me hoped, *knew*, that I was waiting for you."

He reached over and took her hand, pulling her until he she was alongside him. He squeezed her hand gently, feeling in the night wind the promise of many more days with this woman beside him. His soul soared with the knowledge that he was abundantly and beyond all rational thought blessed in his life. But could he say the same for Clara?

He grew quiet. When she quirked a brow at him, he blew out a long breath. "Are you sure, Clara? That you want this? That you want everything that comes with having me? The women who won't speak to you but will sure enough whisper behind your back? People like Lowell putting you in danger? The trials of our children?"

"Stop," she said sternly, and she popped her hands on her hips, beyond frustrated with this man. "Of course I want this. Don't you?"

"Of course, I do." His voice rose defiantly, and he repeated, "I do. But above that, I want what *you* want, what will make *you* happy."

"You," she replied loudly. "*You* make me happy. *You're* what I want." She sounded accusatory. She heard it herself.

"And I want you. But I also want you safe." His voice rose more. "I want to protect you from ridicule, from losing friendships, from a lonely existence... and from danger."

"Lonesome Wolf..." She took a deep breath and blew it slowly out, calming herself. "Those people who have an issue with us being together aren't my friends. If they want to talk, let them talk. If they want to say mean things, let them say them. It isn't going to change my life for the bad. I have my friends, who have been very supportive – cautious maybe, but supportive. The only lonely existence I would have is if I didn't have *you*." She smacked him in the chest. "I can't believe you're saying all of this on the night before our wedding."

"I just want you to be sure, Clara," he defended himself.

"So you said. But, Lonesome Wolf, you are not the one who can keep me safe. That is God's job. Losing Robert taught me that our lives are firmly in God's hands. Let's leave them there."

That's when the rain returned. The sky opened up and the water dumped down on them. Lonesome Wolf grabbed Clara and ran for the barn. As soon as they passed the threshold he slammed the door shut on the driving rain.

They were both drenched. The heavy mood of moments before gave way to the rush of running through a rain shower. Clara had that glint in her eye that always meant something interesting was about to happen.

"You look mighty fine there, sir, with your shirt plastered to your chest like that."

Lonesome Wolf looked into her laughing eyes. He eyed her narrowly, but any menace the look would have lent to his face was completely eradicated by the grin he simply could not suppress. "Clara, are you flirting with me?"

She clasped her hands behind her back, green eyes dancing with mirth, and bobbed her head up and down. "Mmhmm."

He leaned in to whisper in her ear, making sure she could feel his breath on her and his lips move against her skin, "And what, exactly, am I supposed to do about it?"

"I dunno," was her distracted reply.

He looked at her until her attention was focused on him and she could see the passion fully alight in his gaze. Then he leaned in as if to kiss her but instead warned her in a quiet voice, "After tomorrow you won't be able to get away with this."

She tilted her head up until their lips brushed and softly, invitingly said, "What makes you think that after tomorrow I'm going to want to get away with anything?"

In a flash, Lonesome Wolf caught her up in his arms. "If I'd known you were going to act like this, I would've asked you to marry me weeks ago."

Giving him a saucy smile, she turned to leave the barn.

"Clara." She looked over her shoulder, and he beckoned her back with his finger. When she stood obediently in front of him, he told her simply, "I love you."

He was rewarded with a heart-catching smile. "And I love you." With that, ran out into the pour raining.

As he watched her dash back up to the cabin, Lonesome Wolf felt happier than he thought a person should probably feel.

⌘

Finally, the day had come. It was a simple ceremony for a not so simple couple – the pair who half the town loved and supported and the other half wanted to keep apart, the out-going girl and the man whose wont was to keep to himself, the Indian and the auburn-haired white woman.

The skies were clear and the breeze was slight but blessedly cool. The leaves around them rustled in that crinkly, comforting sound that only cottonwoods can produce.

Lonesome Wolf looked into Clara's eyes, soul touching soul, as they recited their vows and Reynolds pronounced them man and wife.

EPILOGUE

The others were joyously inside having a wedding brunch. But John sat out under the trees, tears streaming down his face in silent proclamation of the pain in his spirit. At some point during the ceremony, he had made a decision. Clara and Lonesome Wolf needed time alone to start their lives together. They certainly didn't need him there to cast a constant pall of sorrow over their marriage. It was time for him to go. He would head out West where he could grieve alone. And maybe, in a good long while, where he could heal.

After, he would come back.

But he couldn't think that far into the future. Right now was all he could handle, and he wasn't doing a very good job of handling that.

As soon as the service had ended, he'd slipped into the back bedroom to gather up his belongings. He was supposed to stay with the Eldons so Clara and Lonesome Wolf could have privacy on their wedding night. He could say goodbye, and they'd think he just meant for the night. But it was the time for him to leave. And stay left for a good long while. He would follow the Kellers into Klein Creek – surely they'd open their store to him so he could buy a few supplies – and then he'd be able to get at least a few miles down the road before he had to stop and make camp, a camp far enough down the road that when Clara sent Lonesome Wolf out after him again it would be clear he was really leaving and not planning on coming back for a while.

Yes, a trip West would give him some much needed time alone to think, to remember, to grieve.